ONE
CHILD
ALIVE

ELLERY KANE

bookouture

Published by Bookouture in 2021

An imprint of Storyfire Ltd.
Carmelite House
50 Victoria Embankment
London EC4Y 0DZ

www.bookouture.com

ISBN: 978-1-83888-864-0
eBook ISBN: 978-1-83888-863-3

For Gar
My partner in crime

The axe forgets; the tree remembers.
—African proverb

PROLOGUE

Hannah Fox leaned against the cold marble of the bathroom counter, examining the fine smile lines visible at the corners of her eyes in the magnifying makeup mirror. She pulled at her skin, stretching it smooth, imagining herself twenty-something again, before she applied another layer of the La Prairie concealer that cost more than she cared to admit. A spritz of hairspray and a dab of her signature scent, Chanel No. 5, to finish. She wiped a rogue spot of concealer from the bathroom counter just in case Marie Abbott requested a tour of the house. Journalists could be nosy, even those who worked for froufrou lifestyle magazines like *Santa Barbara Living*. She stood back, admiring the Theory dress she'd carefully selected for this occasion—the perfect emerald shade to complement her red hair—and pronounced herself camera-ready. Even if she still felt like a little girl playing dress-up.

Hannah nudged open the bathroom door, planning to reveal herself slowly, knowing her husband, Peter, would be waiting in the bedroom to admire her. She'd convinced him to come home early from the law office—a rare feat—so the magazine's photographer could take advantage of the golden hour. Following the family interview with Ms. Abbott, the renowned Claude Cappo would snap the cover shot in their backyard just after seven o'clock. Hannah had overlooked no detail.

Peter met her eyes in the dresser mirror, where he stood lacing the necktie she had picked out for him.

"Whoa." He let out a low whistle as he turned to her.

"Does that mean you like it?" Not wanting to ruin her lipstick, she offered her cheek for a quick peck.

"You look beautiful, Hannah. You always do."

She took over, straightening his tie and smoothing the shoulders of his matching sports coat. "Thanks for agreeing to do the interview. I know it's not your cup of tea, but Marie insisted. And it will be great publicity for the Children's Hospital. Not to mention for the law practice."

He chuckled. "I'm happy to talk up the charity work you're doing for the hospital. But if I get any busier at the office, I might have to set up a bedroom there. The DA agreed to a plea deal in the Markum case, by the way."

"You're a genius." Hannah beamed. Peter had been voted Top Defense Attorney in Santa Barbara five years running. A skilled trial lawyer with a book of high-profile cases, he always had the DA running scared. That kind of influence attracted attention, hence today's interview and the tightness in her throat. "So, an office bedroom, huh? Will you let me sleep over sometimes?"

She wiggled her eyebrows at him, giving him a quick swat on the butt before she left to wrangle the children.

Hannah checked four-year-old Thomas's room first, sighing at the mess she found there. His navy plaid shirt and little blazer lay on the bed just where she'd placed them over an hour ago, overtaken by his green plastic army men. She scooped the soldiers up by the handful and tossed them into the plastic bin, hoping Thomas hadn't gone far.

Next, she knocked on Dylan's door, pounding hard enough to jar him from his adolescent stupor—video games, cell phones, and the surge of testosterone that had turned him overnight from a boy into a gangly, pimple-faced zombie. At fourteen, he was the spitting image of his father and just as stubborn. "Ten minutes and counting, Dylan. You need to look presentable."

"Alright, alright." A groan, then silence.

"And comb your hair."

Hannah hurried downstairs, where she spotted eleven-year-old Lily already dressed and seated on the plush sofa that had set them back for more than Hannah's first car. She could always count on her daughter in a pinch.

Gritting her teeth in frustration, Lily looked up at her. "Will you put this on for me?"

Lily opened her hand, revealing the charm bracelet she'd unwrapped at Christmas. As Hannah looped it around her daughter's slim wrist and fastened the delicate clasp, a single butterfly charm dangled from the gold band. Hannah had promised Lily another—a pair of ballet slippers—for her birthday in August.

"Where is your little brother?" Hannah asked.

Lily shrugged, mirroring Hannah's annoyance. "I haven't seen Thomas since he asked Dylan to play with him. Dylan called him a baby and made him cry."

Sighing deeply, Hannah glanced at the oversized wall clock that hung above the stone fireplace. It had been a wedding gift from her sister, Nora. Lovely, but a little tongue-in-cheek, since Nora knew she'd never been late—and never would be—a day in her life.

"Will you help me look for him, Lily-bear?" Hannah began back up the staircase. "Be careful with your dress though. It's silk."

While Lily searched downstairs, Hannah met Peter on the landing, greeting him with an exasperated smile. She wanted today to be perfect, to finally prove to herself she belonged here. In a neighborhood with a gate and a security booth. In a house three times the size of the one where she and Nora had grown up. In clothes with fancy designer labels. With a husband everyone admired.

"Are you alright?" he asked, squeezing her shoulder.

"Thomas is missing."

"Again?"

"You know how he gets." Already, Hannah felt the first signs of panic. A flutter in her chest, dampness beneath her armpits. A sense that time had run out. Because it had, in fact, nearly. In exactly eight minutes, Marie Abbott would appear on the doorbell camera, looking effortlessly chic and expecting the Fox family to be present in their entirety to regale her with tales of their success. Hannah felt like a total impostor.

With tunnel vision, Hannah led the search through the house. They checked all the usual places. Beneath the coffee table and behind the sofa. In the well-stocked pantry and under the bed. Closet doors, flung open. Curtains, pulled back. But Thomas had left no trace.

When the bell rang, Hannah winced as if she'd been struck. Still, she composed herself, took a breath, and followed Peter to the door. He laughed as he opened it. Next to Marie and Claude and their assistant, Thomas shuffled from one bare foot to the other, his red hair wild as the weeds. In his hand, his very favorite toy soldier, Ranger Rob.

"I take it this charming fellow belongs to you." Marie gazed down at the little boy adoringly, while Hannah plastered a smile onto her own face. Thomas troubled her, with his quiet sensitivity. She feared the world would break him. "Claude discovered him stowed away in the hedge. He gave us quite a scare."

"That's Thomas," Hannah managed. "Always finding the best hiding places."

Later, after Thomas had been cleaned up and dressed to match the rest of the family, after the interview and the photo shoot by the pool in the golden hour, Marie pulled Hannah aside, showing her a digital mock-up of the cover. "Next month's issue," she pronounced. "We'll call it *Santa Barbara's Perfect Family*. What do you think?"

Hannah nodded her approval dispassionately. But in all her life, she had never been more pleased.

CHAPTER ONE

Olivia Rockwell flinched at the first explosion. Fireworks bloomed in the night sky, sending ripples of color across the black ocean water and lighting the freckles on her sister's face. Olivia paused briefly, watching the crowd gasp and cheer, before tugging Emily toward the car.

"But Liv, this is the good part."

"You're *drunk*." That word had history, and it zipped off Olivia's tongue, keen as a blade.

"So?" Em shrugged off her hand but followed behind. "That's the whole point of summer break. I'm only here for a few weeks. Let me have a little fun."

"Fun?" How many times had their mother used that line, sloshed drunk from a long night at the Hickory Pit? "You asked Warden Blevins for a piggyback ride."

Another blast illuminated the parking lot and muffled Emily's sharp scoff. "Well, he didn't say no."

"Because he was mortified."

Pushing thoughts of the red-faced warden from her mind, Olivia unlocked the Buick station wagon she'd inherited from their mother. She was stone-cold sober and, unbelievably, her sister's antics hadn't been the most embarrassing moment of her night. Still, she directed a stern finger at the passenger seat that Emily promptly ignored. "He's my *boss*, Em."

"It's not like I have a thing for him." In the tradition of little sisters, she raised her voice with one purpose: big sister's abject humiliation. "You're the one who's got the hots for—"

"Car. Now."

Em groaned as she joined Olivia inside the airless Buick, still stuffy from the warmth of the day. "You're not hiding it from anyone, you know. And neither is Deck. He barely took his eyes off you the whole night. I told you that sundress would turn his head."

Though Olivia couldn't deny Detective Will Decker looked damn good in a swimsuit, she ignored the wiggle of Emily's eyebrows. She busied herself instead, rolling down the windows, starting the car, pulling out of the crowded lot, and steering for home. Pine Grove Road could be crowded with tourists this time of year, so she opted for the dirt road cut-through instead. "Can you believe Graham Bauer punched that lawyer? I'm pretty sure Deck was too busy reining him in to notice my outfit."

"Oh, he noticed." Em giggled. "But nice try changing the subject. Do you think that lawyer guy could really get Graham kicked off the force?"

Olivia didn't answer. As the car rumbled down the path, her heart drummed faster and louder, matching the distant sounds of the fireworks. "Is that smoke?"

Em leaned out the passenger window, letting the breeze blow back her strawberry-blonde curls. She scrunched her nose. "It smells like it."

"Look." Olivia maneuvered off the road, pointing in horror at the silhouette of a sports utility vehicle parked on the shoulder. The bright orange flames transfixed her, flaring from the back seat and licking at the tree trunks like angry waves against the sheer cliffs. Black smoke plumed from its center, signaling doom.

"There's someone inside." Olivia's throat burned.

She cracked her door open.

The fire threw sparks at her, its embers glowing in the grass, warning her to come no closer.

But still, she charged forward until she felt its simmering heat.

Through the open driver's window, the man lay still in the seat. Only the fire moved, flicking like a snake's tongue at his back.

Neither the heat nor Olivia's frantic shouting roused him. She looked back to where Emily stood, wide-eyed and talking hurriedly into her cell phone. At least she'd be safe.

Olivia pulled her thin sweater tight around her body, covered her nose and mouth with her forearm, and darted nearer to the flames. The heat met her like a brick wall. She started to sweat, the soft fabric of her blue sundress clinging to her skin.

Still secured by his seat belt, the man's body had slumped sideways onto the console. When she shook his shoulder, he made no sound. She reached inside, disconnected the belt, and grabbed his arm, struggling to maneuver him through the door as the fire slithered closer and closer to the cab. The flames taunted her in a dangerous game of strike and retreat.

"Leave him!" Emily yelled.

Olivia's eyes burned as she choked on the thick smoke, already feeling lightheaded. But she nearly had him. She held the man beneath his armpits, dragging him out and to the ground. His feet dropped heavy as boulders into the grass.

The greedy fire moved faster now. But Olivia's body refused to move. The man lay half on top of her, his head lolling on her stomach. Though she didn't know him, she recognized his face in an instant, and she couldn't look away from the vicious wound in his left temple. The blood, wet and red on her hands, took her right back there to the Double Rock projects, with her father standing over Tina Solomon's dead body, a knife in his hands. She was eight years old and helpless, her legs useless as stumps.

Olivia gasped for breath, her vision blurring. Above her, the black sky stretched forever. Pinpricks of light danced at its periphery, flickering like stars.

A distant wailing cut through the roar in her head. From somewhere, her sister screamed her name.

She imagined her father scooping her up and carrying her far from this place, the same way he'd taken her from Apartment E that night twenty-seven years ago.

When a pair of strong arms lifted her, she latched on and surrendered to them completely. With the last of her effort, she tilted her head, expecting to see her father's face. No matter that he'd been dead four months now.

"Deck?"

CHAPTER TWO

Detective Will Decker pondered the ridiculousness of his tan boat shoes and navy swim trunks. Entirely appropriate for the Hickory Pit's Barbecue Bash, but completely out of place at a crime scene. The only barbecue here the charred remains of the victim's SUV that had been doused ten minutes ago by Fog Harbor Fire and Rescue.

Will studied the body near his feet while he waited for the medical examiner, Chet Clancy, to arrive. Already, he could imagine Chet's practiced voice pronouncing, *Single gunshot wound to the head.*

Olivia had risked her life to rescue a dead man. Will let his eyes wander to the back of the ambulance, where she sat by Emily, wrapped in a blanket and inhaling oxygen through a mask. Half her mouth twisted at him in an ironic smile, and her dimple tugged at his heart like she held it by a string.

Olivia had nearly *died* rescuing a dead man.

Finally, Will spotted Detective Jimmy Benson's blue Camaro skirting the police barricade. JB and his fourth ex-wife, Tammy—they'd remarried in June at the Little White Chapel in Vegas—had been stuck in traffic on the main road for twenty minutes trying to bypass the tourists who'd left the fireworks show. He'd been buzzing Will's cell every five minutes to unleash a string of expletives while Tammy *tsk, tsk*ed in the background.

Will had been fortunate he'd left the beach early, even if he had been running away. He'd heard the call over the portable radio in his truck as the last of the sparklers illuminated the sky. He glanced back to Olivia and shook his head at her, returning her dim smile.

"Damn tourists!" JB ran an exasperated hand through his graying buzz cut and let out a heavy breath. "I'd like to beat them senseless with their selfie sticks."

Will could always count on JB to reach new heights of inappropriateness. But tonight he seemed especially rattled. "You okay, partner? You look a little flushed."

After a few raps of his fist against his breastbone, JB belched. "I shouldn't have had that third plate of ribs, but Tammy okayed it. She let me call it a cheat day, it being the Fourth and all."

Will motioned Chet over with a grim wave before returning his attention to JB. "Did you tell her every day is a cheat day?" Since mid-March, JB had been living on the edge, lying to Tammy about his strict adherence to her diet regimen. *Low-carb at home, carb-load at work* had become JB's secret motto, most often uttered between mouthfuls.

"Now why the hell would I do that?" He glanced back at the Camaro, where Tammy had taken a seat on the hood, and lowered his voice. "Come to think of it, I'll tell Tammy the truth when you tell Olivia you want to join her in the horizontal tango."

"Horizontal *what*?" With his cheeks burning—Will knew exactly what JB meant—he heaved a grateful sigh as Chet approached.

"What do we have, gentlemen?"

Will stepped aside, gesturing to the dead man. "Doctor Rockwell pulled him out of the car before the whole thing caught fire. It looks to me like he's been shot in the head."

As Chet dropped to one knee in the damp grass, JB gawked at the body awash in the lights from the emergency vehicles as if he'd only just noticed the man, sunburned and slack-jawed. Still clad in his beach gear, one flip-flop had been lost to the fire. The other lay in the grass, its strap broken. On the man's left ring finger, a slim gold band. On his right wrist, a Rolex watch.

"Sheesh, City Boy. *Him*? When were you gonna tell me?"

Chet peered up at them while he examined the man's head with a gloved hand. "You two know this man?"

Will grimaced at the irony of it. Chief Flack was going to blow a gasket. "I wouldn't go that far. But he and Graham Bauer got into it today at the beach in front of that B&B, Shells-by-the-Sea. His kid ran up to catch a football and plowed into Bauer. The guy came over and they exchanged a few words. Then Bauer hauled off and punched him. When he came to, he was understandably pissed off. He announced himself as some big-shot attorney and threatened to sue Bauer and take his badge. JB and I had to help security escort them both to their cars."

The entire incident had left Will with a bad feeling, a familiar kind of dread. Because as much as he wanted to pass judgment on Graham Bauer, he knew a thing or two about the kind of bad decisions that sprouted from a brain pickled in alcohol. One of many reasons he'd sworn off drinking years ago.

"What time was that?" Chet asked, glancing back at the burned shell of the SUV.

"Late afternoon. Around three o'clock, I'd say. I'm fairly certain the B&B security guard, Wade Coffman, wrote an incident report."

"Any firearms in the vehicle?"

Will shook his head, distracted by his thoughts unspooling back to the crowded beach parking lot.

"Then it's highly unlikely he committed suicide." Chet pointed to the circular hole on the victim's left temple. "Perforating entrance wound to the right temporal scalp. Medium caliber, I'd say. Fired at close range. Exit wound on the left occipital. Any chance forensics found the bullet?"

"They're waiting for Fire and Rescue to give us the all-clear before we search the area." Will nodded at the fire engine parked at the scene. Though the car's remains had been extinguished, the heady smell of smoke still lingered from the small patch of smoldering grass beneath it.

"Got a name for this guy?"

Will turned to JB, his partner's worried face matching his own. The dead man had a name, of course. A name and a family—a wife and three kids. He'd been too drunk to drive himself, so Will had taken the keys from him and placed them in his wife's hand.

"Peter Fox."

CHAPTER THREE

"Don't you think you should thank Detective Decker?" A mischievous Emily nudged Olivia with her elbow before she hopped off the back of the ambulance and waved Deck over. "It's only polite."

Olivia's head ached; her eyes burned too. The arm of her favorite sweater bore a small singe mark and a bloodstain. But she could breathe well enough to hiss at her sister, "Em. No. Stop."

Deck made a straight line toward her, his brow furrowed with concern.

"Too late."

Olivia flashed Em a death stare before he arrived, which she promptly disregarded with a shrug—*typical*—and slunk away to eavesdrop from the shadows.

"You feeling alright, Red Adair?"

"Ha ha. Very funny." She tried not to stare at his hand on the tailgate mere inches from her thigh. When he moved it and stuck it in the pocket of his shorts, she knew he'd read her mind. She forced herself to think of anything but what had happened between them tonight on the beach. "Is that…?"

"The guy that had a fight with Graham? Yeah."

"He had a nasty head wound. Gunshot?"

"Chet says so."

After an awkward silence, they both spoke at once.

"Are you sure you're—"

"About earlier—" Olivia stopped short, uncertain what she'd intended to say. She took the easy out he'd given her. "Am I okay? Right as rain, thanks to you."

He nodded, looking down at his boat shoes. "I suppose it was a good thing then, leaving when you did."

"And you. It's lucky you were right behind us."

"Damn lucky." Deck retrieved the edge of the blanket that had fallen from her shoulder and returned it there. She gave in and let her eyes meet his. Between them, the cool night air felt weighted with all that went unspoken.

The fire engine suddenly roared to life, its siren wailing through the trees like a banshee and sending a shiver straight through Olivia. Pulling in alongside it, she spotted Graham in a patrol car, his partner nowhere in sight. Only in a small town like Fog Harbor could a cop be drunk on the beach in the afternoon and back on duty by the evening. Still, it rattled her, the way his eyes darted.

Deck shouted to JB. "What's going on?"

"Another fire." JB jogged up the side of the road toward the ambulance.

"Where?"

Breathless, he rested his hands on his knees, spitting out the words with effort. "That fancy rental up by Shell Beach."

"Ocean's Song?" Olivia knew it well since her friend, Leah, owned the B&B next door.

Will's face paled. "Shit."

"What is it?" she asked.

"That's where Peter Fox and his family were staying."

CHAPTER FOUR

The sky caught fire and burned. A tower of flame and smoke grew above the redwoods, casting an eerie orange glow in the dark as if the sun had risen too early.

Pedal to the floorboard, Will followed behind the red engine racing toward Shell Beach, gaping out his truck's front windshield at the menacing inferno. He didn't like leaving the scene of a murder, especially with Graham showing up. Though Graham had sobered, he'd still acted like an ass, insisting he'd take over in their absence.

"Pull over here." JB directed him into the ditch, twenty or so yards from the BEACH ACCESS sign.

While the engine sped toward the turnoff, Will steered the truck to a stop and flung open the door, ignoring the smell of smoke that rushed in to meet him. Anxious to lay eyes on the place, he jogged through the tall grass, stopping to wait for JB.

"No offense, but could you move any slower?"

JB raised his middle finger. "It'll still be on fire when we get there, City Boy."

The dirt access road led straight to the sands of Shell Beach. Out of place on the rocky coastline of Fog Harbor, it boasted a smooth, white shore, a functioning lifeguard stand, and the best sand dollar-picking in Northern California. The perfect place for a family vacation.

Sharp as a blade, that thought pierced Will's stomach and twisted, the moment he caught sight of Ocean's Song through the haze.

Flames engulfed the north end of the house, greedily consuming the bungalow one room at a time. A crew of firemen battled the monster, beating it back with a hose, even as it leapt to life again.

As Will looked on from a distance, the blaze broke through the picture window, and the small crowd of onlookers gasped and moved back, briefly abandoning their cell phone recordings of the devastation.

"Damn." JB whistled. "That's one hell of a fire. You think we have a second crime scene?"

Will didn't answer him. The whole night had begun to feel like an awful dream, the kind that leaves you breathless and drenched in your own sweat. Now, he could only watch and wonder what they'd find upon waking.

CHAPTER FIVE

For the second time that night, Olivia stared into the fiendish face of a fire, her sister at her side. She felt safe next to Em on the back porch of Shells-by-the-Sea, but the flames hinted otherwise, flaring high into the night sky and threatening to jump the stretch of sand that separated Ocean's Song from the rest of Shell Beach.

"That is way too close for comfort." Leah swaddled a crying baby Liam against her chest while her husband, Jake, looked out with trepidation. A few of the guests milled about, having heard the commotion and abandoned their rooms.

"Did you see anything?" Olivia asked him.

Jake shook his head. "I was still half asleep when the fire trucks pulled up."

"Lucky you," Leah teased. "I know this sounds crazy, but I could've sworn I heard gunshots. Liam woke up screaming bloody murder."

"Gunshots?" Emily widened her eyes at her sister. An expert eavesdropper, Olivia knew she'd heard Deck's every word earlier too.

"I heard them." The voice materialized from the doorway. From the solemn mouth of the security guard Leah and Jake had hired months ago, in the wake of the highest murder tally Fog Harbor had ever seen. His starched uniform identified him as Wade Coffman of Steadfast Security. "At least three—*bang, bang, bang*—but spread apart. Like the guy took his time to think about it."

Olivia shivered. She'd made a point to clean her hands, splashing them with water from a cold bottle one of the EMTs gave her and rubbing them dry with the blanket they'd wrapped around her. But when she looked down at them now, she could still see the red stains of Peter Fox's blood.

CHAPTER SIX

With the fire finally doused, Will and JB approached the charred remains of Ocean's Song. While most of the sprawling house had been spared due to its sturdy cinder block construction, the back had burned beyond recognition. Near the swimming pool deck, ashes blackened the usually pristine sand.

From the periphery of the scene, Fire Lieutenant Jeff Hunt waved them over. The waxing moon spotlighted his tired eyes and drooping shoulders. No surprise to Will since he'd heard the old guy worked himself to the bone, doing double duty as the fire investigator. He even coached the local high school wrestling team on his off days. "Walk with me, Detectives."

The lieutenant led them up the access road, past the remaining fire engines, and around to the front of the house. "What a night. And I was thinking my biggest problem would be the kiddos getting drunk and setting off illegal fireworks. We usually have at least two grass fires and one lost finger. Hell, I'd take a missing appendage any day over this."

Will waited for JB to insert his foot in his mouth like usual, but his partner kept it shut instead, wiping a sheen of sweat from his brow as they walked.

"What can you tell us?" Will glanced over Lieutenant Hunt's shoulder at the intact front door. It yawned open, a warm yellow light glowing from within the foyer and beckoning them inside. From here, nothing seemed amiss. But Will could smell the lingering smoke, caught in his nose like a hideous perfume. A persistent reminder of the hidden devastation.

"For starters, we've got three dead bodies."

"Three?" JB sucked in a breath. "Jiminy Christmas!"

His worst fears confirmed, Will's heart lurched in his throat. "Burned?"

"Shot in the head from what I was told, but Doc Clancy's on his way. We'll let him make the call. Fortunately, only one of the victims was impacted by the fire. We were able to contain the blaze to the back portion of the house. The other two were found just inside the door and moved out here by the firemen. No signs of life."

Lieutenant Hunt made quick work of the front lawn. Quicker than JB could manage. Quicker than Will wanted to go. His thoughts slowed him down, left him standing there, talking to himself, while they went on ahead of him. "*Only* three?"

Mrs. Fox lay on the grass nearest the doorway, flat on her back and clad in her pajamas. Her copper-red hair fell messily around her face. Her dull blue eyes, still open but unseeing. In the center of her forehead, the cause of her death. A single bullet hole.

"The wife." Will made a mental checkmark on a grim list.

Next to her, the teenaged boy from the beach. His patchy stubble and wiry muscles and SpongeBob T-shirt pinned him squarely in the middle: not a boy, not yet a man. Will could still hear his mother chastising him. *Dylan, take your brother and sister to the car. Now.* All signs of the troublemaker he'd been had drained from his body. The wound on his head appeared identical to his mother's.

"That's the kid who smacked into Bauer, right?"

Will nodded at his partner. "He probably heard the first shot and came to the door to investigate."

"Good lord." Chet appeared on the lawn, looking as beleaguered as the lieutenant. "When dispatch said multiple victims, I never imagined this." He stooped down over Dylan's body, releasing a weary sigh.

An unsmiling procession, they moved single file up the steps and inside the house, with Lieutenant Hunt leading them.

"The crew found the adult female victim here." He pointed just past the threshold, where a bowl of half-spilled popcorn had landed, scattering its contents across the hardwood. The bowl itself had broken into four uneven pieces of ceramic. A fifth piece sat in the dustpan near the broom resting against the wall. "The boy was a few steps away. At first, we suspected they'd succumbed to the smoke, but…"

Clad in a pair of crime scene booties, Will stepped carefully to avoid the blood-slick floor, though the firefighters had already left a trail of bloody footprints. The walls, too, bore the red spatter evidence of the crime.

As they moved down the hall, past the kitchen, smoke stained the walls black. By the time they'd reached the remnants of the hard-hit living room, soot carpeted the floor. Empty hooks hung from a curtain rod above the missing picture window, the curtains themselves burned to nothing. Outside, ash and debris floated in the pool, eerily spotlighted by the LEDs below.

"Any idea what caused the fire?"

"It's arson. We'll get the fire dog in here to take a sniff but I'd stake my life on it." Lieutenant Hunt pointed to a half-melted plastic bottle of lighter fluid discarded beneath the charred coffee table. "There's another one of those just inside the master bedroom."

Will approached the debris of ground zero with trepidation. The third body rested on the sofa.

"Lily." Chet gently lifted the burned wrist, where a gold charm dangled, unharmed, from its bracelet. The girl's name had been engraved on a small butterfly. Then, he examined the head, the grisly conclusion visible on his face.

"What about the little boy?" Will remembered him best of the Foxes' three children. Because he'd clung to his mother's leg like a monkey in the throes of a massive meltdown, whining and desperate not to leave the beach. "Three or four years old, maybe. Red hair, freckles."

"The crew checked all the bedrooms. Let me—"

But Will had already taken off for the far wing of the house, passing the shell of the master suite, where the bed frame loomed like a dark skeleton and smoke stains wept down the walls.

He poked his head into the next bedroom, finding it largely untouched by the fire. A pair of boy's swim trunks hung from the top post of a bunk bed erected in the corner. Hidden partway beneath it, Will spotted a plastic police car with one of its tiny tires missing. He peered up at the unmade bed. Empty.

"Hello?" Will's voice sounded small, the way he'd intended. The poor kid probably felt scared out of his mind. But the only answer came from his partner across the hall.

"Got anything?" JB asked.

"Nothing. You?"

JB wobbled, catching himself against the doorframe. Grimacing, he shook his head.

"Are you sure you're okay, man? You look—"

From down the hall, Lieutenant Hunt yelled to them with newfound urgency. "You two need to see this."

They found the lieutenant in another bedroom. This one, with a view of the water. A pile of green plastic army men littered the bedspread and the carpet in front of the partially open sliding glass door.

Lieutenant Hunt pointed to the sand abutting the house, where a single soldier had been left behind, half buried, and a set of small footprints led into the night.

CHAPTER SEVEN

Olivia found a seat in one of the oversized wooden rocking chairs on the back porch of Shells-by-the-Sea, soothing herself with the predictable rhythm and the sounds of the ocean. Emily had taken Leah up on her offer to stay the night in the only available guest room, left vacant by a last-minute cancellation. But Olivia felt too wired to sleep and too unnerved to return to their house secluded in the watchful redwoods.

Leah returned to the porch, baby-less. She placed a hot cup of tea in Olivia's hands and joined her in the adjacent chair, which creaked as Leah started it rocking. That plaintive whine sent a jolt of unease up Olivia's back. "So, I hear you've got a new patient."

Olivia nodded, avoiding Leah's eyes. She knew exactly where the conversation was headed. Now that Leah had returned from maternity leave—with a chic short haircut and fierce maternal instincts—she couldn't get anything past her. Especially not this. "It's not a big deal."

"I've got room on my caseload. I could've taken him."

"And let you have all the fun?" Olivia hoped Leah would laugh and let it go. "You know I'm a sucker for the lost causes."

"Or better yet, give him to an intern."

They both chuckled, knowing inmate Javier Mendez ate interns for breakfast. But Leah sobered quick.

"Seriously, Liv? Mendez? That guy creeps me out." Leah had given her the same speech about Drake Devere, the serial killer who'd escaped from Crescent Bay State Prison in December. And in Leah's defense, she hadn't been wrong. Olivia had nearly lost her little sister thanks to Drake's twisted schemes.

"You do realize we work in a prison." Olivia grinned. "Our patients are not exactly upstanding citizens."

"True. But there's bad and there's seriously bad…"

Olivia thought back to her first session with Javier, the way he'd studied her like an insect in a jar. She didn't dare tell Leah how, when he'd finally dropped his predatory gaze, he'd winked at her.

"…And then, there are the monsters. Like chupacabra-level bad," Leah continued. "That's Javier Mendez."

Sipping her tea, Olivia cast an ironic side-eye at her friend. "Well, you know I'm not afraid of monsters."

"Not to mention I know the real reason you volunteered to therapize that guy."

Olivia nearly choked on her chamomile as her heart skipped like a pebble then sank to the deep, dark bottom of her stomach. No one knew the real reason. Not Leah. Not Deck. Not even Emily. "Which *is*?"

"Doctor Carrie Brown-nose Stanley. You want to put her in her place. Remind her you're the big dog in the MHU."

"Exactly." In the two-plus years since Olivia had returned to Fog Harbor and accepted the job as chief psychologist at Crescent Bay, Carrie still hadn't gotten over the warden's snub, and lately, she'd made it her mission to discredit Olivia at every turn, all the while doing her fair share of sucking up to Warden Blevins. "If anybody can get Mendez to talk, it's the big dog."

Leah sighed. "Just remember what happened to the last woman who tried that."

Olivia stopped rocking, held up her hand for Leah to do the same. "Do you hear that?"

Above the rumble of the waves and the gentle swish of the wind, Olivia heard someone crying.

*

Wade Coffman pointed his flashlight toward the beach, the beam spotlighting the still-warm sand and the black water beyond it. Keeping his free hand on the mace canister affixed to his belt, he walked in the direction of the lifeguard stand.

"Should I wake Jake?" Leah asked. "Or call the cops?"

"Not necessary." Wade didn't bother to turn around. "I'm sure it's just a drunk gal with a broken heart. Nothing I can't handle."

Olivia bundled herself tighter inside her sweater, listening again for the muffled cries. It sounded like a child to her, not a drunk girl. She stepped off the porch and hurried to catch up. "I'm going with you."

"Well, you're not leaving me here all alone." Leah jogged along behind her, both of them following Wade and the deep footprints of his boots in the sand.

As they neared the lifeguard stand, the crying intensified. Little sobs, broken by desperate gasps for breath. Wade held up a closed fist, directing his foot soldiers to halt. He looked like a military man with a graying buzz cut and a square jaw, arms accustomed to carrying a rucksack through the jungle.

But Olivia couldn't wait. That child needed help. She felt certain of it. She ran ahead of Wade and up the wooden plank leading to the door.

Peering in through the window, her eyes adjusting to the dark, she saw a little boy, barefoot and huddled in the corner, his head down on his knees. His whole body trembled, scared as a rabbit.

Hoping not to spook him, Olivia tapped the door before she cracked it open. He looked up and sniffled. He wiped at his splotchy face with the sleeve of his dinosaur pajamas.

"It's okay." She didn't dare move toward him. Not yet. She wondered where he'd come from and what led him to a dark lifeguard stand in the middle of the night. "You're okay."

As she took the first step inside, she felt someone behind her. She kept her gaze locked on the boy as a pair of familiar boat shoes appeared in her lower periphery, alongside Wade's sturdy boots.

"I got this." Deck pushed ahead of her. Olivia tried to shake off her irritation as he dropped to his knee, lowering himself to the boy's level. Of course he thought he knew better.

"You're safe now," he said softly as he produced his badge from his pocket. It shined, even in the dark, and the little boy's eyes widened as they fixed on it. "I'm a policeman."

The boy gasped and scrambled back as if the badge had sharp teeth that would bite. Then he opened his mouth and screamed.

CHAPTER EIGHT

Terror had a sound. Raw and ugly. The sound of the boy's sudden screams pierced the tense quiet of the beach like an icepick, sending Will reeling.

He backed away as fast as he could, bumping into Olivia and skirting past Wade. Olivia reached for the boy, and he latched onto her, still frantic. His sobs muffled by her shoulder, she carried him out of the lifeguard stand with Wade a few steps behind her, leaving Will alone. He'd done nothing wrong, but he felt like an ogre anyway.

Will stooped in the corner, where the boy had been sitting, and pocketed another toy soldier. An infantryman lying on his stomach, his tiny rifle aimed at an imaginary bad guy. Later, he'd make the kid a peace offering.

By the time Will emerged, still flummoxed, Olivia had nearly made it back to the house, trudging up the beach with the boy's legs wrapped around her waist. The others waited on the beach, dumbfounded.

Will felt an inexplicable relief at the sight of JB's smart-ass grin. His partner had barely made the run from the house, laboring as he'd discarded his crime scene booties on the sand. By the time Will had ascended the lifeguard platform, JB had been doubled over and wheezing.

"That went well, City Boy. You're a regular Mister Rogers." JB chuckled but it came out one-note, clunky as a dead piano key. He took a halting step and clutched at his chest. Opened his mouth to speak again but only managed a groan.

Before Will could register his own shock, JB staggered forward and collapsed onto the beach. He lay there, stone-like, even after Will dropped to his knees to try to rouse him. His pulse raced beneath Will's fingers. His face, blanched and sweaty, felt cold to the touch.

Lieutenant Hunt radioed for assistance, as the hellish night dragged on with no promise of morning.

Fog Harbor Gazette

"Police Suspect Arson in Ocean's Song Fire; Multiple Victims
Found Deceased"

by Jeanie Turtletaub

Authorities in Fog Harbor, California, are investigating
two suspicious fires that started late Saturday night,
following the July Fourth festivities at Shell Beach. At
approximately 9:30 p.m., Fog Harbor Fire and Rescue
responded to reports of a car fire on an unmarked dirt road
near the beach parking lot. A good Samaritan discovered
the victim inside the vehicle and attempted to pull him
to safety. Police later discovered he had sustained a fatal
gunshot wound to the head. The victim has since been
identified as fifty-one-year-old prominent Santa Barbara
defense attorney, Peter Fox. According to his professional
website, Fox spent ten years as a public defender before
moving to private practice, where he was known for his
tenacity, guile, and legal acumen.

While responding to the first scene, Fire and Rescue
received a second call of a house fire burning at Shell
Beach. Upon arrival, firefighters discovered the lavish vacation rental, known as Ocean's Song, ablaze. Fortunately,
due to the home's cinder block construction, the fire was
quickly contained to the back portion of the house, and
the property sustained minimal structural damage. Three
victims, all members of the Fox family, were discovered

deceased inside the dwelling having sustained fatal gunshot wounds. They have since been identified as forty-four-year-old Hannah Fox and her children, fourteen-year-old Dylan and eleven-year-old Lily. A third child, age four, was found unharmed and has been placed in the custody of Child Protective Services. Sources close to the investigation revealed that the Fox family had been vacationing in Fog Harbor since July 1st and briefly attended the Hickory Pit's Twentieth Annual Barbecue Bash.

Police Chief Sheila Flack is expected to issue a statement on the investigation early Monday morning. Anyone with information regarding either crime is asked to contact the Fog Harbor Police Department. Marta Gregori, the owner of Ocean's Song, could not be reached for comment.

CHAPTER NINE

JB didn't move. He rested in the hospital bed, still as a stopped heart, an IV snaking from his arm onto the stand beside him. It unnerved Will, seeing him like that, but the steady beat of the monitor reassured him.

"Hey, partner."

No response.

Will plunked into the chair in the corner, watching the rise and fall of JB's chest. "I told you those Twinkies were a bad idea."

Not even an eyelash flutter.

"It figures. You bailing out on me now. When I've got two crime scenes and four bodies to deal with."

Despite the chair's stiff back, Will's eyes grew heavy. After stopping off at home to change his clothes and feed Cyclops, the one-eyed stray cat that had claimed Will as his own, he'd had no time for a nap. Fueled by weak hospital coffee, his body sputtered like an old engine on a cold day. He kept talking to stay awake, unburdening himself to a man who couldn't hear a single word.

"Something weird happened last night with Olivia. I blame it on that damn sundress. Those things should be outlawed. Anyway, we went for a walk down the beach. Just a walk, no biggie. But then she—"

"Detective Decker?"

Will jolted upright to see Tammy standing beside him, still dressed in last night's clothes.

"How are you?" He catalogued the evidence, the answer obvious. The dark circles beneath her eyes. The balled-up tissue in her hand. The thin hospital blanket draped messily on the pull-out sofa.

"I'm as fried as a chicken leg."

Will chuckled, glancing over her shoulder at JB, the king of ridiculous metaphors. Tammy didn't crack a smile. "This whole thing is my fault. I pressured him too much about sticking to the damn diet. This morning, I found a stash of peanut butter cups and a bottle of Zero Smoke odor eliminator in the glove box. Do you think he's been cheating the whole time?"

"Uh…" Will spun around, certain he'd heard JB grunt, but he found him unchanged and unmoving. "He tried his best. I'm sure this will scare him straight."

"Speaking of, I just saw the doctor."

"And? What's the word?"

"Atrial fibrillation."

"Fib who?" JB spoke up, suddenly wide-eyed.

"It's caused by your high blood pressure, Jimmy. And that's not all. The doc said you're prediabetic and well on your way to a heart attack. You're on the bad side of fifty. It's time to get serious about your—"

Will cleared his throat.

"What I mean is, I want us to grow old together." She clasped JB's hand, taking a seat on the bed beside him, and he pulled her in close. "I can't bear the thought of losing you. Not after we've found each other again."

"I'll leave you two alone." Will shuffled for the exit, averting his eyes from JB and Tammy, who'd already started locking lips like a pair of teenagers.

"The hell you will."

JB grinned, propping another pillow behind his head as Tammy offered him a sip of water.

"You can't leave me hanging. I need to hear more about that sundress."

CHAPTER TEN

Olivia peered through the two-way mirror at Thomas Fox. The little red-haired boy sat cross-legged on the floor opposite Dr. Lucy Berry. He stared vacantly, pulling at his shoelace, while Dr. Lucy built the tallest—and possibly, the only—block tower the Fog Harbor Police Department interview room had ever seen.

As the tower teetered and threatened to fall, Olivia held her breath. Thomas appeared preoccupied, barely glancing at Dr. Lucy when she offered him the last square-shaped block. He wound the shoelace around his finger, pulling it so tight he winced. With no choice, Lucy did the honors herself, carefully placing the block atop the structure and clapping her hands at her achievement like a deranged wind-up toy.

"Are you sure she knows what she's doing?" Chief Flack punctuated the question with a healthy dose of skepticism.

When the chief had arrived on the scene at Ocean's Song early that morning, Olivia had recommended she contact Fog Harbor's only child psychologist. After all, picking the brains of convicted criminals didn't exactly translate to getting little boys to give up the secrets locked in theirs, no matter how much Olivia wanted to help. But if Dr. Lucy crashed and burned—which seemed more and more likely by the minute—Olivia had promised to take a crack at him.

"Give her a chance, Chief. She's just trying to build some rapport." But already Olivia felt anxious. Thomas trusted her; she couldn't let him down.

Chief Flack raised an eyebrow. "She's building something, alright. I'm just not sure what it is."

On cue, the tower toppled, sending an avalanche of blocks scattering within a four foot radius.

"Oh, no!" Dr. Lucy met Thomas's indifference with an exaggerated frown and began collecting the pieces. "Shall we build another?"

"For the love of God." Chief Flack sighed and stood up, making a break for the door. She pointed at the telephone mounted on the observation room wall. "Call me if anything exciting happens. Decker should be back from the hospital any minute now. I'll have him check on you when he arrives."

Olivia nodded, turning her attention back to Thomas. It felt easier than sorting her thoughts about Deck. Her brain, fogged by exhaustion, could only manage one issue at a time.

"I want to go home. I hate this place." Thomas planted himself in front of the door, his small hands balled at the waist of his blue striped shorts. He wore the clothes Olivia had picked out from the drawer in the room with the bunk beds while Deck had looked on. She'd put them in a plastic bag, along with a stuffed dog she'd found, and handed them to the social worker, while Thomas waited in the car seat.

Dr. Lucy cast a desperate glance up at the mirror. With her bobbed hair and red-framed glasses, she could've been a child herself. "First, we need to talk about what happened last night. Will you tell me about it?"

"Where's Mommy?"

Olivia groaned. That made five now. Five times Dr. Lucy had posed the same question. Five times Thomas had answered with a question of his own. But she couldn't blame him. Her own mother had taken her to a therapist once, after what she'd witnessed at the Double Rock, and it had gone no better. She'd spent the fifty-minute session with her head buried in a dollhouse, ignoring the therapist's well-meaning questions.

"Your mommy is in heaven, remember? With Daddy and Dylan and Lily."

"But when is she coming back?" The insistent edge in his voice broke Olivia's heart. "I want to give her my Superman so she won't cry anymore."

He pointed to his shirt, where Dr. Lucy had affixed a small sticker, hoping to encourage him.

"Your mommy was crying?"

Ignoring her, Thomas peeled off the sticker, pushing out his lower lip. "I want to give it to her."

"She's not coming back, Thomas. But she'll always be with you." Dr. Lucy laid a hand on her own chest. "In here. With the rest of your family."

Thomas looked down at himself, confused. "In *here*?"

The door to the observation room opened, startling Olivia and jangling her over-caffeinated nerves. When she dropped the pen she'd been holding, it somersaulted, skittering toward the door, and landed on the toe of Deck's dress boot.

Deck looked more tired than surprised. Unshaven and bleary-eyed, she wondered if he'd slept at all. He bent to retrieve her pen, holding it out to her shyly. In a flash, she travelled back to the beach. To last night, before the whole world went sideways.

"How's JB?"

Deck slumped into the chair the chief had left vacant. "As ornery as ever. The doc said he'll be fine. With a few lifestyle changes. And a little time off. I'm under strict orders from Tammy to clean out his stash."

"Oof. How's he taking it?"

"Well, he offered me a hundred bucks for a day-old hospital cafeteria doughnut."

"That well, huh?"

He patted his pocket with a sly grin. "I'm thinking I found myself a new racket."

Olivia shook her head at him and smiled, relieved to fall back into the rhythm of their usual banter. Maybe they could pretend *it* hadn't happened.

"Is this as disastrous as it looks?" he asked, gesturing to the two-way mirror.

Thomas had retreated to the corner of the room and hidden beneath the table. Dr. Lucy sat in the center of the floor, laboring over a new block tower. "Worse."

"I thought you said Dr. Lucy was one of a kind. That there was no one else like her."

"Yeah. *Literally.* As in the only child psychologist in Fog Harbor. I can't vouch for her clinical skills."

Dr. Lucy leaned her head to the side, trying to coax out Thomas. "When scary things happen, it helps to talk about it."

The boy averted his eyes, curling himself into a ball like one of those roly-poly bugs.

Olivia grimaced at Deck. "I can't watch this anymore. Thomas looks miserable, and she's not getting anywhere with him. He's not ready to talk. Pushing him too hard will only make it worse."

"How long have they been in there?"

She glanced at her watch, shocked that only fifteen minutes had passed since Lucy had introduced herself as a doctor who talks to boys and girls to help the police catch the bad guys. "Long enough."

"Alright. We can try again after his aunt gets into town. Maybe a familiar face will be a comfort." Chief Flack had informed Olivia that she'd contacted Hannah's sister, Nora, herself. With Hannah and Peter's parents deceased, Nora was the closest next of kin.

Olivia hurried to the door, fully aware she'd just committed the therapist's cardinal sin. Letting her own stuff dictate her actions. They had a word for that. *Countertransference.* But right now, looking at poor Thomas, she didn't care. The boy needed rescuing. "Would you like me to tell them?"

"I can do it." Deck stood too, suddenly far too close to her in the cramped observation room. She felt unsteady on her feet, like she might bump into him. Still, she clung to the doorknob, refusing to let him win.

"Are you sure that's a good idea, Detective?"

"It sounds like you're saying it's not." He took another step toward her, and she swallowed hard.

"Well, if I remember correctly, Thomas wasn't exactly fond of you."

Deck rolled his eyes. "Kids love me. *Usually.*"

"The evidence would suggest otherwise."

"Anyway, I brought something for him." He withdrew a plastic army man from his pocket. "He left it behind last night in the lifeguard tower. I thought it might be his favorite."

Olivia studied the toy in his palm, feeling guilty for teasing him.

"You really shouldn't have just run off like that," he said.

"I ran off for a good reason."

"Which was?"

His face inches from hers, she felt certain they weren't talking about Thomas anymore, and it made her cheeks flame. "You know why."

"I came after you. I was—"

Before he said something he didn't mean, she fled into the hallway and rapped her knuckles against the solid wood of the interview room door.

Moments later, Dr. Lucy opened the door, holding a block in her hand. She blinked up at Olivia, while Thomas watched curiously from beneath the table. "Is everything okay?"

Olivia lowered her voice, hopeful Thomas wouldn't hear her discussing him like he wasn't there. "Detective Decker and I thought it might be better to wait until his aunt has arrived."

Dr. Lucy closed the door behind her, her sunny disposition darkening. "That child witnessed something awful, and I need more time with him. You can't expect miracles, Doctor Rockwell. Surely you know that, working with a criminal population. If Thomas doesn't want to talk, I certainly can't force him. I'll need to earn his trust."

"But perhaps you could try a more directive approach. He doesn't seem too keen on building block towers."

She looked down at the block she'd carried out, her cheeks pinkening. "I'll bring some crayons and paper with me tomorrow. Children communicate more easily through drawing. It's like a window to the subconscious mind."

Just then, Thomas tugged on the door, opening it a crack. "Can I go home now?"

Olivia wondered what home he meant.

CHAPTER ELEVEN

Will returned the soldier to his pocket and stole a moment alone in the quiet observation room. He leaned against the wall, listening to Olivia deliver the news to a frustrated Dr. Lucy, who agreed to return to the station the following day. Then he watched through the two-way mirror as the social worker retied Thomas's shoelace, took him by the hand, and led him away.

The boy followed along obediently, holding the stuffed dog Olivia had found tangled in the sheets on the bunk bed. At the doorway, he stopped and looked around, lost and confused. Like he'd discovered himself alone on an alien planet.

While Olivia reassured Thomas, Will looked on with recognition. Thomas reminded him of his thirteen-year-old self, the moment he'd realized his mother wouldn't be coming home. She would never have missed the birthday tradition of marking her boy's ever-growing height in pencil on the kitchen doorframe. And yet, that year and every year after, it had gone undone. As if he and his brothers had simply stopped growing, frozen in time in 1992. He knew July Fourth would forever be sullied for Thomas. A dark day that would divide his life into the before and the after.

When Will poked his head around the corner, Olivia had gone. So, that settled it. She wanted him to forget all about last night. *Fine*. He had plenty else to think about besides her kissing him out of the blue. Of course he'd balked. What did she expect? She'd gone and changed her own stupid rules without telling him.

He flopped into his desk chair and began purging JB's drawers on impulse, anxious for a distraction, for a way to rein in his thoughts that swarmed like bees, flitting from one poisonous flower to another. In an hour or so, he planned to head down to the police garage to watch the crime scene techs examine the burned-out shell of the SUV Peter Fox had rented six days ago. He hoped like hell Fox's cell phone would be recovered. His wife's had been located early this morning on what remained of the coffee table. The device, completely melted. Though Will had put in a call to the cell company for the records, it would take at least twenty-four hours to get his hands on them.

Will busied his mind, inventorying JB's indiscretions. One pack of Marlboros. Two half-eaten Snickers. A bag of Halloween candy Will felt certain JB had stolen from the break room. He popped a peanut butter cup in his mouth in JB's honor and dumped the rest in the trash can with a sigh, ending the unceremonious burial.

Then he turned his attention to his computer, searching for the website belonging to Peter Fox, attorney-at-law. The sleek web design and glossy photos confirmed what Will had already gleaned. Peter, a private defense attorney, had a booming law practice in Santa Barbara. According to Peter's bio, he'd cut his teeth in the public defender's office and prided himself on the relationships he'd maintained there. No wonder he boasted of his ability to secure favorable sentencing terms for his clients. He had an in.

Will scrolled down the page, stopping when a photograph hit him head-on. The entire Fox family, barefoot and clad in white button-down shirts, posed together on the beach in front of Little Gull lighthouse. Arm in arm with matching white smiles, it struck Will as one of those candid photos that's anything but. In the photograph, Thomas barely reached his father's knees.

On Hannah's Facebook page, he located the same image with a worrisome caption: FOXES' FOURTH OF JULY AT OCEAN'S SONG... SEVEN YEARS AND COUNTING!

Will shook his head at how naive people could be, giving up their life's details in a public forum for anyone to mine. His suspect pool, growing larger by the minute. And the Foxes looking more and more like the ideal family. Between the photos of Lily's ballet recitals, Dylan's first high school dance, and Thomas's fourth birthday at Disneyland, Will could find no evidence of trouble in paradise. Even the candid selfies of Peter and Hannah gleamed with the kind of mutual admiration of a couple in a jewelry store commercial.

The ringing of the desk phone startled him. "Morning, Chief."

"My office, Decker. ASAP. We need to discuss the Fox case."

Will trudged toward Chief Flack's office, his legs heavy with the knowledge that he had a dead family, an ailing partner, and no leads. Her door stood wide open, and he stopped short of the threshold in shock. One of the chairs was already taken.

"What's *he* doing here?"

"JB's going to be out of commission for at least a week. You need a partner."

"*Him*? Chief, can I speak to you in private?"

With a smirk, Graham Bauer stood and brushed past him as he left the office, forcing Will to step aside. Tonight, Will would be picturing that same smart-ass grin on the heavy bag in his garage. A couple of hard right hooks would set him straight.

As Graham lingered in the hallway, Will entered the office and shut the door firmly behind him. "With all due respect, Chief, you've got to be kidding me. Bauer is an overturned conviction waiting to happen."

She sighed. "I don't disagree."

"What about Milner? I sent her to interview Coffman this morning." Will had texted Jessie on the way over. He hoped the Shells-by-the-Sea security guard could shed light on the timeline between the gunshots he'd heard and the fire at Ocean's Song.

"Jessie's sharp. But she's way too green for this case."

"C'mon. I can't work with that guy." Will resisted the urge to drop to his knees and beg. "It's a conflict of interest. He punched the victim in the face."

"According to Graham, it was self-defense. He said Fox came at him."

"Of course. What else is he gonna say?"

"Listen, I don't like it any more than you do. But you're not in San Francisco anymore. This is all small-town politics. Between you and me, Graham's uncle, Marvin, donated a shitload of money to the mayor's re-election campaign. And guess who appointed yours truly as chief? Unless you want some other yahoo telling you what to do, we've got to keep Marv happy. Which means keeping Graham happy. So, put your big-boy panties on, give him some busy work, and keep him out of trouble. JB will be back in a week's time at the most. No harm, no foul."

"I'll do my best. But I'm telling you, it's a bad idea. The worst you've ever had."

"Noted."

Will knew when to keep his mouth shut. Besides, he couldn't say it out loud. Not without evidence to back it up. But he'd already thought it a hundred times. Graham Bauer was a suspect.

Will returned to find Graham spinning in JB's desk chair, pontificating to his unamused partner, Jessie Milner. "If you ask me, the old man should call it a day. We have standards to maintain in this department, and he's what you might call a weak link. To be honest, that porker should thank his lucky stars Chief Flack did away with the yearly fitness test."

Jessie poked her head over the partition, mouthing *save me* when Graham turned his back.

Will stopped the chair with a firm hand. "Get up, Bauer."

Graham didn't budge. "Hey, Deck. You know, I was thinking that you should come up with a catchy nickname for me, since I am your new partner."

"Temporary partner. And I already have a few nicknames for you that I can't repeat."

"Ouch. Why so salty? You worried I might out-police you?"

Will gritted his teeth. His head already pounding, he took one last swig of coffee and grabbed the keys to the Crown Vic. "Let's go."

With a mock salute, Graham finally rose from the chair and fell into step behind him.

When they reached the car, Will stopped and took a breath while Graham waited in the passenger seat. His moment of respite allowed the added advantage of watching Graham suffer in the stuffy hotbox.

"Alright, I've got three rules. One, I drive… the car and this investigation. Two, you don't touch evidence without my permission. Three, you don't bad-mouth JB. *Ever*." As frustrating as JB could be sometimes, he'd grown on Will like a barnacle. Crusty and relentless.

"And what happens if I break the rules?"

Will grinned and produced his cell phone. As he'd left Chief Flack's office, a text had arrived from JB—*Chief told me the news about Tweedledum. Don't say I never gave you anything*—with a link to a video. Will clicked it for the second time and displayed it for Graham, not even trying to contain his glee.

In the frame, Graham sat on a barstool, straining, as he arm-wrestled his partner. A small group of local cops looked on, hooting and cheering. Though he had a good fifty pounds on Jessie, she held his arm upright. While he struggled, she smiled. With a primal grunt, Graham gave it one last try, his celebrated biceps stretching his shirtsleeves. Jessie waited until he'd exhausted himself before she muscled his arm to the counter, raising her hands in victory.

"I'm waiting," she said, above the drunken whooping. *"Make it loud, Bauer."*

Graham stood atop a chair and cleared his throat. *"Can I get your attention, please? I'd like you all to know I was just defeated in arm-wrestling by my female partner."*

"And?"

"And in high school, I auditioned to be a member of a boy band." After video-Graham had belted out the first verse of a Backstreet Boys' classic, Will hit pause.

"One word, Bauer. Viral."

CHAPTER TWELVE

After leaving the station, Olivia drove to Leah's on autopilot. She couldn't shake the image of Thomas's face, his lip quivering slightly as she'd waved to him from the hallway. He'd barely lifted his small hand before he'd been whisked out the exit door by the social worker. Even now, Olivia rolled her eyes at Dr. Lucy's psychobabble. *A window to the subconscious mind.* But she'd been right about one thing: Thomas had seen something. Something that had sent him running for his life.

Olivia stopped short of the crime scene tape blocking off the road to Ocean's Song and turned into the Shells-by-the-Sea lot. She parked between a police cruiser and a Steadfast Security car and made her way inside to pick up her sister. Already, she couldn't wait to be home, to collapse onto the sofa for a much-needed nap.

"And you said you heard the shots around nine forty last night?" Jessie Milner sat across the shell-shaped coffee table from Wade, jotting notes onto a pad.

"Yes, ma'am. I was heading back from my patrol around the perimeter of the hotel when I heard three blasts, each about thirty seconds apart. At the time, I thought the sound might be fireworks. But then, I realized the show had already ended. A few minutes later, when I saw the flames, I knew it was the devil's work."

Fighting off the impulse to eavesdrop, Olivia continued through the common room to the back porch deck, where Emily had told her she'd be waiting. All of the wooden rockers were taken, with no Em in sight.

"Looking for your sister?" Jake approached from the beach, carrying a picnic basket and a large umbrella, all part of the Shells-by-the-Sea beachside service.

"Have you seen her?"

He pointed in the direction of Ocean's Song. "She walked off with a beach towel about twenty minutes ago."

"Of course she did." Olivia sighed. Since their father had died under suspicious circumstances at Valley View State Prison, the coroner ruling it a suicide, Emily had become even more devil-may-care, like blowing off her classes at San Francisco Art Institute to hang out with her new chic friends in Dolores Park.

Olivia's shoes sank into the soft sand of Shell Beach as she set off to find Em. The tourists flocked here in droves every summer, laying out their striped beach towels, building castles, and plunging into the waters of the chilly Pacific. While she walked among them, she marveled at the way they frolicked, undeterred by the hulking remains of Ocean's Song that loomed over them like a dead beast.

In the light of day, the destruction shocked her. While most of the house remained intact, the burned portion faced outward, scarring the otherwise picturesque beachfront. Olivia stopped outside the lifeguard stand and texted Emily again.

Helllooo?
Tired big sister here.
Where are you?

With no immediate response and no sign of her sister, she walked up the beach toward Ocean's Song, hoping for a closer look. Equal parts drawn and repulsed, she lingered outside the compound.

The gate to the pool stood slightly open, inviting her inside. The crime scene tape that had been stretched across it had collapsed in the wind and lay half-buried in the sand. After a quick glance over her shoulder, she stepped over it and slipped behind the gate, wondering if the killer had exited the house this way. Straight onto the beach and lost in the crowd of revelers leaving the fireworks show, hidden in plain sight.

The pool deck had the scattered look of life interrupted. Several of the lounge chairs had overturned in the chaos of the evening, and remnants of ash floated in the pool alongside a colorful beach ball.

Careful to avoid the shattered glass that littered the wooden planks, Olivia approached the empty window frame. Police tape crisscrossed the gaping hole that had yet to be boarded up by the owner. The charred sofa lay just inside it, spotlighted by a sunbeam, and Olivia stared for a moment, imagining the horrors that had taken place there. Her work as a psychologist had taught her anyone was capable of murder. But to shoot a child in the head, to burn her body, that required the absence of a soul. Poor Lily and Dylan, their lives cut impossibly short in the most brutal way.

From behind Olivia came a whispery-soft sound that raised the hair on her neck and silenced her breath. Even as she blamed the wind, she spun toward it, certain she'd see the killer standing there, ready to silence her as he'd done with the others. The deck was empty; the gate shut. The pool water shimmered beneath the sunlight. But she couldn't shake the feeling of being watched, or the primal undercurrent of fear that came with it.

Olivia moved along the perimeter of the pool, anxious to be rid of this place. She didn't make it far before she spotted something twinkling at the bottom of the water, where it caught the sun's reflection.

The skimmer in hand, she knelt at the pool's edge and peered down at the object. It glinted like a coin but had a strange inverted U-shape. Perhaps it had fallen into the pool by accident. She had to have a look at it.

Maneuvering the net deep beneath the surface, she angled for it, scooping it up after a few tries. She laid the pole on the deck and examined her catch—a small, shimmery horseshoe—that would fit in the palm of her hand.

It made no sense here, at the bottom of a pool in Fog Harbor, and she began to ask herself if it *had* been left deliberately. But what did it mean?

A quick Google search told her the horseshoe was a symbol of luck, its crescent moon shape meant to protect against the curse of the evil eye. She sat back on the warm deck and released a shaky breath.

The Fox family's luck had finally run out.

CHAPTER THIRTEEN

Crime scene tech Kelly Munroe moved around the shell of the silver SUV snapping photographs of the burned interior, while her partner, Steve Li, had begun the painstaking excavation.

Fire Lieutenant Hunt greeted Will with a handshake and a weary smile. Graham hung back, exactly as Will instructed, following the rules like a schoolboy. Or a guilty perp flying under the radar. No matter; Will preferred him like this. Quiet, out of the way, and absorbed in his cell phone.

"Take a look inside." The lieutenant pointed toward the open cargo space which had been reduced to ash. "As you can probably tell, the fire started here, in the rear compartment. The even burn pattern suggests the use of an accelerant, probably poured along the back and middle seats."

Will followed Lieutenant Hunt as he talked, peering in the open doors at the destruction. He found the charred car seat on the rear driver's side particularly unsettling.

"Then, the flames spread up to the front of the car. Fortunately, we were able to extinguish the fire before it destroyed the entire front cabin. Your killer didn't plan on anybody showing up so fast. Not on that road at that time of night. He probably figured most of the town would be occupied for at least another twenty minutes at the fireworks show. In that time, the whole SUV would've been destroyed."

Turning to Steve, Will said, "Give me some good news, man."

"Well, we lifted a ton of fingerprints from the exterior but that's to be expected with a rental car. Larry, the head mechanic at the police impound lot, took a look-see under the hood. Said he didn't see any mechanical issues with the vehicle. No reason for the victim to be stopped on the shoulder in the middle of nowhere."

Will nodded. Stopped on the shoulder *and* still seat-belted in, according to Olivia. The SUV's nose pointed east, away from Ocean's Song. Peter had been headed somewhere.

Steve made his way to the driver's-side door, pointing to a six-inch dent in the aluminum. "Larry also says this appears to be fresh damage."

Will examined the indentation, looking for paint transfer. "A fender bender?"

"Doesn't look like it. But your guess is as good as mine."

"Did you recover anything from the vehicle?"

Steve gestured to the table beside him, covered in plastic sheeting. The refuse of Peter Fox's life laid bare. "A cooler, a couple of fishing poles, and a set of Callaway golf clubs. The driver was out of the bag and tossed in the back seat."

Will surveyed the items with obvious disappointment.

"And we found the bullet."

"Now you're talkin'." Will rubbed his hands together eagerly.

"It was lodged in the side panel between the front and rear passenger windows."

"Caliber?"

"Looks like a nine millimeter."

"Anything else?"

Steve directed a flashlight into the dark cave beneath the middle row of seats. "Stay tuned."

While Will made his way around the vehicle, Graham materialized beside him. "How's it going, partner? Need a hand?"

Though Will said nothing to encourage him, Graham stuck to him like a shadow until they'd reached the driver's door. Then, he craned his neck to see inside it. "Have you looked under this one yet?"

Will watched in horror as Graham's ungloved hand advanced toward the seat like a heat-seeking missile. He seized him by the shoulder and pulled him back. "Rule number two, remember?"

"We already checked there," Steve said. For a by-the-book tech, he remained remarkably calm. "It's the first place I looked."

"Alright, alright." Graham took a step back. But as Will fielded his buzzing cell phone, he kept his eyes on him while he found a quiet spot in the corner to answer.

"Will Decker, Homicide."

"Hello, Detective. This is Marcia Russell, Mr. Fox's personal secretary and office manager. I received your message." No wonder Peter Fox had hired her. Marcia had the sweet and disarming voice of an innocent. She sniffled before she continued. "I heard about the tragedy on the news this morning. Do you know I worked for him for the last fifteen years? It still doesn't feel real. I just saw him last Tuesday before he and his family left on vacation. To tell the truth, I've been worried sick something like this might happen."

Her words felled Will like an axe, and he steadied himself against the wall. "What do you mean?"

"A day after they'd left for Fog Harbor, Peter received an email. A notification from the parole board at Crescent Bay State Prison. An inmate he'd represented as a public defender some twenty-five years ago had just been released on parole. I told Peter it wasn't smart to make the trip up there—not with Elvis Bastidas on the streets again—but he wanted to make Hannah happy. Lord knows, that was a full-time job."

As Will penned the name into his notebook, Graham's booming voice drowned out soft-spoken Marcia. "Hey, I think you missed something, Steve-o."

"One second." Will cursed himself for letting Graham out of his sight. He lowered the phone to find him already rummaging beneath the driver's seat. Grinning from ear to ear, Graham raised his hand high.

"Ms. Russell, I'll have to call you back."

Will stared in disbelief. Not at Graham but at the cell phone he held aloft like a championship trophy.

Will would've paid good money to watch pretty boy Graham attend his first autopsy, but after the stunt he'd pulled at the police garage, he had no choice but to banish his temporary partner to the hallway while Chet examined the bodies of the Fox family one by one. He couldn't afford to lose focus. Not now. But Will planned to read him the riot act the moment they left.

"It's a near-contact wound." Chet ran a gloved finger alongside the hole on Peter's left temple. "See those blackened edges, the searing of the skin? The muzzle of the gun would have likely been less than half an inch or so away from his skin to cause that type of injury."

Will nodded, trying not to appear overeager. He didn't want to hurry Chet but at the same time, the victim's cell phone was practically burning a hole in his pocket. He pulled it out, unable to withstand the wait.

Before Chet made the first incision, Will waved the phone at him and blurted, "Can we do it now?" reminding himself of his younger brother, Petey, who'd always gone hunting for his birthday presents weeks in advance, only to get them all grounded.

Chet sighed. "Give it to me."

Will watched him press Peter's cold thumb against the screen, bringing it to life. The newly visible background image—a candid shot of Lily in ballet slippers and a pink tutu—made Will shake his head. Some parts of the job were harder than others. Parts like this, impossible. At least he'd thought to charge the phone on the way over, giving him ample time to sift through its contents.

After he'd reset the passcode, Will knew the exact place to start. *Where were you going, Peter Fox?* He opened the mapping application, frowning at the destination of the most recent trip logged in the history, which had concluded at 8 p.m. The destination, the Sand Dunes Motel on the outskirts of downtown Fog Harbor.

"What is it?" Chet asked. "You look spooked."

"More like confused." Will knew the Sand Dunes. All the local cops did. It was the seediest motel in Fog Harbor. With his Rolex watch and oversized SUV, Peter Fox would've stuck out like a sore thumb. "He was at the Sand Dunes earlier last night. An hour and a half or so before Olivia found him."

Chet lowered his face shield and retrieved the bone saw from its resting place. He approached Peter's lifeless body. "The only folks who stay at that motel are either breaking the law or running from it."

Will turned away to scan Peter's text messages, hoping to take his mind from the shearing grind of the saw as it worked Peter's chest open. But he could *feel* the sound anyway, the juddering vibrations, shaking him right down to his bones.

Peter's last texts had come in from his wife, Hannah, in quick succession between 7:45 and 7:46 p.m. just prior to his arrival at the Sand Dunes.

Please come back. Think about what you're doing.
It's not safe. He's crazy. He'll destroy you.

An hour and a half later, at 9:15 p.m., she'd phoned him, and they'd spoken for exactly forty-three seconds. The last call Will guessed either would ever have. He felt strangely grateful for it though, since it narrowed the time of death to a fifteen-minute window and pointed like a neon arrow to the Sand Dunes and whoever Peter had encountered there.

*

Will waited until they'd left the cold sterility of the medical examiner's office. He'd been holding back the tide for hours now; the dead deserved respect. But as soon as Graham had buckled himself into the Crown Vic, Will laid into him, taking out his pent-up frustration, the smell of death still clinging to him like a hellish cologne. The sight of a child on an autopsy table never got easier. "What the hell were you thinking, rummaging through the car like that? I told you not to touch the evidence."

Graham never backed down from a fight. Especially not with Will. Not since that first night months ago when he'd seen Will and Olivia sitting together at the Hickory Pit. "I found the cell phone, didn't I?"

Will welcomed the challenge. "I don't know. *Did* you? Or did you plant it there?"

"What? You're out of your mind."

"Steve doesn't miss evidence. Do you really expect me to believe he overlooked a large-screen smartphone?"

"You can believe whatever you want. That's what happened. Maybe Steve got distracted by Kelly. I heard those two were an item once. Nasty breakup."

Will groaned. Trying to talk to Graham required the patience of a kindergarten teacher. But he couldn't leave it alone. "We need to talk about your fight with the victim. I want to know what happened. All of it. Including what you did after you left the beach up until the time you showed up at the crime scene. I assume you have an alibi."

"I don't have to tell you anything."

Will started the car, wishing he could demand Graham get out. He heeded Chief Flack's advice instead. One of them had to be mature about this. "You're right, Graham. You don't have to tell me anything."

The victorious smirk on Graham's face was Will's undoing.

"But until you do, I consider you a suspect."

CHAPTER FOURTEEN

Olivia snapped a photo of the small horseshoe drying in the sunlight on the pool deck of Ocean's Song. She composed a quick text to Deck, letting him know what she'd found, and attached the picture. Predictably, he responded:

Why are you roaming around an active crime scene?

And then, before she could answer him:

I'll be there in fifteen minutes. Don't let that thing out of your sight.

While she waited, Olivia studied the house, trying to understand what had happened there and why. The timing of the two fires suggested Peter had been murdered first. The assailant had known the location of his family and come here to finish the job while the rest of Fog Harbor stared up at the exploding night sky, clueless. The magnitude of the violence—an entire family, gone in the span of thirty minutes—communicated a singular and undeniable message. For the killer, this was personal. And it left Olivia with a new and horrifying worry that Thomas may yet still be a target.

"Liv?" Olivia spun around to the sound of her sister's voice. Emily peered over the top of the gate, her curls blown ragged by the wind. "What are you doing?"

"I was looking for you."

"Here?"

Olivia shrugged, uncertain how to explain the pull she'd felt to see the damage up close. She knew it had to do with her father, what she'd witnessed as a girl, but she couldn't stop herself from trying to rescue Thomas. From trying to understand how a soul could become so twisted not even the best psychologist could unwind the knots. "I couldn't find you, so…"

"So, you blatantly disregarded the crime scene tape?" Deck emerged from the other direction, stepping through the windowless hole in the side of the house and out onto the deck. To Olivia's surprise, Graham trailed behind him.

"In her defense, it's covered in sand." Emily opened the gate and stepped inside, holding up the wilted yellow tape as proof. On her other arm, a rolled beach towel protruded from the top of her tote bag.

Deck gave her sister a withering look as he donned a pair of gloves and retrieved the horseshoe. He examined it briefly before placing it in a plastic evidence bag.

"What is it?" Graham asked.

"I'm not sure, but it's unusual. The shape, that shimmery green stone." Olivia decided to ignore Deck for now. No better way to infuriate him. "It might've been dropped by the killer. It could even be a calling card."

"That's a little far-fetched." Graham laughed at her. As if he knew better. Olivia couldn't believe she'd ever considered him worthy of a second glance, much less seven regrettable dates. Obviously, she'd been lonely and blinded by his strong jaw and perfect hair and drool-worthy biceps. "It probably belongs to one of the thirty or so firefighters who traipsed through here. Doesn't that sound more likely to you?"

Olivia opened her mouth to give Graham a piece of her mind, but Deck butted right in, like usual.

"If Doctor Rockwell says it's important, then it's important."
Clearly, he knew there was no better way to infuriate her than
to stick up for her when she was perfectly capable of defending
herself. She'd show him.

"What're you doing here anyway, Graham?" Her voice came
out exactly as she'd intended. Dripping with contempt.

"Didn't you hear? I work with Detective Decker now."

"*Temporarily.* Only until JB comes back."

Olivia hadn't expected that. Her eyes cut to Deck, who seemed
to be on the verge of implosion. Then, to a mildly amused Emily.

"I thought you got into a fight with the guy who got killed. Is
it even ethical for you to work the case?" Leave it to her sister to
call a spade a spade.

"You're misinformed, Emily. Fox's son plowed into me. I told
that rude little shit he needed to be taught some manners. I can't
help it if his dad got offended and threatened to have my badge. If
you ask me, the whole situation was blown way out of proportion."

As far as Olivia remembered, Graham had been the one in
Fox's face, slurring his words and jutting his chest out like a drunk
frat boy. Peter Fox hadn't helped matters. They'd both been three
sheets to the wind.

"But you threw the first punch," Emily said.

"Well, he started it." With a huffing breath, Graham spun
around and stormed back toward the broken window, calling over
his shoulder, "And I certainly didn't kill him."

After Graham had tromped through the burned shell of the
living room and disappeared, Emily let out a low whistle. "What
a hothead."

Olivia turned to Deck, only to find his brown eyes on her
already. She couldn't be irritated with him now. Not knowing
he'd been stuck with Graham. "You don't really think he killed
anyone, do you?"

"He *found* the victim's phone." He said the word as if he hardly believed it. "*After* Steve finished searching the car. I think he's hiding something."

Graham was a bully. But a killer? "If that's true, then maybe it's a good thing you're keeping him close."

"I wouldn't go that far. Though the phone did turn out to be useful. Peter drove to the Sand Dunes last night to meet someone. And his wife wasn't happy about it."

"I assume you're headed there now."

Deck nodded, then patted his pants pocket, where he'd tucked the plastic baggie with the horseshoe inside. "Nice work spotting this, by the way. But—"

"I know. I know. Keep out of your crime scene."

With a shrug and a smirk, he headed back the way he'd come, stopping after a few steps. "You free later?"

"She's free."

Olivia whipped her head around and glared at Emily. Damn little sisters, always sticking their noses in.

"Apparently, I'm free."

"Want to go a couple rounds on the bag? I have a feeling I'm gonna need it. And I wouldn't mind picking your brain."

"Pick away," Emily said, still grinning.

CHAPTER FIFTEEN

As Will exited the beach house, he puzzled over the horseshoe. *Now that's what you call an old-fashioned clue*, his father would say. With Will's luck, it would probably turn out to be nothing more than a red herring with no useable prints. Still, he marveled at Olivia's knack for discovery, all the while wishing she would stay safely on the sidelines.

A young man had approached Graham outside the Crown Vic. His face bright red from the sun, he looked as if he'd come straight from the beach. Up close though, the bags under his eyes told Will he'd had a sleepless night. "Are you Detective Decker?" the man asked Graham. "I called the station. They said you might be here."

"Hell no, he's not." Will shuddered at the thought of being confused for that nitwit. He couldn't resist a dig. "Wishes he was though."

"Hmph." With that, Graham shut himself inside the car, which was fine by Will, since Will had the keys to the ignition. No keys, no AC. And he knew Graham's pride would never permit him to crack a window.

"What can I do for you?"

"Those murders last night... My girlfriend and I might have heard something. I mean, it's probably nothing, but—"

"Let me be the judge of that." Already, Will felt a twinge of excitement. The thrill of the chase. He withdrew his notepad, steely-eyed, in the same purposeful way he would unholster his gun. "What's your name?"

"Kurt Miles. My girlfriend, Rachel, and I were at the Barbecue Bash last night with her parents. They live in Fog Harbor, and she thought it would be a fun way to spent the Fourth. She didn't tell me that Mom and Dad are extremely old-fashioned. As in, sleep-in-separate-rooms old-fashioned. So, Rachel and I took a long walk down the beach last night, if you catch my drift."

Will nodded, hoping this guy wasn't about to lead him down a rabbit hole to nowhere.

"We set up a blanket between the dunes about fifty yards from Ocean's Song. That far out, the beach was deserted. Quiet. Romantic. Until they started going at it like cats and dogs."

"*Who* started going at it?"

Kurt waved his hand back in the direction of the house. "That couple who got killed, I guess. The Foxes. We could hear them clear as day from their pool deck. Couldn't see over the fence, though."

"What were they arguing about?" Will asked, jotting down a few notes.

"What *weren't* they arguing about? At first, the woman—Mrs. Fox, I assume—was saying how they needed to try to get along for the kids. And then Mr. Fox told her that the kids weren't clueless and he didn't want to come to Fog Harbor anyway, and he was tired of pretending that everything was fine when it obviously wasn't. Mrs. Fox sort of implied he was the reason their whole marriage had gone to hell in a handbasket, and he sort of implied he didn't love her anymore. That was the gist of it."

Will took a breath, trying to reconcile it all with the images he'd seen on Hannah's Facebook page, but the juxtaposition didn't surprise him. Real life was messy. It couldn't be posed, cropped, and filtered. "Then what happened?"

Kurt grimaced. "Mrs. Fox said, 'Please don't go over there. You don't know what he's capable of.' Then Mr. Fox yelled, 'I'm tired of living a lie.' As best we could tell, he stormed out. Mrs. Fox stayed on the deck for a while, crying. Well, sobbing would be a better word. Then she went back inside too."

"Do you remember about what time you heard the arguing?"

"Sure do. We promised Rachel's parents we'd be back by eight, so I'd say it was around seven twenty or seven thirty at the latest."

The timeline of that brutal night had begun to fall into place. Peter and Hannah had argued on the deck at 7:30. He'd left for the motel in a fit of anger, with Hannah begging him to come back. "Do you think Rachel would be willing to swing by the station? She might remember something you didn't."

Kurt's face turned sour. "She went back to Portland this morning. We broke up."

Will knew he'd regret it but he couldn't help asking. Especially when he noticed Graham in the passenger seat, fanning himself with the morning newspaper. Let him suffer. "Broke up? Why?"

"The Foxes. It sounds ridiculous, I know. But Rachel said Mr. Fox sounded like a complete asshole, not even trying to save his marriage or talk it out for the sake of the kids. I pointed out that Mrs. Fox seemed like a real control freak, and sometimes it's better to get divorced than to live in misery. Before I knew it, *we* were the ones arguing like cats and dogs. Rachel said I wasn't committed to the relationship. That I'd jump ship if the seas got too rocky."

"I'm sorry, man. It sounds like you had a rough night. Anything else you can tell me that might be important?"

Kurt shrugged. "Not anything factual. But seeing that story on the news this morning was like a punch to the gut. Those poor kids. I can't say I was surprised though. Not with parents like that. Those two hated each other. Whatever happened to them, they brought it on themselves."

Graham pouted all the way back to the station, where Will gave him his marching orders. Deliver the sealed evidence bag containing

Peter's cell phone to Jessie. Do not pass go. No way in hell was he letting Graham tag along to the Sand Dunes. With a crowd of hungry reporters gathering, Will watched until Jessie met Graham at the door, not trusting him to keep his word. Or his big mouth shut. Especially when Will saw Graham's ex-girlfriend, Heather Hoffman, holding a microphone. Even if word on the street was they'd broken up, Graham had a bad habit of blabbing police business to the leggy blonde.

On the drive over to the motel, Will scarfed a granola bar while he telephoned Marcia Russell, Peter's long-time assistant. He'd cut her off earlier just after she'd revealed her worries about her boss. If this Elvis Bastidas character she'd mentioned had met Peter at the motel, Will felt certain he could wrap up the case in less than twenty-four hours. Even better, he could rub that in JB's face for the foreseeable future.

Marcia answered on the first ring, as if she'd been waiting for him to call back.

"What can you tell me about Elvis Bastidas?"

She let out a trembling sigh. "Nothing good. When Mr. Fox worked for the public defender's office, he represented Bastidas on a murder case. The shooting of a rival gang member. Mr. Fox convinced him to take a twenty-five-year plea deal for manslaughter. Apparently, they disagreed about case strategy. Bastidas wanted to testify on his own behalf—he said it was self-defense—but Mr. Fox talked him out of it. Anyway, the case was settled well before my time."

"Was Peter afraid of him?"

"With good reason. Bastidas had threatened him before."

"From prison?" Will doubted it. Prison officials read, censored, and inspected all mail for evidence of threatening language and contraband.

"Mr. Fox received several letters with no return address and signed by Bastidas, telling him he'd had plenty of time to plan the perfect murder. Of course, we alerted the prison authorities and Bastidas earned himself an additional one-year sentence for criminal threats. Mr. Fox figured he'd asked one of his gang associates to mail the correspondence."

"Do you happen to have those letters?"

"I'll send you the entire case file right away." Marcia's voice brightened with the prospect that she could make a difference. "If you think it will help catch the killer."

Will spotted the Sand Dunes Motel up ahead with its dingy white plaster façade and its flashing red NO VACANCY sign, the V bulb flickering on and off in the fading light of the late afternoon. "I do, Marcia. I really do."

"Right away, Detective."

"One more thing." Will paused, trying to soft-shoe his way into the question. "Since Peter was your boss, this may be a bit awkward for you. But, was he happy in his marriage to Hannah?"

Marcia stayed quiet for so long that Will checked his screen, wondering if she'd hung up.

"Bless his heart, he tried. He really did. Hannah did too, in her way. They were different people. Peter liked to kick back, go surfing, toss the football with Dylan. Have a few beers with his buddies on the weekends. Sure, he worked hard, but he knew how to have fun."

"And Hannah?"

Another sigh. This one, beleaguered. "Hannah didn't do anything just for the sake of doing it. If it served no purpose, she wasn't interested. That woman had no room in her life for fun."

Will pushed through the double doors into the motel lobby, which seemed too fancy a word for a room so small and barren it resembled his brother's cell at Crescent Bay State Prison. Behind the mud-brown countertop, the middle-aged clerk smacked her bubblegum and batted her false eyelashes at him.

"Hi, Betty." Betty Smoot had been working reception—and flirting with cops—since the Sand Dunes had opened its doors in the early nineties. Rumor had it she'd relocated to Fog Harbor for a steamy prison romance that turned cold when she'd fallen for the correctional officer in charge of the visiting room instead.

"To what do I owe this pleasure, Detective Decker?"

He steeled himself for her usual come-ons, starting with her seductive hair-flip. Betty had the subtlety of a bowling ball. "I'm investigating a homicide."

"That quadruple murder?" She clutched her chest. "How awful. An entire family gunned down. It's unspeakable."

"And I need to view the motel security footage from last night between seven and nine thirty."

Betty ushered him through the swinging door and behind the counter with a whisper. "Say no more."

Inside the motel office, Betty offered him the lone seat in a green pleather desk chair. She positioned herself behind him, fast-forwarding through multiple screens of footage. When Will saw Peter's black SUV glide into the parking lot, he pointed. "There. That's him."

Peter piloted the vehicle around the side of the motel and parked in front of a long row of rooms. Each of the doors bore the image of a lone palm tree. "Where's he going?" Will asked, as they watched Peter exit the car and stalk hurriedly toward a guest room.

"Looks like 135. We call it the bridal suite. It's the biggest room we've got, and there's one of them vibrating beds. You know, the Magic Fingers."

Will scooted his chair out of reach of Betty's own fingers, which had found his too-tight shoulders.

On the screen, the motel room door opened, blocking Will's view of the occupant. Then, Peter disappeared inside the room.

"Do you remember who rented the bridal suite?" Will didn't dare take his eyes from the video as Betty scrolled ahead, an hour lapsing in the span of a few seconds.

"Do I *remember*? I remember every handsome face that walks in here… but yours especially, Detective. Don't tell your crotchety old partner, but you're the best-looking detective Fog Harbor has ever—"

Will gestured to the screen, grateful to see the room door swing open wide. Peter ran out, opening the back door of the SUV and retrieving a golf club. He held the club menacingly, two-fisted like a baseball bat as he approached the door again.

"Oh my." Betty stepped toward the screen and placed her long, glittery fingernail on the other man. Just a shadow made of pixels. "This one's got a gun."

The gunman strode toward Peter, who dropped the club on the pavement behind him, stumbling over the curb and falling on his ass. As Peter sat there, the man stooped to retrieve the golf club. Returning the gun to his waistband, he lorded the club over Peter before taking a single swing at the front door. Will had seen the vicious dent it left.

Satisfied with his work, the gunman returned to the bridal suite, and Peter scrambled into the SUV, tossing the club into the back seat and fleeing in a hurry.

"Back up," Will said. "To the part where he falls down."

Betty rewound the video, freezing on a still shot of Peter, splayed like a dead bug on the pavement. "Do those look like flip-flops to you?" Will asked, thinking of Peter's lone black Havaianas sandal lying in the grass at the scene of the fire.

Squinting at the screen, Betty replied, "Don't think so. Those look more like loafers to me. See there," she pointed, "the top of his foot is covered."

"Let it run. Let's see what happens next."

Twenty minutes later, the gunman emerged from his room and drove away in a hurry, nearly bottoming out at the exit. Betty fast-forwarded until they spotted him again, returning in the pitch-black of the early morning.

Betty pressed pause, widening her eyes at Will. "I can't believe no one called the front office. I worked the night shift. Two to ten. Didn't hear a thing."

Will played along. But he knew the score at the Sand Dunes. Snitches weren't welcome among guests or employees. "You said you remember the guy?"

"Jonah Montgomery." Betty flipped through the old-school reservation book, displaying the man's signature and address—Santa Barbara. "He paid in cash. Drove a red Dodge Challenger. Planned to stay through Tuesday, but he checked out first thing this morning. Probably around 5 a.m."

Will flashed her a grin and hurried out of the office. Jonah had a big head start, but with any luck, Highway Patrol could catch him before he went off the grid. "You're a lifesaver, Betty."

"Wait. There's something you should know."

Hand on the door, Will's stomach plummeted at the gravity of her usually breathy voice.

"He dropped his wallet on the floor. Cards and cash scattered everywhere. Naturally, I came out from behind the counter to help him pick it up. I should've known. A good-looking guy like that—"

Will motioned at her to hurry. To spit it out.

"He's a cop."

Adrenaline had already spiked Will's blood before he got on the radio to dispatch, requesting a BOLO for a red Dodge Challenger. *Driver may be armed and dangerous.* He couldn't sit still waiting for somebody else to find his man, so he circled the parking lot twice—nothing—then took off down the highway headed south, driving as the sun began its slow afternoon descent. The dappled light cast flitting shadows in the spaces between the trees, making Will nervous.

When the call came in—someone had spotted the Challenger outside a convenience store north of Brookings, Oregon—Will pulled off the road and smacked the steering wheel with his palm. He'd gambled wrong, thinking Jonah would head home to Santa Barbara. His prime suspect could be well on his way to Canada by now.

CHAPTER SIXTEEN

Olivia walked side by side with her sister, retracing her path from the remains of Ocean's Song up the beach toward Shells-by-the-Sea. The tourist crowd always dwindled in the late afternoon, heading back to their hotels and travel trailers to prepare dinner on the grill and stare up at a black canvas speckled with stars. Olivia never tired of the Fog Harbor sky. She'd missed it during the years she'd spent teaching criminal psychology in Palo Alto.

"Where were you earlier?" After Emily had embarrassed her in front of Deck, Olivia couldn't resist prodding her sister. Since Em had moved to San Francisco, she felt the distance between them growing. "I looked everywhere."

"Laying out a ways down the beach. It was too crowded up here."

"You don't look like you got any sun." With the fair complexion and freckles they shared, the proof should have been obvious on her cheeks, her shoulders, the bridge of her nose.

As they approached Leah's B&B, Em reached inside her bag, displaying a bottle of sunscreen. "SPF 55."

"Fine. But next time, tell me exactly where you're going, okay?"

"You should be thanking me. You found that clue, didn't you? You impressed Detective Decker."

"Hardly. And that's not the point."

Wade waved to them from his post alongside the back deck. His bald head glistened with sweat, his ocean-blue shirt wet beneath his armpits. He lowered the volume on the radio clipped to his waist. "How's the poor little guy you rescued last night? Have you heard anything?"

Olivia wasn't sure how to answer. She hardly felt like a rescuer. Not the way Thomas had cowered under the table in the interview room. But Wade had helped her, lighting her path up the beach to safety, while Thomas trembled in her arms. She owed him something. "His aunt should be here by now. So far, he hasn't said much about what happened."

Wade gave a rueful shake of his head. "Something like that, you never get over. No matter how many years pass by. He'll still be reliving this Fourth of July when he's my age."

"You'd be surprised how resilient children can be." But Olivia knew the past never healed. Not really. Though the wound scabbed over, the cut stung as deep and as raw as ever. Maybe worse, now that her father was gone, and she had little hope of learning the truth about what happened that night at the Double Rock. For a boy like Thomas, who'd lost so much in an instant, resilience sounded like nothing more than a fancy word in one of her psychology textbooks.

"I just hope the cops can find whoever did this," Emily said. "A person like that is capable of anything."

Wade took a swig of water from the bottle he kept in the shade of the eaves. "Well, I think they might have a suspect."

Even with the sun beating down on them, Olivia went cold. "How do you know?"

Patting his radio, Wade answered, "Fog Harbor PD put out a BOLO about ten minutes ago for a red Dodge Challenger."

"Do they have a name?"

"Jonah Montgomery."

Olivia avoided the shortcut home. She couldn't bear to drive past the patch of scorched earth where Peter Fox had drawn his last breath. Surely he'd been familiar with his assailant; he'd looked into a pair of dark eyes he recognized in his final moments. But had he realized what would come next? That his family would be a target? She hoped not.

On the way, Olivia made small talk with Emily, anything to stop her fingers from twitching. As soon as they pulled into the driveway, she hoofed it inside and opened her laptop, typing the suspect's name into the search bar.

Thirty-three million results. *Seriously?*

If the killer knew the Fox family, it stood to reason he might also reside in Santa Barbara. She revised her search, clicking on the first listing. A Facebook page for Jonah Montgomery.

Though he'd been smart about his privacy settings, the little she saw told a story, and she stared, dumbfounded, at his profile picture. A dark-haired man, who looked to be in his late twenties, grinned back at her shamelessly. Even through the cold lens of the camera, he exuded charisma. He held open his uniform shirt, the middle two buttons undone, revealing a Superman logo on his bulletproof vest.

Olivia opened another search window, navigating to the Santa Barbara Police Department web page, where she located Jonah and his mischievous eyes in a picture of the most recent class of rookie officers.

"Who's the hottie?" Emily leaned down over her shoulder, crunching into a pretzel stick.

"Officer Jonah Montgomery of the Santa Barbara Police Department. And apparently, a suspect in a multiple homicide."

"He doesn't look like a murderer."

Olivia raised her eyebrows at Em. They both knew all too well looks had nothing to do with it.

CHAPTER SEVENTEEN

Will didn't bother to return to the police station. Jessie had already emailed him the link to Peter Fox's cell phone data, and after the day he'd had, seeing his new partner, Graham, in the flesh would only cause unnecessary torment. The station would probably still be crawling with reporters anyway. A quick call to Steve Li confirmed that Peter Fox's loafers had been inventoried in the hall closet inside Ocean's Song, next to a pair of his wife's sandals. And just as Will had feared, the horseshoe had no useable prints.

Will pondered the location of those shoes and what it meant, as he passed the town square—the quaint cobblestone courthouse decorated in patriotic red, white, and blue—and turned onto Primrose Avenue. He parked on the street, across from the little white house with the red door and the blue Camaro in the driveway.

Holding the pink box he'd picked up at Myrtle's Café, he rang the doorbell and waited.

Tammy greeted him, looking uncharacteristically frazzled with her oversized sweatpants and her bleach-blonde locks piled into a messy bun atop her head. She scrutinized the box in Will's hands as JB waved him inside from his perch on the sofa.

Will made his way into the living room, ignoring the excited yaps from JB's dachshund, Princess. Tammy had wasted no time transforming JB's bachelor pad. A *home sweet home* cross-stitch hung adjacent to JB's taxidermied bass. "I heard they let you out."

Tammy laughed, scooping the dog up. "More like they couldn't wait to get rid of him. Isn't that right, Princess?"

"I know the feeling."

JB grumbled at both of them. "Are you two ganging up on a sickly old man?"

Will placed the box on the table, meeting Tammy's dictatorial gaze. "Vegan, gluten-free, low-fat doughnuts, courtesy of Myrtle. The icing is sweetened with a sugar substitute."

"You shouldn't have." JB lifted the lid and took a whiff.

"It's no problem. I stopped on the way."

He wrinkled his nose. "No, *really*. You shouldn't have. These things smell like cardboard."

Tammy shook her head, exasperated, but planted a kiss on JB's forehead, leaving a red lipstick mark. "I'll leave you boys to it."

When Tammy had disappeared into the kitchen, JB scrubbed his forehead. "Spill it. Every last detail."

"No way. You're supposed to be taking a break, remember?"

"I know you, City Boy. And you didn't come here to bring me counterfeit doughnuts. Lay it on me."

After Will filled JB in on the day's events—from Graham's coincidental discovery of the cell phone to his own revelatory trip to the Sand Dunes—he helped himself to one of JB's cardboard doughnuts, scarfing it down so quickly he barely registered the taste. He'd hardly eaten all day.

"So, you're saying you've got three suspects, and you need a little assistance from the Detective of the Year. Is that about the size of it?"

"Three?"

"Bastidas. Montgomery. Bauer." JB ticked them off one by one.

"You're giving Graham way too much credit. There's no way that guy pulls off a quadruple murder. I'm surprised he can pin his badge on straight. But now that you mention it, I do need your help."

"I knew it." JB rubbed his hands together eagerly. The same way he approached a sandwich from the Hickory Pit. "What can I do? Interview a suspect? Stake out a location? Chase down a lead?"

"Not exactly." Will pointed to JB's laptop, propped at the edge of the coffee table. A sign-up form for Fog Harbor Beginners CrossFit rested beside it. Tammy had already begun to pencil in JB's details. "I have to warn you, partner. Tammy might be trying to kill you."

"Of course she is. That's marriage for you."

"I sent you a link to Peter Fox's cell phone download."

"Files? You're wasting these powers of deduction on a paper trail?"

Will raised his eyebrows, giving JB an uneven smile. "If Graham planted that cell phone, there was something on it he didn't want anyone to see. You're the only one I trust to find it."

"Because I'm a better detective? C'mon. You can admit it."

Tammy poked her head in from the kitchen. "Because he knows you're already bored out of your mind. As far as I'm concerned, you're saving me, Deck."

"So you'll do it?" Will asked.

JB reached for his laptop. Popping the footrest on his recliner, he set the computer atop his belly and stretched his fingers. "Of course I'll do it. You had me at doughnuts."

Will braced the heavy bag against his shoulder, waiting for Olivia to throw the first punch. She'd been coming over to box for months now, but Will still hadn't grown accustomed to the sight of her swinging auburn ponytail in his garage. Neither had Cy, apparently. The orange tabby watched warily from the warm spot on the hood of Will's pickup truck. Somehow, even with one eye, that damn cat managed to look cynical. As if it was only a matter of time before Will messed things up again.

"I heard you might have a suspect." Olivia tugged on her boxing gloves and tightened the Velcro around her wrists. "Jonah Montgomery?"

"We hit the bag first, then we talk shop." Will marveled at her uncanny ability to find stuff out. She always seemed one step ahead.

"Yes, sir." Olivia landed a vicious jab-cross to the center of the bag, startling him. Like that kiss on the beach. But he dug in and held firm, letting the juddering of her punches quiet his nerves.

"Don't forget to go to the body." He peeked his head around the bag to coach her. "Mix it up a little. A jab to the head and a right hook to the gut. That'll drop 'em every time."

She wiped the sweat from her face with her forearm and grinned. When Will let down his guard and lost himself in her smile, she drilled a punishing right hook to the side of the bag that sent him stumbling. "Like that?"

He pushed the heavy bag back toward her, and it creaked as it swung on the ceiling hook.

"You forgot to bob and weave," she said, her grin broadening. "My turn."

Twenty minutes later and out of breath, Will stepped back from the bag, exhausted but clear-headed. Boxing required the kind of singular focus that always set his mind right. He stripped off his gloves and tossed them into the corner. "How'd you know about Montgomery?"

Olivia threw him the towel he'd left by the door. "Wade Coffman. The security guard at Shells-by-the-Sea. He heard the BOLO come in over the radio. Did they find him?"

"Not yet." Will wiped his face and took a seat on the tailgate. "But he's got a lot of explaining to do."

After Will shared what he'd seen on the Sand Dunes video footage and what he'd learned from Betty, Olivia reached into her bag, frowning as she retrieved her cell phone. "So, he is a cop then?"

"It certainly seems that way."

Joining him on the tailgate, she displayed a Facebook page on her screen. The profile picture belonged to a cocky rookie cop who resembled the golf club-wielding man on the video. "Did you call Santa Barbara PD?" Olivia asked.

He gave her a look, trying to rile her up. "This isn't my first homicide case. Of course I did. He joined the force last year. Clean disciplinary record. No citizen complaints. They told me he took a few days of vacation. He's due back at work on Wednesday."

Showing off now, Will added, "I also spoke with Fire Lieutenant Hunt about the horseshoe. None of his crew reported losing it."

"Well, wise guy, I'll bet no one told you this." Will felt the heat from Olivia's body as she moved closer to him, could see the sweat glistening in the tendrils that had escaped her ponytail. She seemed to sense it too, pulling back and extending her phone instead. He studied the Facebook post on the screen, trying to make sense of it. Jonah stood at the center of a stage, with a shiny red holiday bow pinned to his uniform.

"What am I looking at here?"

"Jonah's privacy settings don't allow us to view most of his posts, but he was tagged in this one at Christmas. It's a charity date auction to benefit the Santa Barbara Children's Hospital. You know, bid a few bucks to have dinner with a handsome cop. I'm sure you've been asked to do that sort of thing."

Will's cheeks warmed but Olivia appeared not to notice.

"And guess who chairs the fundraisers for the hospital?" She clicked to another web page and waited for his reaction. He recognized the woman immediately—the trendy haircut, the gray-blue eyes, the perfect white teeth—though she hadn't been smiling when he'd met her in the Shell Beach parking lot. According to Peter's assistant, Marcia, smiling didn't come naturally.

"Hannah Fox," he answered.

CHAPTER EIGHTEEN

While Deck mulled over the Facebook post, Olivia cursed herself. She'd all but called him handsome. She'd made him blush. He was probably embarrassed for her, especially after that kiss last night. After the way he'd pulled away from her, leaving her no choice but to run.

"Do you think she and Jonah were having an affair?" Deck slid her phone across the tailgate, maintaining his distance. "From what I've heard so far—Peter's assistant, the couple on the beach—it certainly sounds like the Fox marriage was on the rocks."

"It's one of my working hypotheses. Unlike you and JB, always jumping to conclusions, I prefer the scientific method."

He heaved an exasperated sigh. "So, what was Jonah doing in Fog Harbor then?"

"Crashing the family vacation? You said yourself that Hannah called him crazy in her last text to Peter. He might've been stalking her."

Deck nodded his agreement, bolstering her confidence. This Olivia could do, and she wondered what it said about her that she felt more comfortable delving inside the mind of a brutal murderer than talking about her feelings for the man in front of her.

"So, hit me with a profile, Doctor."

"Well, I think we can both agree these murders were highly personal. The killer was known to them and was likely aware they vacationed here on a regular basis. Killing a family in the middle of summer vacation, that makes an emphatic statement. *You're not safe anywhere*. Since Peter was killed first and apart from his wife and children, I'd guess he was the primary target. The killer must've been watching the family since he anticipated they wouldn't be at the fireworks show with the rest of Fog Harbor. He picked the perfect opportunity, but he'd been planning it for a while. Still, he didn't quite get it right, did he? He didn't plan on the bodies being discovered so soon. I don't think he's killed before."

"And the fire? Just covering his tracks?"

"Maybe. Fire means complete obliteration. The ultimate power and control over the victims. A fire rages just like a person. It destroys everything. The ultimate revenge. I'd say you're looking for a very angry individual."

"Damn. I might sleep with the light on tonight."

Olivia laughed uneasily. The profile unnerved her too.

"Do you have time to come inside?" Deck hopped off the tailgate, and Cy followed him, meowing impatiently at the door. "I have something else I want to show you. In the interest of the scientific method."

"Well, when you put it like that. How could I resist?"

After Deck vanished to the back of the house, Olivia splashed her face with water from the kitchen sink. She examined her reflection in the microwave door and smoothed her hair. Passable. Then she took a seat at the kitchen table on one of the vintage red vinyl chairs Deck had bought from a secondhand store, telling her they reminded him of his mother.

He returned in a clean T-shirt, a laptop computer in his hands. "Meet my other suspect."

Olivia read the file name on the computer screen. "Elvis Bastidas."

While Deck ran through the basics on the ex-con, she began scrolling the scanned documents. With every word that caught her eye—*parole, threat, murder*—she felt less and less certain about Jonah Montgomery. "Have you looked at this already?"

He shook his head. "You're the first to see it since Peter's assistant emailed it to me this afternoon. I didn't want to sway your opinion."

She scoffed teasingly. "As if."

"Right. What was I thinking? You're harder to sway than a concrete block."

Grinning, she remarked, "JB is wearing off on you."

Olivia studied the most recent entries in the file. Three letters, printed in the neat script of a man with time on his hands. Bastidas had probably written several drafts so as not to have a single mistake. No cross-outs. No scribbles. "These letters are intense."

Deck pulled his chair closer to her, reading over her shoulder. The last correspondence had arrived a few months ago.

Hello Mr. Fox,

Me again. The sucker you fucked over back in '95. The one you wouldn't let talk to the jury and tell his story like a man. The one who's been biding his time in this shithole prison. Did you think I forgot about you? I think about you and your family every day. I know everything about you. Where you live. Where you work. The kind of car you drive. The fancy schools your kiddies go to. How often you screw your pretty little red-headed wife. I know who you really are... a dead man walking. You took twenty-five years from me. You owe me everything. And I plan on taking it... the easy way or the hard way. I'll be seeing you.

"And you said he got out of Crescent Bay State Prison last week?"

"That's what Marcia said. Apparently, she was more worried about it than Peter since he brought his family here anyway. I put a call in to Bastidas's parole agent."

Olivia couldn't help but think of her late father and her half-brother, Termite. Both members of the Oaktown Boys, they'd always relied on the gang to settle their scores. Mercifully, Termite had gone back underground since she'd last seen him. If she never laid eyes on him again, it would be too soon. "A guy like that never does his own dirty work. You should check out his known associates. Try to figure out how he got those letters past the prison gates to Fox."

He leaned back, smirking at her. "You should've been a cop."

"Psychologists live in the shades of gray. Law enforcement is too black and white for me. Right or wrong. Good or bad. Guilt or innocence." Sometimes she wished she could see the world so dichotomously.

"Friends or lovers."

He may as well have landed an upper cut just beneath her rib cage. The words sucked the air right out of her, and she couldn't speak. Unfortunately, Deck continued without mercy, and there was nowhere to escape to.

"We should talk about what happened last night." No way to bob and weave.

"What's there to talk about? Nothing happened." Though Olivia's memory claimed otherwise.

They'd been halfway down the beach, in the heat of a debate about the upcoming parole hearing of a member of the Manson family with Olivia arguing that, after fifty years in prison, the woman deserved a chance to prove herself outside prison walls. No surprise, Deck had disagreed. When Olivia's fingertips had brushed his hand by accident, a current of undeniable anticipation had zinged through her, a not-so-subtle reminder that she found him both insufferable and irresistible.

"It didn't feel like nothing."

"You stopped us from making a stupid mistake. Clearly, I broke my own rules and you're not interested anyway."

"Not interested?"

Olivia kept her eyes on the table, safe from his pitying gaze. "You pushed me away."

"And then you ran off. You didn't even give me a chance to explain."

She stood up and retreated to the corner of the kitchen. Unable to bear her discomfort any longer, she turned away, hiding her face. "Explain what? That you don't see me like that anymore?"

Deck's chair scraped the linoleum. She heard his footsteps approaching behind her and tried to focus on what to do next. But his hand on her shoulder stirred her thoughts like a witch's brew.

"Olivia, look at me."

She looked.

"Can I have a do-over?"

She rested her hands on his hips, and he took another step toward her, cradling her cheek. His lips meandered along her jaw, marking the space between her ear and chin with soft, torturous kisses. Olivia slid her hands along his back, pulling him closer. Stupid mistake, be damned. Until finally he pressed his mouth to hers.

It felt inevitable as the tides, this kiss. The first time, last March, when she'd shown up on his doorstep, and he'd kissed her breathless, Olivia had known it would happen again. No matter what she'd told herself. What lines she'd drawn. What silly oaths she'd sworn. Now, with his lips on her neck and his hands on her body, she couldn't remember why she'd ever thought this was a bad idea.

Behind them, Deck's cell phone buzzed, rattling against the hard tabletop. He hardly seemed to notice.

"Should you—"

He buried her question against his mouth. Apparently it could wait.

A loud crash from the garage joined the cell phone's insistent nagging.

"What the hell?" Deck breathed against her cheek. He pressed his brow to hers.

She followed behind him as he flung open the door that led from the house to the garage. Everything appeared exactly as they'd left it. Olivia's boxing gloves rested on the cement. The bag swayed slightly. The overhead door stood partially open, her Buick parked outside, and the starry night beyond.

Like one of those tricky *what's wrong with this picture* puzzles, it took them both a moment to spot it.

"Weird." Deck examined the box that had tumbled open. He righted it, hurriedly stacking the spilled contents back inside.

Olivia shivered in the warm garage, gripped by a sudden feeling that crawled like a spider up her spine. Someone was watching. "Is anything missing?"

"No. It must've just fallen over."

He ignored her skeptical frown and answered his persistent cell phone which had started its buzzing again.

"Will Decker, Homicide." A few moments later, he hung up and gave her a solemn look.

"What is it?"

"They arrested Jonah Montgomery trying to cross the Canadian border. He was armed with his service weapon. The US marshals are transporting him back to Fog Harbor."

CHAPTER NINETEEN

Will's heartbeat drummed like the hooves of a racehorse as he walked Olivia to her car. He wanted to kiss her again but thought better of it, certain she'd read him like a book. Already, she'd looked at him strangely when he'd insisted the box had fallen over.

But Will couldn't have her thinking he regretted any of it, so he drew her to his chest, resting his chin on her head. "For the record, I was never *not interested.*"

As soon as Olivia's taillights disappeared down Pine Grove Road, he rushed back to the garage. Cy had followed them out of the house and made his way over to the box. The cat inspected it with his nose before rubbing his head against the corner.

Will approached the box with caution, imagining a dark winged creature springing from inside like a demented jack-in-the-box toy. When he reached it, he gave it a little kick, startling Cy. Though he felt silly, the nervous churning in his gut was undeniable.

He knelt beside it and examined the items again, more closely this time. The things he hadn't wanted Olivia to see belonged to their shared past. To Drake Devere, the serial killer who'd wreaked havoc on Fog Harbor months ago and then vanished, taking a sizeable portion of Will's pride with him. Drake's book, *Hawk's Revenge*, sat atop the pile. On the cover, a bird's talons, dripping red. He'd sent it to Will, the printed dedication inside it meant for him.

For Will
What you did to me will be done to you ten times over.

A small noise came from behind him. Will snapped the book shut, his breath quickening, and spun to look over his shoulder at the half-open garage door, certain he'd see Drake himself casting a long, black shadow.

Only Cy sat there, licking his paw. The tag of the new collar Will had purchased for him jangled as he moved his head.

It would take most of the night—at least nine hours—before the marshals reached Fog Harbor, and Will knew he would lie awake for all of it.

CHAPTER TWENTY

On Monday morning, Olivia left Emily sleeping at home and headed to work at Crescent Bay State Prison two hours ahead of schedule. She couldn't sleep anyway. No point tossing and turning, replaying that kiss and what had come after. The box overturned in the garage, Drake Devere's book tumbling out like a sign from the universe. A tarot card.

It didn't help that Javier Mendez—the man Leah had branded *chupacabra-level bad*—had been assigned to her 9 a.m. Monday slot, the date looming like the man himself. Larger than life. Later, she would drive to the police station for Thomas's second interview with Dr. Lucy. A part of her felt excited at the prospect of Thomas's revelations, but she also dreaded seeing him again. His innocent little face stirred up her own traumas like a stick dredging a mud puddle.

After Olivia had retrieved the push-button alarm from the Mental Health Unit desk, she retreated to her office to sift through the rest of the Bastidas file. Will had emailed it to her late last night, the time stamp 3:45 a.m. So they'd both be running on fumes, then.

Elvis Bastidas had never denied his guilt. He'd freely confessed to detectives his involvement in the shooting death of Tim McKenzie, a long-time member of the Oaktown Boys. As a member of the rival Los Diabolitos street gang, Bastidas alleged McKenzie had called him out at a party and brandished a gun at him. In fear for his life, he'd had no choice but to fire three shots at the nineteen-

year-old victim. The last one, a kill shot to the head. No wonder
Peter Fox hadn't wanted Bastidas to testify. In Olivia's opinion, a
twenty-five-year plea deal for manslaughter had been a lucky break.

Olivia paged through the rest of the file, taking notes to share
with Deck. At exactly nine o'clock, she watched through her door's
small window as Sergeant Shanice Weber left the officer's station
and approached the front door of the MHU for the daily unlock.

The men filed in, clad in their denim-blue jumpsuits, and
took their positions on the metal benches in the lobby. Javier
did not walk among them. Rather, he trailed behind, his colossal
frame towering like one of the ancient redwoods that bordered
the prison. His graying black hair hung in a thick braid down his
back. A mustache of the same color framed his upper lip. A snake
tattoo coiled around his neck. The head of the creature—fangs
exposed—appeared just beneath his right ear.

"Mr. Mendez?" Securing her alarm to her waistband, Olivia
steeled herself. Men like him could sense weakness. "Are you
ready?"

He sauntered toward the door without speaking or breaking
eye contact. Olivia mirrored him, while her heart cowered like a
mouse inside her chest. She reminded herself why she'd wanted
this job—chief psychologist at Crescent Bay—in the first place.
To understand these kinds of men. To understand her father. Now,
more than ever, she needed Javier to help her do both.

After her father's supposed suicide, she'd learned he'd been
informing for the FBI. That he'd been close to IDing "the General",
the enigma responsible for the drugs and cell phones that made
their way through the prison gates every day. Though her father's
digging had gotten him killed, she had no intention of stopping
until she'd unmasked the General and figured out exactly who'd
robbed her dad of his second chance and why.

Having just arrived at the office across the hall, Leah waved to
her. She looked worried. The last female therapist who'd worked

with Javier at the maximum security Desert Canyon State Prison had ended up on the floor of her office with a telephone cord wrapped around her neck.

"Come in. Have a seat."

For forty-five minutes, Olivia listened to Javier ramble non-stop, recounting the gory details of his recently filed lawsuit against the state prison system. They'd wrongfully branded him a shot caller for Los Diabolitos. They'd wrongfully housed him in Administrative Segregation. They'd wrongfully fed him an unhealthy diet that led to his Type 2 diabetes. For years, he'd denied the crime that put him behind bars—the brutal rape and murder of his estranged wife.

"Is there anything you *do* take responsibility for?"

Avoiding her question, Javier's dark eyes looked her up and down, then scanned the room until they landed on her desk, homing in on the empty space next to her computer where her telephone usually sat. She'd unplugged it from the wall and tucked the whole apparatus inside the desk drawer. "Don't you think it's unwise for a female psychologist to meet one-on-one with an inmate without a functioning telephone?"

"That depends on the inmate."

His smile oozed. "Touché."

When the timer on her desk dinged, alerting Olivia that their fifty-minute session was over, she felt a wave of relief. She had no idea how she'd ever get Javier to talk about anything other than himself. But if she couldn't get the truth about her father from the Oaktown Boys, she hoped rival gang member Javier would be willing to spill their secrets. Olivia knew he'd keep showing up to his appointments. Inmates who participated in mental health treatment received favorable placements. And Javier wasn't about to exchange his ticket to Crescent Bay for a ride down south to Corcoran. Which meant she'd have time to devise a strategy.

Javier stood up, dwarfing her, and pointed to her computer screen, which she regretfully realized had been partially visible to him. "Elvis Bastidas, huh? If you see that lucky SOB, tell him *venganza dulce*."

Javier left the office without a word, parting the crowd of inmates in the lobby like Moses in the Red Sea. Olivia let out a long, shaky breath. Working in the prison, she'd picked up enough Spanish to translate his words. *Sweet revenge*. What the hell did that mean? Did Javier Mendez know what happened to Peter Fox?

After Javier had left the MHU, Leah poked her head into Olivia's office. "Shall I get the sage?"

"He's not *that* bad."

The raise of Leah's eyebrows indicated her clear disagreement.

"Okay. He is that bad." Olivia grinned. "But at least he's long-winded. And narcissistic."

"Antisocial, narcissistic, *and* long-winded. The holy trinity of therapy clients." Leah smirked, making the sign of the cross. Then she narrowed her eyes, scrutinizing Olivia's face. "And yet, you seem happy. Glowing, even."

"That's the glow of sleep deprivation."

"Right. Sure, it is."

Carrie Stanley, the psychologist who'd been gunning for the chief psychologist job since before Olivia arrived in Fog Harbor, stopped outside the office door looking smug. "How did it go with Javier Mendez? He can be a handful even for an experienced clinician."

"Excellent." Olivia didn't miss a beat. "I think we made some real breakthroughs."

CHAPTER TWENTY-ONE

Will sat on JB's sofa, exhausted, with Princess's head resting on his thigh. Tammy had left for her job at the crime lab five minutes ago, leaving them to review the result of JB's deep-dive investigation into Peter Fox's cell phone. But Will's thoughts drifted elsewhere.

"She likes you." JB sounded surprised.

"You think? She didn't even text me when she got home."

"Wait—*what*? Are we still talking about Princess?"

Will blinked a few times, wondering if he'd fallen asleep. Princess gazed up at him adoringly. "Uh, can we stay focused here? We've got a case to solve."

"*You* have a case to solve. Until the doc gives me the go-ahead, the only thing I have to do is put my feet up and binge-watch *The Golden Girls*. That Blanche really gets my blood pumping."

"I thought you said we were in this together. We're partners, remember?"

"Yeah. Partners. That's only if you solve it, City Boy."

JB dismissed Will's aggrieved expression, producing his laptop and a sheaf of paper from the end table. "Don't worry. You'll be fine. I taught you everything I know."

"And if I don't solve the case?"

"Then we'll let Graham take the blame. If he's not in jail, that is."

"Did you find something?"

JB scrolled through the records on the laptop, displaying the content of Peter's text messages, starting in May. "No. That's the point. It's what I *didn't* find."

"You lost me."

"Every Saturday afternoon at four o'clock, Peter received a text message from La Cumbre Country Club notifying him of Sunday's available tee times. Look. May 2, 9, 16, 23, 30. Same for June. But on July Fourth, the only messages he received are the two from his wife. Nothing else."

"Maybe the text didn't go out because of the holiday. Can you call the club?"

"Exactly what I thought. But Frederick at the pro shop assured me the text went out as usual to all their regular golfers. Peter played his last round this past Sunday."

Will studied the messages, thinking of Peter and all the *last times* he'd had without knowing. "What do you make of it?"

"Jeez, City Boy, do I have to do all the heavy lifting? We need to get the records from the cell phone company. I think some of Peter's messages may have been deleted."

Will nodded. "In the meantime, I've got something else to keep you busy. Check your email."

After a few clicks, JB gaped at the screen. The exact reaction Will had had when he'd received the same email from Marcia Russell, with a link to a file hosting service. "What the hell is all this?"

"That's what twenty-six years of client files looks like, partner. Our guy could be in there. A needle in a haystack. Since you're basically on desk duty, you know what that means."

JB raised his middle finger.

"You're it."

Will had reviewed the same paragraphs in Chet's autopsy report for a full hour now, waiting for the marshals to arrive with Jonah Montgomery. Like black magic, the words conjured images he couldn't unsee. A dark contrast to the photos on Hannah's Facebook page, where eleven-year-old Lily had played Clara the last two Christmases in the Santa Barbara Youth Ballet's production of *The Nutcracker*.

> *The body of the deceased child was partially burned with charring of the bone underneath. The pugilistic position of the body and degree of burning suggested approximately ten minutes exposure to fire.*

Fourteen-year-old Dylan, sweaty and grinning in his football uniform, his arm flung around the shoulders of a teammate. Hannah had written: *Another victory for the Stingrays! Two touchdown passes for this star QB!*

> *A small entrance wound is located on the center forehead of the adolescent male. The projectile entered the front of the skull and passed through the cerebrum."*

Will tensed when Chief Flack joined him at his desk. "I've got Montgomery in room one for you. Don't screw it up."

Graham pumped his fist in the air from across the partition. "Finally!"

"Remember the rules. No talking to the suspects."

"Hey, that wasn't a rule."

"It is now." Will gestured to the break room. Sure, he'd already had three cups, but no one was counting. "Get me a fresh coffee. I'll meet you inside."

As Graham disappeared from view, Chief Flack grabbed his arm. "Before you go in there, there's something you should know…"

Jonah Montgomery looked light-years from the Facebook photo Olivia had shown him. His eyes were now sunken like blackened pits and his arms and face scratched by brambles. According to the

Canadian Border Services, he'd run from them when spotted and had been found hiding in a thicket. Clearly, the thicket had won.

Before Will could open his manila folder and launch into it, Graham materialized at the doorway, out of breath and holding two steaming cups of coffee.

"This one's for you." Graham placed the cup on the table in front of Jonah, passing the other to Will as an afterthought.

"C'mon, dude. I'm a cop. I know the whole routine. That buddy-buddy shit isn't going to fly with me."

When Graham shrank back, Will fought the urge to high-five his suspect. A first time for everything, apparently.

"Alright, Mr. Montgomery, you're a straight shooter. I can work with that." Will lowered himself into the chair closest to Jonah, pushing Graham's seat into the corner. Then, he placed the family photo he'd enlarged and printed from Peter's website smack dab between them. "Right now, you're the main suspect in the quadruple murders of the Fox family. Do you want to talk to me?"

Graham cleared his throat. "To us, you mean."

Will gave him a pointed look, and he slunk into the chair, quiet as a mouse.

"Look, I'm sure you've seen the motel security footage by now." Jonah waited for Will's confirmation but he remained tight-lipped. "You're not going to like what I have to say. You probably won't believe me."

Will opened his notepad to a fresh page. Seeing the clean white surface, ready to be filled with answers, always quickened his heartbeat.

"Try me."

"First off, I didn't kill anyone. I took an oath to uphold the law, not to break it. Plus, I'd never hurt a kid. Especially not those two. Dylan and Lily were great. The only thing I'm guilty of is being suckered into the middle of that train wreck of a marriage."

"Suckered in how? Were you having an affair with Hannah Fox?"

Jonah sat back in the chair, looking even more uncomfortable than Will had expected. He pushed the photo away from him. Then he reached for it, turning it face down. "Try again."

"With Peter?" Will sipped his scalding-hot coffee too fast. He hadn't seen that coming. "Starting when?"

"A couple of weeks after the charity auction for the children's hospital. Hannah always recruited the rookie officers for the dates. I guess you could say I caught Peter's eye. He came by the Lazy Dog. It's a bar downtown where all the cops hang out. I always had a thing for older men."

"Did Hannah know?"

"That Peter prefers dudes? What do you think? He told me she looked the other way. That they stayed together for the kids, lived separate lives. The whole clichéd speech. Then, when we started to get serious, he promised me he'd leave her. Like a fool I believed him."

Jonah took a deep breath, as if a heavy weight rested on his chest. "A friend of Hannah's came to the house one day looking for her. She walked in on us. Of course, she told Hannah. It turned out his wife had no clue about any of it. Peter made us both look like fools."

"How did Hannah react? Was she upset?"

"That's putting it mildly. I don't even think she cared about the affair so much as the idea that he might get found out. That her precious position in Santa Barbara society was in jeopardy. They did a spread in a local magazine—about her and Peter and the kids. You wanna know the headline? *Santa Barbara's Perfect Family*." Jonah scoffed.

Will saw it then, the pain in his eyes. Sparking like flint on steel.

"Can you believe Hannah tried to pay me off? She offered me fifty thousand dollars to stay away from Peter. God knows, on a cop's salary I needed the money."

"Why didn't you take it?"

"Knowing what I know now, I probably should have. But Peter did the full sales job on me. He kept telling me what I wanted to hear. That he wanted to be with me, and he just had to find a way to make it happen. He begged me to be patient. When Hannah saw that her payoff didn't work, she told Peter I'd gotten physical with her. That I'd grabbed her by the throat and told her to back off."

"Did you?"

"Hell, no. Now ask me if I wanted to." Jonah flipped the photograph face up again, folding it so that Hannah was completely covered. "I hate—*hated*—that bitch. Everyone thinks she's so amazing. So charitable. She's a controlling snake who refused to let Peter go."

"He believed her then? About the assault?"

"She faked her own injuries. She had pictures and everything. It was only a matter of time before she tried to have me kicked off the force. I've been dreaming of being a cop since our house got broken into when I was five years old. No way I was letting her take that from me too."

Will could relate to that. He remembered riding in the back of his dad's squad car, smushed between Ben and Petey, begging their dad to use the siren. Even then, he'd known he would follow in Captain Henry Decker's colossal footsteps.

"And that's when I threatened to go public with what I knew. I told him it would destroy him—his career, his family, everything—and he knew it was true. Look what happened to that congressman."

A laugh burst out of Graham's closed lips. "The guy who sent the—"

"*Bauer*." Confirmation that his partner had the maturity of a fifth grade boy. "Please continue, Mr. Montgomery."

"Peter trusted me. We talked about growing up gay. How hard it was for him compared to me. Different generations, ya know. He admitted he'd had a few dalliances with younger guys. Underage guys. Before me, there was this one in particular he met online. After exchanging some racy pictures and hooking up a couple times, the kid told him he was only seventeen. Peter ended it right away. Except this one time, he was lonely, and he sent one more nude pic. He cried when he told me. His biggest fear was being found out, and I…"

Jonah slumped forward, hiding his eyes. His shoulders shook. "I used it against him."

Showing the empathy of a gnat, Graham piped up again. "Why would you want to be with a perverted guy like that?"

Another poison glance from Will that he promptly ignored. "I'm just sayin'."

"No, you're right. I guess I fell hard. He's a good-looking guy and a smooth talker. You've seen his website. He calls himself Sly Fox for a reason. *Called*, I mean… Jesus Christ, I can't believe he's really gone."

"Did anyone else know about Peter's secret?"

"Just that underage kid. But he's not talking."

Will frowned, uneasy.

"I looked him up after Peter told me. Marty Ricks. He offed himself a couple of years ago. You're welcome to check into it yourself."

"Guess we can rule him out," Graham muttered. Will actually found himself wishing JB back. The sooner, the better.

"I can't imagine Peter took it very well that you supposedly roughed up his wife. Or when you threatened to go public. A powerful guy like that could have done you a lot of damage."

With a sad nod, Jonah continued. "He went ballistic. All of a sudden, it was the two of them against me. I think Peter even had me followed. I never intended to go through with it. I was just hurt and angry, but I still cared about Peter. Stupid me, I came here to convince him to leave with me. I was going to drive up to the Redwoods State Park and camp there for a few days. Maybe I was as naive as Peter said I was."

Or as crazy as Hannah claimed. Will hoped he would know soon enough. "So, what happened the night of the Fourth?"

Jonah sighed like he'd been dreading this question all along. "I checked in to the Sand Dunes that afternoon and sent Peter a message asking him to come to the motel."

"A text?" JB's investigation had made it clear. Aside from Hannah's, Peter had received no other texts that day. Will wondered if he'd finally tripped Jonah up.

"No. We used Snapchat because the messages disappear after a few seconds. He was always terrified of his wife finding out about us. At first, he refused to meet me. He said he needed to get his life together. That Hannah was close to forgiving him, and he couldn't screw up again. But later, I guess he got drunk and Hannah got pissy about some fight he had on the beach and he changed his mind. All of a sudden he couldn't wait to see me. He even told Hannah where he was going. Like he wanted her to suffer."

"Then what? What went wrong?"

"When he came over, he was drunk. He just wanted sex. I poured my heart out, tried to give him this fancy watch I'd bought for him. Hell, I couldn't even afford it. But it was the same old story, different day. *I can't leave my wife and kids. I can't go public. If you tell anybody about me, I'll destroy you.* The usual. We got into an argument, and you know the rest. It's all there on the security footage."

"You threatened him with a gun. Your service weapon, I assume?"

"You're welcome to run the ballistics." Jonah cocked his head and Will caught a glimpse of his other self—the confident and brash officer who'd emblazoned a Superman logo on his police gear. "And he brandished a golf club."

"You swung it at his car." Chief Flack had already sent Jonah's gun—a 9 mm Glock—to the lab for testing.

"His *car*. Not him. I just lost it. I needed to hit something."

Will had felt the same urge, tugging on his boxing gloves. Anger had to go somewhere, or it would turn his heart bitter, like his father's. He slid another photograph from the folder on his lap. "Ever seen this before?"

Jonah studied the image briefly before pushing it away. "It's a horseshoe." He pointed to the ruler beside it, where the branches measured one and a half inches from the toe. "Clearly not full size. A toy or a replica. And it's not mine."

"That's not what I asked."

"No, I've never seen it before. It's unusual though, this material. Looks like tourmaline. They sell this crap in some of the tourist shops in downtown Santa Barbara."

"Tourmaline," Will repeated. He'd scrawled the same on his notepad this morning, when Steve had called from the lab. Classified as a semi-precious stone, tourmaline was common to California and could be found in a variety of colors, including the iridescent green shade of the horseshoe. "Do you know where Peter went after he left?"

Jonah scoffed. "Home to her, I suspect. Where he always went."

"And you?"

"I drove down to that tourist trap, the haunted lighthouse. Little Gull, I think it's called. I got loaded in the parking lot and passed out drunk reading this letter I'd written for Peter. Woke up around 4:30 a.m. and drove back to the motel. I saw the news story a little while later and I panicked."

"I assume there's no one to verify your story."

"Not unless those ghosts start talking. And before you start combing my cell phone data, I left it at the room. I figured he'd change his mind, come crawling back. I didn't want to be tempted to answer."

Will had heard worse alibis. Sometimes, a story could sound so bad it had the ring of truth. Still, he had to follow the breadcrumbs of evidence. He remembered what Chief Flack had told him. What the marshals had discovered in Jonah's car, trapped between the seat and the console. "What about the lighter fluid?"

"The what?"

"The lighter fluid you purchased on your way to Fog Harbor. We found the receipt."

Jonah swallowed hard. "Camping."

"And where did those two bottles of lighter fluid go? I suppose they just walked off by themselves."

For the first time in the interview, Jonah didn't offer a quick reply. He picked up the photo again, looking at it with a mixture of anguish and regret. "I'd like to speak with an attorney."

CHAPTER TWENTY-TWO

Olivia arrived at the station for Thomas's second interview, parking near the door to avoid the reporters who lingered like vultures, eager to pick through the scraps of someone else's trauma. As she walked toward them, they briefly raised their eyes, ready to swoop in. Determining her to be no one of consequence, they lost interest, quickly redirecting their attention—and their cameras—to the white SUV that pulled in behind her.

Olivia recognized the woman behind the steering wheel from Hannah's social media accounts as Nora Goodwin, her only sister. Though she had five years and twenty pounds on Hannah, they shared the same auburn hair and delicate nose. Newly divorced and childless, Nora worked as a pharmacist in San Luis Obispo and took too many pictures of her bulldog, Bruiser, who she'd named after the dog in *Legally Blonde*. Amazing the details you could pluck online.

Nora exited the car, keeping her head down. *Smart woman.* After unbuckling Thomas from his car seat, she stepped aside, beckoning him. He shook his head with fervor. The reporters seemed to sense the brewing drama and turned to each other in frustration. Thomas's name hadn't been made public, so journalistic ethics dictated they maintain his anonymity. Otherwise, Olivia felt certain their cameras would be whirring, greedily capturing every moment.

Just then, Olivia's cell buzzed with several incoming texts from Deck, and her stomach dropped.

Dr. Lucy has a stomach bug. She won't be coming.
Chief Flack wants you to give it a go.
Thomas and his aunt just arrived.

Before Olivia could type a response, Deck strode out the station door, scanning the parking lot.

"White SUV," she told him. Then, more shyly, "Hi."

One corner of his mouth turned up slightly, and she couldn't stop herself imagining kissing it.

"I assume you got my texts."

She held up her phone, her response half typed.

"So you'll do it?"

"I'll try my best. But there's one little problem." Olivia gestured to the lot. Thomas still hadn't budged. He'd latched his small arms around the headrest of the passenger seat, as Nora tried simultaneously to cajole him and to forcibly remove him from the car.

As they approached, Thomas's fear became palpable in the clawing grasp of his fingers and his quiet sobs.

Deck gently tapped Nora's shoulder, and she spun toward them, frazzled. Her eyes welled with her own bottomless grief. "You must be Hannah's sister, Nora. I'm Detective Decker. I'm very sorry about the loss of your family. We're doing everything we can to solve the case as quickly as possible. Hopefully, you and I can find some time to talk as well."

Olivia extended her hand and introduced herself. "It looks like you need some help."

Tears already spilling from her eyes, Nora nodded. "He was fine until we pulled into the parking lot."

"Hi, Thomas. Remember me?" Olivia leaned her head down to see his face.

A small nod. But his grip on the headrest remained firm. Even the stuffed dog he cherished had been abandoned, falling to the floor at his feet.

"Dr. Lucy won't be here today. It's just you and me. Would you come inside?"

Another violent head shake, his shaggy red hair flying across his face.

From his pocket, Deck produced the army man. He held it out in his palm. "I think this soldier belongs to you."

Thomas eyed it suspiciously for a moment, before he relinquished his grip on the seat and took it from Deck, marching it across his leg. "Ranger Rob," he corrected.

"How about you and Ranger Rob talk to Dr. Rockwell out here? Is that better?"

Thomas sniffled.

"Is that okay with you?" Deck asked Nora, waving over a couple of patrol officers who had just gone off duty.

"I think it's for the best. He's terrified of this place."

As the officers kept an eye on the media vultures circling at the periphery, Olivia touched Thomas's shoulder. "Is that true, Thomas? You're scared of the police station?"

He looked toward the front door with apprehension. As if a monster might break it down and come lumbering toward them. Then, he aimed his gun-toting army man. "*Pow. Pow. Pow.*"

"Who are you shooting?" Olivia asked.

"The bad man." Thomas gestured back to the station, whispering, "That's where he lives."

Unsettled, Olivia followed his gaze past the reporters to the front doors. "And how do you know the bad man?"

"He hurt Mommy and Dylan and Lily. I saw him. He had a gun, like in the movies. I ran and hid."

"Then what happened? Where did you go?"

"To hide in my secret fort on the beach. Dylan said it wasn't really a fort because the lifeguard lived there. But the bad man couldn't find me. Ranger Rob used his invisible shield so the bad man couldn't see me."

Olivia nodded, encouraging Thomas. "Do you think you could recognize the bad man if you saw him again?"

Thomas's eyes widened; his little body stiffened, and Ranger Rob disappeared into his hand, his knuckles white. "I don't want to see him again. Never ever."

"What did he look like?"

In a voice so quiet, Olivia had to strain to hear it. "A policeman. The bad man is a policeman."

CHAPTER TWENTY-THREE

While Olivia reassured Thomas, Will pulled Nora aside, all of them still reeling from Thomas's revelation. Will, most of all. He regretted not pressing Jonah harder before he'd lawyered up. But Jonah would have nothing but time to think. He'd been booked on charges of brandishing a weapon. Maybe a night or two in the city jail would get him talking again.

"A policeman?" Nora shook her head, lowered the eyes that looked a lot like Hannah's. "I don't understand. Do you think my nephew is confused? He's been through so much. He told me his mom and dad were arguing that night. They hadn't been getting along."

"It's certainly possible Thomas is imagining things. But that wouldn't explain his reaction on the night we found him. He took one look at my badge and all hell broke loose. And you saw how he acted today. He's afraid of the station. I think we have to believe him until we know otherwise."

Will had seen the terror in Thomas's eyes that night in the lifeguard stand, had heard the tremble in his voice just now when he'd uttered the word "policeman." No one would convince Will it was a product of the boy's imagination.

Nora cast a concerned glance back to the vehicle, where Thomas sat with Olivia. "The medical examiner's office called this morning. They want to release the…"

Will contemplated the difficulty in finishing that sentence. Her loss, immeasurable, indescribable, and yet she had to stay upright. Had to keep putting one foot in front of the other. She had to carry on for Thomas. "We'll need you to stick around a bit longer. Where are you staying?"

"Everything was sold out. I had to pay double for an Airbnb in the middle of nowhere. For Thomas's sake, I pray this part will be over soon. I want to get him as far from here as possible."

"I totally understand. We're in the process of developing a suspect. I'll be able to put together a photo lineup soon, and we'll have Thomas take a look."

"It's so much pressure for him. Poor kid. He's already had it rough. Hannah was planning to enroll him in this fancy pre-school—the number one ranked in Southern California—but his IQ score wasn't quite up to par. She had him doing math workbooks right up until the time they left on vacation."

Will recalled his own preschool days, certain he and his friends had been eating playdough and running with scissors. "I didn't realize preschools had rankings."

"If it didn't have a ranking, Hannah wasn't interested. She always was the achiever of the two of us. The prettiest, the skinniest, the richest. She already had Dylan slaving away in SAT prep and Lily taking private ballet lessons from a former prima ballerina. To her, everything was a competition. It's no surprise she picked Peter, with his handsome face and his law degree and his fat pocketbook. A trophy husband, if I ever saw one."

"So Peter had already left the public defender's office by the time he met Hannah?"

Nora's derisive laugh confirmed Will's suspicion. "Hannah, with a public defender? That'd be the day. Peter was one of the top defense attorneys in Santa Barbara when they started dating. By the time they had Lily, he was fielding calls from all over the country."

"How *did* they meet?" Will asked.

"Oh, that's right. I guess you wouldn't know. Hannah graduated from USC law school herself. She and Peter both applied for a teaching position at UC Santa Barbara. Hannah liked to joke that she won the job and Peter won her."

"She was an attorney too?" Will sighed. The more he learned, the more unwieldy the case became. Even on four cups of coffee, he felt outmatched.

"Not practicing. She stopped teaching after she got pregnant with Dylan. But Peter would send her to interview potential clients. She always had the final say. She loved that."

"Any enemies? Feuds? Disgruntled clients? We have reason to believe this crime was personal, carried out by someone who knew the family. Perhaps even knew they would be vacationing in Fog Harbor."

"If Hannah had problems, she never shared them with me. She took great pains to make sure her life looked perfect from the outside. Lately, something seemed off. I couldn't quite put my finger on it, but she seemed less chatty on our weekly calls. Then, about a month ago, I asked her if she was okay. If she was happy. With Peter, with the kids, with life in general. She just laughed it off. God knows, she'd never admit any weakness. But I wondered if things were starting to fall apart."

"And? How did Hannah respond when you asked?"

"'Grow up,' she said. 'Happy is for children and puppies.'"

Thomas pressed his face to the glass while they drove away. He advanced the army man in his hand across the bottom of the window. Then, he raised his eyes and waved. No joy in his face, but at least his terror had subsided.

Will turned to face Olivia, watching as she smiled after Thomas. "Did he say anything more about the policeman?"

"Only that he wore a badge and a uniform, but..." Her face was a warning. He wouldn't like what came next.

"*But...?*"

"The more we talked, the more fantastical his story became. By the end of it, he was chasing the bad man from the house with his army of green soldiers."

Will's stomach knotted. "You don't believe him?"

"I'm not saying that. Children can make excellent witnesses depending on the circumstances. I just want to be cautious about taking him too literally, especially after what he's been through."

"Pretty hard to do that when one of our suspects is an actual policeman." Though Will didn't say it out loud, he couldn't help but think of Graham as well. That guy could not be trusted. "The policeman theory makes sense, too. With Peter being parked on the side of the road and still seat-belted in. Like he was pulled over."

Olivia nodded, noncommittal. "And I presume your best suspect is Jonah Montgomery."

"Of course. Who else?"

She raised her eyebrows, ready to school him yet again, and began walking toward the station. Will jogged to catch up with her, resisting the impulse to take her hand.

"What aren't you telling me?"

"I need to show you something I found in the Bastidas file. You may have more prime suspects than you think."

SANTA BARBARA POLICE DEPARTMENT

ARREST REPORT

NAME: Elvis Bastidas
ADDRESS: 21 Rule Avenue, Apt 144, Santa Barbara, CA
DOB: 8/23/74   AGE: 20   SEX: M   RACE: HISPANIC
ARRESTING OFFICER: CHARLES SHEN
INCIDENT TYPE: ROBBERY;
IMPERSONATING A POLICE OFFICER; USE OF A
FIREARM

NARRATIVE:
AT 8 P.M. ON OCTOBER 31, 1994, ELVIS BASTIDAS
WAS PLACED UNDER ARREST OUTSIDE OF THE PALM
COURT APARTMENTS ON SUSPICION OF ROBBERY AND
IMPERSONATING A POLICE OFFICER.

ON THE ABOVE TIME AND DATE, I WAS ON UNIFORMED
DUTY IN A MARKED PATROL CAR, ASSIGNED TO WEST FOG
HARBOR. AT THAT TIME, I RECEIVED AN ECC BROADCAST
FOR A POSSIBLE ROBBERY IN PROGRESS AT THE PALM
COURT APARTMENTS. THE SUSPECT WAS DESCRIBED AS
A WELL-BUILT HISPANIC MALE IN A POLICE UNIFORM AND
WAS THOUGHT TO BE IN POSSESSION OF A FIREARM.

THE CALLER, JASMINE GOODE, MET ME AT THE FRONT
ENTRANCE OF HER RESIDENCE, APARTMENT 65. SHE
REPORTED THAT SHE HAD JUST RETURNED FROM TRICK-
OR-TREATING WITH HER CHILDREN WHEN THE SUSPECT
KNOCKED ON HER DOOR CLAIMING TO BE A SANTA

BARBARA POLICE OFFICER. HE INSISTED HE NEEDED
TO SEARCH HER RESIDENCE FOR A SUSPECT WHO HAD
ESCAPED FROM CUSTODY NEARBY. ONCE HE HAD GAINED
ENTRY TO HER HOME, BASTIDAS BRANDISHED A GUN AND
DEMANDED HER MONEY AND VALUABLES. HE FLED THE
APARTMENT WITH TWENTY DOLLARS IN CASH AND SEVERAL
PIECES OF COSTUME JEWELRY.

I SEARCHED THE PREMISES OF THE PALM COURT
APARTMENTS AND FOUND THE SUSPECT HIDING IN A
MAINTENANCE SHED. HE WAS STILL WEARING A MOCK
POLICE UNIFORM WHICH HE INFORMED ME HE HAD
PURCHASED AS A HALLOWEEN COSTUME. I PLACED
HIM UNDER ARREST WITHOUT INCIDENT. THE HANDGUN
BELIEVED TO BE USED BY BASTIDAS IN THE COMMISSION
OF THE ROBBERY WAS NOT RECOVERED.

SHORTLY AFTER MY ARRIVAL ON THE SCENE, TWO
OTHER PALM COURT RESIDENTS CAME FORWARD,
ALLEGING THEY HAD BEEN ROBBED UNDER SIMILAR
CIRCUMSTANCES.

CHAPTER TWENTY-FOUR

Olivia sat in JB's vacant desk chair watching Deck's eyes scan the ancient arrest report and waiting for his reaction. She'd really started to enjoy one-upping him but she didn't want to rub it in. Not if she intended to put her lips on his again in the not-so-distant future.

"I know it's old," she said. "At least two years before he got arrested for murder. It could be nothing."

"Impersonating an officer? *Shit.*" Somehow he managed to looked pissed off and awestruck simultaneously. "That's what you meant about not taking Thomas literally. Why didn't you tell me sooner?"

"It's a big file. I didn't even think of it until Thomas said what he said about the bad man."

Deck sat back, both hands behind his head, looking defeated. Then he flashed a sudden frown at the stack of files on his desk. "Hey, Milner. Did you take the phone records from my desk?"

Jessie peered over the cubicle partition and shook her head. "Haven't seen them. But Graham was carrying a stack of files when he walked out a few minutes ago. I think he's in the break room."

Before Olivia could say a word, Deck sprang to his feet. She followed him down the hallway past the lieutenant's office, where Graham had commandeered a table inside the sad little break room, with its prehistoric coffeemaker and grumbling fridge. His feet propped on a chair, he didn't look up from the papers in his lap.

"You took evidence from my desk?"

With a smirk, Graham raised his eyes. Olivia figured he'd been expecting this, relished it even. "Chill, Decker. I am your partner. I just wanted to help out." He cast a surprised glance her way, as if he'd just noticed her there. "Oh, hey, Liv."

Ugh. From his mouth, that nickname rankled. She barely smiled at him.

"Hand it over, Graham."

Predictably, Graham made a show of it, huffing as he dropped the files onto the table, sending one of the folders tumbling to the ground. "Suit yourself."

Then he proceeded to the countertop, taking his time filling his coffee cup and swirling in two sugars. "How've you been?" Graham asked her, chewing on the end of the stirrer. "I didn't get a chance to talk to you on the Fourth. It would be nice to catch up, talk shop. Maybe share a few ribs at the Pit."

Olivia contemplated how best to tell him she had no interest in any of the above.

"Get out." Will pointed at the door, emphatic.

"What?"

"You heard me. Leave. Now."

"Since when do you call the shots around here?" Graham stalked toward Will, the same way he'd ended up chest to chest with Peter Fox, before he'd hauled off and punched him.

"Since you tampered with evidence at a crime scene. I know you lifted the cell phone off our victim."

"Prove it."

Olivia rolled her eyes, stepping between them, though she didn't mind seeing Graham put in his place. "You two are ridiculous."

Graham shrugged, knocking Will off balance with a bump to the shoulder. "I get it. You want a little alone time. Can't say I blame you. But Liv knows who's the bigger man here."

He stomped off before Olivia could remind him that she could speak for herself.

"That guy is insufferable." Deck quickly shut the break room door. Turning to her, he grinned. "But he's not entirely wrong."

"About which part?" Olivia felt the heat from his dark eyes as he walked toward her. She could already feel his back muscles beneath her fingers, the roughness of his stubble against her mouth. She braced for it, welcomed it.

He zipped right past her without an answer, dropping to his knees in front of the locked shred bin. Once a week, Fog Harbor Mobile Shredding collected the contents of the bin for disposal. "Help me get this thing open before anyone else comes in."

Two bent paper clips later and the box yielded, the door swinging open in Deck's hand.

"Should I be concerned that an officer of the law is remarkably skilled at lock-picking?"

He looked back at her, smug and annoyingly irresistible. "I'm a man of many hidden talents, Doctor Rockwell."

"Humility is apparently not one of them."

Chuckling, he lifted the bin from inside, setting it on the table and sifting through the papers at the top of the pile, plucking one from the refuse.

"Anything?" She peered over his shoulder, the EasyTalk cell logo visible at the top of the page. Her heart sank as she read. As much as she despised Graham and lamented that she'd ever been suckered in by him, she'd never expected this. "That's Graham's cell number."

At 3:53 p.m., Graham had laid down the gauntlet via text message.

Okay, asshole. You name the time and place, and we'll finish this. You want my badge? You're going to have to pry it from my cold, dead fingers.

Peter had wasted no time in responding one minute later. The exchange reeked of booze and testosterone.

Thank you for threatening me. Now I have even more evidence to present to your chief in the morning. You think I'm scared of a police officer in Hicksville, USA? I'll have your badge in my pocket before you can say Barney Fife.

The final text had come from Graham at 4:15 p.m.

Be careful. I know where you're staying. I'll make you and your family wish you'd never set foot in Fog Harbor.

Deck let out a long, slow breath. "Looks like we have another, *other* prime suspect."

"What will you do?"

"I need to talk to the chief ASAP. At a minimum, he's got to be put on desk duty until we can rule him out." He reached for the doorknob, when she stopped him with a finger in his belt loop.

"Doctor Rockwell." His voice squeaked out, a little hoarse. "What are you doing?"

She leaned in toward him, bringing her mouth mere inches from his. "Don't leave the evidence behind," she whispered, pointing behind him to the shred bin he'd forgotten to return to its place.

He nearly brushed his lips against hers, before stepping out of her reach. "Wouldn't dream of it."

CHAPTER TWENTY-FIVE

After walking Olivia to the door, Will headed to Chief Flack's office. Even as he pondered the horrific notion that Graham had murdered the Fox family, his body wouldn't stop tingling. He felt like a teenager. He seriously needed to keep his hands to himself and his head in the game.

"What did you say to Graham?" Jessie called out from her desk. "He stormed out of here madder than a hornet."

Will gave a cryptic shrug, tucking the incriminating phone records under his arm. "Can you follow up with Bastidas's parole officer? Find out if he works today."

"Sure thing."

Chief Flack beckoned Will into the lion's den while she finished a phone call. "Yes, Mayor Crawley. I understand your position. I'll be sure to let him know."

When she hung up the phone, she closed her eyes and began counting. Very. Very. Slowly.

"Uh, Chief?"

A quick shake of her head silenced him. After she reached ten, she opened her eyes and plastered a smile on her face. "I take it you had a disagreement with Bauer again. The mayor would like to remind you of the importance of the Bauer family to the city of Fog Harbor."

Will's mouth dropped. He knew that Graham's uncle Marvin had donated a tidy sum to Crawley's re-election campaign, but that didn't earn Graham carte blanche to do whatever he pleased, up to and including murder. He slid the page of deleted text messages across the chief's desk. "Well, you let Crawley know that his crowned prince is a suspect in a quadruple homicide. I caught him tampering with evidence."

Chief Flack studied the page, her expression darkening. The well-worn grooves in her forehead deepened.

"That's Graham's cell number," Will explained. "He sent those messages to Peter Fox on the afternoon leading up to the murders. Then, he stole the phone off Peter's body and deleted them. And today, he took the records off my desk and stuck this in the shred box."

"Where is he now?"

"Jessie said he took off. Probably to cover more of his tracks." Will waited for the chief's head to explode. For her to throw her desk placard. To yell. Anything but the placid face he saw right now. "Please tell me you're pulling him from the case."

She nodded. "That seems prudent. But let me deliver the news. We have to be delicate about it. Besides, you don't really think he's behind all this, do you?"

"Why does everyone keep asking that?" He hadn't deemed Graham capable, but he couldn't close his eyes to the facts. "It's not about what I think. I go where the evidence leads me."

"I've known Graham since he moved to Fog Harbor to live with Uncle Marvin. Fresh out of community college, he was determined to be a cop. Youngest rookie we've ever had on the force at age twenty-three. He even got a commendation a few years back for interrupting a robbery at First National. I know he's a disaster, but—"

Will felt nauseous. In a mere five minutes, he'd become alarmingly earthbound. "Please don't make excuses for him."

"No excuses," Chief Flack agreed. "But he's not as different from you as you think. Ambitious. Competitive. Family history of law enforcement."

"Oh, please."

"I just don't see him as a cold-blooded killer, Decker. I want to make sure we stay focused on what's important here. Getting justice for that family. For that little boy."

Will recognized defeat. Sometimes, you had to concede a battle to win the war. "You're absolutely right, Chief. I'm heading over to interview Bastidas now, and I'm taking Jessie with me."

Will found Elvis Bastidas exactly where his parole agent told Jessie he would be. Sweating buckets at a construction site on the outskirts of town. The man lumbering in a stained tank top on the roof of the soon-to-be Tasty Treat didn't bear the faintest resemblance to his mug shot. His time in the joint—twenty-five-plus years—had been unkind. He'd lost his full head of black hair and gained fifty pounds, a chest full of bad tattoos, and a nasty knife scar beneath his chin.

"I think that's his wife's car." Jessie pointed at a beat-up Chevy suburban with a bad paint job and two bullet holes in the rear hatch. "His parole officer said it was a beater."

"Go check it out. Let me know if there's anything worth taking a looking at."

With her swingy blonde ponytail and sweet smile, Jessie reminded Will of a kindergarten teacher. But he'd watched her clock a sub-five-minute mile in the Fog Harbor Turkey Trot last year, and she always outgunned Graham at the range. Her disarming appearance gave her a leg-up. No one ever saw her coming. Case in point, Bastidas didn't notice her scoping out his ride.

But when he spotted Will standing at the bottom of the ladder, he unleashed a string of curse words in Spanish.

"I know why you're here, and you got the wrong guy, *ese*," Bastidas yelled down to him. "I've been keeping my nose clean. Ask my PO."

"We did." According to Bastidas's parole officer, he'd reported right on time after his release and had found a job almost immediately. "And if you're telling the truth, you've got nothing to worry about."

Bastidas began a slow and awkward climb down the ladder. His pants struggled to stay in place beneath his belly. Finally, he planted his work boots in front of Will, giving said pants one more hopeful tug. "Did you have to show up here at my job?"

"Would you rather come down to the station?"

He groaned and wiped the sweat from his forehead with a black handkerchief. The color of Los Diabolitos. "Just hurry it up. I've got work to do."

"It'll be quick and painless," Will promised.

"Yeah. Like a bullet to the head."

An image flashed in Will's mind. Hannah Fox and her oldest son laid out on the lawn, matching bullet wounds to the center of their foreheads. "Tell me about your relationship with Peter Fox."

"There ain't one. Unless you count me hating the guy's guts. He represented me—if you want to call it that. Sorry excuse for a public defender, and that's really sayin' something. He convinced me to accept a plea deal and wouldn't let me take the stand. I know those jurors would've seen it my way. That shooting was self-defense."

"So, you admit you had beef with him?"

"Ain't no secret. I'm sure you read my love letters. That's why you're here. Am I right?"

Will pulled up a copy of the most recent correspondence on his phone and read it out loud for Bastidas. "Pretty graphic. You can understand why I'd feel compelled to talk to you. You threatened him, called him a dead man walking. Implied you'd been stalking his wife and kids. You get out of prison and the whole family turns up dead. I'd say you've got some explaining to do, starting with where you were the night of the Fourth."

"At Shell Beach with my old lady watching the fireworks show. You can ask her. She'll vouch for me."

Will had been at this detective gig long enough to have a practiced poker face, but Bastidas putting himself at the crime scene warranted a twitch of his eyebrows. If his only alibi was the woman who laid her head on the pillow next to his, he was in big trouble. "Anybody else see you there?"

"Yeah. A whole beach full of white people. Tourists."

"Did you interact with any of them? Have a conversation?"

"Look at me. What do you think?"

Bastidas didn't want to know what Will thought. That the chip on his shoulder wasn't going to get him very far. "You ever impersonate a cop?"

"What would I want to do that for?"

Will shrugged. "Police report says you did. Back in the early nineties. A couple of robberies at the Palm Court Apartments."

"They dismissed that shit."

Unfortunately, the charges had been dismissed due to the victims' lack of cooperation. Will couldn't blame them. Los Diabolitos would just as soon put a bullet in your back than let you get away with telling tales.

Jessie joined them, flashing Will a look of disappointment that told him she hadn't spotted anything worthwhile. Not surprising though. After a quarter century in prison, Bastidas wouldn't make it easy. He'd earned his PhD in criminal sophistication. Still, Will planned to have a look inside. As an active parolee, Bastidas—and his vehicle—were subject to search at any time for any reason.

"I love your tattoo." Will contained his amusement at the innocent lilt in Jessie's voice, knowing she could drop him to his knees with an arm bar. She pointed to the Spanish script across his collarbone. *Venganza dulce*. Unlike Bastidas's other tattoos—most of them symbolic of his loyalty to his gang—this ink looked fresh. "Did you get it in the joint?"

"A month ago." Bastidas grinned, his teeth a crooked fence beneath his thin mustache, holding up his paper-thin tank top as Jessie moved closer. "You can look, but you can't touch. Gabriella wouldn't like that."

"Sweet revenge," she said, eyeing Will as Bastidas preened. "What does that mean to you?"

"My freedom. A life lived well is always the best revenge. That's what *mi abuelo* used to say."

A life lived well? Will imagined Bastidas's grandfather rolling in his grave. "How did you feel when you heard about Fox and his family?"

"I didn't shed any tears, if that's what you're asking. Hell, I'm proud of the SOB who had the cojones to send Fox to hell. But I didn't do it—the guy had a long line of enemies—and if I had I would've gone about it another way."

Will waited for the explanation, dreading it all the while.

"Me, personally, I would have done the wife and kids. Left that sorry SOB alive to suffer alone."

Not glimpsing a trace of a soul in his dark, beady eyes—time hadn't changed that—Will studied the rest of him. He wore a slim gold band on his ring finger and a thick gold chain around his neck, a cross dangling over the tattoo Jessie had asked about. Along with the scar on his neck, he had a few other shank marks on his upper chest. "How'd you get that burn on your hand?"

"This?" Bastidas turned his right hand to the side, where the flesh had been stripped away. "I'm a roofer. Ever heard of hot tar? Well, it's damn hot."

"When did it happen?"

"A couple days ago."

"Looks pretty nasty. You get any medical treatment?"

Bastidas scoffed. "Gabriella put some mineral oil on it. Dissolved the tar. Lost a little skin with it. No big deal."

Will held up his phone. "Do you mind if I snap a picture of it?"

Bastidas didn't hesitate. He raised his right hand toward the eye of the camera, flashing the sign for Los Diabolitos. "Whatever gets your rocks off, *ese*."

Thirty minutes later, and Will had excavated the Chevy suburban with the meticulous enthusiasm of an archaeologist. All he'd managed to unearth were a few discarded food wrappers—apparently, Bastidas shared JB's sweet tooth—and an old marijuana roach slipped beneath the floormat. Though Will could've busted him on a violation of his parole conditions, it hardly seemed worth the paperwork.

"Lovely guy." Jessie shook her head, lamenting, while Will drove them back to the station. Any hope he had of ruling Bastidas out had been crushed beneath the ex-con's work boots.

"A real gentleman. But, did he murder the Foxes?"

"I wouldn't bet against it," she said. "I can talk to Gabriella, if you want. Confirm his alibi."

Will nodded, though he doubted it would be a fruitful conversation. "What do we know about her?"

"His parole officer told me they got married in the county jail before Elvis transferred to state prison. No criminal history, but she's on disability for mental health issues."

"Be sure to ask her about the burn." Will intended to show the pictures to Chet as well. To determine if the injury was consistent with a tar burn.

"And the tattoo," she added.

"Yeah, about that... Good catch. I didn't know you spoke Spanish."

She laughed. "You can thank my mom for that one. She's a high school Spanish teacher. Her and my dad were always using it as their secret code, so naturally my brother and I became fluent. Though I'm sure she never thought I'd be using my language skills to translate a parolee's tattoo."

"She'd be so proud," he teased. "And hey, if Graham asks, you don't know anything about the case."

She pressed two fingers together, zipped them across her lips. "*Mis labios están sellados.*"

CHAPTER TWENTY-SIX

Back at the prison, the rest of Olivia's Monday afternoon crawled until she couldn't stand it any longer. She said goodbye to Leah and Sergeant Weber and escaped the MHU, anxious to get home, throw on her running shoes, and hit the trail behind her house. She needed to think. About Thomas and Graham and Elvis Bastidas. About the horseshoe and the policeman and what it all meant. About Javier Mendez and her father.

But mostly, she needed to outrun her own fear. Now that she'd finally admitted her feelings for Deck—to herself, anyway—she'd started to count the ways one of them would inevitably mess it up. After all, the odds weren't in their favor with her failed marriage and his broken engagement between them.

"Em?" Olivia saw no signs of her sister in the house. No dishes on the coffee table. No shoes tossed in the hallway. The television regarded her with its unremitting dead eye. And yet, the rental car her sister had commandeered in San Francisco for the trip back to Fog Harbor sat unmoved in the driveway.

Telling herself she'd be ridiculous to panic, Olivia checked the kitchen counter for a note that might explain where Em had disappeared to. Nothing. Not even a breadcrumb. Feeling decidedly guilty, she glanced over her shoulder before she cracked the door to her sister's room, waiting for someone to stop her.

Next to her unmade bed, Emily had propped her easel and started another painting—the firework-lit sky above Shell Beach. The paint, still wet. Olivia gathered a pile of her sister's clothes and tossed them on the rocking chair near the window. A business card fluttered from the pocket of the jean shorts Em had worn yesterday.

Spade Investigations
Nick Spade, Private Investigator
SpadePI@spadeinvestigations.net

Just then, Olivia heard the rumble of an engine outside. The front door opened, and her sister called to her. Before she left the bedroom, Olivia tucked the card into her pocket, safeguarding it until she could figure out what to do with it.

"Hey, Liv." Em had already kicked off her pointy-toed flats and plopped into a chair at the kitchen table. "Did you get my note?"

"What note?"

"The note I left on the kitchen counter. Remember Tara from the prison?" Emily had worked as a dental hygienist at Crescent Bay for a while before she'd made the move to San Francisco. "We went for coffee at Myrtle's."

"You didn't leave a note."

Emily frowned, huffing out an annoyed breath. "I definitely did. Trust me, I know how you freak out if I go off the grid for a split second."

"Can you really blame me?" The past flashed between them like a lightning strike. She'd almost lost Em to Drake Devere. The truth of that had wormed itself into her heart and mind, burrowed so deep she couldn't unknow it, couldn't unfeel it.

"It's not like I'm going to get kidnapped again. That's a once-in-a-lifetime kind of thing."

"You're right." Olivia's voice dripped with sarcasm. "I'll be sure to give the bad guys the message."

She spun around, determined to get into her running clothes and tear out the door as quickly as possible.

"Liv." No matter how angry she was, she never could ignore her sister's voice. "I really did leave a note. I swear it."

Her mind finally blown clear, Olivia slowed her pace as she traced the river's edge leading to the rocky beach by Little Gull lighthouse. In another quarter mile, the redwood cover would lessen, the dirt, tree-lined path giving way to sandy shores. Already she could smell the brine of the ocean. Maybe she'd take off her shoes and wade in. The sea, a cure-all for her worries.

While Olivia walked, she thought of her sister, of that rogue business card she'd slipped into her sock drawer with plans to do her own investigation. Why would her sister hire a PI? And without telling her? It unnerved Olivia the same way little Thomas had with his strange accusations.

From somewhere in the woods, Olivia heard the sudden snap of a twig, and her head jerked toward the sound. The sun had already begun its steady descent, with the dappled light turning to shadow deeper in the forest. She peered into the darkness between the tree trunks, waiting to discern the slightest movement, listening for the smallest sound.

Seeing nothing, she kept walking, forcing herself to look straight ahead, no matter how terrified she felt. If she didn't look, it couldn't be real. Even so, her body telegraphed the signs of danger. The fine hairs prickled at the back of her neck. Unease fisted her stomach. Hot as it was out, a chill coursed through her, as it seemed a pair of eyes followed her step for step, a presence flitting in and out of her periphery.

By the time she'd reached the clearing and spotted the lighthouse, she felt remarkably silly. But she knew one thing for certain. She'd take the long way back. Up the stairs, through the parking lot where she always did her best thinking, and back down Pine Grove Road to home.

Olivia watched the waves roll in and out, leaving a trail of white foam behind them. In the quiet gloaming, a new horror gripped her. If Emily *had* left a note, where had it gone?

With a half mile to go down Pine Grove Road, Olivia heard the growl of an engine behind her, a pair of headlamps illuminating her path. Already jumpy, she stepped off into the ditch, breathing hard and squinting into the brightness until the shiny black truck with its monster tires had stopped alongside her.

Graham Bauer lowered his window. "Need a ride?"

"Sure." In a way, she felt relieved, preferring the devil she knew to the one who might be lurking in the shadows. She forced a smile, knowing it would soften him to her questions. Deck had his interrogation style. She had hers.

"Your sister told me I might find you out here. She said you went for a run."

Olivia climbed up into the cab, disquieted by his admission and the gun in the holster on his waist. He'd been looking for her. The truck rumbled on, beast-like, down the deserted road.

"I need to talk to you about Detective Decker. He's barking up the wrong tree. I think the guy's got it in for me." Graham took his eyes from the road and settled them on her thighs, bare in her running shorts. "He trusts you. Can you talk to him for me?"

"And tell him what, exactly?" Olivia slid her legs out of Graham's reach, crossing them toward the door.

"That I didn't have a goddamned thing to do with those murders."

She thought of the phone records Deck had dug out of the shred box, where Graham had left them to die. "Are you sure about that?"

"C'mon, Liv. You know me."

"Then, tell me what happened between you and Peter Fox. And don't say 'nothing.'"

Graham steered the truck off the road and into a turnout. He parked and cut the engine. The sudden silence dropped like a curtain around them, and Olivia warded off the sudden and irrational need to escape. "I was drunk. Drunk people say things they don't mean."

"Drunk people also do things they regret." Olivia recalled their one night together. How he'd insisted she have that third glass of wine.

"I didn't *do* anything." And there it was. His hand on her knee. Like a chess game, she moved it aside.

"Why did you shred those pages from the phone record?" Checkmate. But then, he rested it on his gun instead.

"Because it made me look guilty. And to be honest, Liv, I don't have an alibi. I went home, and yeah, I texted the guy like an idiot. I got his cell number from the incident report. Then, I laid on the couch for a couple of hours, eating potato chips, flipping through the channels, and feeling sorry for myself. I watched that movie you like—*National Treasure*. They show it on SFTV every Fourth. That's when I heard the call on the radio. About the SUV on fire."

"You should've just told Deck the truth. Now, he doesn't believe a word you say."

"What about you? Do you believe me?"

"Honestly, I'm not sure."

Graham groaned like she'd punched him in the gut. "Are you sleeping with him?"

"*What?*"

"You heard me. You can't trust that guy. Remember he snitched on his own brother. And he's trying to make me look bad to impress you."

Olivia pulled on the door handle, ready to end the conversation one way or another. It didn't budge. "Let me out."

She tugged again, feeling panic rise in her throat. Graham's mouth kept moving but she couldn't hear a word over the white noise in her brain. All she saw was his hand coming toward her with intention.

Desperate, she slung her elbow at his face. It glanced off his chin and she screamed as he reached across her. Pressed the button she'd been too fear-blind to see.

Click.

She flung herself out the open door and slammed it shut behind her. The truck roared to life and left her standing on shaky legs in a cloud of dust.

CHAPTER TWENTY-SEVEN

Will barreled down Pine Grove Road toward the turnoff for home, distracted by the slipperiness of his suspect list. He couldn't put his finger on any one of them. Not for very long. Bastidas had given them a convenient alibi. And ballistics had tested Jonah's service weapon and determined that gun had not fired the fatal headshots. Which left Will with exactly nothing.

A flash of movement in the ditch distracted him for an instant. When he turned his head to the road again, the startled white eyes of a deer blinked back at him. Will cursed, slammed on his brakes, and watched his bag from the Hickory Pit go flying.

His trunk screeched to a stop. The deer, already vanished in the thicket.

Standing on the side of the road, in the glow of his high beams, a familiar pair of legs.

Will leaned out his open window. "What in the hell are you doing? You almost got me killed."

"You, or the deer?"

"Well, you certainly annihilated my number five, to go." Will glanced despairingly at the floorboard.

"Side of mac and cheese?" The corner of her mouth lifted, revealing that single dimple that drove Will crazy.

"Of course."

She hung her head. "Then, that is a tragedy."

"Seriously, though." He cocked his head toward the passenger seat. "Get in. It's not safe for you to be jogging out here at night."

Will detected a trace of trouble in her eyes. She offered no reply, just hurried around and hopped inside, collecting the Hickory Pit bag and returning it to the seat between them.

"Are you okay?" Though he felt pulled to look at her, he kept his focus on the road this time.

"I'm fine." But the way she said it made Will nervous.

"What happened?"

"If I tell you, will you promise not to go full cop on me?"

"What does that mean? I *am* a cop." Will pulled into Olivia's driveway, comforted by the sight of the warm yellow light through the windows. He parked behind the Buick and turned to her, taking her in. Her face, flushed. Her hair, damp with sweat. A tendril had escaped her ponytail and latched itself to her cheek.

"Just don't make a big deal out of it. I ran into Graham, and I think I overreacted."

"Already, I don't like this." He white-knuckled the steering wheel. "Did he hurt you?"

"See. You're doing it."

Will sighed hard and leaned back against the seat, resting his hands in his lap. "Alright. Cop mode disengaged. Proceed."

When Olivia stopped talking, Will shook his head in disbelief. He told himself to stay calm and pull it together, but he couldn't stand the idea of Graham trying to bully her, to turn her against him. "I can't believe the nerve of that guy."

"Right. Like he needs you to make him look bad."

Will gave her a sideways glance. "Like I'm so desperate to impress you."

"Well…" She smiled, soothing the flare of indignation in his chest.

"But he's wrong about everything else," Will countered. "And I don't believe his story."

"I don't either. *National Treasure* ended at noon on the Fourth. Em and I watched it before we headed to the beach."

Will took in the revelation, questioning his own instincts. "I didn't think Graham was capable of something like this. I should've known better."

"Don't beat yourself up. I still don't think Graham did it. Sure, his ego was bruised, and he was ticked off. But he hardly knew the Foxes. That kind of brutality requires something more intimate. The kind of deep-seated anger that comes from stewing in your own juices for a very long time."

Still uncertain, Will set about distracting himself. "My turn. If I ask you something, will you promise not to go full shrink on me?"

He never tired of hearing her laugh. "Deal."

But suddenly, he clammed up, not sure he had the guts to spit it out. "I really wish you'd dropped Graham with a jab-hook."

"That's not a question."

Busted. "Why did you change your mind about…" He volleyed his hand back and forth between them, as his face warmed. He could interview a murder suspect no problem, but Olivia and her teasing green eyes made him nervous. "Us? The *just friends* thing."

"Who said I changed my mind?"

Flustered, he stammered out a, "Well—I…" before he pulled it together. "Your lips did. Pretty emphatically, actually."

Olivia tried to hide her smile, but it showed through her eyes, glinting with flecks of gold. "Maybe my lips were just desperate to keep yours quiet. It's quite an arduous task, you know."

When she cocked her head at him, Will countered, tucking that stray tendril behind her ear and cupping her cheek.

"Yeah. It seemed like a real chore."

She leaned in, just teasing him now. "Like doing the dishes."

"Vacuuming," he whispered, his mouth grazing hers. "Folding the—"

Her hand in his hair, Olivia pulled Will in.

"Laundry," she finished, before kissing him hard.

No sooner had Will opened the front door, letting himself and Cyclops inside, than the landline rang. Only one person had ever called him at that number.

"Hello, Dad."

"Where have you been, William? This is my fourth call." Retired Captain Henry Decker managed to make him feel like a kid again. Ten years old and in trouble, bracing himself as his dad snatched the belt off the brass hook in the bedroom. Since Will's visit in March, they'd been on speaking terms again.

"Kinda busy with work right now. You have my cell, if you need to reach me."

Grumbling, his father continued, "I hear you've got yourself quite a case. Four victims, two of them children. That's a damn shame."

"We made an arrest. I think we're close to solving it." Will hated the way he sounded, still anxious for his father's approval. Telling lies to make him proud.

His father harrumphed. "I saw it on the news. Sounds like you're pinning it on a fellow officer."

Ignoring that not-so-subtle dig, Will replied, "I'm not *pinning* anything on anyone. I'm following the evidence, like you taught me. We have video of Officer Montgomery arguing with Peter Fox right before the murders. It got physical. Besides, innocent men don't make a run for the Canadian border."

"You sound like John Q. Public, son. Everybody wants to blame the cops these days. But looking guilty and *being* guilty are two different things. Don't forget that."

Will bit his tongue, taking satisfaction in knowing his father would blow a gasket if he saw his list of suspects, two cops' names writ large.

"What does your girlfriend think about it?"

"Olivia's not my girlfriend. She's a forensic psychologist. Chief Flack hired her to help."

"Mm-hmm."

Will sighed.

"Is that where you were tonight?"

"I've gotta go, Dad. It's getting late."

"Just be careful, son. You don't know how much of her daddy she's got in her. Until the shit hits the fan, you never can tell if a woman will be there for you when it counts."

Resisting the urge to slam the phone back into its cradle, Will mumbled a goodbye. Leave it to Henry Decker to bring him right back down to earth.

The Downtown Star

Secrets Exposed! Murdered Attorney Caught in Love Triangle
with Hot Cop!

Peter and Hannah Fox appeared to have the perfect marriage. Three beautiful children, a lavish mansion in the hills, and a successful law practice. Sadly, *Santa Barbara's perfect family* met a tragic end on July Fourth weekend, when Peter, Hannah, and two of their children were shot and killed while on vacation in the sleepy town of Fog Harbor, leading many to wonder about the dark secrets that led to their demise.

Stunning revelations in the days following the brutal slayings suggest the Foxes' picture-perfect façade was nothing more than a well-crafted illusion to disguise Peter's multiple affairs with much younger men. Twenty-eight-year-old Jonah Montgomery, dubbed by Santa Barbara locals as the "hot cop," was arrested at the Canadian border after reports that he brandished a weapon at Fox at a seedy Fog Harbor motel. In still shots of security footage obtained exclusively by *The Downtown Star* (see below) Fox, age fifty-one, can be seen wielding a golf club at the door of the bridal suite, where Montgomery was a registered guest. Another photo appears to show Montgomery threatening Fox with a gun in an apparent lovers' quarrel. Police have not officially charged Montgomery in the murders of the Fox family but he remains in a Fog Harbor jail, having been denied bond.

An inside source tells *The Downtown Star* that Fox had a history of seducing younger men online which went far beyond his dalliance with Montgomery and occasionally crossed the line of legality, with him sending nude pictures to adolescent boys he met in a barely legal chatroom. "Peter paid off more than a few young men," the source adds. "No price was too high to keep his dirty little secrets. It's not surprising his lies finally caught up with him, but his family suffered too, paying the ultimate price. That's the real tragedy here."

CHAPTER TWENTY-EIGHT

The morning sun warmed Will's back as he knocked on JB's front door. JB greeted him with a wheat bagel in one hand and a gossip magazine in the other, Princess dancing at his feet. He broke off a piece of bagel that Princess gobbled in one gulp.

Behind him, Tammy rolled her eyes. "People food isn't good for her, remember?"

"Wheat bagels are not people food," JB argued, sneaking Princess another bite. "So, big day today, City Boy."

"Yeah. The photo lineup." Will had lain awake half the night thinking about it. That and Olivia's hands finding their way beneath his blue button-down. "I hope Thomas pulls through. We really need something concrete to go on."

"I was talking about my doctor's appointment. If I get the all-clear, I can resume a moderate level of physical activity. You know what that means?"

"You can finally get your ass off the sofa and help Detective Decker solve this case?" Tammy gave Will a wink.

JB wiggled his eyebrows at her, giving her a playful swat. "Not exactly."

Chuckling, Will made his way inside and pointed to JB's laptop, which sat open on the coffee table. "Speaking of, did you find anything in Fox's files yet?"

"Just a lot of guilty-as-sin clients. The guy sure had a knack for finding loopholes. It's no wonder he made bank defending the scum of the earth."

His curiosity piqued, Will took a seat in the armchair. "Loop-holes?"

"Get this. Fox defended an inmate at Valley View on a murder rap. The guy had killed another inmate who came into his cell uninvited. Fox argued he should get off the hook because a man is allowed to defend his dwelling from intruders."

"The jury bought that?"

"Didn't need to. The DA pled down to voluntary manslaughter to be served concurrent to the drug case the guy was already doing time for. He got out in five years."

Will grimaced. "Sheesh."

"And check this out." JB revealed his copy of *The Downtown Star*, slapping it on the coffee table in front of Will. "Tammy picked up a copy at the bagel shop. Underage boys? It sounds like Peter had a lot in common with those dirtbags he defended."

"Is this what it's come to?" Will scanned the front page story skeptically. "If we're building our case on rumors from *The Downtown Star*, we're in big trouble. It's not exactly the bastion of journalistic integrity."

"*Your* case, City Boy. And I thought you could probably use the help, bastion or not."

"I'm doing perfectly fine."

"That bad, huh?" JB returned to his spot on the sofa, carting Princess under his arm. "So, about this lineup. Are we taking bets?"

Jessie waited for Will at his desk. "What's the word?" he asked her, hoping to start the day with some good news. Though he'd already spotted Graham over her shoulder, brooding. "You talk to Bastidas's wife?"

Jessie nodded, a worried furrow marking her usually sunny face. "She confirmed his alibi. Fourth of July fireworks, just the two of them."

"How sweet."

"And his story about the burn. She said her father worked as a roofer too, so she knew exactly how to handle it. According to Gabriella, Elvis's boss begged him not to go to the doctor. I guess the work site isn't entirely OSHA compliant, if you know what I mean."

Will nodded glumly. Chet had emailed his reply to the photograph Will had sent him, confirming that the mark on Bastidas's hand appeared consistent with a tar burn.

"What about the tattoo?" Will asked Jessie. "Did Gabriella know when he'd gotten it?"

"She wasn't sure. But she said that it wasn't there during their last family visit a few months ago. She admitted Elvis had beef with a lot of people, Fox included, but he'd calmed down in recent years. He was trying to set a good example for her younger brother, Pedro, who lives with them. Trying to help Pedro avoid making the same mistakes."

"Why do I get the feeling there's a *but* here?"

Jessie lowered her voice. "Gabriella told me she's been worried sick ever since Elvis was released. Word on the street is that Oaktown's got a price on his head. Payback for the murder of Tim McKenzie. Apparently, those bullet holes on the Chevy are fresh. Elvis refuses to leave Fog Harbor. He thinks it'll make him look like a coward. He didn't even tell his PO about it, and she's worried her brother may do something stupid to try to impress him."

Will contemplated banging his head against his wall. The last thing he needed in the middle of a quadruple murder was a gang shootout. "Alright. Get in touch with Bastidas's parole agent. Let him know what's going on. I'll stop by and see Gabriella this afternoon."

After Jessie had returned to her desk, Will slumped into his seat and began preparing three photographic arrays for Thomas, selecting offenders with similar physical characteristics to his suspects. As he worked, he detected a noticeable absence.

Graham had never been so quiet. He sat there with his perfect coif, keeping his mouth shut and his eyes fixed on his computer screen. Resentment wafted from him, filling the six feet between their desks with the kind of noxious tension that Will hadn't suffered through since his days in San Francisco. Back when he'd been branded a snitch and worse for testifying against his brother—and fellow cop—in the wrongful death trial that sent Ben to prison for six years.

When Lieutenant Gary Wheeler appeared in the doorway and gave Will a single nod of his head, his stomach flip-flopped. Thomas had arrived. Chief Flack already waited in the observation room with Olivia. Will collected the photo arrays, tucking them inside a plain folder that gave away nothing of its life-altering contents.

Graham finally lifted his face, shooting daggers at Will as he stood.

"This is where the rubber meets the road, Bauer." Will couldn't resist goading him. Though he would've preferred something less subtle—slapping handcuffs on the guy or cold-clocking him in the face—the chief would not approve.

"What's that supposed to mean?"

Will walked away without an explanation, relishing Graham's frustration.

He poked his head into the observation room, giving Olivia a small wave.

Chief Flack met his smile with indifference. "Ready, Decker?"

"As ready as I'm going to be."

"You prepared two photo arrays, correct?"

He barely nodded, preferring not to outright lie to her. No way in hell would the chief approve of his third suspect.

She gestured to the folder. "Let me see them."

Will slipped the first two pages out and handed them to the chief. She studied the photos, nodding to herself, satisfied. Then, she pointed to the door. "You wait with Doctor Rockwell."

"Wait with... *what*?"

"You're heavily invested in this case, Decker, and I am too. I think it's best if we take a back seat, especially with such a vulnerable witness. We both know the gold standard of lineups is double-blind procedure, so I asked Officer Bullock to administer."

Will saw him, then, over her shoulder, waddling toward them. Bulldog Bullock, aptly named for his prominent jowls, his underbite, and his stocky, bow-legged frame. His temper too.

"Chief, are you sure?"

She raised her eyebrows in warning, and he knew better than to ask again. He slunk away, taking the folder with him, the third suspect burning a hole right through it.

CHAPTER TWENTY-NINE

Olivia positioned herself directly behind the two-way mirror, her heart heavy with worry for little Thomas. He sat in a chair that was much too big for him, his small blue sneakers swinging inches from the ground. Officer Bullock plopped into the chair beside him, while Thomas held tight onto Aunt Nora's hand. In the other, he gripped his stuffed dog. His favorite army man, Ranger Rob, stood guard on the table. Olivia felt proud of him for being brave. He must've remembered what she'd told him yesterday. No one would let the bad man hurt him or his aunt. Even so, she felt guilty for making empty promises. Until they'd found the Foxes' killer, Thomas was in danger.

Deck paced like a lion in a cage behind her, while Chief Flack stood by, his watchful keeper.

"Okay, Thomas. I'm going to show you some pictures. I want you to take your time and have a close look at them." Bullock placed the first photo array on the table facing the boy.

Thomas's face remained an unreadable blank.

"Do you recognize anyone?" Bullock asked.

Thomas cast an uncertain glance at Nora.

"Go ahead, honey. Answer the question."

He returned his eyes to the photographs, scanning right past Bastidas's most recent prison photo, and shook his head *no*.

Olivia watched as Bullock collected the photo stoically. In its place, he set the second array, Jonah's picture at the bottom center. The officer repeated the instructions and waited while Thomas studied the photographs one by one. He paused, placing his finger on Jonah's face.

Nora's breath hitched. Behind Olivia, Deck stopped moving. His regular footfalls suddenly still.

"You recognize him?" Bullock asked.

Again, Thomas looked to Nora, who offered him a nod of encouragement. "That's Daddy's friend," he said.

"Daddy's friend," Bullock echoed. "Tell me about Daddy's friend."

"His name is Jonah. He came over to the house before to talk to Daddy. He told me I could ride one of his horses."

Olivia turned to Deck, who'd joined her at the mirror. *Horses?* she mouthed, thinking of the tourmaline horseshoe she'd found sunk at the bottom of the Ocean's Song swimming pool.

"Did Jonah hurt your family?"

Thomas scrunched his face. He looked like he might cry, gripping the stuffed dog to his chest. "The bad man did it. He showed Mommy his badge, and she couldn't tell he was the bad man. And then, he came inside and it was loud and Mommy screamed and Dylan fell down. But me and Ranger Rob chased him away. We went to the fort to get more ammo."

Bullock thumped his fat finger against Jonah's picture. "Is this the bad man, Thomas? Is Daddy's friend the bad man?"

Thomas whimpered, a gut-wrenching sound. "Can we go get ice cream now?"

"Not yet, honey. Soon." Aunt Nora smoothed his hair and put an arm around his small shoulders. "Is Daddy's friend Jonah the bad man you saw?"

The little boy leaned into her for a moment, gathering himself. Then, he took an audible breath and spoke so fast Olivia had to focus to understand him. "I don't think so 'cause he wouldn't have hurt Daddy and he's nice to me and he promised I could ride his horse named Ginger in the parade…"

While Thomas rambled about feeding apples to Ginger, Olivia retrieved her phone from her pocket and typed a few words into the search bar on a hunch. She clicked the link on the screen and scrolled through the website, half-heartedly searching for Jonah's name. When she actually found it, accompanied by a photo, she stared in disbelief at the caption.

Santa Barbara County Sheriff's Office Mounted Unit Reserve Member Jonah Montgomery and his mount, Ginger, assist with a search-and-rescue operation near Cathedral Peak

Olivia passed the phone to Deck, just as Officer Bullock collected the second photo array. Thomas had finally run out of words. Ignoring the officer's last-ditch questions about the bad man, Thomas marched the army man across the table, pointed his tiny gun at Bullock, and made shooting noises until Bullock surrendered.

"Give me a second," Bullock told Nora, hoisting himself to his feet.

Seconds later, he opened the door to the observation room and heaved a sigh, tossing the photo arrays on the nearest chair. He ran a hand across his head, disturbing his combover. "Kids are exhausting. Give me a coked-out criminal any day."

"So, what do you think?" Chief Flack asked.

Bullock threw up his hands, his beady eyes widening. "I think he's four years old and doesn't have a goddamned clue what he saw. If he's your star witness, you're in big trouble."

Olivia winced. Thomas wasn't just the star witness. He was the only witness.

Without a word, Deck headed out the door and into the interview room, greeting Nora with a sad smile. "Let me walk you both out."

Chief Flack and Officer Bullock followed behind him, stopping in the hallway to debrief. Bullock's grumbling was still audible. After they left, Olivia stood there flummoxed, replaying what Thomas had said. The little boy had seen far more than she'd imagined. He had witnessed the murders of his mom and brother, possibly his sister too. Chilling in its own right but made worse by a single realization. If Thomas had seen the killer, the killer had seen him.

Olivia turned away from the empty interview room and spotted the folder Deck had left behind, resting beneath a chair. An edge of white paper protruded from the top. She knew she shouldn't open it. She should simply return it to Deck. She should keep her civilian nose out of official police business. And yet, after taking a cautionary glance at the door, she peeked inside at a third photo array. No need to scan the two rows of suspects; her eyes were drawn straight to the face familiar to her. The one belonging to Graham Bauer.

CHAPTER THIRTY

"Let's go this way." Will directed Nora down the corridor that led back to his desk. Thomas tagged along behind her, clinging to her hand and his stuffed dog. Will had seen him carefully tuck Ranger Rob in his jeans pocket.

"What happens now?" Nora asked, the pained expression on her face giving her away. She struck him as the stiff upper lip sort of woman who would wait until Thomas had fallen asleep before she lost it, bearing the burden of her grief as stolidly as Will's father had. Nearly thirty years after his mother had vanished like a ghost, and Will hadn't witnessed a single tear.

"We keep investigating." Will peered around the corner, searching the cubicles. "It's possible Thomas didn't get a clear look at the perpetrator's face."

"What's a purple tator?" Thomas asked, looking up at Will with those sad eyes, blue as the sea itself.

"A bad man." Will disguised his disappointment. Graham's desk chair sat empty. In his mind, it had gone differently. In his mind, Thomas had turned the corner and gasped, burying his face in his aunt's side. In his mind, Thomas had held out a shaky finger and declared Graham Bauer the worst bad man of all.

Instead, the little boy glanced up at Nora, unsure of himself and of Will and of the entire awful situation. "Oh."

Will escorted them out of the station and into the parking lot, still scanning for a sign of Graham. The coward had probably taken an early lunch. "I understand if you need to return home.

We'll contact you as soon as we have news to report. If Thomas remembers anything more, or if you think of something—even if it doesn't seem important—you have my card and Doctor Rockwell's. Please let us know."

She nodded, helping Thomas into the back, buckling him in the car seat, and shutting the door. "Of course. Whatever I can do to help. At some point, I'm sure this will all seem real. But right now, it's like living in a nightmare. For both of us. Last night, Thomas woke up screaming. I almost had a heart attack right then and there. He keeps asking for his mom and his big brother. I can't wrap my head around the fact that he saw the whole thing. That they're all really gone."

Will watched Thomas through the window. Ranger Rob had been stationed behind the headrest, the perfect spot for an ambush. Suddenly, the glass shushed down and Thomas turned to them in earnest. Whatever horrors he'd witnessed and kept locked up in the attic of his head, Will imagined him releasing them. They'd fly from his small red mouth like black winged birds and take the shape of a face. A name. A killer Will could hunt down.

"Can we get ice cream now?"

When Will turned back for the station, Olivia headed toward him. Her grim expression matched his own.

"Why didn't you show him the third photo array?" She held the folder out to him.

Realizing then he'd left it behind in his rush, Will's heart stuttered for a beat or two before he snatched up the folder and tucked it beneath his arm. "You saw it?"

She nodded.

"Did anyone else?"

"I don't think so."

Will let himself breathe. "Chief Flack said we didn't have enough evidence to name Graham as a suspect. Apparently, his TV show mix-up isn't sufficient."

"But what about those texts?"

"Also not sufficient. She doesn't want to ruffle any feathers unnecessarily." It still burned Will to say it.

"Then why'd you stick him in a lineup to begin with?" Olivia scrutinized his face. He watched her puzzle for a moment before her eyes lit up. "You thought you were going in there, didn't you?"

He shrugged, feeling like a hapless sucker.

"You were going to pull one over on Chief Flack, and she outsmarted you."

"Are you trying to make me feel better or worse?"

Olivia laughed, but rubbed his shoulder to ease the sting. "I'm sorry. You're right. It's just that Wise Guy Detective doesn't usually get played like a fiddle."

He rolled his eyes, walking back toward the station.

"Wait," she called after him. Sucker that he was, he stopped, allowing her to catch up. "What did you think about Thomas? It wasn't a total bust, you know."

"How do you figure? He didn't identify either of our prime suspects, and the more we talk to him, the more confused he seems."

"But we learned that Jonah owns a horse. That he's a reserve member of the mounted unit. He never told you that. Which is especially interesting since I found that small horseshoe in the bottom of the pool."

"All circumstantial." Will wished he could share in her excitement, but he knew too much. He'd seen too many cases go to shit. And his gut instinct—the cop clairvoyance that always steered him right—had gone woefully silent. "Plus, the gun we found on him isn't a match."

"But circumstantial doesn't mean inconsequential." She nudged him with her elbow, still trying to make him smile. "You know as well as I do that every killer makes at least one mistake. This one is no different. That's how you'll catch him."

"True," Will conceded. "Killers make mistakes. The problem is, so do detectives."

Will mulled over Olivia's words of encouragement as he showed his badge to the officer at the control booth of Crescent Bay State Prison. He'd come here, behind the concrete walls and barbed wire, to kill two birds.

The iron gate swung open, and the usual stench knocked him back like a palm strike to the nose. It had been a while. Two months, to be exact, since he'd visited his brother, Ben, here. But the smell never changed. Beneath the heady scent of bleach, a mixture of bodily fluids and despair. Long-dead dreams and sweaty socks.

When he'd come here last, he'd gone through the visitors' entrance with the rest of the civilians and been ushered into a large room that reminded him of his high school cafeteria. Even more so after Ben had taken a seat across from him, sharing the M&Ms he'd wrangled from the vending machine. This time, he had official business with the warden.

Will approached the administrative office and asked a correctional officer to buzz him inside, already wrestling with the demons of the past that seemed to haunt this place. Ben, of course. But not only Ben. Drake Devere too. Will still blamed himself for Devere's escape from Crescent Bay. Frankly, so did Warden Blevins.

"Good afternoon, Detective." The warden appeared in the doorway of his office, with a smile so wide and toothy it promised menace. "You're here about Mr. Bastidas."

Will gave Blevins a nod, looking past him to his secretary's desk and to the small, sad table and folding chair beside it reserved for the inmate clerk who just happened to be his brother. Warden Blevins had recruited Ben for the job for reasons unknown, reasons which Will regarded with wariness. After he and Olivia had seen the warden brokering deals with the Oaktown Boys, it seemed wise to maintain a healthy dose of suspicion.

Ben raised his eyes, disguising his exclamation of surprise with a cough. At least he looked better than he had the last time. He'd gained a few pounds on his lean frame and lost the bags under his eyes.

"I had Ben tag the files of Bastidas's known Los Diabolitos associates for your perusal. I presume you trust your brother's level of thoroughness, as well as his discretion."

Will caught Ben's eye, Blevins's words poised between them like a loaded gun. Once upon a time, Will *had* trusted Ben with his life. But that trust had been blown to bits by Ben's service weapon in a single, fateful night.

"Of course," Will said, ignoring Ben's mirthless snort. He retrieved another folding chair from the corner and dragged it to Ben's desk, where he took a seat facing the older, harder version of himself.

Ben swiveled the computer screen toward him and placed a stack of envelopes on his desk. "Have at it. I've got mail to sort."

Warden Blevins nodded at them both. "If you discover anything that could reflect poorly on this institution, I'll expect the courtesy of a full debrief."

Will agreed again, the lie rolling off his tongue. He owed Blevins nothing.

As soon as the warden had locked himself inside his ivory tower, Will pointed to the empty desk where his secretary usually sat. "Where's Leeza?"

"Early lunch." Ben's voice oozed sarcasm, even as he lowered it to a whisper. "Ever since Blevins hired me, she's got me doing her job too. I'm working overtime."

"What do you expect, man? You're cheap labor." Though Will didn't like the idea of Ben spending so much time alone with the warden, he supposed Ben was safer here out of the direct reach of the Oaktown thugs. "I still can't believe you took this job."

Ben shrugged, his eyes shifting to the door and back to Will again. "Blevins said he'd put in a good word for me with the Classification Committee. I might be able to shave some time off my sentence."

That churned Will's stomach. Every favor Blevins gave came with strings attached. "Just keep your eyes open."

After giving a stiff salute, Ben winked at him. "Aye, aye, Captain. Both eyes wide open."

Will quickly scrolled through the files Ben had marked, getting a lay of the land. All of the men had been validated by the Institutional Gang Investigators as members of Los Diabolitos. Most had worked their way up the ranks to hold positions of authority. If there was a hit on an attorney and his family, these were the guys who'd okayed it. But sorting through reams of useless information and trying to decipher the gang's lingo seemed like a colossal waste of time.

Will pushed back from the desk. Then, realizing he had no better leads, returned to the files with a sigh of resignation.

"Looks like you've got yourself a tough case." Ben raised his head from the heaping pile of mail.

"What makes you say that?"

"You're doing that thing with your face." Ben squinted, scrunched his forehead, and poked his head out like a turtle. "The *my evidence is shit* face."

Will couldn't deny it. "So, what's your take on it then? I'm sure it's been all over the news. Enlighten me."

"A rich defense attorney. Dead wife and kids. Fancy beach house set on fire. Uh, yeah. There's been a little media coverage." Ben stared at him until Will squirmed under the weight of his gaze. "Seriously? You want my opinion? Damn, you must be desperate."

"Well, when you put it that way, I guess I am."

Ben huffed out a laugh and went back to mail sorting. Will waited him out.

"If you're looking at Bastidas, no way in hell that guy did the deed himself. Guys like Bastidas and Mendez don't get their hands dirty."

"Mendez?" Will swallowed hard, the name slithering up his throat. "As in Javier Mendez?"

The Javier Mendez case had been the stuff of legend in the San Francisco Police Department. Both for the brutality of the crime scene—he'd staked his wife's severed head on a bedpost—and for his utter lack of remorse.

"See for yourself," Ben said, with a shrug. "His file is in there. I thought you knew."

"Knew what?"

"That he and Bastidas are homeboys. Apparently, they go all the way back to the streets of Santa Barbara. They grew up together."

"How would I know that?"

Ben raised an eyebrow, paving the road for the smart-ass comment that followed. "I figured you put your girl up to sussing him out."

"My *girl*?"

"Doctor Rockwell. *Olivia*."

Will wanted to put Ben in a headlock just to wipe the smirk off him, though secretly he liked thinking of Olivia that way. "What does she have to do with it?"

"Rumor is that she's therapizing the guy. Which is pretty weird since he's got no soul. And even weirder since the last bleeding heart who tried to find one ended up with a telephone cord around her neck."

Will ignored his brain's blaring alarm bells. He could think of one reason Olivia wanted inside the head of Javier Mendez, and it had nothing to do with saving that bastard's soul. He paged down until he located the tab for Mendez's file and began to compare it against what he knew about Bastidas. They'd done time together at Desert Canyon State Prison, a maximum security facility down south. In fact, they'd even been cellmates for a while. Both had ended up at Crescent Bay eventually, Mendez most recently, after the unfortunate incident with the aforementioned bleeding heart.

When Will reached the old section of Mendez's file, where some of the faded pages had been stamped POOR ORIGINAL, he slowed down, took his time. Came to a complete and utter stop on a name in the Family History portion of Mendez's post-sentencing report.

Gabriella Mendez Bastidas, sister, age 26.

Mendez had seven brothers. One sister. Who just happened to be married to one of his suspects.

"Find something?" Ben asked.

"Let me guess. I've got that—"

"*Jinkies* face." Ben widened his eyes, holding his mouth in a perfect O, before he chuckled. "Straight out of *Scooby-Doo*."

"Whatever, Shaggy. Can I print this page?"

Ben nodded, suddenly serious. "Watch yourself, Deck. Los Diabolitos is nothing to mess with."

With a handful of printed pages on the passenger seat of the Crown Vic, Will drove away from the prison. He avoided the rearview mirror, preferring not to think of Ben back there behind the razor wire in prison garb. No matter what his brother had done, it still hit him like a punch to the gut every time he saw him there.

Will's ringing phone came as a welcome distraction. Even if the appearance of Chief Flack's number ratcheted his anxiety up a notch. "What's up, Chief?"

"Did Thomas Fox leave his stuffed animal in the interview room?"

"Not that I know of. Have you checked the lost and found?"

She released a pained sigh. "I'm an officer of the law, Decker. And a woman. I know where to look for missing things, even if it is below my pay grade."

"Just asking." Will heard the beep of an incoming call. "JB's on the other line. I'll check for the dog when I get back to the station."

Chief Flack murmured her agreement, and Will swapped calls. Before he could speak, JB launched into his one-man show.

"*Bow chicka wow wow.* The love machine is back in business, baby."

Will half groaned, half snorted. "*Baby?*"

"Oh. City Boy. It's you. I could've sworn I dialed Tammy's number. How'd the photo lineup go?"

"Total bust. I'm assuming the doc gave you the all-clear."

"Detective of the Year reporting for duty." Will imagined he'd said it with a straight face. "No stairs. No running. No jumping. No climbing. Not even a vigorous walk."

"So, business as usual then?" Will whipped the Crown Vic around, U-turning toward Primrose Avenue, a smile spreading across his face. "I'll pick you up in ten."

CHAPTER THIRTY-ONE

Olivia struggled through her late-morning client session, anxiously awaiting the ding of the fifty-minute timer. She had a plan for her lunch break that didn't involve the turkey sandwich and raisins she'd packed.

Olivia printed the memo she'd typed—authorizing Mendez for a coveted single cell due to mental health symptoms—and plucked it from the printer. The paper, still warm to the touch, made her feel cold inside. Because of what it meant. What it said about her. Since her father had died, leaving her to uncover all of his secrets, she understood desperation in a new way. How she might be convinced to break the rules, to play with fire, if it meant getting the answers she needed.

Leah had taken the day off for Liam's well-baby check-up, so she didn't need to sneak around. Still, she felt like a criminal among criminals leaving the MHU and making her way to A Yard.

Outside, the air smelled different. Like freedom. The stench of the prison blown away in the breeze. Sometimes, when the wind picked up, the inmates swore they could smell the sea. Cruelty or justice, depending on which side of the fence you resided.

Javier Mendez was unmissable, basking in the sun atop a picnic table by the racquetball courts. No one sat next to him, but a group of younger inmates flanked the table like courtiers surrounding their king. They closed ranks, leering at her as she approached, and she suddenly wished she'd worn more layers. Her silk blouse and slacks were woefully insufficient against their predatory gazes.

With men like these, confidence could be wielded like a weapon. She stood up straight, broadened her shoulders, and held her ground, the way she'd been taught to handle the mountain lions that occasionally roamed the running trail behind her house.

Maintaining eye contact with Mendez, Olivia walked a straight line to the table. He nodded at the men, who retreated back to their positions. They kept watching her, though. She felt it in the fine hairs that raised on her arms and at the back of her neck.

Olivia said nothing. Because when you throw caution to the wind and toss the rules out the window, there's nothing to be said. She simply placed the memo in his hand and strode away.

When she reached the track on the perimeter of the yard, she glanced over her shoulder. The memo had already disappeared, into his pocket perhaps. But he wore a tiny smile that confirmed he'd read it. She smiled too. Favors like that didn't come free.

Olivia returned to her desk feeling lighter. At least she'd done something. For months, she'd felt powerless, helpless, resigned to accept the bogus story the prison had told her. That her father had killed himself. Even though she knew it was complete BS.

Still riding her high, Olivia studied the business card she'd found in Em's pocket. Last night, she'd scoured the Internet, only to discover that Nick Spade had no website. But she had been able to confirm he'd been licensed as a PI for three years.

With fifteen minutes until her next patient, Olivia picked up the phone and dialed. Time to unmask Nick Spade and find out why her little sister needed to speak to him.

"Spade Investigations, Nick speaking."

"Hi, Nick." Olivia forced her voice up an octave to match her sister's flirty tone. "It's Emily... Emily Rockwell. I was hoping you'd have an update for me."

"Unfortunately, I don't work miracles. Cases like this take time."

"Well, what *have* you done?"

Nick laughed unabashedly, raising Olivia's protective big sister hackles. "Can we talk about this tonight? An early dinner, remember? Five thirty at the Hickory Pit. My treat."

"Of course. I totally spaced." Olivia didn't know which worried her more. Her sister hiring a private investigator or dating one. "I'll be there."

"And hey, bring that drawing of your father's. I got a tip from my contact at the Feds and scrounged up my old black light from storage."

Olivia must've mumbled a response, but in her panicked brain the only words she could hear—*black light*—repeated like the cry of a banshee, summoning the memory of the March afternoon when she'd discovered her father's hidden message on a piece of drawing paper he'd kept in his cell. No way that Em had it now, since Olivia had to surrender the entire sketchbook to two suits from the FBI. Which could only mean one thing.

Somehow, her little sister had gotten her hands on another drawing with another hidden message.

CHAPTER THIRTY-TWO

"Damn, City Boy. You sure made it here in a hurry." As soon as JB had fastened his seat belt, he picked up right where he'd left off, dedicated to his life's work of ribbing Will incessantly. "Missed me, huh?"

"Like a headache."

"You sweet talker, you. No wonder Olivia finally came around."

Will felt a flush creep up his neck. "What do you know about it?"

"I know plenty. There's only one man who can keep a secret in Fog Harbor."

Will waited quietly, without giving JB the satisfaction of asking. He knew his partner couldn't resist delivering a punchline. Best not to encourage him.

"The gravedigger." JB paused for a beat, then nudged Will with his elbow. "Oh, c'mon. That was funny."

With a mirthless eye-roll, Will consulted his GPS, making a right turn toward the outskirts of town. Elvis Bastidas, his wife, Gabriella, and her twenty-three-year-old brother, Pedro, lived off a dirt road in a small trailer park known for gang activity. "Alright, Jay Leno. Let's stay focused."

JB gave a smart-ass salute. "How 'bout you tell me where the hell we're going?"

Will flashed his phone screen in JB's direction.

"Sunrise Canyon?" He groaned. "My first ten minutes back on the job, and that's where you take me? I was hoping for someplace a little more classy. Where the trailers don't have bullet holes."

While Will filled JB in on his morning—Jessie's discussion with Gabriella, the anticlimactic photo array, and the connection he'd discovered between Bastidas and Mendez—the Crown Vic rumbled over the bumps in the road, juddering his teeth.

The road dead-ended at a clearing in the redwoods, where a semicircle of run-down trailers dotted the landscape. Most of them appeared completely abandoned, with water-stained furniture in their weedy yards and trash bags for windows. An uneasy chill passed over Will when a frightened face disappeared behind the curtains of a mud-brown trailer at the heart of the park.

"He's already home from work." Will brought the car to a stop between Bastidas's suburban and his trailer, painted a pallid shade of blue that echoed the sky.

The whole place seemed too quiet. The sort of delicate calm that teetered on a razor's edge, ready to tumble and break wide open.

As if he'd read Will's mind, JB pulled his Glock from its holster. "Is it just me, or is your Spidey sense tingling?"

A sudden gust of wind blew the door to the trailer wide open—cracked linoleum, a shock of slick red, a pair of bare feet—and started Will's heart pumping. He pointed to the glove box, where he'd stashed a set of handcuffs that JB slipped into his pocket.

Without another word, they exited the car, taking cover alongside it.

Will moved first, gun drawn, toward the doorway, where a shadow flitted at the edge of his vision. "Hands where I can see them."

As he moved closer, the shadow took the shape of a woman. Gabriella, he guessed. Her long black hair fell like a curtain around her face, while she crouched at Bastidas's side, crying, repeating his name. "Elvis, Elvis. *Quédate conmigo.*"

"Hands," Will repeated, taking in the whole scene, one garish segment at a time. Beside Gabriella, Bastidas slumped against the wall, grimacing. Sweat beaded on his pale forehead. Gabriella had tied a dish towel around his wound but blood soaked through his pants leg. It pooled on the floor beneath him, covered the soles of his feet.

Slowly, Gabriella registered their presence. She stood, splaying her red palms.

"What happened?" Will asked, holstering his gun. "Where's your brother?"

She pointed, raising her finger over Will's shoulder. When he glanced back, he saw JB had returned to the car to radio for help. Behind him, the dirt road was laid out, long and lonely. "Oaktown Boys. Pedro went after them."

"Is he armed?"

Gabriella nodded gravely, showing Will a bullet hole that had pierced the flimsy trailer door. "They rode up on their bikes a few minutes ago and started shooting. Everybody ran inside. But Pedro, he—"

Bastidas groaned, tried to stand up.

"Easy there, big guy." Will stepped inside the trailer and took a quick glance around, scanning Bastidas's waistband for weapons. "Keep pressure on that leg until the paramedics get here."

Gabriella blinked a few times before springing into action, balling another towel at the site of the wound. As Will descended the concrete steps, leaving his bloody shoeprints, she called out to him.

"Don't hurt him, please. He's just a dumb kid. He didn't know any better."

Just then, a hail of rapid-fire bullets pierced the air. The staccato sound zipped right up his spine when he recognized it as a high-powered automatic rifle. The kind that had no business in the hands of Bastidas or his kid brother-in-law. Will ran down the path in the direction of the noise, which came from deep in the redwoods. Though he couldn't imagine a motorcycle gang fleeing through the thick forest, he couldn't deny his own ears. Pedro must've taken a shortcut to the main road in hopes of catching them.

"Take the car," he yelled to JB. "I'll meet you down there."

Will plunged into the tree cover, while JB took off in the Crown Vic, leaving a cloud of dust in his wake.

The gunfire had gone quiet now. Only the rat-tat-tat of Will's heart pinging in his chest, and the heavy sounds of his own breathing. His footfalls breaking against the detritus of the forest floor. Twigs snapping like small bones under his boots.

The sun didn't quite reach here. Though he'd begun to sweat through his dress shirt, Will shivered against the sudden cold. He had the distinct sense of being watched. Being hunted by something or someone just beyond his view. He ducked behind the nearest redwood, pressing his back to the rough bark and listening as hard as he ever had.

When the silence became unbearable, he readied his gun and whipped around, certain he'd see Pedro—or worse—ready to end him.

JB's voice interrupted his relief. "Put the gun down! Slow and steady."

Sprinting again, Will headed back toward the road with his Glock raised and ready. Pedro had already dropped to his knees near the path, an automatic rifle discarded ten feet away from him. The redwoods cast their long shadows, darkening his face. When Pedro looked up, his eyes burned, black as coal.

"Get on the ground," JB directed. "All the way."

Once Pedro had lowered himself to the dirt, Will patted him down, pulling a six-inch blade from his boot and two handfuls of spent shell casings from the pockets of his utility pants. "Any other weapons on you?"

Pedro shook his head. The same black hair as his sister's flopping against his sweaty face.

JB cuffed him up while Will cleared the weapon, discharging a single round from the chamber, before he dropped the empty magazine into the grass. Pedro had meant business. But when Will sat him up and looked him in the face, he saw just how young he was. Twenty-three going on seventeen with those chubby cheeks and that wise-ass smirk nobody had wiped off his face yet.

Scanning the forest, Will spotted a redwood trunk peppered with gunfire. He squinted at it for a moment, distracted.

"Got anything to say for yourself?" JB stood over Pedro, sirens audible in the distance.

"I did it."

"Did *what*?"

It took a lot to surprise Will these days. Even more to shock him. It had been a long time since he'd been shaken to the bone.

"The murder of that family. The fucking Foxes. Shot 'em in the head and burned 'em up. Sent 'em straight to hell where they belong. Nobody does Los Diabolitos that way and gets away with it. *Venganza dulce.*"

CHAPTER THIRTY-THREE

Olivia sent Emily a text telling her she'd be home late, that she had to cover an evening treatment group at the prison. Then she parked in the turnout on the way to the Hickory Pit, hunkering down until her sister blazed past in her rental car, going way too fast for Olivia's liking.

Olivia tailed her from a distance, parking in the overflow lot across the street, and waiting for Nick Spade to show his face. Knowing her sister, it would be dangerously handsome.

At 5:30 p.m. on the dot, a gray Toyota Corolla pulled into the spot next to Emily. Though Olivia couldn't see the driver through the tinted windows, she would've bet money it belonged to Nick. The perfect car for a PI, a Corolla could blend in anywhere, especially at the Hickory Pit during Tuesday's popular live music happy hour, rife with blue-collar workers and off-duty cops. Stay-at-home moms and the nine-to-five crowd.

When the man stepped out of the driver's side, she groaned audibly. She recognized Nick Spade. In fact, he'd sat behind her in tenth grade algebra where she'd endured his constant need to throw spitballs in her hair. Back then, she'd known him as Nicholas Spadoni, world-class troublemaker. He'd grown into his thick black curls and put on twenty pounds of muscle, none of which changed the fact that he was entirely too old for her little sister. Certainly too old to have his slimy hand on the small of Em's back, guiding her into the Hickory Pit.

A thousand worms crawling under her skin, Olivia made herself stay seated. She couldn't barge in there like gangbusters. She had to think this through. Once her blood had stopped boiling, she'd go in level-headed, act surprised to find her sister there, and calmly inquire as to why in the hell she'd felt it necessary to hire a private investigator.

The double doors to the Hickory Pit burst open, stilling her heart. A blur of red hair caught her eye, streaking across the parking lot. Little legs in little blue jeans barreled haphazard down the asphalt, as an oversized pickup rumbled toward him. Panicked, Olivia hurried out of the Buick.

"Thomas! Watch out!"

She held out her palm, like it had the power to stop him. Instead, the truck squealed to a halt as the boy scampered in front of the grille, oblivious. He flung himself against her, sobbing. His hands tightened in a death grip on her shirt. His body, shuddering. His breath was coming in high-pitched gasps.

A frantic Nora emerged from the Pit. Her eyes darted like a wild animal's, searching for Thomas.

"Over here," Olivia called to her. Thomas didn't let go.

The truck glided forward, the beefy driver shaking his head through the window at them, obviously annoyed. *Damn kids*, he mouthed at her.

Even after Nora plucked Thomas from Olivia's arms, he remained inconsolable.

"What happened?" Olivia asked, when his crying had quieted.

"I… I don't know." Nora glanced warily at the Hickory Pit, as if its dingy red awning dripped with blood. "He's been off ever since we left the station. And then, Woofie disappeared."

"Woofie?"

"His stuffed dog. He must've lost it at the rental cabin."

Thomas whimpered as Nora smoothed his hair. "Anyway, we were sitting in a back booth. We'd finished our meal, and Thomas was finally eating the ice cream he's been talking about all day. I looked down at my phone for a split second and the next thing I know he's white as a sheet. He ran out of the place before I could get my head around what was happening."

Thomas had wriggled out of Nora's arms. One of his shoelaces had come untied. He crouched down, pulling at it anxiously, the same way he'd done in the interview room with Dr. Lucy.

Olivia bent down to his level, looked him in his watery blue eyes. "Can you tell me and Aunt Nora why you got upset?"

He tugged even harder, wrapping the lace around one finger. Olivia marveled at the strength in his small hand. She covered it with her own. "You're safe now. Nobody can hurt you."

A rapid shake of his head. "The bad man can."

"Did you see him? Did you see the bad man?"

His wide gaze fixed on the double doors, Olivia wondered if he'd stopped breathing. "Thomas?"

"He's in there."

With Nora and Thomas waiting in the parking lot, Olivia jogged to the entrance of the restaurant, her black flats thwacking against the pavement. She pushed through the doors and straight into the crowd, standing on tiptoe to get a bird's eye view of the bar.

Thomas had left no room for doubt. The bad man was a policeman. The bad man was inside the Hickory Pit. Unfortunately, so was most of Fog Harbor PD. There were at least twenty cops who fit the bill, gathered around the bar slinging back beers in clear view of the booths. The whole place was packed with bodies, their eyes fixed on a pretty brunette in a cowboy hat strumming a guitar in the corner. Near the makeshift stage, she caught sight of Emily and Nick talking, their heads close together.

Olivia sighed.

"Is the little guy okay?" She spun toward the deep voice, running right into Wade Coffman's barrel chest. "I came over here to grab a quick bite on my break, and I saw him take off. Tried to stop him. He looked like he'd seen a ghost."

"Did you happen to notice where he and his aunt were sitting?"

Wade easily parted the sea of people, guiding her toward the middle of the restaurant. Finally, she could breathe again. He pointed to Olivia's favorite spot. She'd sat there too many times to count. "The very back booth on the far right. He had a clear view of the bar. Do you think he saw…"

His voice trailed as she nodded solemnly.

With Wade in the lead, Olivia made her way down the aisle so she could take a look from Thomas's perspective. She wanted to see with his eyes.

The booth sat, unclaimed. Only Thomas's soupy dish of ice cream and a basket of wilted French fries remained. After she lowered herself into the seat, she spotted something else. Ranger Rob had been left behind, face down between the salt and pepper shakers.

Olivia tucked the soldier into the pocket of her slacks, then squinted up at the bar. Though she tried to make her face an unreadable blank, she failed miserably.

"You see somebody suspicious?" Wade asked.

She wanted to run. To get outside as fast as she could. To call Deck.

"No," she answered, though her whole body railed against it, screamed *yes*. She stood, already slipping her cell from her pocket. "Stay here. I'll go get Thomas so he can have a look."

CHAPTER THIRTY-FOUR

Will studied Pedro from behind the two-way mirror. In the same spot where he'd stood that morning, watching helplessly as Thomas dashed his hopes with a little shake of his head. It seemed a lifetime ago. But at least he'd cleared one case: Thomas had not left his stuffed dog behind at the station. He planned to phone Nora as soon as they took Pedro's statement.

Patrol hadn't located the group of Oaktown Boys who'd opened fire at Sunrise Canyon, leaving a through-and-through bullet hole in Bastidas's calf. But a few gang members on the loose and a little blood spilled seemed a small price to pay for finding their killer. Even if it meant Will might have to eat crow with Graham. Thankfully, said meal of crow had been delayed until tomorrow, since Graham had already taken off for the night, probably planning to drink himself into a stupor at the Hickory Pit.

Pedro slumped forward. His arms tucked inside his T-shirt, he rested his head, eyes closed, against the table as if he'd fallen asleep. Will had seen it before. Young punks who pretended to nod off in the interrogation room. Like being accused of murder was no more than a snuggle in a warm fuzzy blanket; the thought of spending the rest of their lives in prison, the perfect firm pillow. But in Pedro's case, that pillow would come with a set of leather straps that would fix him to a gurney while the state slipped a lethal cocktail into his vein.

"You're welcome." JB sidled up and patted him on the shoulder, snickering. "Less than thirty minutes back on the job and I solve your case. Hell, I might as well have wrapped him up in a shiny bow."

Will shrugged him off, frustrated with himself more than anything. "Let's just get his statement, alright? Save the gloating for later."

"Whatever you say, City Boy. I'll even let you have the first go at him. Give you a chance to redeem yourself."

When they entered the room, Pedro didn't look up, but he opened one dark eye. It followed Will as he took the chair nearest his suspect. He moved it even closer, until he could smell Pedro's oniony sweat. "You wanna be a tough guy? Sit up. Put your shirt on."

Reluctantly, Pedro pulled himself upright, stretching his arms through the thin white fabric. Will searched Pedro's arms for the devil tattoo that would've branded him a member of Los Diabolitos but came up empty. Only a badly drawn and brightly colored dragon extending down one bicep and the words *Mi Familia* on the other. A smattering of small circular scars dotted his forearms.

JB positioned himself in the corner, scribbling on a notepad. Probably noting his Detective of the Year victory speech.

"Why am I in here?" Pedro spit out the words, twisting his mouth, like he tasted something sour. "I already told you. I did it. I would've killed those Oaktown *cabróns* too, but I didn't have a clear shot and I ran out of ammo. What more do you want to know?"

"The whole story. From beginning to end. Starting with who put you up to it."

"Nobody."

"Bullshit." Every entry on Pedro's rap sheet had a crime partner. Like his brother-in-law, he'd grown up in Santa Barbara too. Spent his teen years boosting cars and volleying in and out of juvie. "No way you pulled that off by yourself without Uncle Elvis holding your hand."

"He's not my uncle."

"Might as well be. Because from where I'm sitting, you're just a kid. Have you even started shaving yet?"

Pedro's fists clenched. "*¡Chinga tú madre!*"

JB's pen stopped moving. He barely glanced up. "Easy there, *pendejo*. Save the insults for your girlfriend."

"I don't have a girlfriend."

"You will tonight." JB grinned. "You've got a one-way ticket to big-boy jail, my friend."

Fuming, Pedro ground his teeth. "The only thing I did for Elvis was mail a few letters to that *pendejo*, Fox. Elvis tried to warn him that he would have to pay for what he'd done. He should've done his job right in the first place. I wanted to put in work for my brother-in-law, to prove I'm not some chump, but Elvis had no clue about what I had planned. I only told him after the fact. After it went down."

Will didn't buy it for one second. "So, how did it go down exactly?"

Pedro shrugged like he couldn't be bothered, and Will fought the recurring urge to slam his suspect's head against the table. "You really want the gory details?"

Though he could think of nothing he wanted less, Will nodded.

"First, I shot that asshole in the head. Then, I went back to the beach house and did the wife and kids. Laid down some gasoline and watched the place go up in smoke. End of story."

"The kids too, huh? You shot them all?"

"Except the one who got away."

"Did the kid see you?"

"How the hell would I know what she saw?"

With a quick, knowing glance, Will and JB spoke simultaneously. "*She?*"

"She. He. Whatever. It was dark, and I was busy. I couldn't tell."

"What were you wearing?"

"Wearing?" Another castoff shrug from Pedro. "I don't remember. I tossed it all, though. Right into a dumpster outside the supermarket the next day. It's probably in the landfill by now."

"And after you left the beach house?" Will asked. "Where did you go?"

"I met up with Elvis and my sister in the parking lot. Gabriella drove us home. I slept like a baby."

"And the gun?"

"Watched it sink to the bottom of the Earl River with the fishes."

Will sat back and shook his head at JB. "Can I talk to you for a minute?"

Once the door had shut behind them, Will let out a heavy sigh. He leaned against the wall, suddenly exhausted. The last few days catching up with him all at once, heavy on his shoulders. "I hate to put a damper on your party, but Pedro is full of shit."

"What makes you say that?"

Will smacked his palm against his own forehead. "Seriously? Were you even paying attention? The guy doesn't know anything about the crimes that wasn't in the *Gazette* a few days ago. He told the vaguest account of a quadruple homicide I've ever heard. And we found bottles of *lighter fluid* at the crime scene. Not gasoline. Besides, you saw it for yourself. He didn't even realize Thomas was a boy. The paper left that part out, you know."

"He confessed. What kind of moron confesses to one murder, much less four of them?"

"A moron who wants to impress his brother-in-law, a shot caller for Los Diabolitos. Just like this afternoon. I guarantee you he fired every shot from that AR into a redwood trunk. He's a wannabe gangster desperate for Bastidas's approval."

"If that's true, why didn't Bastidas tell you and Jessie that Pedro was with them at the fireworks show that night at the beach? It sounds to me like he's covering for the kid."

Will pondered JB's question before the answer came to him. Once, as a boy, he'd lied to Ben. Told his older brother he'd beaten up the meanest bully at Bernal Heights Junior High School just to feel the sting of Ben's high five. He understood Pedro even if he didn't want to. "You're right. Bastidas *is* covering for Pedro. Because Pedro lied to him too."

While JB tried to find a way to prove himself right, Will's phone buzzed. *Olivia*, he mouthed to JB, turning away when his asinine partner puckered his lips.

"Hey, what's up?"

He didn't like the hitch he heard in her breath, even above the background noise. "You have to get down here. To the Hickory Pit. Thomas saw the killer inside."

"Bastidas's brother-in-law, Pedro, just confessed."

"*What?*" She sounded as confused as he felt. Like a blind man stumbling in the dark. "That's not possible. Deck, I saw…"

"You saw…"

She said it fast. So fast he thought he'd misunderstood her. "Who?"

"Graham. Graham's at the bar. In Thomas's eyeline. I'm looking right at him."

Will took off, motioning for JB to follow. "Don't go anywhere. We'll be there as soon as we can."

CHAPTER THIRTY-FIVE

Olivia left Wade sitting in the booth and made her way back toward the door. The country singer had started another set, crooning about beer and broken hearts while Graham and his drunken buddies mooned over her. But at least he'd been too busy to notice Olivia. So had Em, apparently. Arms wrapped around Nick's neck, they swayed together on the dance floor to the beat of the music.

As she pocketed her cell, Ranger Rob tumbled from her pocket and skittered across the hardwood. Kicked by a boot, the toy soldier went flying, just as she'd reached for it. She maneuvered through the mob, crouching to retrieve Thomas's prized possession. The moment she stood up, Ranger Rob in hand, the fire alarm began to blare.

The singing trailed off, stopped. Bar patrons set down their drinks. The folks who'd been lucky enough to score a booth sat still, their dinners abandoned. Raucous laughter turned to nervous chatter. No one seemed sure what to do. The alarm wailed on, insistent.

Olivia covered her ears, the urgent sound like a hammer to her brain.

Jane, the bartender, boosted herself onto the countertop, whistling to get the crowd's attention. "Everybody out. Now."

For a split second, an eerie quiet blanketed the Hickory Pit. Then, the place erupted into chaos. Everyone headed for the same double doors, the memory of the Ocean's Song fire fresh in their minds.

Olivia, too, hurried for the exit, only to be swept sideways by the pulsing crowd that had taken on a life of its own. She glanced over her shoulder, searching for Wade or for Emily. But they'd been subsumed by the sweaty mass of people clamoring for the door, hands sticky with barbecue sauce and beer on their breath. Finally, she spotted a slice of sky, sucked in a bit of fresh air.

The Hickory Pit spat her out onto the sidewalk, stumbling. When she found her balance, she searched the crowded parking lot for Nora and Thomas. Came up empty.

"Liv? What are you doing here?"

Emily had no right to sound so indignant. Not when she was the one who'd been sneaking around and withholding information. "I could ask the same of you."

"I'm just meeting a friend." Behind her, Nick flushed. "This is—"

"Nicholas Spadoni. Aka Nick Spade. Yeah, I know him. We went to high school together."

Raising a hand to wave at her, Nick shuffled from one foot to the other as the crowd milled about around him. Inside, the fire alarm still blared its warning.

"You know my sister?" Emily looked mortified.

"I was going to tell you."

"So, you're a private investigator now?" Olivia asked, piling it on. "I'm confused. Is my sister your date or your client?"

Em groaned, pulling Nick by the arm. "You don't have to answer that. Let's go. We'll find another spot to talk."

But Nick had rooted himself to the pavement. Olivia wondered if he remembered their senior year, when she and her friends had embarrassed him royally on a regular basis, calling him Poodle Head as he flounced down the hallway. It wasn't one of her finer moments. "It's none of your business, Olivia."

So, that was a yes, then. Memories of humiliation fully intact.

"My sister is my business. She's a little young for you, don't you think?"

Emily shot her a look, clearly contemplating the best methods to murder her annoying big sister. "You're just mad because you have no love life," she hissed. "Why don't you just grow up and kiss *him* already?"

"*Who?*" Although she could already guess, judging by the smug look on Em's face, that Deck was standing behind her. She turned around slowly, feeling an uncomfortable heat creep up her neck.

Sure enough, Deck's brown eyes sized her up. His brow creased in confusion as he gestured to the restless mob. "What the hell is going on?"

The corner of JB's mouth turned up in amusement. "I think Doctor Rockwell's sister just dared her to kiss you."

While Olivia wondered if death by mortification was a legitimate possibility, Will chivalrously ignored his loud-mouthed partner. "Why is half of Fog Harbor standing outside the Hickory Pit? And where are Thomas and his aunt?"

"Fire alarm." At the edge of the crowd, Olivia suddenly spotted Nora's auburn hair. She tried to signal to her, but Nora seemed distracted, frantic even, her eyes pinballing across the expanse of the parking lot. It didn't take long for Olivia to realize why.

"Where *is* Thomas?" She repeated Deck's words, each one leveling the world like a small earthquake.

"I lost him." Nora sounded on the verge of a breakdown, her voice fragile as a flower petal. Looked it, too. Her hand, shaking as she pointed to the empty spot next to her. "He was right *here*. And I lost him."

"What happened?" Olivia scanned the parking lot for Thomas.

"He must've gotten scared again when the fire alarm sounded. For a split second he let go of my hand and took off running toward the field. But I got jostled by the crowd and couldn't see him anymore. Then, I panicked. He's done this before, but—"

"Before?" Olivia asked.

"With Hannah and Peter." Nora hung her head. "Whenever he'd get anxious or upset, he'd run and hide from them. Once, it took her two hours to find him. He'd crawled into the dryer."

"I'm sure he hasn't gone far." Deck guided Nora to his car, helped her into the passenger seat. "Olivia, can you stay with her?"

Olivia nodded, comforting Nora with a pat to the shoulder, though she had no intention of standing by while Thomas was out there alone and frightened.

"First Lily and Dylan, and now Thomas too." Nora finally broke, grabbing onto Olivia like a life raft in stormy waters. "I loved those kids as if they were my own."

While Olivia watched over Nora's trembling shoulder, Deck made his way to the front entrance of the Pit, put two fingers in his mouth and whistled once, twice, three times, bringing the din to a halt. "Anybody seen a little boy out here, four years old, with red hair?"

A few nervous whispers and worried head shakes. Fingers pointing in the direction of the forest. The group of off-duty cops instantly sobered, a couple of them joining Deck by the door. Wade, too, had appeared there, fitting right in with his buzz cut and his burly arms. His look of intense concentration.

Graham stepped forward from the edge of the crowd, and Olivia didn't breathe until he spoke. "I saw him."

CHAPTER THIRTY-SIX

Will watched over Graham's shoulder while volunteers from the crowd—off-duty cops and civilians alike—began to search for Thomas. Minutes ago, the fire department had cleared the call. False alarm.

Feeling sick inside, Will returned his focus to his least favorite suspect. "So, tell me again exactly when you saw Thomas?"

"Like I already said, I was sitting at the bar drinking, and I noticed him with his aunt in the corner. Is that a crime?" With a seething glare, Graham whipped his badge from his back pocket and looked at it in astonishment. "Oh, wait. I *am* a cop. And no, it's *not* a crime."

Will breathed through it, holding himself together. "Did Thomas see you?"

"How the hell would I know?"

"He told Olivia he'd spotted the perpetrator inside the Pit. The bad man, the policeman who killed his family. That's why I hightailed it down here. Olivia said he had a clear view of you from the booth."

Will noticed a single bead of sweat forming on Graham's hairline. It fattened until it rolled down his temple.

"Me and twenty other cops. Remember, the kid is four years old. He's barely out of diapers. Besides, didn't Bastidas's brother-in-law already confess?"

"Yeah, he did. But you're sweating. You never sweat."

Graham swallowed, his Adam's apple sticking for a moment, bulging. Then he wiped his brow. "Newsflash. It's July, man. It's freaking hot out here."

Will consulted his cell phone. "Actually, it's a very pleasant seventy degrees today."

"Am I free to leave, Detective? Because last I heard there's a missing kid, and I don't think your witch hunt is helping anybody find him."

Will glanced up, watching the first group of volunteers cross the road into the grassy field across from the Pit. "Fine. Just don't go too far. When Thomas shows up, I want him to take a good long look at you."

After dismissing Graham, Will found Nora in the parking lot, staring ahead blankly with Olivia and JB stanchioned beside her. The slight tremble of her lower lip spoke for her, as her weary eyes searched down the lonely stretch of road adjacent to the restaurant.

"He just wandered off," Will assured her. "There are plenty of places out here for kids to hide. We'll keep looking."

"The police will find him," Olivia said, offering her Thomas's Ranger Rob. "And he'll be missing his lucky soldier."

It disappeared into Nora's palm before she spoke. "What if someone saw him run away and snatched him up?"

JB beat Will to the answer. "We don't know that, ma'am. In fact, there's no reason to think that at all."

Olivia flashed Will a pointed look that communicated her vehement disagreement. And she wasn't wrong. Even if the supposed killer was in jail, Thomas had vanished just minutes after he'd ID'd the bad man inside the Hickory Pit.

Will lifted his shoulders in a small, sad shrug. "My partner's right. We arrested someone this afternoon. He confessed to the murders."

"*What?*"

"But we're verifying his story. Sometimes people confess to things they didn't do."

Nora looked to Olivia. For solace or for explanation, he couldn't tell. "It's true," Olivia said. "False confessions are not uncommon in high-profile crimes like this. I believe Thomas saw someone inside the restaurant. Someone critical to solving this case. Is there anything else you can tell us that might help us find him?"

A single tear escaped from the corner of Nora's eye down her cheek, and she wiped it away. "There is one thing I remember."

Olivia nodded her encouragement, while Will joined JB in closing ranks around Nora. He didn't want to miss a word. "Right before Thomas screamed and ran out, a couple of those officers had started an arm-wrestling match at the bar. They were hooting and hollering, drawing attention to themselves. I think Thomas might have been watching them."

Will could hardly believe what he'd heard. "Arm-wrestling?"

"Arm-wrestling," Nora repeated. "Is that important?"

"It might be."

JB's eyes scanned the parking lot, where a few of the off-duty officers had gathered.

"Do you see the men who were involved?" JB asked.

Taking a few quiet breaths, Nora looked around, zeroing in on the group. On a pair of broad shoulders and perfectly sculpted hair. When the man held up a hand to wave at Olivia, misunderstanding, Will could barely contain himself.

"Him," Nora said. "He was one of them."

CHAPTER THIRTY-SEVEN

"No way in hell." Deck clenched his stubbled jaw like Olivia had just offered herself up as a ritual sacrifice. "Not after the way he treated you yesterday. He scared you."

Though she couldn't argue with that last part, Olivia groaned, side-eyeing JB. She'd need his help to convince Deck she could get Graham to fess up whatever secrets he'd been keeping.

"I think Doctor Rockwell has a point. Bauer loathes the both of us. She'll certainly get further than we will, City Boy."

"You can't be serious." Will directed his words at his partner, but Olivia felt every single one of them like a barb to the skin. "You want a civilian to interrogate a possible murder suspect who just happens to be a cop himself? Are you sure those blood pressure pills aren't messing with your head?"

"She *is* a psychologist. Talking is practically in the job description."

Sensing a turn of the tide, Olivia heaped on her reassurances. "It's not an interrogation, Deck. Just a conversation. For whatever reason, Graham trusts me. He came to me for help last night. Besides, you and JB will be close by if anything goes wrong."

"*When* something goes wrong."

"Are you worried I'll do a better job than you?"

JB cackled. "Of course he is."

"Fine. We'll see about that." Deck looked her dead in the eyes, his glinting in the sunlight like he couldn't decide whether to chastise her or kiss her senseless. "You've got five minutes. Then let the professionals take over."

Graham already looked defeated. Instead of helping with the search, he'd taken a seat on the concrete step outside the front door of the Hickory Pit. Olivia joined him there, deciding to take the soft approach she'd use with an inmate patient in denial. Just to get him talking.

"I'm sorry about last night." She offered him a sympathetic look. "I didn't mean to—"

"No. You meant it. And I deserved it. I was way out of line. I just thought you knew me better than that. I realize I've got a temper, especially when I've been drinking. But to kill someone? C'mon, Liv."

She nodded, noncommittal. Under the wrong circumstances, anyone could be capable of murder. Surely Graham knew that.

"Did Decker put you up to this? To see if you can Jedi mind-trick me into confessing to something I didn't do?"

She wished she had a few mind tricks up her sleeve, but working with inmates had taught her there was no truth serum. "What is it with you two? He's not your enemy."

"That's news to me. He thinks he's so smart, so by-the-book. Just because he worked homicide at SFPD doesn't make him any better than the rest of us. He's all about the job, Liv."

"So am I." But his words discomfited, nagging at her like a pebble in her shoe.

"He'll let you down. Maybe not now, but eventually. Cops aren't good at relationships as a general rule. Ask Heather."

"The breakup rumors are true then?"

He wiggled his eyebrows. "I'm back on the market."

She laughed, despite the heaviness of the question stuck inside her throat. Now seemed as good a time as any to ask it. "Why did you lie about your alibi?"

His smile flattened in an instant, face hard as chiseled granite. This was the Graham from the truck. Icicle eyes; the rest of him, pure heat. "Excuse me?"

"You weren't home watching *National Treasure* like you said. It had already aired. Where were you really at, Graham?"

"Okay, so maybe it was a different movie. The sequel, or something. I wasn't taking notes. Besides, they show that film all the time. They probably replayed it."

Olivia let her silence speak for her. If she called him a liar the way Deck would, he'd shut down. But she'd double-checked the television schedule last night. *National Treasure* had run only once on the Fourth, from 9:30 a.m. to noon.

"You told Decker, didn't you? That I don't have an alibi." Graham cut his eyes across the lot to JB and Deck. Thankfully, they'd busied themselves talking to the patrol officers who had arrived to aid in the search for Thomas. With only a few hours of daylight left and the forest filled with hiding places, they needed all the help they could get.

"Thomas's aunt said he was looking up at the bar, watching you arm-wrestle, when he freaked out and ran."

Graham cursed under his breath.

"Is it possible he recognized you?"

"I'm sure he saw me that afternoon at the beach getting into it with his dad. He could've easily seen me at the station too."

"Maybe Thomas is confused about what he saw, thinking it was a cop who killed his mom and brother and sister. You're the only one who can clear this up. I know you're not a bad guy, but when you hide things you look like it. There's a little boy missing."

"Yeah. He got scared and ran away. Obviously I had nothing to do with it."

"Obviously." Olivia hoisted herself to her feet, disgusted and disappointed. Mostly in herself for thinking she could wrangle the truth from Graham. Like squeezing blood from a turnip, her father used to say.

"Wait."

She wondered if she'd misheard him, but when she glanced back he jerked his head at the Hickory Pit, motioning her inside.

Most of the crowd had cleared out to help with the search for Thomas or to return to the safety of their homes to hold their own children a little tighter. The band had packed up too, leaving the place strangely quiet.

Olivia gasped when Graham gripped her by the wrist and tugged her into the shadowy corner near the restrooms.

"You okay?" Jane looked up at her from the bar—a perfunctory glance—as she wiped down the counter and collected the dirty glasses. She knew Olivia could handle herself, even with a part-time asshole like Graham.

"Fine." But Olivia jerked her arm away from him anyway just to prove a point. "Get off me. What're we doing in here?"

"I don't want Decker listening in. I need to be discreet. I've got a career to think about. My uncle told me to get a lawyer."

"A lawyer?" *Don't push. Don't push.* But she couldn't help it. "Discreet about what?"

His face in his hands, Graham groaned. "I can't believe I'm telling you this."

"Better me than Deck. He's going to get nervous if we don't come out soon." Olivia couldn't see the door but she half expected him to burst through it at any moment.

"Okay. You're right. I need to get this off my chest. I erased the texts between me and Peter Fox, because I called the cell phone company and they told me that deleted texts can't be retrieved after forty-eight hours. I lied about the movie. I have a shit alibi. The truth is, I went to Ocean's Song that night. Maybe around nine fifteen."

And just like that, she imagined Graham on the front porch, still drunk and angry. The Fox family, minus Peter, tucked inside, kids piled on the sofa, watching television, while their mother, Hannah, buttered a bowl of hot popcorn and tried to distract herself from her disintegrating marriage. Graham's gun, heavy as a hot stone in his hand, when he raised it to her head and pulled the trigger. Olivia closed her eyes, and the dark images scattered like crows.

"Fox had texted me, saying he'd filed a report against me. That my days on the force were numbered. I went there to give him a piece of my mind. Yeah, I put on the uniform. I brought my gun. Banged on the door. I thought I'd scare him a little. Get him to back off. Sometimes, seeing the badge puts it all in perspective. Makes the big talkers think twice."

"Did anyone answer?"

She'd seen that look before on her inmate patients. A mixture of shame and resignation. Knowing what's done is done. "Thomas."

CHAPTER THIRTY-EIGHT

Through the small crack in the back window of the Hickory Pit, Graham's pitiful voice travelled to Will's ear. "But I swear to God I didn't hurt them. I heard yelling from behind him that sounded like Fox and his wife arguing and then, a loud crash. A bowl broke and popcorn went flying. Thomas freaked, so I shut the door in his face and I got the hell out of there. I drove around for a while, asking myself what the hell I was thinking, and that's when dispatch came on the radio about the fire."

Will had heard about enough. Giving JB a nod, they rushed around to the front entrance and pushed through the double doors.

"You were saying...?" Will couldn't resist being an asshole. After all his unconvincing denials, Graham had just put himself at the scene of a triple murder and had admitted to destroying evidence. He'd also confirmed Will's suspicions that Peter had returned home after the incident at the Sand Dunes, only to leave again. "What happened, Bauer? Cat got your tongue?"

Dumbfounded, Graham shot daggers at Olivia, his eyes darting from her to the window and back again. "You set me up."

"Like hell I did. You pulled me back here. I had no idea the window was open." Olivia directed her venom at Graham, but Will felt the sting. He figured she'd be pissed at him. But he'd listened in for good reason, and her indignation was a small price to pay for the pleasure of cuffing Graham Bauer.

Will strode toward Graham on a mission. "You're under arrest for obstruction."

"Don't forget tampering with evidence," JB added gleefully.

"Who knows?" Will piled on. "By the end of tonight, you might be on the hook for first-degree murder. Four counts."

No response. Only the blue of Graham's eyes, clear and flat as washed glass. Will had finally shocked him into silence.

He motioned for Graham to turn around, already trying to fit this piece of the puzzle. Would Graham have had enough time to murder the Foxes, set the place on fire, and show up back at the first crime scene without a hair out of place?

Maybe.

Graham nodded, as if he'd read Will's mind. He took a single step, then reared back. It had been a long time since Will had taken a shot to the face. A hard right that juddered his skull, rattled his teeth like marbles in a jar.

JB moved in fast, securing Graham's hands behind his back and steering him away from Will.

Will put a hand to his nose. Still intact. But he could taste the blood in the back of his throat, and his fingers came back stained with it. He wiped them on his slacks.

"Looks like you're gonna have to add resisting to that, Decker." Graham had found his voice again. His smirk too. Tossing both over his shoulder as JB pushed him out the front door. "Totally worth it."

"Are you okay?" Olivia asked.

Will's eyes watered, and he tilted his head back, squeezing the bridge of his nose. "Been better."

Jane appeared beside him, shaking her head and offering an ice-filled rag from the bar. Wincing, he pressed it to his face.

"Why didn't you tell me you planned on eavesdropping?" Olivia asked, sounding more amused than irritated. Maybe she'd go easy on him now that he'd paid for his subterfuge with a fist to his nose bridge.

"I didn't *plan* on it. I saw an opportunity. That window's been busted for a while. With the place all but empty, I figured we might get lucky."

She grimaced at the bloody fingerprints on his pants leg. "If that's what you want to call it."

"Are you mocking my pain?"

"Never." She moved in closer to examine his face. Her gentle hand on his temple made Will feel a lot better about the shiner he'd have tomorrow. "But how does a guy with a heavy bag in his garage get sucker-punched?"

"I guess I forgot to bob and weave."

Once JB had secured Graham in the back of a patrol car and sent him on his way to booking, Will motioned his partner over to the staging area, where the officers had begun handing out orange reflective vests. The stress of the afternoon had already settled onto JB's haggard face, worrying Will a little. He hoped JB hadn't come back to work too early, wasn't pushing too hard. "You should go home and get some rest. I'll get a lift back to the station with patrol."

JB twisted his mouth at Will like he tasted something rotten. "You're benching me already? I just got back in the game, City Boy. I feel fine. At least let me get Bauer's full statement."

Will tried to shake his head but it already hurt like hell. A dull pain throbbed from his eye socket. "I think we should let him marinate overnight. We need to get a better handle on this before we start asking any more questions. We only get one shot at him."

It was a bill of goods, and Will knew it. As soon as Graham stepped foot in Del Norte County Jail, he'd be lawyered up and posting bail. But right now, finding Thomas was more important.

"Fair enough." JB sighed and shuffled toward the Crown Vic, his shoulders drooping. Will had never seen him give up so easily.

"There is one thing you can do for me," Will called after him.

"If you ask me to feed that damn cat of yours, or write up an incident report, you may as well just take my badge and put me out to pasture. I don't need you to load me with busy work because you feel sorry for me."

"C'mon, man. Cy loves you." Will chuckled as JB slumped back toward him. "Keep looking through Fox's old client files. I can't help but get the feeling we missed something."

"What am I looking for exactly?"

Will shrugged, donning one of the orange vests. No matter what he'd told Nora, he had to assume the worst. That Thomas had been taken. But with Jonah and Pedro in jail, Elvis at the hospital, and Graham in plain sight at the bar, his suspect list had dwindled. It didn't sit right with him. "You're Detective of the Year. You figure it out."

"Now I know you feel sorry for me." But JB's eyes looked brighter. "Alright, alright. I'll feed the cat too."

"Well, you're not getting rid of *me* so easily, Detective." Olivia appeared beside him. She'd swapped her blouse for a Hickory Pit T-shirt and her feet were now clad in running shoes. "Good thing I had a spare pair in the trunk. Don't even try to convince me otherwise."

"Us either. C'mon, Nick." Emily tugged at the hand of the guy Olivia had declared much too old for her. Still sensing tension, Will wondered what he'd missed. A fight between sisters, clearly. With Nick stuck in the unenviable middle of it.

As Will tossed out three vests, Emily frowned at him. "What happened to your face?"

He shrugged. "I ran into Graham's fist."

*

With Olivia and her sister leading the way, Will trekked into the grassy field adjacent to the Hickory Pit parking lot, where the search volunteers had scattered like ants. Fifty yards or so out, the field turned to forest. One of its boundaries apparently cleared years ago for construction on a gas station that never came. The rest seemed to go on forever, leaving Will with a sinking feeling. How far could a little boy go on his own? Where would he hide?

"Do you really think he ran away?" Olivia's haunted eyes met his, and he worried for her too. He didn't need a PhD to recognize this whole case had gotten under her skin and unearthed memories best left buried. What she'd witnessed as a kid. What happened to her father, then and now. Thomas and his family had brought it all back. The corpse of her past staggering to life and lumbering behind her. Will knew all too well there was no escaping it.

"He's a little boy. They do that kind of thing. It sounds like Thomas had a knack for it."

She stopped walking, letting Emily and Nick walk on ahead. "I should have never left him in the first place. Or sent Wade out to get him instead. He would've pushed through the crowd and made it out faster. He would've seen where Thomas ran."

Will didn't try to argue, just put his hand on her shoulder and squeezed. "Let's keep looking."

"Hey, Liv! Deck! Over here!" Emily waved to them excitedly from the far corner of the field, where the grass met the road. A group of searchers had surrounded the bone-dry culvert. Nick crouched down, peering inside.

Olivia took off, moving faster than he'd expected. He caught up to her just as they reached the road.

"It's him." Her relief was palpable and contagious.

When Will spotted Thomas near the center of the tunnel, huddled with a handful of rocks, he took a long, deep breath. "Come on out, buddy. Everybody's looking for you."

Olivia beckoned to him too, dropping to her hands and knees. "What're you doing in there?"

Thomas shook his head, put a finger to his lips. His small voice carried down the culvert like the whisper of a ghost. "Hiding from the bad man."

CHAPTER THIRTY-NINE

Thomas's right hand was sticky with dirt and sweat but Olivia dared not let go. It had taken twenty minutes to coax him from the tunnel big enough for a boy but too small for a man. Finally, after his aunt Nora had produced Ranger Rob, Thomas had reluctantly scooted to the edge of the culvert and allowed her to pluck him out. His clothes were a little worse for wear and he had a few bramble scratches on his arms, but he was otherwise unscathed.

Now, Nora walked on the other side of him, her hand latched tightly onto his left wrist like he might take flight again without a moment's notice.

As they traipsed back across the field toward the Hickory Pit parking lot, Thomas looked up at Olivia. "Do you think Ranger Rob can help me find Woofie?"

"Woofie is probably off having a great adventure. He'll turn up when you least expect him."

Thomas's lower lip protruded.

"Doctor Rockwell is right," Nora said, her voice strained. "When Woofie does turn up, he'll be very disappointed if we can't find *you*." To Deck, she added, "You didn't happen to find his stuffed toy at the station, did you?"

"No, I'm sorry. I meant to call you. I'll keep checking the lost and found."

Thomas stopped walking, grinding them all to a halt in the grass. "What if the bad man has Woofie?"

Olivia gave Deck a worried look. At some point, when Thomas felt a little braver, he'd have to take a look at Graham's photo. At least for right now, all but one of Deck's suspects sat in a jail cell. Still, Olivia didn't feel reassured.

"You let me worry about the bad man, okay?" Deck motioned for Thomas to keep moving. And he did, his little legs skipping now, the bad man momentarily forgotten.

When they finally reached the lot, the small group of remaining searchers, including Emily and Nick, let out a whooping cheer. Jane brought Thomas a glass of orange juice from the bar.

"Am I famous?" he asked, gulping down his drink.

"All these people were worried about you." Olivia swept her hand across the parking lot, noticing the old Buick, parked exactly where she'd left it a lifetime ago. When the main thing on her mind had been spying on her sister. Though only an hour had passed, the strange episode stretched out between then and now like the ocean at high tide, leaving her standing disoriented on the other side. "Aunt Nora is right. You can't go running off every time you get scared. Find a grownup next time, alright?"

"But the bad man *is* a grownup. Just like you and Aunt Nora. Mommy let him inside."

Olivia nodded at Thomas sympathetically. She remembered that feeling. Her safe place to fall ripped out from beneath her.

"Most grownups are good, kiddo." Deck rescued Olivia from her own awful memories. "We are doing everything we can to find the bad man and to keep you and your aunt safe."

Thomas wiped his mouth with the back of his hand and turned his summer-sky eyes to Deck. "How do you tell the good grownups from the bad ones?"

"The truth is, sometimes you can't."

*

Olivia leaned down into the open driver's window of Emily's car, frowning at her sister. Thankfully, Nick had already taken the hint and left. "I'm not done with you."

"Are you ever?"

"I worry. I can't help it. I don't want you getting involved with Nick Spadoni and—"

"*Spade*." Fire in her eyes, Emily keyed on the ignition. "We're just friends."

"I mean, professionally." Of course, Olivia had meant both, but she knew when to pick her battles. "You need to steer clear of Dad's case. You're in over your head."

"Who said anything about Dad?"

"Nick did. He also mentioned something about a black light."

Emily's face scrunched in confusion. The same way it had, years ago, when Olivia had tried to teach her little sister long division. That hadn't ended well either, with Olivia frustrated and Emily in tears, her pencil broken in half. "No, he didn't."

Olivia raised her eyebrows, daring her sister to lie to her. Her own lie of omission—that she'd posed as Em on the phone—would never see the light of day.

"Even if he did, it's none of your business." She jerked the gear into drive. "That's why they call him a *private* investigator. It's private."

As Emily screeched out of the parking lot and sped down Pine Grove Road, sending Olivia's heart into her throat, Deck approached. A purple crescent-shaped bruise had already materialized beneath his eye.

"Don't say a word," she warned him, walking toward the Buick.

"Wasn't gonna."

"Can you believe she hired a PI? To look into our father's murder?" She paused for a beat, gaining steam. She could still remember pulling one disgusting spitball from her hair, only to feel another thwack her head minutes later.

"Do you want me to answer, or—"

"A guy I went to high school with, at that? He wasn't even that smart."

Deck smirked at her, hands raised. "Just listening then. Got it."

"I'm pretty sure he failed PE. How does anyone fail PE?"

"Uh…"

"And she's been sneaking around with him. She likes him. I can tell. He's exactly her type. Dark and mysterious. But trust me, he's no Tom Selleck."

Deck laughed. "So, you had a thing for Magnum PI, huh? Was it the mustache?"

She rolled her eyes at him, while she unlocked the Buick and climbed inside.

"I get it." Musing, he put a hand on her door. "Us regular detectives are so boring with our policies and procedures. Our chain of custody."

"That pesky adherence to the law."

They both laughed, and the knots in Olivia's neck loosened. Instant guilt followed, when she recalled Nora's pale face as they'd driven away. Olivia couldn't rid herself of the awful feeling that the bad man who haunted Thomas still walked among them, slippery as a shadow.

"What're you thinking about?" he asked.

"Nora and Thomas. This whole ordeal. I overheard you talking to JB. Do you really believe you missed something?"

Deck's sigh confirmed her own fears. "Nora agreed I'd stop by the house tomorrow to show Thomas a lineup with Graham and Pedro. I'm hoping that will shed some light on what really happened that night. You said yourself, people confess to things they didn't do. Care to venture a guess as to how many fake Zodiac killers tried to turn themselves in to Homicide in San Francisco?"

"That many, huh?" But it made a sick kind of sense. Sometimes, the only way to be seen in the world was to claim to be a monster. "Where are you headed now?"

"To get inside the head of a man who confesses to not one, but *four* murders he probably didn't commit."

"Are you gunning for my job now?" she asked.

"I assumed you were coming with me." Deck made his way around the passenger side and opened the door, smiling down at her. "Besides, I'll need a ride back to the station."

CHAPTER FORTY

As the last orange slice of sunlight sank toward the horizon, Will directed Olivia back to Sunrise Canyon trailer park.

"Pull off here," he told her, pointing into the ditch near the spot where they'd ordered Pedro down to the dirt. "By that big redwood."

Olivia steered the Buick off the dirt road and cut the engine. "What're we doing here?"

"Elvis Bastidas lives with Gabriella and Pedro in a trailer about a half mile up. When we arrived, Pedro was already down here in the trees, supposedly shooting at the Oaktown Boys, as they fled for their lives on their bikes."

Will headed into the forest, wishing he'd marked the tree somehow. The fading light would make it harder to spot, and he couldn't trust his adrenaline-soaked memories.

"Here's the part that doesn't make sense. There's only one way in and out of Sunrise Canyon, and JB and I didn't pass a single soul. Didn't see anyone on the main road either. That means Oaktown had already headed west by the time we'd arrived. But we heard Pedro shooting off his AR-15 well after we found Bastidas."

"Who was he shooting at, then?"

"Exactly." Will produced his cell phone, activating the flashlight, and aimed it into the shadowy woods. Its thin beam swallowed by the thick canopy, the massive trunks stanchioned around them like the legs of giants.

Olivia followed behind him, her footfalls mirroring his own. "Did you find any shell casings?"

"Twenty-eight. All in Pedro's pants pockets. Apparently, he collected them after he fired."

"Sounds pretty criminally sophisticated then, if he knows how to cover his tracks."

"Hardly. He talks a big game. But I don't buy it. I think he was covering up something else."

A twig snapped in the darkness, and Will shone the light at the sound. Two yellow eyes stared back at him, then vanished into the thicket. When he glanced back over his shoulder to catch Olivia laughing at him, he spotted it.

"There. That's the tree." Up close, Will could see the bullet holes in the redwood's splintered flesh. He pressed his hand to the trunk, still warm from the sun.

"You think he unloaded the gun into that tree trunk?"

"I do." Will walked backward from the tree, keeping his eyes trained on the ground. "He wanted to brag to his brother-in-law about being a tough guy."

"Look." Olivia crouched down a few paces from where he stood, spotting the brass of a shell casing in the weeds. "He missed one."

Will peered through the forest in the direction of the main road, imagining himself as Pedro, unleashing a hail of bullets, the casings discharging as he fired. A slight slope of the terrain prevented him from seeing anything beyond the trees. "Assuming the shell casing dropped here when he fired the gun, there's no way he had sight of anything. That hill blocks the view of the main road."

Olivia stood beside him in the near dark, her gaze following his. "You're right..."

"But?"

"But just because he lied about shooting at the Oaktown Boys, doesn't mean he's fabricating his story about the murders."

Will had expected her to say that. If he hadn't heard Pedro's flimsy confession himself, he would've agreed. "Everything he knew was straight from the papers. He said he used gasoline. He thought the kid that got away was a girl."

When Olivia *hmm*ed, Will decided now was as good a time as any to tell her everything he knew about Pedro Mendez and his big brother, Javier. To call her on her crazy decision to therapize the creep. Out here in the middle of nowhere, she couldn't run away from him. She had to listen.

"There's something else about Pedro that you should know." He headed in the direction of the Buick, training his flashlight up ahead of them. "He and Gabriella have a brother in prison here at Crescent Bay. I think you know him."

Olivia kept moving forward but he sensed her hesitation, the slight change in the weight of her footsteps in the brush.

"Javier Mendez. Ring a bell?"

"Should it?"

Will stopped short, and she almost ran into him. His hand steadied her, his frustration dissipating when he saw the panic in her eyes. "Why don't you trust me? You don't have to lie."

"But I do." She hung her head.

"What does that even mean?"

"I *do* trust you. And I *do* have to lie. Termite made that clear. Anybody who knows anything about my dad ends up dead."

Just his luck. Will had managed to fall for the one woman as stubborn as him. "You decided you'd do it all by yourself then? You'd figure out who killed your father and why. You'd single-handedly take on the Oaktown Boys and the General. And you'd start by trying to squeeze information from Javier Mendez, a shot caller for Los Diabolitos, one of the Oaktown Boys' biggest rivals. The guy who happened to choke out his last therapist?"

A strangled laugh escaped Olivia's throat. "Yes?"

"Is that a question?"

"It's just that it sounds so bad when you put it like that."

"You mean, when I tell the truth."

She groaned, exasperated, but he wouldn't let her wriggle away from him. With nowhere else to go, she finally gave in, leveling him with a glance.

"I don't want to risk you getting hurt," she said. "I couldn't live with that."

Olivia's eyes, glistening in the light from his cell phone, transfixed him.

"That makes two of us," he said, reaching for her hand.

A sharp crack of gunfire shattered the stillness, sending them both scrambling for cover. Will reached for the Glock at his waist.

"That was a warning. You're trespassing on private property." Gabriella stood on the path alongside the Buick, clad in a bathrobe and men's work boots. Her flashlight at her feet, she swept a shotgun across the trees. "Next time, I won't miss."

"Detective Will Decker. My partner and I stopped by this afternoon, right after Elvis was shot. Remember?" He stepped forward, his hands raised, hoping Olivia would stay hidden in the woods behind him. Setting his gun in the grass, he told her, "We're just taking a look around."

"You got a search warrant?" The frightened woman from the trailer had disappeared, leaving a force of nature in her place. Her dark hair fell around her face. Her eyes, two hollow pits.

"Your brother was arrested down here firing off rounds from an assault rifle. As far as I'm concerned, it's still an active crime scene."

She didn't lower the shotgun as he'd expected, its sights aimed unnervingly close to his vital bits.

"Did Elvis send you down here?" he asked.

Her head tipped skyward while she cackled. "I sent that *pendejo* packing as soon as Pedro called from jail. I'm done with him.

Acabado. I told him that he can get his own damn ride from the hospital. Do you know he actually believes my brother murdered that family? For him and his stupid gang."

"What do you believe?" Will heard Olivia's voice at his shoulder and dared to look at her, her hands raised like his own. "We want to hear your side of it, Gabriella. The only way you can help Pedro is to tell the truth."

Finally, Gabriella lowered her weapon. She leaned against the Buick, her shoulders slumped. "Pedro moved in with me three years ago, after our mother died, back when Elvis was still in prison. I was so depressed that I needed help around the house, and Pedro needed to get away from our old neighborhood in Santa Barbara. Elvis promised me he wouldn't let Pedro get mixed up in his nonsense. Next thing you know, Pedro's his little errand boy, sending letters to that attorney. Since Elvis got out, he's been pressuring Pedro to do his dirty work. All I do is feel guilty. It's my fault he's here in the first place. I've lost too damn much to that gang. First, my dad—gunned down in a shootout with Oaktown. Then, my older brothers—every one of them in prison or dead. And my husband. Now, Pedro too."

Will took her sobs as his cue, making his way out of the redwood grove toward her and securing her weapon. He kept his sympathy locked in a box, knowing it would leave him vulnerable. She was still Bastidas's wife, and he didn't trust her.

"Pedro is a follower. Always has been. My brother Javier had him running drugs for the gang before he turned thirteen. That way, if he got caught, he'd only get a little time in juvie, a slap on the wrist. But Pedro isn't like Javier or Elvis. He doesn't have an evil bone in his body. This past winter, he rescued a litter of kittens, brought them all back to the house wrapped in his hoodie. He cried when the runt didn't live through the night."

Olivia nodded, taking a position beside Gabriella. In full therapist mode, she mirrored Gabriella's tone. "Did Elvis ask him to do something to the Foxes?"

Gabriella sighed in reply. "Mind if I smoke?"

When neither of them protested, she slipped a pack of Newports from the pocket of her robe and held it up to Will—*see, not a weapon*—before plucking a cigarette and placing it between her pursed lips.

"Elvis and Javier don't ask. They give orders." In her shaky hands, the lighter sparked; the flame instantly doused. "All Pedro ever wanted was a man's approval. Didn't matter which man. Didn't matter what he had to do to get it."

"What did he have to do?" Olivia practically whispered the question, her voice no louder than the rustle of the leaves.

"They had a plan." Gabriella struck the lighter again and again, the little flashes briefly revealing tear tracks in her makeup. "Javier and Elvis concocted the whole scheme in prison. All they needed was someone to carry it out."

Will began to doubt his instincts. Maybe Pedro's babyface was a clever disguise. After all, he had Mendez blood in his veins, and so did Gabriella.

"Let me." He held his hand out, and Gabriella surrendered the lighter to him. With one firm rub of his thumb, a flame appeared. She leaned in toward it, taking a few desperate drags from the cigarette before she spoke again.

"Fox vacationed here every year. Elvis knew it. He thought it was fate, him getting out right before the Fourth. His personal Independence Day. I tried to tell him it wasn't worth it. Revenge never is. But he had his mind made up. He bought that AR-15 for Pedro from an old buddy of Javier's the day he got released from Crescent Bay. He told Pedro this was his chance to finally put in some real work for Los Diabolitos. Blood in, blood out, you know?"

"What happened?" Olivia asked.

Another long drag from the Newport. A thin smile. "Nothing."

Will scanned the forest, peered down the dirt path into the unknown, starting to wonder if they'd been set up. "I don't understand."

"I think what Gabriella is saying is that they never got a chance to carry out their plan. The Foxes were already dead."

"*Chica muy lista*. She's right. I woke up on the morning of the fifth and heard the story on the news. Pedro had insisted on staying home from the fireworks that night; he doesn't like crowds. But he lied and told Elvis he'd done the murders. Elvis made him out to be some kind of vigilante hero. Javier even called from prison to congratulate him. *Venganza dulce*."

"How do you know Pedro was lying?"

"For a million reasons. A sister knows." Gabriella dropped her cigarette, snuffing it out with the toe of the work boot. "But mostly because our father was a mean son of a bitch who burned us with cigarettes every time he had one too many *cervezas*. Pedro is deathly afraid of fire."

CHAPTER FORTY-ONE

Olivia piloted the old Buick back down the dirt road, letting Deck simmer in silence. When they turned onto the highway, he swore under his breath, his anger at Bastidas slowly bubbling to the surface.

"What a coward, getting Pedro to do his dirty work. You would hope the man might've changed a little in a quarter century behind bars."

Olivia understood better than she cared to admit. Before her father had been carted off to prison, he'd done the same, recruiting the Oaktown minions to get their fists bloodied. "Do you think Gabriella told us the truth?"

He shrugged. "Hell if I know. But Pedro had a bunch of scars on his arms. Looked just like cigarette burns. This case is a twisty road with no end in sight."

Olivia nodded her agreement. Every lead seemed to wind up at a dead end with the *bad man* lurking unseen. And that miniature tourmaline horseshoe in the pool still nagged at her. "Who would've thought that a defense attorney could have so many enemies? It's usually the DAs and the judges these guys go after."

"That's why I asked JB to keep digging through Fox's old client files. With Thomas spotting this mysterious bad man, I can't help feeling I missed something big."

As they entered the downtown, Olivia tapped the brakes. Though it was only a little past eight, the streets had emptied. Even the grocery store parking lot stretched out like a vast ocean of unfettered concrete, with light pole shadows looming like misshapen monsters. All of Fog Harbor had been swallowed by the dusky quiet. "I'd be happy to help with the files. I'm sure it's a lot for JB to manage on his own."

"A lot for him to complain about, you mean." He added, "I'll send over the link to the files."

Just then, Deck's cell phone rang. They both startled, then laughed. Olivia's heart pattered faster than a snare drum roll, while Deck listened to the voice on the other end of the line.

"Change of plans," he said, with a sudden urgency. "Take me down to Little Gull."

Olivia veered off the road, preparing to turn the Buick in the other direction. "What happened?"

"That was Chief Flack. Apparently, the lighthouse keeper saw someone in the parking lot on the night of the murders." Deck focused up ahead but Olivia could see his wheels spinning a hundred miles a minute. "He thinks it might be one of our suspects."

Lighthouse keeper Guthrie Smalls waved his flashlight at them from the base of Little Gull, the wind whipping what remained of his hair into a frenzy.

"Come on over." The old man's voice thin as a reed, he beckoned them across the rock jetty that gave safe passage over the water below to the slope of the island on the other side. Years ago, the city had erected a steel railing along the path, after a young girl had fallen and cracked her head on the craggy ocean bottom.

Olivia followed close behind Deck, holding tight to the rail and measuring every step in the beam of the light from her cell phone. She tasted the saltwater mist on her mouth, felt the cold ocean spray against her cheeks. Though she considered the bluffs overlooking Little Gull as the spot where she did her best thinking, it had been years since she'd made the trek to the lighthouse itself. When the cold water sloshed over her feet and a sudden gust jostled her off balance, she remembered why. No surprise, Deck had told her to wait in the car. But sitting alone in the dark had seemed much worse with Thomas's *bad man* still on the loose and an uneasy feeling she couldn't name swirling in her stomach.

After hustling up the hillside where the pink ice plants grew wild, Guthrie ushered them into the warmth of the lighthouse and up the narrow stairs to the keeper's quarters, where a twin-size bed fit snugly alongside a chest of drawers and a wooden desk. He retrieved a pair of binoculars from his bedside before leading them to another winding staircase that deposited them in the tower.

Beyond the glow of the beacon, Olivia couldn't tell where the sky ended and the ocean began. She stood in awe in front of the panoramic windows, feeling comforted by her insignificance.

"Amazing, isn't it?" Guthrie joined her there, while Deck positioned himself opposite the view, looking back toward the parking lot.

"The chief tells me you saw something out here on the night of the Fourth," Deck said.

Guthrie heaved a sigh and turned to him, pointing an arthritic finger at the beach. "I don't get out here as often as I used to, now that the lighthouse is automated. But I always spend the night on the Fourth to watch the fireworks. It was a tradition for my wife and me. After she passed a few years ago, I didn't have the heart to stop. When I see those sparklers brightening up the sky, it makes me feel close to her again."

All business, Deck ignored the old man's reminiscing and produced a notepad from his pocket. "You watched the fireworks that night?"

"Started to. It was a fantastic show. My Rose always loved the way the fireworks colored the water. She'd say it looked like God had spilled paint on the ocean."

"Something interrupted you?"

"Some*one* is more like it. A drunken hoodlum down on the shoreline. He pulled into the lot around nine o'clock, radio blaring, just before the show started." Guthrie's frown lines deepened as he shook his head. "A man can't get any peace these days."

"Did you notice what kind of car he drove?" Will asked.

"Sure did. A real hot rod. One of those Dodge Challengers. Bright red."

Olivia caught Deck's eye, wondering if the old man had just confirmed Jonah's story.

"What happened next?"

"Well, he got out of his car and started stumbling up and down the beach. Lucky it was a full moon that night, so I followed him with the binoculars for a while. He seemed pretty upset, tossing rocks into the water. Just your standard Little Gull Lamenter. That's what Rose and I would call the guys and gals who came out here broken-hearted and three sheets to the wind. As soon as the show got started, I didn't pay him much attention. I figured he'd sleep it off on the beach the way most of the Lamenters do in the summer. Then, the fire caught my eye."

Olivia sucked in a breath, remembering that night. The singed hole in her sweater, the bloodstains. The weight of Peter Fox's dead body slumped against her.

Deck moved to the westward-facing windows, borrowing Guthrie's binoculars. "You can see Ocean's Song from here?"

"Oh, no. Not *that* fire. That poor sucker set one of those beach trash cans ablaze and sacrificed a few mementos to the flames. That's about the time I got a real good look at him. When I saw that Jonah Montgomery fella last night on the evening news, I got to wondering if I should tell somebody what I saw. Rose always nagged me about being a busybody, but—"

"You did the right thing." Deck clapped Guthrie's shoulder with the same kind of excitement Olivia felt when she made a breakthrough with one of her inmate patients. "Which trash can was it?"

"Probably passed it on your way out to the jetty. But it's Tuesday. The garbage men came this afternoon, so it'll be empty now."

Olivia watched Deck deflate, his smile flat as a punctured tire.

"Cheer up, Detective." Guthrie flashed a boyish smile. "I figured it might be important. I emptied the can myself before I called the station. Kept the bag downstairs for you, in case you wanted it. Just remember, the tide's coming in, so you won't have long."

Deck donned the work gloves Guthrie had loaned him and gingerly opened the black plastic. Olivia peered over his shoulder, directing Guthrie's flashlight into the littered bowels of the trash bag. "Just a peek," Deck reminded her. "We'll let the techs do the rest."

But as Deck began poking through the refuse, they both hunkered down, taking their time to carefully separate the items and examine them one by one. Dozens of soda cans and candy wrappers. Two empty bottles of sunscreen and a half-eaten hot dog. Olivia wondered if they'd find anything worthwhile.

Just when her heart started to sink, Olivia saw it, spotlighting it with the beam. "Look."

A melted bottle of lighter fluid had settled at the bottom of the bag. Deck nudged it with his glove, revealing what lay beneath. A gold watch, still ticking, even with its face cracked and blackened with ash.

CHAPTER FORTY-TWO

Will stared at the watch. Now that he could see it, he could hear it too. Each tick seemed impossibly loud, filling him with dread. First, Guthrie's story. Then, the watch, the bottle of lighter fluid. Even if Jonah hadn't told him the whole story, all the evidence added up to a big fat *F* on Will's detective work. Another suspect eliminated.

"Damn," Will muttered to Olivia. "Jonah was telling the truth."

"Yoo-hoo." Guthrie's voice echoed along the winding stairwell to where they stood. "Are you two still down there?"

"Just finishing up," Olivia called back to him, as Will cinched the top of the plastic bag into a knot. "We'll be out of your hair in no time."

Guthrie hobbled down one step at a time, the creaking of the stairs announcing his arrival. "Did you forget about the tide schedule?"

Will glanced at his own watch, a present from his father on the day he'd taken his sworn oath as an officer of the law. It seemed to mock him. "It's eight fifteen."

"That can't be right." Olivia frowned at him as she spoke, and panic took hold. Will looked closer at the face of the Omega, gaping at the unmoving second hand.

"Oh dear. I thought you'd left." Guthrie shook his head. "It's nearly ten o'clock. Tide's been rising. You won't be able to make it back safely until early morning."

"What?" Incredulous, Will dropped the bag and ran to the door, peering out at the water sweeping across the jetty. In the moonlight, he could make out the sudden swell of the ocean. Its crests licked up and over the sides, reminding him of the flames that had started this whole mess of a case. He turned back to Olivia, exasperated. "How could you not know this?"

"Me? I knew about the tide. I just... I got caught up in hearing Guthrie's story. I lost track of time. But you can't seriously blame me for this. Why didn't you realize your watch had stopped? Couldn't you see the time on your cell phone?"

Will groaned, running his hand through his hair. "I'm not a local. I had no idea the whole jetty would be underwater. That we were on the clock. Are you sure we can't make it across?"

"Not unless you plan on swimming a few hundred yards in fifty-degree water."

"She's right." Guthrie passed Will the binoculars. "Have a closer look, Detective."

Will headed back to the door, Olivia on his heels. He looked one more time, already knowing he'd find only roiling black water between Little Gull and the shoreline. Guthrie had taken care of the lighthouse for years. He knew the tides the same way Will knew the shifty eyes of a guilty suspect.

"Don't fret." Guthrie joined them outside, where the grassy island sloped down to the water. "Rose and I got stuck out here more times than we could count. We always made the best of it."

"I suppose there are worse ways to spend an evening." When the corner of Olivia's mouth turned up at Will, he rolled his eyes at her. "I better text Emily though, so she doesn't worry. Shouldn't you call JB? Tell him about Jonah?"

"Are you kidding? You can't breathe a word about this to him. I'll never live it down. I can fill him in on Jonah in the morning."

"What about Graham?" she asked.

Will removed his cell phone from his pocket. Before he unlocked it, he glared at the bright screen as if it had betrayed him, the time writ large across it. The battery, alarmingly low. He scanned his messages, regarding the newest text from Lieutenant Wheeler with the same disdain. He held it up for Olivia to read.

Good ole Uncle Marvin called in a favor with the judge. Bauer posted bail.

Will lay awake, his stomach growling, unsatisfied by the peanut butter and jelly sandwiches Guthrie had prepared for them. Thanks to Graham's fist, his head had started to throb. His work attire—slacks and an untucked button-down—felt about as comfortable as a straitjacket. No matter which direction he shifted, his back ached, the thin carpet like a concrete slab beneath him.

Guthrie lay on the recliner near the desk, covered in one of Rose's quilts he'd pulled out of the small linen closet. His snoring grew louder and louder, until it eclipsed the roar of the ocean. Then, he gurgled awake, snuffling, before falling back under the spell of the kind of deep sleep that had always eluded Will. *Cops sleep best with one eye open*, his dad had told him once.

"You awake?" Olivia whispered.

He flipped on his side, toward the twin-sized bed that chivalrous Guthrie had insisted should be claimed by the fairer sex. After tossing and turning for a while, that pancake-flat mattress had started to resemble a little slice of heaven. "What does it look like?"

Her teeth flashed white in the dark. Her laugh all breath, like her voice. "Guthrie said low tide is at four a.m. That's only a couple more hours."

"Super." He turned again, flat on his back, staring up at the pole in the center of the room, a crocheted throw pillow beneath his head. "I'll just keep counting sheep then. One million *one*, one million *two*…"

"It's not like I'm doing much better up here. This bed isn't exactly comfortable. It's one step down from a college dorm room. One step up from a prison bunk."

"Right. I can see that. You look like you're suffering."

Olivia sighed. When the bed creaked, he cast a sidelong glance at her. She patted the empty space she'd cleared for him. "Come on, then. If you're going to whine about it."

Will swallowed hard. All the times he'd imagined spending the night with her, it hadn't gone down like this. With an old man rumbling like a freight train and organic peanut butter on his breath. He dragged himself to his feet, bringing his poor excuse for a pillow with him.

"Fine." But he definitely wasn't. His heart pounded in his throat as he pulled back the quilt and carefully climbed in, the bed sagging with his weight. As he lay back, he felt every point of contact between them—elbow, shoulder, foot—like a live wire pressed to his skin.

Olivia rolled onto her side, facing him. She scooted toward the wall, letting Will occupy the empty space, the sheets still warm from her body. "Better?" she asked.

He felt her reach for him, her hand set upon his chest.

"Like sleeping on a cloud." He covered it with his own, lightly squeezing her fingers. "For the record, I wasn't whining."

CHAPTER FORTY-THREE

The obnoxious squawking of a seagull outside the window forced Olivia to open her eyes. Not that she'd slept a wink since Deck had passed out, slinging his arm across her waist and pulling her right into ground zero, where her back fit so snugly against his chest she could feel the solid thump of his heart. At least Guthrie's snore had quieted to a soft reverberation.

The small clock on the desk near the recliner read 4:15 a.m. The tide was low enough now that they could cross the jetty safely. She desperately needed a shower, a change of clothes, and a nap before work. But she preferred it here, nestled in Deck's arms.

Olivia turned onto her back, Deck's hand sliding across her stomach, and took a moment to study him in the moonlight before she nudged him with her elbow.

Stubble shadowed his jaw, and the bruise under his right eye had begun to darken at the edge. His hair askew, his lashes fluttering, she felt a tenderness she couldn't explain. Only that she wanted to touch him but suddenly felt too shy to follow through.

"Deck. Wake up."

He moaned softly.

"It's low tide."

Olivia lifted his arm, heavy as driftwood, and freed herself from beneath it. "Hey, Sleeping Beauty."

"Stop yelling." He offered her a lazy grin before hoisting himself up and planting his socked feet on the floor. "I hear you."

While they quietly retucked and straightened their clothing and slipped on their shoes, Olivia checked her phone. As she feared, it had gone the way of Deck's and died during the night. At least she'd been able to text Emily first—*Stuck at Little Gull with Deck. Tide rising*—even if Em's response, a smiley face emoji with red heart eyes, had been lacking an appropriate amount of sisterly concern.

"Should we let him sleep?" Olivia tiptoed around Guthrie in the dark, watching the rise and fall of his chest beneath the quilt. She wondered how many nights he'd spent here sardined in that twin bed with Rose. That must be why he preferred the recliner.

The moment Deck nodded at her, he banged his knee against the leg of the desk. He winced, hobbling toward the staircase. Even as Olivia bit back her laughter, Guthrie didn't stir.

She scribbled a note on the pad in the corner of the desk, thanking him for his hospitality, and followed Deck down to the ground level, where he'd secured the plastic bag containing Jonah's kindling.

The biting air of early morning nipped at Olivia's skin, awakening her instantly. The ocean had retreated again, leaving the path across the jetty slick but clear. When they crested the hill, Deck stopped walking and directed Guthrie's flashlight up ahead of them, across the rocks to the other side. A jolt of panic coursed through Olivia, razing the last of her sleepy cobwebs.

She squinted at the shadowy figures in the parking lot. Spotlighted by the single light pole, their faces began to take shape. She wondered how long they'd been waiting and what awful news had brought them here before the dawn.

CHAPTER FORTY-FOUR

Will gripped the plastic bag in one hand, the railing in the other, the cold steel a tangible reminder he wasn't dreaming. Even though the sea smoke hung over the water like a gossamer web, and he had the sickening feeling his reality had shifted without him knowing.

He couldn't move as fast as he wanted, not with the rocky path strewn with kelp and still damp beneath his feet. With Olivia behind him, he took careful steps, glancing over his shoulder to reassure himself. But it worried him seeing JB pacing between the cars, cell phone pressed to his ear, while Emily stood watch.

"I've been calling you for over an hour." The hard edge of JB's voice, the fact that he hadn't pointed out Will's complete incompetence with tide tables or inquired about the trash bag beside him, confirmed it.

"Me too." Emily matched JB's tone.

"Our cell batteries died overnight," Olivia told her. "I assumed you knew that would happen."

Will met his partner's troubled eyes. "What's wrong?"

"Your cat is missing."

"That's why you're here?" Unease twisted Will's empty stomach but he refused to give in to it. "Cy does his own thing. You know that. He'll turn up in a day or two. Probably leave something dead on my tailgate."

JB didn't laugh. Instead, he measured his words, and each one cut to the quick. "There's more. Nora called 911 early this morning. Thomas ran off again."

"Where are they staying?" Olivia hustled toward the Buick, JB to the Crown Vic. Even Emily had already unlocked her rental. But Will lingered there, feeling one step behind. Like he'd left himself sleeping in the lighthouse.

"At an Airbnb in the woods off Pine Grove Road. We've already called in the state police to help organize a search. We've got search dogs headed down here on loan from Brookings PD."

"Search dogs?" The news hit Will like another sucker punch. "Are you positive he left the house? The kid likes to hide."

JB raised an incredulous eyebrow. Will couldn't tell if it was the question that surprised him or his own slow-on-the-uptake demeanor. He wasn't used to playing catch-up. "That cabin is crawling with cops right now. So yeah, positive. He's not there."

Finally, the adrenaline kicked him in the ass and cleared his brain fog. He hurried to the trunk, slinging the trash bag inside. "Let's go, then."

Will cinched his seat belt while JB floored it down the empty highway toward Pine Grove Road, with Emily and Olivia speeding behind them. As they neared the Airbnb, he shook his head at Will, disappointed. "I can't believe you pulled a stunt like this in the middle of a quadruple murder case."

"You think I planned it?"

"C'mon, City Boy. No self-respecting resident of Fog Harbor forgets about the tide tables. How else are you gonna get Doctor Rockwell to spend the night alone with you? Your charm and good looks? You're sneakier than I gave you credit for, though. A lighthouse. That's some Nicholas Sparks shit. Hell, it sounds like something I would've thought of."

"If I planned it—which I didn't, for the record—I certainly wouldn't have marooned us out there with the seventy-year-old lighthouse keeper. Listening to him snoring all night. Let me tell you, it wasn't exactly my idea of romance."

Will's thoughts betrayed him, going straight to the 3:25 a.m. moment when he'd deliberately reached for Olivia and pulled her close to him, inhaling the vanilla scent of her shampoo like his life depended on it. Coward that he was, he'd pretended to be asleep.

As JB turned down the dirt road to the rental cabin, he busted out a laugh. "Guthrie Smalls, huh?"

"You *knew*?"

"Of course I knew. Chief Flack filled me in. She told me you went out there to talk to him. Besides, there's no way you're smart enough to come up with a scheme like that. So, what did the old guy have to say? I assume he's the reason you were lugging that trash bag like a broke-down Santa Claus."

"I'll give you the details later. Bottom line, we're running out of suspects. Jonah Montgomery's not our man. And neither is Pedro Mendez." Will side-eyed his partner. "I didn't realize you were a closet Nicholas Sparks fan."

"*The Notebook* is a literary masterpiece. Don't try to convince me otherwise." JB parked in the clearing in front of the cabin, alongside a fleet of police vehicles. Nora waited under the porch light, staring out into the inky spaces between the trees, where the shadows seemed to pulse with life. Will shivered watching her.

"Wouldn't dream of it." He thrust the door open and headed for the house, trying to shake off his lingering worry. About Cy. About Thomas. Most of all, about what they'd find out there in the dark, dark woods.

Will shook the firm hand of California State Police Sergeant Kingsley, a tall black man reminiscent of a redwood. Solid, sturdy, and immovable. Distinguished, too, in his perfectly pressed uniform. Unlike Will, who'd been wearing the same rumpled clothing for nearly twenty-four hours. Kingsley's eyes catalogued the blood spot on Will's slacks, the bruise on his face. Thankfully, he extended Will a small kindness and said nothing.

"Catch me up, Sergeant. Detective Benson said there's been a thorough search of the interior of the house. What about the perimeter?"

When Sergeant Kingsley started walking, flashlight in hand, Will and JB followed. Wordlessly, he guided them around the side of the quaint log cabin—an Airbnber's dream—where the local crime scene techs busied themselves dusting the sill outside Thomas's bedroom for fingerprints. The window had been opened, the curtains parted on the inside.

"Based on his aunt's statement, we suspect he went out this way. The front door was still locked from the inside when she discovered him missing. She said he has a history of running away."

Will frowned at the three feet of distance between the sill and the ground. In the dirt below, he spotted two small footprints. Then, two more. He followed the trail a short distance until it dead-ended at the treeline, where the beam of Kingsley's flashlight revealed the thick underbrush.

"A cursory search of the grove turned up nothing. Now that we've secured the K-9s, we'll head out into the woods to do a more thorough look-see. A little boy couldn't go far out here on his own. We'll probably find him tuckered out and hunting for grasshoppers under a fallen log."

Will opened his mouth to argue. To remind Sergeant Tree Trunk that that little boy was the only witness to the murder of his family. To question whether Thomas would've jumped from a window alone in the pitch-black. To ask the sergeant how he managed to make the search for a missing boy sound like a fairy tale.

JB nudged Will. "Let's go talk to Nora, and get the timeline down before we head out."

As they trekked back to the porch, leaving Sergeant Kingsley at the window, JB shook his head, dismayed. "What kid goes hunting for grasshoppers in the middle of the night?"

Nora had finally run out of tears, and the vacant look in her eyes made Will's heart heavy. Guilt could do that to a person. Suck their pain dry, leaving only a husk behind.

While JB plopped onto the nearby rocker and removed his pocket notepad, Will stood by Nora's side, following her empty gaze into the redwood grove. "I know you've already spoken to the state police, but it's important that Detective Benson and I understand exactly what you saw and heard this morning."

Nora's heartbreak consumed the space between them, making it hard to breathe.

"What happened?" Will asked gently.

His words took forever to reach her. Hers, when they came, brittle as the dry summer grass. "Like I told the other officer, I put Thomas to bed around eight like usual. We read his favorite story, and he fell right to sleep. He must've been exhausted from the day. I checked on him again before I laid down."

"What time was that?"

"Ten thirty or so. The news had just started, and I couldn't deal with hearing about it all again, so I downed the rest of my glass of wine and took a shower. Before I headed into the bedroom, I peeked inside. Thomas had taken Ranger Rob from the nightstand and laid him on the pillow next to his head."

A laugh clunked from her throat, flightless and broken as a dead bird. "I remember thinking how lucky I was that we found him today. *Lucky*. Can you believe it?"

"When did you notice he was missing?"

"Around three. I had this awful dream a man was standing in the doorway, watching Thomas sleep. His hands were on fire, and the whole place went up in flames. I woke in a cold sweat, certain I'd heard Thomas cry out. It's silly, but I lay there for a while, too scared to get up. Then, when I couldn't find him, I thought he'd gone to the bathroom or gotten scared and hidden in the closet. I looked for about fifteen minutes before I called the police. That's when I noticed the window was open."

Will swallowed a lump. Fear that went straight down into the pit of him.

"In Thomas's bedroom?"

Nora nodded. "I think I'd been too panicked to notice before."

"Was anything missing? Clothing? Toys?"

"Ranger Rob. That's it. We never did find his stuffed dog." She raised her shaking hand, extending it toward the forest. "That little boy is out there barefoot in his pjs, for God's sake. Oh God, this is all my fault."

CHAPTER FORTY-FIVE

"Nick's on his way here." Emily tossed out the warning as casually as a flip of her strawberry-blonde curls over her shoulder. "He heard the call on his scanner and wanted to help. He's been in these woods before."

"Good for him." Olivia had no right to be upset with her sister. She'd kept plenty of her own secrets. But Emily careened toward bad decisions like a tornado in a wheat field, and Nick had trouble written all over him. "I have, too. Remember that abandoned gold mine?"

"Oh, yeah. What was it called again?"

"Clawfoot." As a teenager, Olivia had trekked out to the mine on a Halloween night dare, she and her giggling friends listening for the scratching of the miners who'd supposedly perished within it when it had collapsed following an earthquake. Since then, there'd been a number of additional cave-ins, leaving the mine a dangerous place. Inhospitable to all living things but a colony of bats.

"That thing has been boarded up for years."

Olivia nodded, her attention drawn to the porch, where Nora wobbled forward. Her face had turned the pale color of the moon, her legs suddenly seesawing beneath her. She swayed like a felled tree. Then, with everyone watching, she crumpled, collapsing into Deck's arms.

Deck caught her and lowered her to the porch.

Olivia hurried up the steps of the cabin, with Emily behind her. She grabbed a cushion from the porch swing and helped slip it beneath Nora's head. Her eyes blinked open, and she struggled to sit up.

"Easy," Olivia cautioned. "You passed out."

Resigned, Nora lay back down. "Promise me you'll find him again. He's all I've got left of my sister. All I've got left."

Olivia patted Nora's hand, raising her eyes to Deck's. It was his promise to make, but his mouth stayed shut in a hard, unforgiving line and his gaze laser-focused behind her. Olivia cringed at the sight of Graham approaching from his pickup truck, Chief Flack at his side.

"What the hell is *he* doing here?" Deck demanded. "He should be in jail right now."

"There's this thing called bail, Decker, and due process. Maybe you've heard of it?"

"I've heard of nepotism. Corruption. Abuse of power. Should I go on?"

"I told you he'd be an asshole about it, Chief." But Graham looked right at Olivia when he said it, even after she shook her head at him in disapproval.

Chief Flack raised her hands between them, trying to hold back the storm. "It was my idea. Graham knows the redwood grove. His uncle, Marvin, owns part of the land."

Olivia could feel Deck's heat. His jaw clenched tight as a vise. "Of course he does."

"He's agreed he won't be directly involved in the search."

"Well, that's a relief."

Graham produced a folded square from his pocket. He approached the cabin, holding it out to Deck like a peace offering. Or a rigged explosive. "After I turned sixteen, I'd drive up to Fog Harbor every weekend from Santa Rosa and stay with my uncle. We'd hunt elk and deer in that grove. I know it like the back of my hand."

When Deck stayed silent and seething, JB spoke up. "I don't like it either, but it would be useful to know where the hell we're going. The troopers said it's more than a thousand acres of dense forest."

"He's right." Graham avoided Deck's eyes. "I want to help, man. Seriously."

Deck sighed, snatching up the paper. He jerked his head toward the periphery, where the other volunteers had begun to gather, Nick and Wade Coffman among them. "Do it over there then. Stay away from me."

Olivia squeezed Nora's hand. "It's okay. We'll find Thomas and bring him home to you. You have my word."

While Nora struggled to her feet, leaning on Olivia, Deck unfolded Graham's rudimentary, hand-drawn map of the grove. Pencil strokes designated its borders and features. A squiggly line for the Earl River bisected the edge of the property. At its center, a small circle marked the Clawfoot Gold Mine that had been abandoned for at least three decades.

After phoning in to work to cancel her patient and intern meetings, Olivia slipped an orange reflective vest over her blouse, hoisted a walking stick, and summoned her courage for the second time in as many days. At the entrance to the grove, the two police K-9 dogs—German shepherds Lucius and Augustus—pulled at their handlers' leashes, yelping with excitement, anxious to track the scent they'd picked up from Thomas's pillow. Their high-pitched whines cut through the stillness of the early morning and raised the hairs on Olivia's arms. But the thought of Thomas alone out there gave her strength.

When Sergeant Kingsley finally signaled to the group, the dogs charged ahead, forging a path through the tangled brush. Emily took her arm and together they walked into the unknown.

CHAPTER FORTY-SIX

The blackbirds' singing marked the first sign of the impending dawn. But deep inside the redwood grove, the night wore on, never-ending. Flashlights flitted like fireflies, skittering across the dank forest floor, searching for signs of life. Above it all, the unwavering spotlight of a helicopter commissioned by the state police guided the way. The soft whir of its blades comforted Will, but not as much as the sound of Olivia's breathing behind him, reminding him he wasn't alone out there. He'd left JB to supervise at the cabin, since tromping through the forest with an irregular heartbeat seemed ill-advised.

Every few minutes, Will glanced over his shoulder to check on Olivia and her sister. Her navy slacks, covered in her own dusty handprints. Auburn hair, whipped back into a ponytail. Her tired eyes, shining and determined in the glow of her flashlight.

"Thomas!" Will added his weary voice to the chorus of weary voices. They'd been trekking through the grove for about thirty minutes now, moving between the ancient trunks that seemed to huddle together, intent on hiding their secrets. In the spaces between, the dark stretched out endlessly.

The police K-9s led them through the underbrush with the rest of the volunteers. Will couldn't shake the feeling someone was one step ahead, laughing while he bumbled around in the woods aimlessly, looking for a black cat in a coal mine. He wondered if Olivia felt the same, but he kept quiet. Left to their own devices, his doubts and fears multiplied.

For a little boy like Thomas, danger lurked everywhere. Behind every tree trunk. Inside every hidden hole in the earth. Under the cold waters of the Earl River. All sorts of predators roamed these woods—bobcats, mountain lions, coyotes, black bears. Even bats. But those weren't the sort on Will's mind, as he poked every mound of leaf cover with his walking stick, half expecting to find the unthinkable.

As they drew nearer to the old mine at the center of the grove, Will kept calling Thomas's name, all the while reminding himself there was no evidence the boy had ventured into the forest at all. No definitive sign he'd been taken either. The further in they walked, the louder Will's cop clairvoyance nagged at him, mocked him. Insisted he'd made a terrible mistake. That he'd missed something essential. His head began to throb again, radiating outward from the eye socket that bore Graham's handiwork.

Will stopped to rest beside a large redwood. Listening to the boots tramp through the brush and the labored sounds of the dogs' breathing, he looked skyward, but the tree's thick canopy blocked the stars.

"You okay?" Olivia asked, joining him beneath the boughs. In the moonlight, the branches looked faintly skeletal. Limbs disembodied and reaching for the sky.

As Will contemplated his answer, Lucius took off at a full gallop, nose to the ground. The dog tugged its leash from its handler and disappeared into the grove with the rest of the searchers in full pursuit.

Will ran as fast as he could in the dark, Olivia maintaining pace beside him. His flashlight could barely keep up with his feet, and he nearly tripped a dozen times. Each almost-fall sent a jolt of primitive fear to his pounding heart until he swore it would burst in his chest.

Up ahead, he spotted the shadowy entrance to the Clawfoot Gold Mine. The other searchers pulled up short at the giant mouth of a hole carved into a large rock face and partially boarded with half-rotted wooden planks. Lucius sat at attention in front of it, fixated on the ground.

"What is it?" Will asked Olivia, before he could see it for himself. She gaped at it in horror.

At the dog's feet, Thomas's stuffed dog lay covered in dirt, found at last.

CHAPTER FORTY-SEVEN

Standing at the entrance to Clawfoot, Olivia stared helplessly at Thomas's lost toy. A stray leaf clung to the dirty gray fur, and one of the ears had nearly torn from the head.

"Woofie." But Deck already knew that. He crouched down to get a closer look at it.

"This belonged to Thomas," he told the others. Slipping on a pair of latex gloves, he placed the toy in a plastic baggie from his pocket. "It's been missing since yesterday."

"How did it get here?" Emily asked.

Olivia shook her head, not wanting to contemplate an answer. She could still remember being here, years ago, terrified, with her silly friends egging her on and squealing with anticipation as they'd pried loose one of the rotting boards. When a twig had snapped behind them, they'd gone running, screaming like wild banshees, back to the road.

"Looks like somebody's gone in there fairly recently." The familiar bellow of Wade Coffman drew her attention. He gestured to the ground where his flashlight revealed three cast-off boards. They sat atop the grass, not beneath it. The forest hadn't reclaimed them yet.

"Probably a bunch of kids," countered Nick Spade. "There's nothing else to do around here."

Nick looked to Olivia for support. *As if.* "We have to check it out," she said. "Thomas might have been curious and wandered inside."

While Nick cast a skeptical eye her way, Deck settled the argument, addressing Sergeant Kingsley with authority. "I agree. We've come this far, and we've got the dogs here. If Thomas went in that mine, this is our best chance to find him."

The officer guiding Lucius nodded. "I say we take a small group, Detective. We don't want anyone else getting lost or injured. These abandoned mines are notoriously unstable. One wrong move, and the whole thing comes crashing down."

Olivia watched as Deck counted off six men, including Wade and Nick, who reluctantly shrugged his agreement. They leveraged their walking sticks to remove the remaining boards from the entrance, tossing them into the thick grass. One of the planks was so decayed, it broke in two. Just as the last board had been cast aside, a sudden, vicious flutter of wings assaulted them.

Directing her flashlight upward, Olivia gulped down a scream. A small colony of bats took to the air. In a horrifying instant, they vanished just as quickly, their bodies camouflaged by the velvet sky and the enveloping darkness of the redwoods.

"I'm going in," she announced to Deck, hoping to sway him with her confidence. Or wear him down with her persistence. Either way, she wasn't about to wait on the sidelines tormented by the ghouls of her imagination. "Thomas trusts me. If he's scared, I can talk him down. Besides, I know this place."

"I don't think that's a good idea."

"You're so predictable."

"Yeah. So are you."

"Well, then I'm in good company."

He groaned. "Fine, but just stay with me, okay?"

Olivia bit back her annoyance. "If you're scared of the dark, just say so."

She waved goodbye to Emily, as the dogs led the way into the cold, craggy mine shaft. Noses fixed to the old steel tracks, where a set of carts had carried wares up from the depths below. Frayed electric wire that had once provided light hung loosely from the wall, affixed by nails. The old bulbs had all gone dark long ago.

"You've been in here before?" Deck asked her, while they followed the group down the long, shadowy tunnel.

Olivia directed her flashlight up ahead, where the mine shaft split into two passages. She stepped carefully, the rock damp beneath her feet. Wade was the first to call out for Thomas, his voice echoing eerily into the unknown.

"Not exactly." She smiled at Deck's back, knowing he couldn't see her. No way she'd recount that story. He didn't need to know how scared she'd been. "Too dangerous."

"I have." Nick appeared beside her, buzzing with energy, like a fly she couldn't swat. "Remember that Halloween when it was the thing to do? The seniors dared all us juniors to spend the night inside Clawfoot. That was right before another section caved in, and they put up no trespassing signs. A buddy of mine and I got drunk and rode one of those mine carts until it fell off the track. If you go far enough in, there are pools of water down there."

"So, you two knew each other in high school, huh?" Deck asked.

Olivia waved her hand dismissively, hoping Nick would stay focused on finding Thomas, not regaling Deck with tales of how awful she'd been to him.

"Olivia was far too cool for me."

"Hardly."

Nick smirked at her protestation. "Still is, it seems."

"I just want to know what you're doing with my sister. She means a lot to me."

"It's confidential. Private investigator privilege."

As Deck went on ahead, Olivia pulled Nick aside and lowered her voice to a whisper. "I know about the black light and your tip from the Feds."

Olivia registered the shock in Nick's eyes, but he played it cooler than Em had, as they hurried to catch up to the others. "I have no idea what you're talking about."

Olivia's eyes grew accustomed to the never-ending darkness, but the sameness of the tunnel disoriented her. She understood how someone could get lost down here and disappear forever. After separating into two groups at the fork in the shaft, they'd been walking for at least fifteen minutes, surrounded by the same rough rock wall, the same ancient track beneath their feet. The same sound, too—silence. So when she spotted an aberration in the distance, she blinked and looked again, wondering if the shadows were playing tricks with her.

Lining the wall, a set of wooden shelves filled haphazard with empty buckets and rusted tools in coffee cans, the dust as thick as snow. An old conveyance cart sat on the trolley tracks ahead, showing its age. Its wheels rusted, its body sagging with rot. As Lucius whined and pulled at the leash, straining against it, a chill zipped up Olivia's spine.

The officer jogged to keep up, jerking Lucius back when they reached the cart. He peered inside and cursed under his breath, sending ripples of a whisper reverberating down the tunnel. Olivia thought of Nora, waiting by her phone for any news, and said a silent prayer.

"Got something?" Deck asked, hurrying toward the car.

The officer nodded. "It's not good."

The nearer Olivia got, the stronger the scent. Metal and sweetness.

Olivia willed her legs to keep moving through the quicksand of her past. It always lingered in the shadows, ready to swallow her heart at a moment's notice. Every bad thing that happened brought her right back to *the* bad thing. But she wasn't eight years old and she wasn't standing in the doorway of Apartment E and her father wasn't there, hunched over the body of a dead woman, with blood on his hands.

She sucked in a breath, took a final step forward, and forced her eyes down into the mine cart.

Blood. Blood, everywhere.

CHAPTER FORTY-EIGHT

Will breathed in through his nose to calm himself. His heart had taken off like a jackrabbit at the sight of the blood puddle in the mine cart. After he radioed to JB to get the crime scene techs down there ASAP, he shined the beam of his flashlight down the tunnel, along the walls.

"Wait." Olivia grabbed his arm, pointed at a spot on the rock face, her voice high and breathy. "Is that...?"

Will redirected the light onto the wall, the horror of the whole scene taking shape. Characters written in blood that dripped like rainwater through the crags and crevices of the rock.

"What does it say?" the K-9 officer asked, pulling a frenetic Lucius to attention.

"That looks like the number ten." Olivia gestured with her flashlight. "And an X."

"Ten X?" Nick suggested.

"Or ten times," Olivia said. "Whatever that means."

Nick grimaced. "Hopefully not ten victims."

Will snapped a photograph of the wall and the cart with his cell phone. Thank goodness he'd thought to charge it in the Crown Vic on the way over. "It'll take a while for CSI to get down here. I'm going to see what's at the end of the tunnel."

Olivia jogged after him. "Do you think that's Thomas's blood?"

Will had no good answer, so he kept his mouth shut and his eyes focused on the sliver of faint light visible ahead. She didn't ask again, which meant she'd probably assumed the worst, like Will, and had no desire to give voice to the awful possibility.

As they drew nearer to the light, Will made out its source: a thin opening between the ancient planks of wood crisscrossed over the exit, similar to those they'd cast off the front entrance. But these hadn't been replaced in some time. The nails he could see had gone rusty.

"Whoever came into Clawfoot didn't go out this way. Are there any other exits?"

The disheartened look on Olivia's face spoke for her. "This place is a maze, with enough tunnels to get lost in. The miners made sure there were plenty of ventilation exits in case of a cave-in."

After they wandered back to the cart, a heavy silence between them, Will forced himself to take another look inside it. The surface of the blood puddle had begun to congeal. Fat drops of it marked the tracks like breadcrumbs, leading to the garish message left behind.

While Lucius and his officer handler headed back down the tunnel to search for signs of Thomas, Olivia and Nick stationed themselves in front of the stony wall, scrutinizing the red letters.

"What're you thinking?" Will asked.

"It's strange," she puzzled. "Why leave a message here? *Now*? Why not at Ocean's Song? Or even near the car, if Peter was the primary target?"

"Maybe that horseshoe you found in the pool was the message."

"Maybe." Olivia sounded unconvinced. "But the mediums are so different. The horseshoe was subtle. But words written in blood, that's blatant. That's undeniable. That's—"

"Brutal," Nick finished. "The guy certainly knows how to make a statement. Albeit a cryptic one."

When Olivia looked at Will, he could practically hear the gears turning behind her fiery eyes.

Just then, Will's radio came alive, filling the tunnel with eerie static. The voice, when it came, echoed down and around them. "Kingsley for Decker. Come in."

"Go for Decker."

"We got one too. A bloody message. Looks like yours. *Ten X*. Or *Ten times*. Over."

Will didn't know why, but as soon as he heard it from Kingsley's mouth, he felt the chill of the familiar. Something told him that message was meant for him.

Three hours later, the crime scene techs had processed five bloody carts in five tunnels. Five scrawled messages, each one bearing the exact same letters—TEN X—but no sign of Thomas.

While the search carried on, past the mine and deeper into the redwood grove, Will and Olivia caught the last ATV ride back to the cabin with Steve Li.

"Anything you can tell us from the blood evidence?" Will asked, as they rumbled over the forest floor.

"Nothing definitive. I don't like to speculate."

"But?" Will prodded.

"But, we'll have an answer for you as soon as possible. First, I want to rule out an animal as the source. Detective Benson already collected a DNA sample from Thomas's aunt if it comes to that."

Will felt sick and tired. Sick and tired of this case. Sick and tired of being wrong. Sick and tired of waiting for the other shoe to drop.

Olivia squeezed his knee but it didn't quiet his chattering nerves. Neither did her words, which she doled out carefully, reluctantly. Like teaspoons of unpleasant medicine. "Whoever has Thomas, I don't think it's the same person who killed his family."

CHAPTER FORTY-NINE

When she returned home mid-morning, Olivia found Emily passed out on the sofa, a cheesy reality show marathon playing on the television. She slumped down beside her sister, wishing she could close her eyes. But Deck had emailed her Peter Fox's client files, and her buzzing curiosity kept her awake.

Freshly showered and armed with a steaming cup of black coffee and a heaping bowl of oatmeal, Olivia returned to the sofa and her sleeping sister and propped her laptop on her knees. She opened a new document and typed TEN X in bold red letters, alongside a list of their mostly exonerated suspects—Jonah, Elvis, and Pedro—and the word *horseshoe*. After a moment's pause, she added a name: Graham.

Then, she started scrolling through Fox's old clients, beginning with his work as a public defender, when he'd had to take what he'd been given, guilty or not. Gangbangers, conmen, small-time criminals. The occasional murderer. The accused, too poor to afford representation from an attorney who didn't have a caseload as long as his arm. Fox had kept fastidious handwritten notes, even on the cases he'd turned down, that had been scanned and filed alongside the legal briefs and filings typed on his fancy letterhead. Peter Fox's handwriting had a distinctive neutrality. Simple script with neat block letters. He cut loose a lot of cases. Mostly, the ones he couldn't win.

A few years after Peter hung up his shingle, he'd won a big case—the acquittal of a pretty boy with a hefty inheritance who'd murdered his college sweetheart—and business started booming. A year or so later, Hannah began interviewing clients on Peter's behalf. Olivia could tell because of the handwriting, his nuanced strokes replaced by her bold loops and cutting dashes that conveyed a subtle bias. Notes like *looks guilty* and *creepy eyes* and *reminds me of Bundy* told the reader she'd clearly made up her mind. But under Hannah's supervision, Peter's acquittal percentage went up. Way up. She obviously knew how to pick a winner.

With Emily nestled next to her, Olivia read file after file until her eyelids grew heavy and her vision started to blur. Just when she'd decided to allow herself a break, possibly even a catnap, a case caught her attention. Made her sit up straight, her skin pricking.

Ten years prior, Peter had defended Tim Overton, a ranch hand who'd claimed he'd been possessed by demons when he executed four members of the Holt family with a single shot to the head, before setting the family ranch house on fire. Peter had been able to convince the jury that, due to his chronic schizophrenia, Overton was not criminally responsible for the murders and should instead be committed to Napa State Hospital. He'd been released only two years later.

Olivia took a screenshot of the summary page and sent it in an email to Deck, typing *For Follow-Up?* in the subject line. The similarities couldn't be ignored, nor the injustice. Getting murderers off scot-free had propelled Peter straight up the ladder of Santa Barbara society, leaving a mob of angry victims in his wake. Maybe one of them had decided to mete out justice the old-fashioned way.

As Olivia pondered the Holts' fate, Emily began dreaming aloud. Her voice, haunted and childlike, she spoke a single word.

"Daddy?"

Restless, she turned away from Olivia, resettling with her head on the couch cushion. Olivia watched the rise and fall of her sister's chest until she felt certain sleep had pulled her back under. Careful not to disturb Em, she stood up, tiptoeing across the living room and down the hall toward her sister's room.

Olivia took one last glance back, before she cracked the door and prepared to snoop again like a textbook big sister. When Emily had enrolled in the art institute, she'd shipped most of her belongings to her studio apartment in downtown San Francisco, leaving her room a shell of its former girly self. But Olivia knew all of her hiding places. Under the mattress. Atop the closet's highest shelf. Stuffed in the toe of her rain boots.

She struck gold pressed between the pages of the first Harry Potter. A well-worn envelope addressed to Emily Rockwell at 222 Golden Gate View Avenue, Apartment 3 in San Francisco. The return address, Valley View State Prison, where their father had spent the last ten years of his incarceration.

Olivia opened the flap with care and removed the letter dated March 1st, just days before her father had supposedly hanged himself from a pipe that seemed too far to reach on his own.

Dear Em,

I enjoyed our recent visit more than you know. This place gets real lonely, and it feels good to have you in my corner. Liv will come around too. I just have to prove it to her. As hard as it was admitting to you the mistakes I made in the past, it was freeing to get that boulder off my chest. Please be patient with your sister. Let her tell you about that day at the Double Rock in her own time. Whatever happens at my parole hearing, just know I love you and believe in you. Keep making art. Art speaks when words can't.

Love,
Dad

Tucked inside the envelope, their father had enclosed one of his own original drawings. As Olivia unfolded the thick paper, the sight knocked the wind from her, and she had to sit down. He'd drawn her and Emily as they were now—though he hadn't been face to face with Olivia in years. Olivia immediately recognized the inspiration from a photo she and Emily had taken at the beach near Little Gull. But their father had drawn them facing the water and added himself between, his arms around them both. He'd titled the drawing *Love*.

Moving quickly, Olivia padded out of Em's room toward her own, in search of the black light she'd purchased from Big Ed's Hardware months ago.

Turning the lights off, she sucked in a breath and held it up to the margin, the same as she'd done with the other drawing. The one that revealed her father had been close to determining the General's identity.

"What are you doing?" Emily demanded.

Olivia dropped the black light and cursed as it tumbled toward the hardwood, landing with a clatter at the bedside.

"There's nothing there. Nick and I already looked."

"When?"

"Last night."

Olivia ignored the implications of her sister's answer, focusing instead on proving her wrong. She retrieved the black light and scanned the drawing, front to back, finding nothing.

"Told you." But there was no joy in Emily's gloating. She dropped to the bed beside her sister, her eyes filling with tears. "I didn't want to be right. I wanted one last message from Dad. Nick thought there would be."

"Why did you get Nick involved in the first place? I thought you believed the whole suicide story." Emily had been the one to encourage Olivia to move on, to accuse her of trying to distract herself with her silly conspiracy theories and ignoring the real issue. That she hadn't made peace with their dad before he died. "And don't say it's private investigator privilege."

"Well, technically, it is. But I know you, and you'll never give up."

"You're right about that."

Emily tucked her feet under the covers and propped a pillow behind her. It reminded Olivia of the old days, when she'd read bedtime stories to her little sister while their mother had drowned her sorrows at the Hickory Pit bar.

"The FBI showed up at my apartment in April, wanting to know if I'd been in contact with Dad before he died. Or if you'd given me any of his drawings. They told me you'd turned over the sketchbook from his property. You know, the one you *said* you couldn't *find*."

Olivia cringed. *Sorry*, she mouthed.

"Anyway, it freaked me out how pushy they were, so I just blurted out a lie. I told them I was angry with Dad for killing himself, and I'd destroyed everything he sent me."

"Did they believe you?"

"I think so. For a second, I thought they were gonna search the place anyway. The one guy stared me down like he was trying to intimidate me. I've always had my doubts about what happened to Dad, but that's when I knew for sure you were right. He didn't kill himself."

Olivia didn't know how to feel. But it wasn't the worst thing in the world to have her sister on her side.

"They were so interested in his drawings, I figured there must be something there. But I wasn't sure what to do about it. When I came back home for summer break, I found Nick online, and he told me he could help me. He knows a guy with an in at the FBI. His contact told him that the black light messages are used a lot with prison informants. So, I figured it was worth a shot."

Placing the drawing on the bed between them, Olivia examined it more closely. Beyond the pencil-shaded lighthouse, the gray strokes of the water broke the horizon. Their father had drawn three naval ships in the distance. On each hull, he'd penciled in the tiny ship numbers, three per vessel and barely visible.

Their gaze met, and Olivia saw the same idea swirling in her sister's eyes, the same vibrant green as her own.

"Do we own a magnifying glass?" Emily asked.

But Olivia had already sprung up from the bed, drawing in hand, and headed for the kitchen. She flung open the junk drawer and retrieved their mother's magnifying glass and a notepad.

"Write this down," she told her sister. "Nine six nine. Four nine five. Three two four."

"What does it mean?" Em chewed on the end of the pencil, as she pondered the numbers.

Olivia returned to their father's artwork. The way he'd drawn them, looking out at the boats on the water. Her heart welled with certainty. "It means Dad left us one last message after all."

CHAPTER FIFTY

Will couldn't stand sitting at his cubicle, twiddling his thumbs while the crime scene techs processed the evidence from the mine shaft and the search party carried on, deeper into the redwood grove. So, he'd avoided the station entirely, telling JB to meet him at Del Norte County Jail, where he planned to have one last go at Jonah to nail down the real story. On the drive over, Will phoned Jonah's attorney and explained they'd found new evidence at Little Gull that would likely exonerate his client.

Will found JB waiting outside the small interview room, looking fresh as a daisy compared to himself. "You take the lead on this one. I'm exhausted."

JB wiggled his eyebrows. "I'll bet you are." But, as they entered the room, he gave Will a fatherly pat on the shoulder that said he understood the unbearable pressure of this case. Four victims and not a single viable suspect left. The only witness, gone.

At least the email from Olivia had given Will a glimmer of hope. With the victims shot in the head and the ranch house set on fire, the Holt case bore many similarities to the Fox murders. But Will had been unable to locate the only surviving member of the Holt family, Dwayne. After the trial, it seemed he'd disappeared entirely.

Jonah grimaced when he saw Will and JB approach. His face shadowed with stubble; his eyes clouded with anguish. In only a couple of days, he'd withered like a tree with no sunlight. But Will spotted a glint of hope in his eyes. "My lawyer says you might have good news."

JB took the seat across from Jonah, while Will stayed on his feet. He worried that if he stopped moving now, he wouldn't have the fortitude to get up again. Or worse, he'd fall asleep in the interview room.

"You're one lucky SOB," JB began. "My partner got a call from the lighthouse keeper down at Little Gull. He saw you start a fire in a trash can on the beach around the same time as the Fox murders. You're no longer a suspect."

"I—what? A fire in a trash can?" Jonah blinked back his surprise. "I honestly don't remember. I got so drunk that I must've blacked out. The next morning, all I could remember was driving out there and reading that damn letter, while I stared out at the water and chugged vodka straight from the bottle, but I couldn't find the letter or the watch I bought for Peter. Then, when Detective Decker asked me about the bottles of lighter fluid, I panicked. I didn't even realize they were missing. In my heart, I knew I didn't do it. Still, I couldn't be sure. You two know as well as I do, anybody's capable of murder."

Will nodded, wishing he didn't. The same way he wished he could erase Nora's haunted look from his mind's eye. And that nagging, dreadful feeling from the pit of his stomach. "Can you tell us about the watch you purchased for Peter?"

"It had an inscription on the back. *Until the end of time.* Stupid, right? I should've known he wouldn't accept it. He never wanted to have any evidence that I existed. It was too risky." He huffed out an ironic laugh. "Now, the story is all over the gossip rags. I suppose I should take some satisfaction in that, but I'd crawl back in my hole and stay there forever if it would bring Peter back."

Will reached into his pocket and removed the evidence bag that contained the gold watch he and Olivia had discovered at the bottom of the trash bag. He laid it on the table, the watch's smoke-stained face visible through the clear plastic. "Look familiar?"

Jonah gasped, wiping away a tear. "Any chance I can have it back?"

"I'll see what I can do. In the meantime, the DA will likely drop the brandishing charge, and you'll be free to go."

"Free," Jonah repeated. "I don't feel free. At this point, I've lost my job as a cop. I lost the man that I loved. My dignity. I blame myself for all of it. If I hadn't come to this godforsaken place, Peter might still be alive. What the hell do I do now?"

Will realized he'd been asking himself that same damn question all morning.

Will hurried out the jail's double doors and into the parking lot, spewing words over his shoulder at JB. "Let's head back to the station and catch up with Chief Flack, see if the search turned up anything more. Then, we can look for that Holt fellow. Or cross-reference the Fox files with any recent releases from Crescent Bay and—"

JB cleared his throat with authority, forcing Will to stop and look at him. "Slow down, City Boy. First things first, you need to go home and take a shower. Put on some clean clothes and run a comb through your hair. Shave those day-old whiskers. Because right now, you look worse than a street bum. No offense."

Will caught sight of himself in his truck window; he had to admit JB made a good point. Surely, a hot shower and a decent meal would set him straight. He would look like a detective, and this case would start making sense again.

"Don't worry. I'll hold down the fort till you get back."

After they parted ways, Will hauled himself into the driver's seat and autopiloted home in a stupor. He went in via the garage, hoping Cy had returned through the hole in the siding, but his food sat untouched, his bed empty.

Feeling worse than ever, Will inhaled a slice of leftover pizza, barely pausing to taste the congealed cheese and stale pepperoni.

Then, he stripped down to nothing, setting the water as hot as he could stand it.

With a towel around his waist and one foot over the tub's edge, his cell phone's ringing stopped him. The familiar number of the crime lab flashed on the screen. He couldn't let this one go to voicemail.

"Tell me you got something good."

"Well, it's not bad. Not worst case, anyway." Steve Li really knew how to sell it. "We've got no useable prints. The messages in the gold mine appear to have been applied with a brush, a rag, or a gloved finger. And the blood that you found in those mine carts doesn't belong to Thomas."

Will withstood a surge of relief, bracing himself with an arm against the wall.

"We ran a precipitin test. It's not human at all. It belongs to an animal."

"What kind of animal?" The steamed bathroom began to close in around him, sweat pricking at his pores. Yet, he felt cold.

"Hard to say. We've overnighted a sample to the forensic veterinarian in San Francisco, but it'll take time to get the results. And yes, before you ask, I told them to rush it."

Will hung up without saying goodbye. He dropped the towel to the floor and let the water pummel him.

Not Thomas's blood.

Not Thomas's blood.

Not Thomas's blood.

That's a good thing, he reminded himself. Still, he found himself dripping water onto the tile floor and heaving into the toilet, upchucking the only decent meal he'd had in twenty-four hours.

CHAPTER FIFTY-ONE

Olivia returned to the sofa, her father's secret numeric code in hand. "Dad probably figured we wouldn't know about the black light. This looks like a simple alphabet cipher."

"How *did* you know?" Emily asked. "About the black light?"

Settling in, Olivia recounted the entire story. The two black suits who had shown up at her door, demanding her father's sketchbook she'd collected from the prison. On a whim, she'd ripped out the last drawing he'd done of their life at the Double Rock, mostly because it filled her with bittersweet nostalgia and made her dad seem not so far away. But, like her sister, she'd suspected the sketch held secrets. Days later, a note had turned up in her office—from Will's brother, Ben, she'd assumed—with two words.

"The note said 'black light.' So I gave it a try. Dad's handwriting glowed in the margins."

"What did it say?" Emily bit at her bottom lip anxiously.

Olivia knew it by heart. "That the officer who escorted him to the holding cell where he died was involved in drug smuggling. That he was getting close to IDing the General and needed more time."

"More time."

They both released a weary sigh, before Olivia forced herself to buck up. If nothing else, for her sister. "Let's see what Dad wanted us to know."

For each number, she called out a corresponding letter of the alphabet that her sister recorded on a sheet of paper. "I... F... I... D... I... E—"

Em gasped. "If I die... Jeez."

"C... B... D."

"If I die, CBD."

Olivia puzzled for a moment until she understood. But her father's instructions didn't make her feel any better. Because she already had. "If I die, *see* BD. Ben Decker."

"Oh. Will's brother. You talked to Ben though, right?"

"It's okay." Olivia rubbed Emily's arm. Big sisters could smooth a bumpy ponytail or mend a loose button. Pop the head back on a favorite doll or correct algebra homework. But some things even big sisters couldn't fix. "Maybe he hoped Ben would tell us about the black light. Which he did."

"Do you think Ben knows more than what he's saying?"

"Possibly. I'm sure he's looking out for himself, too. He doesn't want a target on his back any more than Dad did." She gave her sister a pointed look. "And I don't want a target on yours. You need to steer clear of Nick."

With a groan, Emily shrugged off her hand and slumped off the sofa. "You can't leave it alone, can you? It's not about Dad or a target on my back. You just don't want me to figure anything out on my own. About Dad. About Nick. You want me to be a little girl forever. That way everyone can think you're the capable big sister and I'm helpless without you."

"That's not true, and you know it." But Olivia's protest carried no weight. It flattened like a blade of grass beneath Emily's stony anger.

"You haven't even asked me if I'm interested in Nick. You just assume I'm the same boy-crazy teenager I was years ago. But I'm twenty-five years old, and I can run my life just fine on my own."

Emily disappeared inside her room, banging the door behind her. When she flung it open a minute later, teary-eyed and red-faced, Olivia gaped at the bag in her hand. "Where are you going?"

Slinging it over her shoulder, Emily silenced her with a stake to the heart. "It's none of your business."

*

After Emily stormed out, Olivia retrieved her laptop, searching for a distraction. Truthfully, she knew Em felt heartbroken, wishing their father's last message had firmly pointed a finger at his killer. Or at least had been longer than nine letters. Seeing her own longing mirrored in her sister's eyes, Olivia realized how desperate she'd become in her hunt for answers. So desperate, she'd skirted the prison rules and done a favor for cold-blooded Javier Mendez. A favor that wouldn't be without consequence. Though it ached, she knew she had to be okay with not knowing. It had to be enough that her father died doing the right thing. For once, he'd stood up on the side of the good guys.

As she mindlessly scrolled down the screen, perusing Hannah's notes about various reject clients, Olivia thought, too, of Thomas. Of his stuffed toy flung to the dirt in the middle of the woods. Of the message scrawled in blood on the wall. *Ten X.* With the entire Fox family missing or dead, who was it meant for?

CHAPTER FIFTY-TWO

Will splashed his freshly shaven face with cold water and wiped the steam from the mirror, comforted to find he still bore a vague resemblance to Detective Will Decker. Even with his swollen eye and dark circles and crippling self-doubt. He swiped the razor once more under his chin, cleaning up a missed spot of stubble.

"Shit."

The razor dropped into the sink as blood seeped from the nick in his chin. Will wiped it, blotting the cut with a tissue. Hoping the damn thing would stop, he left a small piece sticking to the wound as he dressed. Black slacks, light blue button-down—his standard detective uniform. Before leaving, he fastened his badge to his belt, right next to his gun holster. Today, he felt the weight of it, the heft of expectation, like never before. Four people, dead. A little boy, missing. Will at the center of it all, trying to make sense of the unimaginable.

He exited the house through the garage to take one more look for Cy. He scanned the periphery of the basement and poked around in all Cy's favorite hiding places—behind the tool chest, inside a bucket where Will stored his boxing gear, atop the highest, dustiest shelf. He called out for the cat, disturbed by how worried he sounded. He'd told JB Cy did his own thing, but that wasn't entirely true. At first, Cy had led the life of a bachelor tomcat, ghosting Will whenever he felt like it. But, the last couple of months, he had solidified his commitment to domestication, spending most nights asleep at Will's feet.

That damn cat should be the last thing on his mind. Still, Will couldn't help himself. As he prepared to slip out beneath the garage door, he took a last glance over his shoulder. His mouth hung slightly open as he gaped at the box in the corner. It hit him like a rogue wave, threatening to knock his feet from beneath him. For the second time that day, bile rose up in Will's throat. He'd been dead right about that message scrawled in blood. It had been meant for him.

Will fired off a message to JB, letting him know he would see him at the station just as soon as he spoke to Olivia. His skin still crawling, Will knocked on her front door. He heard the definitive click of the deadbolt before Olivia's face appeared. Worry clouded her bright green eyes, tugged at the corners of her mouth. She ushered him inside the living room, and, for a moment, he pulled her close on the sofa, hoping that the soft, warm scent of her would calm his nerves.

"What's wrong?" he asked her, trying not to sound panicked.

"Emily and I had an argument. She stormed out of here thirty minutes ago and won't answer my texts." Olivia noticed the book in his hand. "What's that? Why do you—"

He laid the book out in front of her on the coffee table, open to the twisted dedication Drake had intended for him. "'What you did to me will be done to you ten times over.' I think Drake Devere is involved in this somehow."

The subtle crease between her eyebrows sank his heart. She didn't believe him. "Drake is *what*?"

"Drake's exact words to me are written in blood in the mine."

Olivia studied the dedication again. Her face softened in a way he couldn't stand. Like she pitied him. "I'm not saying you're wrong, but…"

"But what?"

"Don't you think you're getting a little ahead of yourself? Why would Drake murder an entire family? Why would he kidnap a little boy? It's not his MO. Besides, he's been in the wind since December."

"It's about *me*. About what I did to him." Will drew her eye to the faded scar between his thumb and forefinger, the raised flesh white and waxy. "I killed Drake's girlfriend, Isabella."

"You *what*?"

"I convinced her to give up evidence on Drake. We knew he'd killed those girls, but we couldn't prove it. Everything we had was circumstantial. So, I bought her one too many drinks at the bar and begged for her help. I promised her we wouldn't pursue the death penalty. I threatened to charge her with obstruction, told her she'd be responsible if any other women died. I'm not proud of it, but I'd probably do it again it if meant putting Drake behind bars."

"How did she end up... *dead*?"

In the long pause that followed, Will wallowed knee-deep in his shame. "After we arrested Drake, Isabella started to feel guilty. She said I coerced her into giving evidence, but nobody bought it. She even tried to reconcile with Drake, but he refused to see her. Then, she found out I lied to her about the death penalty. One night after work, she attacked me and my partner with a knife outside the station, slashed us both. She had him on the ground, with the knife raised, and I shot her."

"You had no choice."

Will raised his shoulders in a sad shrug. "That's not entirely true. By the time it came to that, I'd made a lot of choices. Bad ones."

"So had she."

"I should've known better. I swore an oath to serve and protect, not to manipulate and deceive."

"You did the best you could, Deck. You picked the lesser of two evils. Anyone would have done the same."

Dismayed, he leaned back against the sofa and sighed, as if he'd heard it all before. "It doesn't always feel that way. Especially when I had to explain myself to the Torro family. No father wants to hear that shooting their little girl was justified."

She leaned with him, their shoulders touching. Knees too.

"Drake has been biding his time, and now he's back to get his revenge." Will reached for the book again. It felt heavy as a millstone in his shaky hands. Olivia stopped him, wrapping her fingers around his.

"Have you had a chance to take a nap? To eat?" she asked. "Your hands are shaking. And you've got…" She plucked the piece of tissue from the nick on his chin. "You cut yourself."

Will wrested his hand from hers, staring at the knife scar between his thumb and forefinger. "So it's just a coincidence then? Cy suddenly disappearing. The message written in animal blood. The noise from the garage the other night. He's probably been watching me. You too."

"Oh, Deck. Don't take this the wrong way, but you sound a little paranoid. What about that case file I emailed you? The Holts? Surely, we can come up with a better suspect than Drake."

Stunned, he nodded vacantly, as if he'd suddenly changed his mind. "You're right. I'm running on no sleep and too much caffeine. I lost it there for a minute. Thanks for setting me straight."

Olivia frowned at him, her concern apparent. But he ducked his head to avoid her eyes. She'd see right through him.

"I better get back to the station. Before JB solves this whole thing without me." Will had never counted on her doubting him, not after he'd spilled his guts, and he realized he had no clue what to do next. But Drake's message had made it clear. He would stop at nothing to make Will pay for the past. And the price—he finally dropped his gaze to meet Olivia's—was way too steep.

CHAPTER FIFTY-THREE

Will found JB at his cubicle hunched over the phone. *Sergeant Kingsley*, he mouthed, cupping his hand over the receiver. Then, he tapped the speaker button, filling the station with the sergeant's baritone. The perfect tenor for his doomsday message.

"...The dogs lost the scent at the Earl River. No way a boy of his age and size could cross safely on his own, and his aunt says he can't swim. I reckon our perp dumped him in the water. We may have a floater on our hands. We've got officers combing the banks downstream and a slew of volunteers searching the shallows. I'll let you know what turns up."

As he hung up the phone, JB grimaced while Will shook his head in disgust. No way Drake would end his game of cat and mouse with a body washed ashore. That wasn't his style. Drake would keep Thomas alive as long as he could. All the better to stay one step ahead. To manipulate the pursuit. To steer Will right where he wanted him.

"You two." Chief Flack materialized at her door, her face a map of all that had gone wrong. Deep grooves of worry lined her forehead, eyes sunk like craters in the furrowed earth. "My office. Now."

Like men walking to the guillotine, Will and JB marched on leaden legs, neither eager for the dressing-down that seemed promised to them.

"What's she upset about?" Will whispered.

"Probably your fault, if we're taking bets."

Will didn't doubt it. He'd been off his game since day one of this case. The worst part, he'd been outmaneuvered by Drake Devere again. It twisted his gut to admit it, but he had to consider the possibility his feelings for Olivia were a distraction he couldn't afford. It still ached that she didn't believe him.

Tails between their legs, they took their usual seats across from Chief Flack's desk, right in the line of fire, and prepared for a missile strike.

"Gentlemen, what is my job title?"

So, worse than a missile then. A loaded question.

"Chief of Police," JB answered, without a trace of irony. "And a damn good one, I might add."

"You're absolutely right, Benson. So, why am I the last to know that Pedro Mendez was released from custody this afternoon? Last I heard, we had a confession on a quadruple homicide."

"No argument here, Chief. That was Decker's decision."

Will rolled his eyes at his traitorous partner. "A decision you agreed with. Look, Chief, Mendez's confession was total BS. His sister, Gabriella, confirmed it. He was just trying to impress his big brother and earn street cred with Los Diabolitos."

"I see. So, what you're telling me is we're back to square one. Four dead victims and one missing little boy. That we have no suspects. Zero. Zilch."

"Nada?" JB suggested, before shrinking in his chair at Chief Flack's withering look.

"Actually…"

"Yes, Detective Decker?" Her sharp tone did nothing to calm Will's trepidation, as he readied a bomb for dropping. "Is there something I should know?"

"Well, we're not entirely without a suspect."

Chief Flack raised her eyebrows, her expression eerily calm. Not unlike the landscape of Hiroshima from the bird's eye view of a B-29 bomber.

"I have reason to suspect Drake Devere may be involved."

"What the hell?" JB eyed him as if he'd sprouted a second head. To the chief, he added, "For the record, I have no idea what he's talking about. This is the first I've heard of it."

Chief Flack blinked back at them both, shock settling on her face. "For a second I thought you said 'Drake Devere.'"

"Fire in the hole," JB muttered under his breath.

Will watched the moment her confusion turned to disbelief. Her disbelief to thinly veiled indignation. She sat back, fuming. "Somebody better explain this to me. *Now.*"

"Thomas is just a pawn in his twisted game. This is all about me. The messages in the mine—*ten times.* Ten times over. Drake is trying to take from me like I took from him. Killing the Foxes and kidnapping Thomas is just the start."

JB side-eyed him, before letting out a low whistle. "I'm no Doctor Rockwell, but somebody's a little grandiose."

Reluctantly, Will gestured to the computer on the chief's desk, shame crawling beneath his skin. A flush worked its way up his neck to his freshly shaven face. "Do me a favor, Chief. Type Will Decker and Isabella Torro into the search bar. You'll see I'm not crazy."

Will waited for the results to populate the screen, for the *San Francisco Post* article to load. The headline burned into his brain long ago, along with the events of that day. *Woman Dead in Officer Involved Shooting Outside SFPD Embarcadero Station.*

As JB read over Chief Flack's shoulder, his mouth hung open. "Are you kidding me, City Boy? You shot *Mrs.* Vulture?"

Eyes fixed on the screen, the chief remained expressionless, which unnerved Will even more. He'd rather she curse or yell or throw her keyboard.

"Drake has been communicating with me ever since I put him away. Once a year on the anniversary of his arrest, even after he escaped. I should've told you both sooner. I had no idea he'd take it this far."

In the pin-drop quiet, Chief Flack stared ahead flatly, apparently still shell-shocked. Will kept talking, hoping to bring her back and win her over.

"I'd say we have a golden opportunity here, Chief. To catch our fugitive and put him back behind bars where he belongs."

"What exactly would you recommend we do next, Decker?"

JB drew in a breath through his teeth, a soft noise of trepidation, but it didn't slow Will down. "We need to put out a BOLO on Drake. Probably alert the media. He's out for blood this time. He'll sacrifice anybody who stands in the way of his revenge against me."

Will had barreled ahead straight into the brick wall otherwise known as Chief Flack. He knew it the moment she rose from her chair, indignation still coloring her cheeks, and glared down at JB from across her desk. "Has your partner lost his goddamned mind?"

Smartly, JB avoided her eyes, which were now laser-focused on Will.

"I know you went through the wringer when Drake escaped. Hell, so did I. But a psychopath with a personal vendetta? Where's the evidence? This isn't Drake Devere's MO. He doesn't set fires. He doesn't kill men. And he sure as hell doesn't kidnap kids. Who else knows about your suspicions?"

"Only the two of you." Will lowered his voice, added, "And Olivia Rockwell."

"And what did Doctor Rockwell think?"

Will swallowed hard. "She agrees with you. She thinks I'm paranoid. That I need to take a closer look at one of Fox's client files."

"Damn right you're paranoid. No one else finds out about this. Understood?"

"But—" Another hiss from JB, and Will fell silent, appeasing her with a quick nod.

"Until you have proof that Devere is involved, I don't want to hear another word about it. We don't need another media circus. We don't need more egg on our faces. And we certainly don't need our failures plastered all over SFTV, our tale of woe narrated by that high-heeled windbag reporter, Heather Hoffman. With yours truly taking the brunt of it all."

JB's brow furrowed quizzically. "No offense, Chief. But as pep talks go, that was a bit of a downer. We need some direction here. We've got a missing kid and four dead bodies."

"*Direction*? You need direction?"

Will winced. A mental duck and cover.

"Here's a direction for you. Out!" Chief Flack speared the air with her finger, pointing at the door. "Get off your asses. Find the kid. Arrest the *real* killer. And try not to screw it the hell up."

The chief picked up steam as she wagged her finger at them until finally she boiled over, unleashing a string of expletives before she collapsed back into her chair, spent.

JB reached the door first, leaving Will alone on the battlefield, wondering if his partner had strategically chosen the seat closest to the exit. Will scrambled out behind him before the chief found her second wind.

"I'd say that went well." JB plopped into his desk chair, looking satisfied with himself.

"*Well*? Have you been doubling up on your blood pressure meds again?"

"C'mon, City Boy. We both know Chief Flack is tougher than a boiled owl."

From the cubicles opposite them, Jessie raised her head and grimaced. *A boiled owl?* she mouthed to Will as he flumped into his seat.

JB leaned in conspiratorially. "That there was a lesson in distraction straight out of Sun Tzu's *Art of War*. Confuse the enemy. Create a diversion, so you get out unscathed. And by the way, you're welcome."

"One thing's for sure, JB. You can confuse with the best of them."

"You bet your ass I can." He smacked his desk with gusto. "Now, how the hell are we going to find Devere?"

Will took a deep breath, not wanting to admit how helpless he felt. At least JB had his back. "So, you believe me then?"

"Nah. Not really. But then, it's not the craziest thing I've ever heard. My second ex-wife, Lydia, used to carry a disposable camera in her bra just in case the aliens abducted her."

"Thanks for the vote of confidence."

Jessie cleared her throat, covering a laugh, and motioned them over. "Take a look at this report that patrol sent over for investigation. It happened this morning near the Airbnb where Thomas and his aunt were staying."

Will read over her shoulder, his intuition giving him a firm kick in the ass.

FOG HARBOR POLICE DEPARTMENT
POLICE REPORT

REPORTING PARTY: DOUGLAS JESSUP, DVM
ADDRESS: WHISKERS AND TAILS VETERINARY CLINIC,
39 PINE GROVE RD, FOG HARBOR
DATE: JULY 8
INVESTIGATING OFFICER: SCOTT GREEN
INCIDENT TYPE: BREAKING AND ENTERING

NARRATIVE:

AT 7:00 A.M. ON JULY 8, DR. DOUGLAS JESSUP CONTACTED
POLICE REGARDING A POSSIBLE BURGLARY AT THE
WHISKERS AND TAILS VETERINARY CLINIC.

ON THE ABOVE DATE, I WAS ON UNIFORMED DUTY IN A
MARKED PATROL CAR, ASSIGNED TO WEST FOG HARBOR,
WHEN I RECEIVED AN ECC BROADCAST RELATED TO A
POSSIBLE BURGLARY IN PROGRESS.

UPON MY ARRIVAL, I WAS CONTACTED BY THE CALLER,
DR. JESSUP, WHO MET ME AT THE FRONT ENTRANCE OF THE
BUSINESS. DR. JESSUP REPORTED THAT HE HAD FOUND
MINOR DAMAGE TO THE BACK DOOR WHEN HE ARRIVED
AT WORK THAT MORNING. FEARING HIS BUSINESS HAD
BEEN BURGLARIZED, HE CONTACTED POLICE AND WAITED
OUTSIDE.

I ENTERED THE PREMISES AND CONDUCTED A SEARCH FOR THE POSSIBLE SUSPECT(S) WITH NEGATIVE RESULTS. I CONFIRMED THAT THE LOCKING MECHANISM ON THE BACK DOOR HAD BEEN TAMPERED WITH. DR. JESSUP INFORMED ME THAT THE CLINIC DOES NOT HAVE VIDEO SURVEILLANCE.

CHAPTER FIFTY-FOUR

Will surveyed the crowded Whiskers and Tails waiting room, while JB side-eyed the corgi to his right. Tongue lolling, the dog trotted over and took a long, wet lick of JB's dress shoe, before aggressively sniffing his pants leg. "Sheesh. At least buy me dinner first."

"I'm so sorry, sir." The dog's middle-aged owner grinned apologetically, tugging at the leash. "Wilson has a shoe fetish. The stinkier, the better. Not that yours smell badly, of course."

JB offered Wilson a hearty scratch behind the ears. "My wife agrees, little buddy. She tells me I should own stock in Odor Eaters."

As the dog went in for another taste, Dr. Jessup appeared in the doorway, a monogrammed pet carrier in hand. After delivering a yowling Mr. Whiskers to his owner, the vet ushered them inside. His white coat, a perfect match for his snow-white hair.

"Detectives, thank you for coming."

Will followed the doctor through the halls of the clinic and into his office. JB trailed behind, pausing to encourage a basset hound with a plastic cone around his head. When he'd caught up to them, Dr. Jessup asked, "How's my favorite dachshund, Princess? Has she been sticking with her diet?"

Fighting off a laugh, Will raised his eyebrows at JB. He felt certain bagels were not on Princess's diet. Even the wheat ones JB despised.

"To the letter. Just like her dad." JB patted his belly.

"And how's that scrappy feline of yours, Detective Decker?"

Will moved aside a *Reserved for the Cat* throw pillow and took a seat on the chair opposite Dr. Jessup. "Missing, actually."

"Oh dear."

"I don't suppose anyone brought in a one-eyed orange tabby in the last day or two?"

"Not that I've heard. But I can put a flier up in the office if you'd like. I hope he has a collar."

Will nodded, trying to keep himself focused. It had been easier to compartmentalize in San Francisco. When he'd been a pariah with a broken engagement and no real friends to speak of. When he'd been branded a snitch and a traitor by the very department where he'd taken his oath. Now, he had friends and a cat with a shiny new name tag. A woman who'd captured his heart.

"We're here about the burglary," JB said, breaking the silence. "There's a chance it might be connected to a homicide we're working. Can you tell us more about what happened?"

"Well, like I told Officer Green, it's the darnedest thing. I lock the place up myself every night. In twenty-five years, I've never had a break-in. But yesterday, I left early and all hell broke loose. My granddaughter had a swim meet, and I didn't want to miss it. So, my vet tech, Lauren, agreed to close up shop for me. When I arrived this morning, I parked in the back like I always do. First thing, I noticed the lock sticking a bit when I tried to get in. The frame had some damage, too. Like someone forced it open. Naturally, I called you folks. The locksmith's due out at five to repair the damage and install a deadbolt. I'm even contemplating one of those new-fangled security cameras."

"Would you show us the back door?" Will asked. "We may want to send our techs over to dust for prints."

"Of course." Dr. Jessup led the way past the kennel to a nondescript door that opened to the staff parking lot and the forest beyond. Though Whiskers and Tails abutted the same redwood grove where Thomas had gone missing, the trees looked different here, their branches regal in the dappled light from the late-afternoon sun. A stark contrast to the crooked fingers that had clawed at Will's back on the trek to the mine.

The door itself appeared exactly as the doctor had described. The frame splintered menacingly around the lips of the lock.

"Pried open," Will suggested to his partner. "Maybe a crowbar?"

JB surveyed the damage. "Sure looks that way."

"Did you want to see the fridge too?"

"The fridge?" Will felt a prickle at the back of his neck, skirting the fine line between curious and dreading. "Was something missing?"

Dr. Jessup stepped across the threshold and into the parking lot, closing the marred door behind them. His usually sunny demeanor darkened. "I'd rather the staff not hear this. It would trouble them greatly."

"Now you've got me spooked, Doc." JB patted him on the shoulder. "It can't be that bad."

"After Officer Green left, I did a quick walk-through of the clinic. I didn't notice anything missing. Even the chow chow puppy that we neutered for Mrs. Delacroix. Those little guys can fetch up to three thousand dollars. No pun intended."

"Three *what*? For a *what*?" JB's mouth gaped. "It cost me four bucks for gas money to drive out to Brookings and back to get Princess. *Free to a good home.*"

"I always say the wet kisses come standard no matter how much you pay." Dr. Jessup gave a half-hearted chuckle before he kicked a small pebble across the lot. It bounced and skittered, coming to a stop beneath the doctor's pickup truck. "Around noon, we had a trauma case come in. A Lab named Susie hit by a car off Highway 187. In the middle of surgery prep, that's when I realized."

"Realized what?" Will asked.

Dr. Jessup raised his head from the pavement. Beneath the still water of his kind brown eyes, fear darted like an eel. It made Will nervous. "Five pints of whole feline blood were missing from the medical fridge."

After they'd sent an uneasy Dr. Jessup back inside to tend to his patients, JB regarded Will with the same face he'd pulled when he'd eaten his first sugar-free doughnut. Unadulterated disgust.

"Feline blood?" he repeated. "What the hell would anybody want with—?"

Will cocked his head at his partner, watching the truth of it take shape. "Looks like we may have found the source of our animal blood."

"Whoever did this is one sick puppy."

"No doubt about that." Will tamped down his palpable relief. At least there was a chance the blood hadn't come from his own feline, and he could hold out hope for Cy's safe return. "We'll have to get the techs down here to look for fingerprints."

"How far is Whiskers and Tails from the Airbnb?" JB asked.

Will typed the address into the mapping application on his phone, raising his eyebrows at the answer. "Jessie was right. It's about a quarter mile. Probably closer if you cut through the grove."

"Bingo. I'll bet the perp's holed up here somewhere," JB said. "These guys always operate from a home base. Maybe an abandoned cabin or… What's wrong?"

JB had spotted Will's worry, rolling in like the fog.

"You know what else is near Pine Grove Road?" Will fought off a shiver, imagining her there. The surrounding woods, dense enough to disappear in. "Olivia's house."

"What would the guy want with Olivia?" It took JB half a second to realize. "Damn. You really do think Drake Devere is in on this."

But Will had already pulled out his cell, scrolling through his contacts until he found the number for Officer Bulldog Bullock. That guy was always up for overtime. "Give me a second to make a phone call."

CHAPTER FIFTY-FIVE

Olivia peered out her front window at the police car parked in her driveway, thick-jowled Officer Bullock seated at the wheel. "Unbelievable," she muttered under her breath.

When she'd gone out to talk to Bullock a few minutes ago, he'd gruffly informed her Detective Decker had sent him there to keep an eye out. Though it seemed he'd rather be literally anywhere else, he'd rudely refused to leave—*No can do, Doc. Decker's orders*—and worst of all, she couldn't reach Deck to give him a piece of her mind. His phone rang once, then went to voicemail, and she kept deleting the texts she composed, judging them all too harsh. At least Em had finally texted. Three words meant to wound but still better than radio silence. *Staying at Nick's.*

Olivia tried to take a nap. To watch television. To organize her sock drawer. But her thoughts kept floating away like an untethered balloon. Finally, she busied herself in the kitchen, preparing dinner for Officer Bullock. She knew nothing would tick him off more than a little kindness. Maybe, if she got lucky, she'd even run him off simply by offering.

She started a pot of water boiling for spaghetti, chopped tomatoes for the sauce, and drenched a few dinner rolls in garlic and butter, sliding them into the warm oven. Though she'd never been a fan of Bulldog Bullock, and rarely had time for cooking, it served its purpose now, keeping her occupied. Even so, while she stirred the pot of noodles, her mind drifted again to Deck and his paranoia. To the Foxes, and little Thomas out there alone.

After the profiling work Olivia had done for the FBI, she knew the stats all too well. Many kidnapped children died within the first three hours; most within the first two days. The more time that passed, the less likely Thomas would be found alive.

The more she thought, the more she wondered. Could Drake have killed the Foxes? Kidnapped Thomas? The more she wondered, the more certain she felt she'd been right. Drake didn't set fires. He'd raped and killed women. Five of them, to be exact. All lured to their deaths in the foggy mist of Muir Woods.

The sizzling of the water as it boiled over onto the stovetop jolted her back to the kitchen. So much for a distraction. She cleaned the mess, drained and sauced the pasta, and arranged the table for two.

The drone of talk radio wafted from the window of Officer Bullock's patrol car. He frowned at Olivia as she approached, grumbling under his breath.

"Supposed to be my night off… relegated to babysitting duty."

Olivia bit her tongue and smiled, not giving him the satisfaction of acting like said baby. "Would you like to come inside for dinner? I made you a plate."

His jaw tensed in surprise, accentuating his underbite. "I'm on duty, remember? Detective Decker's orders."

"Cops have to eat too. Surely, Detective Decker would understand." By now, she felt desperate for the company. The house was far too quiet without Emily there, and in the solitude her worries multiplied like gremlins. "Do you like spaghetti?"

Amid his grousing, Officer Bullock mumbled something that sounded like a yes. He huffed his way out of the car and followed her up the driveway toward the house.

"I'm sorry this ruined your plans for the evening. It's really unnecessary, but I do appreciate you looking out for me."

He shrugged, his expression softening. "It's poker night down at the Lion's Head."

Olivia knew the place but only by its reputation. It was one of a few hole-in-the-wall casinos that had opened years ago on the Yurok reservation about fifteen miles outside of Fog Harbor. One of her inmate patients had been a regular there before he'd wound up so far in debt he robbed a string of convenience stores.

Officer Bullock entered the kitchen and sat at the table, taking a whiff of the plate she'd set for him, piled high with spaghetti and garlic bread. "Smells delicious."

"Hold the compliments until after you've tasted it. I'm no Julia Child."

"Well, I guarantee it's better than the canned soup I packed in my thermos." He twirled the first helping of spaghetti and took a messy bite. Olivia did the same, though she hardly felt hungry. "You know, I thought Detective Decker was pulling my chain when he called. Drake Devere back in town? It sounds pretty far-fetched. Devere's crazy as a loon, but he's no dummy."

Olivia nodded, taking another well-timed bite. She felt bad for Bullock, relegated here on his night off with the wild prospect of a serial killer lurking in the shadows.

"Then, I figured, so what if Decker's delusional? It's still a solid ten hours of overtime." Bullock dipped a hunk of bread in the tomato sauce and popped it in his mouth. "Easiest money I ever earned."

Bullock ignored the raise of Olivia's eyebrows and continued talking. "Didn't you help interview that missing boy?"

For a grumpy old man, he sure had a lot to say, and his words affected her more than she cared to admit, stirring up the swarm of bees in the pit of her stomach.

"Thomas. Yes, I did. And I watched you administer the lineup."

"He must've been a better witness than I gave him credit for if the sicko came back to finish the job." Bullock wiped a smear of sauce onto his napkin. The red stain, faintly nauseating. "I hate to say it, but the kid's bound to be long dead by now."

*

After dinner, Officer Bullock accepted Olivia's offer of a cup of coffee. They sat together in companionable silence while night fell around them.

"So, are you any good at poker?" she asked.

"Terrible. I've given that damn place so much of my hard-earned money they call me a high roller." Olivia tried not to stare. She'd never seen Bulldog Bullock crack a smile, much less a chuckle. "But since my wife died a few years back, it passes the time."

"I'm sorry. I didn't realize." Olivia decided she'd misjudged him, mistaking his gruff demeanor for meanness when really it concealed an ache.

"Cindy would've hated it. She always insisted that gambling was the worst of all the sins. The gambling man has no chance of remaining honorable, she'd say. Taking money without earning it. And now look at me. I've even earned the lion's paw."

"Lion's paw? What's that?"

Bullock reached into his pocket and laid a small token on the table. The unusual shade of iridescent green caught her eye. "The casinos hand out these tourmaline tokens to their best patrons. Each casino's token looks a little different. It gets you the VIP treatment. Complimentary food and liquor. Plus, a seat at the high rollers' table on poker night."

"How many do they give?"

Bullock shrugged. "I'm sure there's plenty of sorry suckers like me. Why do you ask?"

Olivia grabbed her phone, searching for a list of the casinos on the reservation. She scanned the names, hoping her hunch would pay off.

Lion's Head.

Lucky Elk.

Ruby Tempest.

And finally, the Golden Steed. Its name made it the most likely choice.

"I found something like it in the Foxes' pool. We think the killer may have dropped it."

He studied the picture, his frown deepening. "Looks like Cindy was right," he said. "Your killer was a sinner just like me."

After Bullock returned to his patrol car, patting his full belly, Olivia raced to her cell phone, dialing the Golden Steed.

"Good evening." The woman's tone, warm as melted butter, oozed the kind of agreeableness Olivia had hoped for. "It's always your lucky day at the Golden Steed. How can I help you?"

"I'm interested in your VIP token. I've been told all the casinos have them."

"You mean the happy horseshoe?"

"The happy horseshoe." Olivia's voice caught in her throat. It had looked anything but, sunk to the bottom of the Ocean's Song ash-filled pool. "That's the one. It's tourmaline, I assume."

"Yes, ma'am. All the casino tokens are made on the reservation and distributed to our most esteemed guests."

"How do I find out if a friend is on the list?"

Olivia heard the woman talking to someone else, her words muffled, as if she'd covered the receiver with her hand. When she returned, she sounded all business.

"I'm sorry, ma'am. Our Happy Horseshoe VIP list is proprietary and confidential. However, I'd be glad to help you with something else. Reservations at the restaurant, perhaps? We have an all-you-can-eat—"

Olivia hung up, hurrying to the bedroom to retrieve her laptop. She sat on the edge of the bed, breathless, and scrolled through Fox's client files once more. This time she went straight to the Holt case. It had already caught her eye, of course, with its striking similarities to the Fox murders, but now she felt thoroughly convinced. Because when he'd been interviewed by police, the family's only surviving member, Dwayne Holt, had told them, "I should've been at home, but I was out doing the devil's work. I went gambling."

Desperate to get her hands on that VIP list, Olivia composed an email to an unlikely ally, hoping he would help.

CHAPTER FIFTY-SIX

Like a gloved hand, darkness descended on Fog Harbor, smothering the last slivers of light beneath the horizon. Will trudged through the thick grass, his flashlight trained on a dilapidated deer stand on the outskirts of the redwood grove. One of several potential hideouts he and JB had searched that afternoon and into the evening, looking for the sicko who had taken Thomas.

A makeshift ladder led to the stand's door four feet off the ground. Its windows were so thick with grime, Will couldn't see through them. Couldn't tell who or what might be concealed inside.

Approaching the ladder with caution, Will directed JB around to the back of the stand. He took the first step on the rung, hoping the wood wouldn't give way. When he'd reached the entrance, he withdrew his gun, tapping the barrel against the door.

"Fog Harbor Police. Show yourself."

His command went unanswered, bleeding into the thick of the trees, just as it had at the last three spots they'd visited. But Will knew better than to relax. Not until he'd flung open the door and scanned the cobwebbed stand floor to ceiling with his flashlight.

"Nothing," he called down to JB. "No signs of life."

"Not even a rabid raccoon," JB answered, rounding the side of the structure.

Will backed down the ladder, feeling defeated. As they trekked back toward civilization, his cell phone buzzed. He wondered how long he'd been without a signal.

"Will Decker, Homicide."

"Decker, it's Sergeant Kingsley. I've been trying to reach you." The urgency in the sergeant's voice perked Will up again. He raised his brows at JB excitedly. "Our search of the river came up empty. But we just got a call from dispatch. A tipster says he spotted a little boy wandering in the ditch near the exit for Crescent Bay State Prison. Units are en route now."

Will started jogging, motioning JB to follow. "We'll meet you there."

Will steered the Crown Vic into the ditch, parking near the road sign. PRISON AREA: DO NOT PICK UP HITCHHIKERS. A fleet of patrol cars had already arrived, their flashing lights illuminating the blacktop in eerie shades of blue and red.

JB spotted Sergeant Kingsley on the periphery of the chaos.

"What do we have?" Will asked, as they approached.

The sergeant pointed to the fence line that abutted the ditch. A half mile from where they stood, the floodlights and barbed wire of the prison warned off intruders. "The caller said he saw a boy matching Thomas's description walking near the fence line."

Will stared out into nothing. "Any sign of him?"

"Nothing so far. But feel free to take a look."

After they'd walked the fence line and back, Will turned around, ready for another go. JB shook his head. "It's a waste of time, City Boy. The kid's not here. My bet is on a long-haul trucker, up all night and seeing things in the shadows."

Will couldn't shake a shadow of his own. Unease had clung to him from the moment he'd arrived here, a stone's throw from the prison Drake had once called home.

They walked back, weaving through the patrol cars, until they found Sergeant Kingsley. Will stood next to him, looking out at the officers combing the grass. "Know anything about the tipster?"

"He didn't give his name. We tried to follow up but dispatch couldn't trace the number."

Will turned to JB, finding a familiar wariness in his eyes. "You still betting on a trucker, partner?"

"Hey!" One of the female officers shouted up at them from the ditch, holding something in her gloved hand. "I got something. It was hidden in the grass."

Stumbling down the embankment, Will's legs turned to lead the moment he saw it. The gray collar, the little silver charm he'd had engraved.

Cyclops
If lost return to Will Decker, Fog Harbor Police Department

Will leaned against the hood of the Crown Vic trying to get his mind right. After they'd bagged up the collar, he fled back to the car before he lost it. Drake had led him here, with the promise of rescuing Thomas, knowing it would be the collar they'd find. He felt like a puppet on a string controlled by an unseen hand.

"You alright?" JB put a solid hand on his shoulder, grounding Will's thoughts. "Cy's a tough little bugger. You said it yourself. Who knows how that thing ended up here?"

It hit Will then like a sudden wave, sweeping his feet from beneath him. A realization. Drake had put him in this exact spot, distracted, for a reason. "We need to check on—"

Inside the car, the radio came to life. "Officer needs assistance at 117 Seawood Lane."

"Shit." Will tossed JB the keys and slid into the passenger seat. "Isn't that Olivia's address?"

"Yeah." Will's heart raced ahead of him at breakneck speed, a runaway train hurtling straight off a cliff. "Get us there, quick."

CHAPTER FIFTY-SEVEN

The rattling of bones juddered Olivia awake. She lay still in the dark, holding her breath, until the sound came again. Not an unearthed skeleton after all, but her cell phone vibrating against the cherrywood nightstand. A text from her little sister had arrived.

I'm sorry about earlier. I was just bummed about Dad. I really thought that message would say... something.

The phone's bright screen claimed it was only nine forty-five. Officer Bullock had been parked outside for just a few hours. But Olivia's brain felt waterlogged. The quiet around her as deep as the ocean. Even the crickets and the whippoorwills outside her window had fallen silent. Only the thud of her heartbeat echoed in her ears.

Me too. On both counts.

After sending her reply, Olivia silenced her cell so it wouldn't disturb her again. Closed her eyes, opened them. Turned to one side, then the other. It was useless. No matter how many sheep she counted, she couldn't stop thinking of the Holt family and the tourmaline horseshoe.

Restless, Olivia tossed off the covers and returned to her laptop, reading Dwayne Holt's words again and again, wondering why his guilt-ridden admission had burrowed itself into her brain and what to do about it. She padded down the hallway through the living room, gulped down a glass of water in the kitchen, and watched a tiny spider scurry across the floor to its home beneath the fridge. Finally, she made her way to the front door and raised herself on tiptoe to peer through the small window at the top.

At first, she thought she might be dreaming. The porchlight cast the entire scene in a strange golden glow, and the world around her seemed to stop, poised like a roller coaster at the top of the lift hill, waiting for the dizzying fall.

The patrol car remained at the end of the driveway. Its headlamps off. Its front window, dark. The driver's door stood open. Officer Bullock was gone.

Olivia scanned the yard, the faint hint of the road barely visible in the distance. When she spotted a silhouette, the fine hair on her arms stood on end. The shadow flitted at the edges of her vision, where the light barely reached, and disappeared again.

Then came another sound. She strained to hear it above the white noise of her own panic. It twisted her gut and wrenched her heart. A child's crying.

Olivia didn't have much time. She rushed into the bedroom and secured her mother's revolver beneath the waistband of her sleeping shorts. Tugged on her sneakers and hurried to the front door, where she stopped again, checking the window once more before she slipped into the cool night air.

She stood on the porch, listening to the symphony of summer. Usually comforting, the sounds unnerved her now. The crickets shrieking. An owl hooting its warning. The occasional howl of a coyote. Unpredictable, they sent her eyes darting into the dark smudges between the trees. Somewhere, close by, the child cried again.

The muffled whimpers called her toward the back of the house, where a dirt path led into the woods and to the Earl River. Her running trail, she knew it like the back of her hand, and she jogged toward the sound, trying to keep her breath steady while her vision adjusted to the darkness.

She strained to see the path ahead, cursing herself for leaving her flashlight behind. The air seemed impossibly still—not even a breeze—and she'd already begun to sweat. Fear seeped from her pores, dampening the back of her T-shirt. Still, she sprinted faster, propelling herself recklessly down the trail, uncertain whether danger lay ahead or behind or all around her.

Suddenly, her foot caught the edge of something large and warm, and she went down hard. Her wrist made a sickening snapping sound as she braced her fall against it. A jolt of pain shot up her arm, and she bit her cheek to keep from howling. If not for the child's plaintive wails, she would've laid there. Instead, she hauled herself up and gaped at Officer Bullock's body, the unnatural angle of his neck. Suppressing a scream, she held her arm like a broken wing against her as she ran.

When she reached the redwoods, Olivia froze. Hiccuping sobs of terror, Thomas stood near the bank of the river, dangerously close to its deep waters. As she started toward him, Olivia heard sirens in the distance, and for a moment, she felt relieved. Judging by the sound, they'd already made the turn off Pine Grove Road toward the house.

"It's going to be okay," she called to him. "You're safe now."

When Thomas pointed, unspeaking, into the shadows, Olivia stared in horror. Because she knew then who had killed the Foxes. She also knew she'd lied. Thomas wasn't safe at all, and neither was she.

CHAPTER FIFTY-EIGHT

JB made a hard left from Pine Grove Road onto Seawood Lane, spitting out gravel as he revved through the turn. At least five patrol cars trailed them down the dark road, lights and sirens blaring.

"Can't you go any faster?" Will gritted his teeth, clenched his fists. Anything to keep himself from throwing open the door and running the rest of the way. He desperately needed to lay eyes on Olivia.

"Maybe if I had a hovercraft." The car jolted forward as JB punched the accelerator, the seat belt tightening across Will's chest. "Did you try her cell again?"

Will dialed for a third time and listened to the incessant ringing, hanging up before the call went to voicemail. He tossed his cell into the center console in disgust. "Still not answering. Something's wrong, man. I know it."

JB pushed the Crown Vic to its limits, the forest whipping by in a blur out the window until Olivia's driveway came into view. Her Buick parked in front of Bullock's patrol car. Emily's rental, gone.

Will cracked the door before the vehicle came to a complete stop. His feet hit the ground running, hurtling him in the direction of the frantic shrieking at the back of the house.

"Olivia!" Will called out, as he swept his flashlight across the trees. When his beam landed on the body of Officer Bullock, he stopped short. Tamping down his panic, he called over his shoulder, "Check on Bulldog and secure the house!"

The yelling stopped suddenly, but Will kept running, trying not to think too much. About Bullock lying in the grass; his neck twisted unnaturally. About the frightened voice that sounded exactly like Olivia's, cut off mid-scream. About the twisted man who waited for him. He felt certain of it now.

By the time Will reached the Earl River, he only heard the remaining sirens, as they turned onto Seawood Lane. As if a hole in the earth had opened and swallowed Olivia whole. The absolute stillness, the moonlit calm, disturbed him even more. He readied his Glock as he scanned the woods across the water, but the all-knowing trees kept their secrets close.

"There!" JB pointed downriver. "The kid!"

In the gleam of JB's flashlight, Will spotted a small hand above the dark water. It grasped a fistful of air before it disappeared again.

Will left his gun and flashlight on the shore and dove in without thinking, the unexpected shock of the cold water propelling him forward. Despite the summer drought, his feet barely touched the bottom, and he felt the tug of the river pulling him toward the ocean. He searched, until he spotted Thomas again, his head popping up like a turtle's. The boy took a gasping breath, before the water sucked him back down.

Will swam toward Thomas, grabbing for him beneath the surface. He caught the boy's leg but it escaped his grasp, his skin slippery as a fish, and they floated further downstream. Will felt his own limbs tiring, his arms heavy as they thrashed through the water.

Finally, Will's fingers found Thomas's slim wrist. He latched onto the boy and didn't let go, scooping his limp body from the cold river. As he feared, Thomas's lips had turned a purple-blue, his face as white as the moon.

Grabbing onto an exposed tree root protruding from the muddy bank, Will anchored himself, while JB and the other officers helped to haul Thomas onto dry land.

Will followed, hoisting himself up with the last bit of strength he had. He collapsed on the dirt path, shivering. It took effort to turn his head to find Thomas lying in the grass.

One of the patrol officers knelt beside the boy, placing his fingers on Thomas's neck. "I've got a faint pulse," he said, and he began breathing into his mouth. After a few rescue breaths, water bubbled up from Thomas's lips, and he started to cough. A good sign, Will thought, wondering how long he had been in the water. Any more than a few minutes, the odds of a full recovery were slim.

"You okay, partner?" JB hovered above him, offering his hand. Over his shoulder, the sky draped like a black curtain, a shroud.

Will stared upward, lightheaded with the certainty Olivia was in danger and that flat on his back and soaking wet was exactly where Drake had wanted him.

Taking JB's hand, he picked himself up off the ground, retrieved his gun and flashlight from the bank, and wrung the water from his button-down. "Bullock?"

JB shook his head, the answer in his eyes.

"I heard Olivia scream. She's in trouble."

Just then, Jessie emerged from the back door, jogging in their direction. "There's no sign of an intruder. No indications of forced entry."

"And her sister?"

"Only one of the beds looked slept in. I assume it was Olivia's. Her computer and phone are in the bedroom, but they're password-protected."

"Take them back to the office. If we can't get access, we'll have computer forensics take a look. And call Thomas's Aunt Nora. Let her know he's on his way to Fog Harbor General."

The arriving paramedics rushed past them to Thomas's aid, cutting away his clothing and drying his slight frame, before wrapping him in a thick blanket. Will watched them through a haze of unreality, until they carted Thomas to the ambulance.

Another medic approached Will, placing a foil blanket around his shoulders. "We should probably take a look at you," she said. "You'll want to change out of those clothes ASAP. We don't want you getting hypothermia."

Will stared deep into the forest beyond the river, where the moonlight didn't reach. Sergeant Kingsley's search team had already dispersed, combing the redwoods for signs of life. Will imagined Olivia out there, Drake looming like a shadow man beside her.

"She's right, City Boy. They've already started looking for Olivia."

It took everything in him to nod. He'd be of no use anyway in his waterlogged dress shoes and soaking wet pants. "Give me ten minutes to find some dry gear. I'm not going anywhere."

CHAPTER FIFTY-NINE

In the back of an ambulance, Will stripped off his wet shirt, pulling on the Fog Harbor PD tee and sweatpants he'd borrowed from patrol. Then, he took off his dress shoes and turned them upside down, emptying out the river water. Discarded his socks. After drying the shoes with a towel, he put them back on, rendering them squishy but passable.

He found Chet and JB crouched by Bullock's lifeless body. He had few visible injuries, but the strange position of his head told Will all he needed to know. Broken neck.

JB frowned up at him. "What's this?"

Will felt certain he didn't want to see it, whatever it was. He wanted to be back in the lighthouse, warm and dry, with his arms around Olivia. He leaned in, following the beam of Chet's flashlight. A small object glinted beneath Bullock's hip.

JB moved aside, allowing him a closer look. Lying in the weeds that had sprung up on the dirt path, a tourmaline token winked back at him, in the shape of a paw.

"Looks similar in shape and color to the horseshoe Olivia found in the pool at Ocean's Song." JB plucked it from the grass with a gloved hand, turning it over in his palm. "What do you make of it?"

Olivia would've had a theory, a hunch. A fresh take on the evidence. All Will could muster: "I have no idea."

"You don't think Bulldog had something to do with the Fox murders, do you? I mean, the guy is about as approachable as a porcupine but I can't see him offing an entire family."

"He sat right across from Thomas when he administered the lineup, so I'd say it's pretty unlikely. But, at this point…" He threw up his hands. "Nothing would surprise me."

From up ahead, near the riverbank, Will heard Jessie call out, "Hey, Decker, Benson, there's a gun here."

Will and JB hurried along the path to find her hunched in the grass, examining the old snub-nosed revolver that Will recognized on sight. "That belongs to Olivia."

"How did it get out here, so far off the trail?" Jessie wondered.

JB shrugged. "The perp probably disarmed her somehow. Maybe he used the boy as a lure."

Guilt took root in Will's heart, sprouting like a poisonous weed. He spun away, fast-walking back toward the house, ignoring JB's footsteps behind him.

"Slow down, City Boy. Heart condition over here. Remember?"

Will paused in the glow of the porchlight but didn't turn around. "I'm gonna take a look inside. Maybe the officers missed something. I have to find Emily, too. She and Olivia had a fight this afternoon, and she must've stayed somewhere else. She needs to know what happened."

"What will you tell her?"

In his mind, Will heard Olivia's scream, brutal as a knife's blade. "The truth."

With most of Fog Harbor PD searching the woods for Olivia and her captor, Will found solace alone in her bedroom. He sat in front of the window looking out to the forest, cradling her desk phone against his ear. On most nights it would've been an idyllic view, with the moonlight shining through the trees. But tonight, listening to Emily's tears and the questions he couldn't answer, the whole scene took on a ghastly appearance. Like something out of a horror film.

"I promise we'll find her. *I'll* find her."

"We had a stupid fight. I went to Nick's just to tick her off." Emily choked back a sob, then gathered herself, sniffling. "I should've been there."

"It's a blessing you weren't."

"Are you sure it's Drake who took her? She was looking at Peter Fox's client files earlier. Maybe she found something in there."

Will replayed the last few days—the intruder in the garage, Cy gone missing, a message written in blood—lamenting all the signs he'd missed. "It's him. I'm positive."

"What can I do to help?"

"Do you know the password for her phone or laptop?"

"Um, she usually used our mom's birthdate for her cell. March 3, 1963. Three, three, six, three. You should try that."

Will grabbed a pen from Olivia's desk drawer and jotted the numbers on his hand. He felt so scattered he'd be hard pressed to remember his own passwords. "Otherwise, I want you to stay put. If anything happened to you, Olivia would never forgive me. This whole mess is already my fault."

"Your fault? *How?* Drake was obsessed with my sister. You know that. This is all part of some sick fantasy of his."

"I think it goes beyond that, Emily. I took someone from Drake. Now he's repaying the favor. The fact that it's Olivia I care about is just icing on Devere's cake."

"Surely he wouldn't risk his freedom for revenge."

Will stared out the window, watching the searchers' flashlights appear and disappear in the tree cover. "One thing I've learned about Drake is to never underestimate how far he'll go to get what he wants. Or how many people he'll take down with him."

A soft knock at the door interrupted him. After Will assured Emily he'd call her as soon as he had more information, he hung up the phone and took a deep breath meant to expel his demons.

"Come in."

JB cracked the door. "I thought I'd find you in here. There's news from the hospital."

Will couldn't remember the last time he'd prayed. He'd stopped talking to God after his mom disappeared, though his dad had forced him and his brothers to show their faces in church every Sunday. Poor Captain Henry Decker and his three motherless boys. But now, thinking of Thomas, Will wondered why he'd stopped.

"Thomas is recovering in the ICU at Fog Harbor General. He's going to be okay."

"Do you think he'll be able to tell us anything about what happened to him?"

"Only one way to find out."

CHAPTER SIXTY

While JB drove them downtown to the hospital to see Thomas, Will made two phone calls. First, to Dr. Lucy's emergency number. She reluctantly agreed to meet them at Fog Harbor General in thirty minutes. Though she hadn't been much help before, Will knew he was way out of his depth interviewing a kid who had been through hell and back. JB had the bedside manner of a cantankerous rhino. Without Dr. Lucy, they'd never manage to get past Nora and the ICU doc.

Next, Will called Jessie back at the station, where she'd returned with Olivia's devices. "I've got the passcode to Olivia's cell," he told her, putting the call on speaker.

After he'd recited the numbers, Jessie released a breath. "We're in."

"Check recent activity. Incoming and outgoing calls. Texts. Web searches."

"Whoa. Slow down. Give me a sec."

Will paused for a moment, his heart pinballing in his chest. "Anything?"

"*Hmm.* Interesting."

"You're killing me here."

JB raised his brows at Will, making a *calm the heck down* gesture with his free hand.

"Alright. She's got the Fox files open to the Holt case. And her last Internet search was for that casino on the Yurok reservation. The Golden Steed. Graham and I helped the tribal police with an auto theft out there last month. The phone number matches the one she dialed. It looks like she spoke to them this evening for about three minutes."

"Any calls after that?"

In the silence, Will white-knuckled the phone, suppressing a primal scream. "Jessie?"

"Three," she said finally. "To you."

JB squeezed the Crown Vic into the first available spot in the parking lot. "You want to talk about it?"

Will shook his head but unleashed anyway, smacking the dash with his palm. "If we hadn't been in the middle of nowhere hunting for Devere, I would've had a cell signal. If I'd had a signal, I wouldn't have missed her calls. I'd know why the hell she was looking up the Golden Steed, and maybe—"

"I know what you need." Reaching across Will's lap, JB popped the glove box. "Emergency Twinkie stash. That'll fix you right up."

Will snapped the glove box shut, nearly clamping JB's hand inside. "Can't you just be serious for one goddamned minute? Olivia is missing."

"I know that." JB hung his head, avoiding Will's glare, and already Will felt guilty for barking at him. He knew his partner meant well.

"You're not supposed to be eating those things anyway."

JB cracked the door, muttering under his breath, "Exactly why I offered them to *you*."

Dr. Lucy met them outside the automatic doors, looking less than pleased. She'd abandoned her put-together professional attire for a coffee-stained T-shirt and jeans. Her bobbed hair askew, dark circles under her red-framed glasses, she gave the impression of a woman who'd gone through her own personal Armageddon.

"Rough day for you too?" JB asked, cutting his eyes at Will.

"Well, let's see. I came back from a couple sick days to two no-shows, three tantrums, and a waiting room full of unhappy parents. My last client had a meltdown and chucked a plastic dinosaur at my head."

"I hope you put the little bastard in timeout."

An aggrieved Dr. Lucy deadpanned, "That was his mother."

"Sheesh."

"So, I went home and had a glass of wine or three. Took a bubble bath. Lost myself in a Lifetime movie. Just when I'm starting to relax, the phone rang, and here I am."

"I'm sorry," Will said. He wondered if she'd even noticed his mismatched clothing, his damp hair. The offensive chorking noise coming from his dress shoes every time he stepped. "I wouldn't have called if it wasn't important."

"It always is, Detective."

The hospital assaulted Will's senses. The antiseptic odor. The harsh fluorescent lights. The constant and urgent sounds of sickness—beeps and alarms, distant moans. It all made Will want to run the other way. He felt sick that Thomas had ended up here. Even sicker that Olivia had vanished.

When the elevator opened to the ICU, Will spotted Nora at the nurses' desk. Her eyes wide, she hurried toward them, wrapping Will in a desperate hug, trapping his arms at his sides.

"Thank you," she murmured through her tears. "They told me you went in after him. You saved my nephew's life. You're a hero."

Will certainly didn't feel like one. But at least he'd done one thing right. "How is Thomas?" he asked, after Nora had released him.

Before she could answer, the doctor approached from down the hallway, a grave look on his already stern face. "Thomas is incredibly lucky to be alive. We're treating him for mild hypoxia and hypothermia, but his vitals are good and his lungs look clear. He's tired and hoarse. Even a minute or two longer in the water, we would be having a very different conversation."

"Can we see him?" Will asked, waving Dr. Lucy over. He hoped she could hide her resentment long enough to convince the doctor of her expertise. "We need him to identify the man who took him. It's critical."

"As I mentioned, he's very lethargic. He may have some trouble talking. He's been through a lot tonight. I'm sure it can wait till morning. We don't want to retraumatize him."

Dr. Lucy smoothed her hair, cleared her throat. "I will have you know that I am a licensed child psychologist. I have twenty years of experience treating the children of Fog Harbor. I think I know a thing or two about retraumatization. It can only help Thomas to talk about what happened to him."

Will piled on. "With all due respect, Doc, it can't wait until morning. We have a dangerous perpetrator at large and a missing woman. Thomas might be able to help us find them."

"It's okay with me," Nora added, slipping Thomas's toy soldier, Ranger Rob, into Will's hand. "Thomas trusts Detective Decker."

"I suppose a few minutes should be fine. But if he shows any signs of distress…"

Dr. Lucy gave a sage nod. "I'm on it."

Like a baby bird fallen from its nest, Thomas looked small and breakable, with his eyes half-opened and a heavy cover draped over his body. JB agreed he would wait outside, while Will accompanied Dr. Lucy behind the curtain to Thomas's bedside. They didn't want to overwhelm him with too many faces, too many questions.

"Remember me?" Dr. Lucy asked, hopeful.

Thomas barely shrugged, glancing past her to Will. His eyes fixed on the army man in Will's hand.

"Hey, buddy. How ya feelin'?" Will stepped forward and produced Ranger Rob, setting him atop the bed's railing. "This guy has been looking for you."

A faint smile of recognition that quickly faded to gray.

"Dr. Lucy is going to ask you some questions about what happened. Ranger Rob and I will be right here if you need us."

When the psychologist approached, Thomas ducked beneath the covers, slowly peeking out at her. This wasn't going to be easy.

"I know it's hard to talk right now. But, it's really important for you to tell me everything you can remember since you were asleep at the cabin with your aunt Nora. A lot has happened since then, and the police need your help."

Beneath the blankets, Thomas shivered. "Is Woofie okay? I tried to save him."

"Woofie is just fine," Will reassured him, hoping they could salvage the stuffed toy from the evidence room once it had been processed.

"I had a bad dream and I thought Daddy was calling me from the woods. I heard him through the window. That's when I saw Woofie. But the bad man got me before me and Woofie could run away."

"What happened tonight? At the river?" Will couldn't contain himself any longer. He had to know. "Did you see Doctor Rockwell?"

Thomas gave a small nod. "She said I would be safe and she would take my place. But the bad man threw me in the water anyway."

Dr. Lucy produced the old photograph of Drake Devere the nurse had printed for them at their request. It came straight from USA News Online. She held it out for Thomas to see. "Do you recognize this person? Is he the bad man?"

Thomas stared at the picture for a moment, his eyes wide. Then he turned away, refusing to look again.

"Is he the one who hurt you and your family?"

Thomas ducked back beneath the covers, prompting a frustrated head shake from Dr. Lucy. She glanced over her shoulder at Will. "Your presence is making him uncomfortable, Detective. It's too much pressure. Give me a few minutes alone with him. I'll get to the bottom of this."

With no dinosaurs to throw himself, Will simply glared at her and offered up the plastic army man to Thomas. "Would it help if Ranger Rob looked with you?"

Though Thomas didn't answer, he poked his head out, his blue eyes dull but alert. Will placed Ranger Rob atop the covers, as Dr. Lucy ushered him out.

"Trust me. I'm a professional."

Relegated behind the curtain, Will listened with JB and Nora as Dr. Lucy whipped out her trusty crayons and construction paper, cajoling Thomas to draw a picture for her. "Show me where you were today."

In the long silence that followed, Will heard the swishing of a marker across the page.

"Can you tell me about this drawing?" Dr. Lucy asked.

No answer.

"If you tell me, I might have a Superman sticker in my bag for you."

Will gritted his teeth. But then, "It's a house made of dirt and rocks and inside there's a train and a lake and..." Thomas ran out of breath, taking a heartbreaking gasp. "Outside I saw a Christmas tree."

"A house made of dirt? Hmm... and what's this here?"

"Can I have my sticker now?"

From behind them, Will heard approaching footsteps. The doctor appeared, a disapproving frown darkening his face.

"Our patient needs his rest, Detective."

Will swept back the curtain. He'd heard about enough anyway. "Alright, Thomas. You and Ranger Rob get some rest. We'll be back to see you tomorrow."

Thomas eyed the army man Dr. Lucy had moved to his bedside table. His little voice, no louder than a whisper, stopped Will cold. "Did you catch the bad man yet?"

After they'd all been escorted back to the nurses' station, leaving Nora to say goodnight, Dr. Lucy offered her two cents and the rudimentary drawing Thomas had made. "I wouldn't put too much faith in anything that little boy says. A house made of dirt? A train? A lake? A Christmas tree, for God's sake. At this point, it's probably all confabulation."

"Confabu-*who*?" JB asked.

"For all we know, the bad man is a figment of Thomas's imagination."

Will paced the floor, huffing out a breath. "I need to go back in there, show him the photo again. Doctor Lucy's right. He must be confused. Drake *is* the bad man. He must be."

JB headed for the door and down the hallway, motioning for Will to follow. Once they were out of earshot, he said, "There's no way you're getting back in there tonight. And I wouldn't trust that shrink to judge Princess's mental health, much less Thomas's."

"You heard him though, right? 'Did you catch the bad man yet?'"

"I heard him."

"And? He looked right at that picture of Devere. He didn't say a word but he looked terrified."

JB shrugged. "Hell if I know. Ranger Rob, Woofie, the Bad Man. This is exactly why I didn't have kids."

"Alright. Well, what now? We can't just do nothing."

JB checked his watch. "It's late. But, you know what? The Golden Steed is open all night. You wait here. I'll get rid of the *professional.*"

Will leaned against the wall, forcing himself to take a breath. He realized then that he still had Thomas's drawing gripped in his hand as if his life depended on it, the edge crinkled in his fist. He held it out and studied the squiggles beneath the bright hospital lights.

Feeling lightheaded, Will rubbed his eyes. He wondered if Olivia had been right. Maybe he was paranoid, seeing things. Maybe he'd lost his damn mind. Because he swore that inside the dirt house, in bright red crayon, Thomas had scribbled 10 X.

CHAPTER SIXTY-ONE

Backdropped by the towering redwoods, the Golden Steed rose up from the earth like a glittering mirage. Its garish bright lights out of place in the wilderness; its glitzy façade outshining the moon. A couple of tribal police cars flanked the ends of the parking lot, the colorful Yurok symbol on the door panel a stark reminder of exactly how far Will's badge would go on Native American land. *Nowhere*. He had to depend on kindness instead.

"Let me do the talking," Will told JB, as they made their way through the crowded lot toward the entrance. "We'll have to charm our way inside."

"Shouldn't I take the lead then?" JB caught himself mid-chuckle, quickly sobering.

"Sorry about before," Will said. "I shouldn't have snapped at you. You were only trying to cheer me up."

JB shrugged. "I should've known better. Twinkies are a special kind of magic. But they can't fix everything."

The tribal policeman stationed at the door held them up, his piercing brown eyes fixed on their gun holsters and badges. His own badge identified him as Officer Jim Featherstone. But the hard edge beneath his thin smile was more stone than feather. Beyond him, Will could see into the belly of the casino, where the seasons never changed, the sun never set.

"Can I help you fellas?"

"Detectives Decker and Benson. We're here on official police business about a missing woman."

While JB bit back a laugh, Will cursed himself for sounding so formal. Turns out, he couldn't do charming. Not right now. On no sleep. With Olivia in danger.

"Oh, really? Because I think we both know Fog Harbor PD's jurisdiction doesn't apply on the Rez."

"C'mon, man. We need to talk to the front desk staff about a phone call they received a few hours ago. It won't take more than five minutes." Sensing his resistance, Will doubled down. "It's extremely important, and you're impeding our investigation."

"No can do. And it's *Officer*."

Will shot a pleading glance at JB. He'd never live this one down.

"Officer Featherstone, you will have to excuse my partner. He's a city slicker still new to the area. He doesn't understand the way things work." JB lowered his voice, cupping his hand to his mouth and standing on tiptoe to reach Featherstone's ear. "To be honest, he's a slow learner. Tries my patience every damn day."

"I know the type."

"Of course you do. You're the first line of defense out here. That's a position of trust. You're doing a mighty fine job. Would you be so kind as to escort us to the front desk so we can get out of your hair?"

Shooting daggers at Will, Featherstone reluctantly accompanied them inside. "Five minutes. No funny business."

The clamor of the casino, the relentless throbbing of the crowd, pushed Will forward. He blinked his tired eyes against the assault of the bright lights. Winced every time the bells sounded, announcing that another sucker had finally won a round. Already, he needed an aspirin.

"Jeez," JB muttered. "If that's your idea of charm, no wonder you're still single."

When they reached the front desk, Officer Featherstone spoke for them, catching the heavily lined eye of the bottle-blonde clerk, Geena. She smacked her gum and winked at him. "Hey, Feather."

Featherstone poked out his chest and cleared his throat, eyeing Will and JB like a pair of cockroaches that had skittered across his shoe. "These two cops want to know if some lady called here a while ago asking questions."

Geena looked equally offended, chewing her gum with new-found intensity. "You do realize this is the front desk. Everyone who calls is asking about something. Got a name?"

"Doctor Olivia Rockwell," JB answered. "She might've been a little—"

"Pushy. Demanding even." Will didn't think Olivia would mind. Desperate times and all.

"Hmph." Featherstone cocked his head at Geena. "Imagine that."

"Don't recall any doctors," she said. "Or any Olivias. It might help if you knew the reason for her call."

Will took a breath, barely holding it together. "That's why we're here. We don't know what it was about. But it might have been unusual. Do you remember anything like that?"

The desk phone rang, and Geena answered it, putting the caller on hold before she turned back to him and shrugged. "I don't. But my shift started at midnight, so... if you don't mind." She flashed a pointed glance at the blinking red phone light. "Good evening. It's always your lucky day at the Golden Steed. How can I help you?"

"Guess you boys got your answer." Officer Featherstone seemed pleased. "Time to hit the road."

Will glanced over his shoulder, waiting for JB's reply. He hoped his partner could sweet-talk the officer into letting them take a look around.

JB rubbed his hands together eagerly, his eyes bright. "You mind if I give her one quick pull just for old times' sake?"

"Excuse me?"

"The slots. C'mon, Featherstone. Don't you ever let your hair down?"

*

Will stood near the row of slots, listening to the hollow clink of coins on metal as JB fed quarters into the machine. Thankfully, a noisy disagreement at the high rollers' poker table had drawn the attention of Officer Featherstone. The young dealer was unable to keep the peace and was in way over her head. But Will knew it wouldn't take Featherstone long to throw a couple of drunken buffoons out on their asses.

"Eyes up and out," JB instructed, as he pulled the lever. "You're supposed to be doing detective work right now."

"*I'm* supposed to be doing detective work. What the hell are you doing?"

"I'm the decoy." JB didn't take his eyes from the spinning reel. "C'mon, Double Diamonds…"

Slumping against the side of the machine, Will released a breath. "This is a waste of time. We need to get back to Olivia's house and help with the search. It's the only thing left to do. Featherstone isn't going to be too keen on us hanging out here."

"With that attitude, I'll be feeding the one-armed bandit all night." He loaded up another quarter. "Now get out there and do what you do best. Figure shit out."

Just then, the poker table went flying, upended in the scuffle that had suddenly turned into a brawl. Stunned, Officer Featherstone struggled to get his footing as he slipped on the playing cards strewn across the floor. The moment he managed to right himself, the bigger of the two combatants reared back and prepared to put him back down with a wallop to the face.

Will wished more than anything he could turn off his sense of duty like a switch. He owed Featherstone nothing. Less than nothing. Even so, he couldn't watch the guy get pummeled.

He ran over and grabbed the patron from behind, securing his grip beneath the man's armpits. "Cool it," he growled, using his knee for leverage. "You don't want to hit a police officer."

"Feather ain't no real cop."

The universe clearly testing him, Will heard himself say, "He's got a badge and a gun. That's real enough for me."

Trying to wriggle himself free, the patron unleashed a string of curse words. Will tilted back and dropped him to the ground, holding him there until the rest of the tribal police rushed in to assist.

"We've got it from here, Detective." Officer Featherstone stood over him, red-faced. At least the poker dealer seemed grateful. She busied herself collecting the cards and chips that had scattered in the melee.

Will took his sweet time getting up. "A 'thank you' would suffice. That guy almost cleaned your clock."

"I had it under control."

"Sure you did." JB extended his hand to Will. "Just like the captain of the *Titanic*."

As Will rose to his feet, half smiling, he spotted it in the debris, partially hidden under a few remaining poker chips. He held it in his palm.

"What is this?" he asked, passing it to Featherstone.

The officer glanced at it. Gave a casual shrug before passing it to the dealer. She slipped it in her pocket. "A happy horseshoe," Featherstone said.

Puzzling, JB scratched his chin.

"It's a token we use at the casino. We hand it out to the VIPs." He pointed at the bright red exit sign, ushering them toward it. "All the casinos do it. The Lion's Head and Ruby Tempest too."

To Will, it had the ring of truth. Everyone on the police force knew Bulldog Bullock spent his off nights at the Yurok casinos. Will surmised that the tourmaline paw in Bullock's possession came courtesy of the Lion's Head. "So, that's it? Just show the token and you're in? Seems pretty low-tech."

"Not exactly. A fingerprint scan is required for confirmation of ID."

"I don't suppose you have a list of those folks? The VIPs."

"Of course we do. It's proprietary." Hands on his hips, he focused his eyes on the doors, waiting for them to get the hell out.

Will turned his attention to the dealer instead. Doe-eyed, she didn't look a day over the requisite twenty-one. "One of your tokens showed up at the scene of our murder. We think it might have belonged to law enforcement or someone pretending to be. Any of your high rollers fit that description?"

"Don't answer that, Casey." Featherstone stepped in between them, so close Will had no choice but to back down. "Most cops know they're not welcome around here. And don't even bother threatening to get a search warrant. You know as well as I do your warrant is worthless here on the Rez."

As they trekked back to the car, JB flashed the cash-out voucher he'd printed from the slot machine and hooted in celebration. "Jackpot!"

"You won fifteen dollars," Will said flatly.

"And a complimentary trip to the all-you-can-eat buffet."

"You're on a diet."

JB wiggled his brows. "They've got a salad bar."

"You hate salad."

Throwing up his hands, JB made an exasperated face at Will. "At least we found the horseshoe. You can't argue with that."

Will opened his mouth again, ready to remind his partner that the token meant nothing without the names on the VIP list. Even then, the horseshoe could've ended up with anyone, anywhere, at any time. Really, the whole trip had been a bust. Meanwhile, they'd gotten no closer to finding Olivia.

"Actually…" Will found himself smiling in spite of it all. "*I* found the horseshoe."

"Hey, Detective!" Casey loud-whispered, as she skirted in between cars, hurrying to catch up to them. "Sorry about Feather. He can be a jerk sometimes, but he means well. Rumor is that his best friend got shot by a local cop when they were teenagers. I don't know if there's any truth to it, but he gets pretty surly when Fog Harbor PD shows up."

"He sure does. Did *you* want to tell us something? Maybe help us identify our killer?"

Will pulled up a few photos on his phone, scrolling through the faces of all his known suspects, while Casey looked on. Keeping a watchful eye on the casino's front doors, she shook her head.

"No one I've seen before. But I work the VIP area most nights. And Feather's lying. There are plenty of high rollers who aren't afraid to flash a badge."

Yawning, JB pulled the Crown Vic into the station parking lot. "We should brief the chief ASAP. Let her know our perp is more than likely a cop. She's going to blow another gasket."

"I'll take care of it," Will said. "You go home and get some rest."

"City boys need sleep too, you know."

Will had been awake for nearly twenty-four hours. His eyes burned. His head ached. At that point, he could've slept in a detention camp with the CIA blasting the *Barney* theme song. "After we find Olivia. *And* arrest Devere. Then I'll sleep."

JB cut the engine and turned to Will. "That's some real hero mumbo-jumbo. If you think I'm gonna tell her you said it, you're sorely mistaken. She wouldn't be impressed anyway. She'd say you were being hard-headed and completely impractical."

Will leaned back against the seat, wishing Olivia was there to take JB's side. To tell him how stupid he was being. "Do you think she's okay?"

"Hey, that woman is a scrapper." JB's smile didn't reach his eyes. "All kidding aside, we're going to find her. I'll see you back here at 6 a.m. I won't tell anybody if you catnap for an hour or two. I know you've got a reputation to uphold."

CHAPTER SIXTY-TWO

With the moon descending in the night sky, Will met Sergeant Kingsley on the dirt path by the Earl River behind Olivia's house. Though they'd suspended the search until first light, he'd begged Kingsley for an update, forgoing the temptation of sleep a little longer. He had gone home though, gearing up in his heavy rubber boots and quick-drying cargo pants. The kind that came in handy in the wet Fog Harbor winters when the Earl River swelled to twice its size, swallowing everything in its path.

Kingsley pointed his flashlight down the trail. "Let's walk further downriver. There's a rocky low point where it's easy to get across. I want to show you something."

Will followed in silence, his tired mind playing tricks. Movement in the trees. *Just a nightingale.* Whispers from the river. *The current pushing toward the sea.* Olivia's frantic screams. *Only in his mind.*

A quarter of a mile downriver, the banks narrowed. Three large rocks formed a passageway across the flowing water.

"Be careful. It's slipperier than it looks." Sergeant Kingsley heeded his own warning, taking his time to cross to the other side. Will matched his steps, scrambling up the grassy bank and onto dry land.

"Take a look." Kingsley spotlighted the muddy area alongside them, where searchers had plunged a metal stake into the earth next to a perfect footprint. The sole of a Nike sneaker, the swoosh still visible at its center.

Will gaped at it. "Olivia wore Nikes."

"We figured as much. The dogs tracked her scent from the house to the dirt trail and across the river right here."

Sergeant Kingsley headed into the grove with Will behind him. After walking about forty paces, he stopped beneath the canopy of an ancient redwood.

"The dogs lost the scent in this area. They circled a few times but couldn't pick it up again."

Will looked around them. Nothing but ferns and dirt and the soft-barked bodies of the trees. He stared up at the nearest redwood, its branches seeming to stretch forever toward the stars. Whatever it had seen, unknowable. "There's nothing here."

Nodding, Kingsley swept his light across the forest floor. "No disturbance in the underbrush. No signs of a vehicle coming in or out. It's as if she walked right into these woods and vanished. No sign of her or anyone else."

"Thomas drew a picture at the hospital. He told the psychologist he'd been inside a house made of dirt and rocks."

"Sounds like Clawfoot."

"That's what I was thinking." Will didn't mention the less believable parts of Thomas's story. Though he figured a little boy like Thomas could have easily imagined a steam engine running down those rusty steel tracks, they certainly hadn't come across any Christmas trees.

"We'll send a team back to the entrance first thing in the morning. In the meantime, you should get some sleep. You look like hell."

"Noted." Will felt like it too. "I'm just going to look around a bit first."

"Suit yourself."

As the beam of Sergeant Kingsley's flashlight dimmed in the distance, Will clicked on his own. He stood motionless, listening. A slight breeze stirred the branches above him, sending a few of its needles fluttering down like snowflakes.

Will wished he'd been smarter. Faster. Better. Now Olivia was gone, and the blame lay squarely at his feet. He waited for a moment, summoning all the strength he had left.

Then, he yelled her name into the night sky, knowing she couldn't hear him.

CHAPTER SIXTY-THREE

Will didn't pass a single car on his drive back to the police station. An eerie fog hovered over the road, shape-shifting like a ghost as he passed through it. His mind, just as murky. He convinced himself he wanted to take another look at the horseshoe they'd discovered in the pool. Compare it to the one near Bullock's body. But really, he couldn't slow down. Couldn't stop. If he did, he'd have to admit just how hopeless he felt.

Will navigated the final turn, frowning at the familiar black truck with its oversized tires hogging three parking spots in the otherwise empty lot. It belonged to the last person on earth he wanted to lay eyes on. Cursing under his breath, Will slogged to the station door and let himself inside.

"Bauer?"

Graham sheepishly poked his head up over the divider, the desk lamp from his cubicle glowing like a homing beacon.

"What the hell are you doing here?" Will stalked toward him, newly energized by the anger zipping through his blood. He pressed a hand to the bridge of his nose, the faint ache a reminder of that asshole's handiwork.

"I heard the news about Liv, and I couldn't sleep. Besides, I could say the same about you. It's two thirty in the morning."

"Yeah. Well, you're the only one of us in a police station out on bail." Will slumped into his chair and glared at the pile of mail strewn across his keyboard.

"Did you put this here?"

Graham grunted.

"Since when are you allowed in the mailroom?"

"Since I'm relegated to desk duty." Graham held up a sheet of paper for Will to see. A bulleted list of tasks assigned by Chief Flack. "Right here. Second line from the top. Mail distribution."

"Well, you did a shitty job of it. Mail goes in a neat stack, not—" Will stopped sorting, his eyes fixed on the envelope in his hand. The small block print that spelled out his name across the front had haunted his nightmares. Because he knew the hand that penned it.

"You okay, Decker?" Graham hoisted himself from his seat, peering over the divider.

Will waved him off. His mouth dry as a bone, he ripped into the thin envelope and emptied the contents. A lone photograph.

Undeterred, Graham rounded the corner of the row of cubicles, sending Will scrambling to hide the picture in his drawer. Though he had no idea what it meant, the message on the back was clear.

> This is between you and me. Come alone—no cell phones, no trackers, no funny business—or you'll be carrying her out in a body bag. Don't take too long. If I get bored, I'll be forced to entertain myself.

"I didn't realize you cared so much about your goddamn mail. Should I tie it up with a little red bow next time?"

"Why are you still talking?"

Before Will could flip the empty envelope over, Graham spotted it on the desk. "Bad news on the test results?"

"What?"

"Come to think of it, is that why you've been so moody lately?"

"What test results?" Graham was making even less sense than usual.

"From the vet. Your cat."

Will's stomach dropped to his knees. He felt his mouth hinge open but no words came out.

"You're acting weird, man. A guy from Fog Harbor Couriers came by with a letter from Doctor Jessup's office. Said he had some test results for Cyclops and left that envelope. Something about a fatal condition."

In an instant, Will jumped out of his seat, pinning Graham against JB's desk. A picture of Tammy in her wedding dress beneath the Welcome to Las Vegas sign toppled forward. "Are you messing with me?"

The shocked whites of Graham's eyes answered for him. Will stepped back, still breathing hard.

"I need to know everything you remember about the courier."

"Not until you tell me what the hell is going on."

Will shook his head, paced to the end of the dark hall. No way he could trust Graham. Not after he'd destroyed evidence, told half-truths. Not after he'd blabbed details of every case to his ex, Heather Hoffman. But what the hell choice did he have?

"That note wasn't from the vet's office. Cyclops has been missing since yesterday. I think Drake Devere could be involved in Olivia's disappearance. Maybe he's the one who dropped off the letter."

Frowning, Graham dropped into JB's seat. Head in his hands, he leaned forward, propping his elbows on the desk. Will listened to the tick of the office clock, mocking them both.

"We can review the video surveillance from the parking lot. But I've looked at Devere's ugly mug on that WANTED poster enough times to know it wasn't him."

Will had already taken off for the IT office. "What time?" he called over his shoulder.

"Uh, I dunno. Seven thirty, maybe. The place was already pretty empty. I'd just picked up dinner for the chief at the Hickory Pit."

His heart hammering against his rib cage, Will scrolled through the footage from the station lot until he saw Graham exit his truck, carrying a large paper bag from the Pit. When he reached the door, the courier hurried toward him, dropping his bicycle on the sidewalk alongside the station. In his hand, he held the envelope.

"Told ya." Graham tapped the screen with his finger. "But we can call the courier service in the morning if you still think he's not legit."

Will couldn't do anything but stare at the man's face, cataloguing the pudgy cheeks, the bulbous nose. He'd never been more disappointed *not* to see Drake Devere.

Will hurried back to his desk, a sense of dread weighing him down like a stone in his pocket. He opened the desk drawer and removed the photograph he'd hidden there, Drake's twisted message penned on the back. In the foreground stood a tree unlike any he'd seen before. Backdropped by the forest, it looked like the ghost of a redwood, rising up tall and thin toward the sky. Its needles a shocking shade of snow white, it seemed to radiate with an unnatural glow.

"A Christmas tree," he muttered, thinking of Thomas. Will went straight to his computer, typing *white redwood* into the search bar. The first article from a website called The Tree Aficionado told him what he needed to know.

Albino redwoods, the ghosts of the forests, are extremely rare, with only fifty or so known in existence. Albino redwoods lack pigmentation, making their leaves white rather than the usual green. They are the only conifers believed to have this mutation. Because of their rarity, their locations are not often disclosed to the public. Though several of these majestic oddities can be found in Humboldt County, California, local legend has it that the largest albino redwood exists in the Clawfoot Grove in nearby Fog Harbor. But good luck finding the rare beast. After a two-day trip to the area, The Tree Aficionado returned without a single photograph of the elusive redwood.

Will flumped back in his chair, disgusted. The clock's incessant ticking like a tap on the shoulder, reminding him what was at stake.

Graham poked his head over the cubicle wall. "You still think Devere might be involved in this?"

Will didn't answer. He sat for a moment, studying the computer screen and contemplating the impossible decision that lay before him. He felt like JB, putting his last quarter in the slot machine and giving it a pull. "You said your uncle Marvin took you hunting in the grove, right? That you know it like the back of your hand?"

Graham nodded, hesitant. As if Will would find some way to use it against him.

"Ever heard of an albino redwood?"

Will followed Graham's taillights as they rumbled down the fire trail adjacent to the redwood grove. When the lights flashed red, he slowed to a stop alongside Graham's truck, and exited his own vehicle.

Graham leaned out the window. "This is as close as we can get on four wheels. You sure you don't want me to come with you?"

Against his better judgment, Will shook his head.

"At least tell me what this is all about."

"If you care about Olivia, it's better you don't know." Will peered out into the grove warily, wondering if Drake could hear him. "It's better no one knows. That includes my partner."

"Suit yourself." But Graham looked worried. He reached behind him, rummaging in the back seat, and tossed something out the window. It landed softly on the dirt trail. "If you're gonna do something stupid, at least protect yourself."

With Graham's tires kicking up dust, Will approached. Lying there in the moonlight was Graham's Kevlar vest.

CHAPTER SIXTY-FOUR

Will directed his flashlight back to the map in his hand, convinced he'd taken a wrong turn at the last marker—a rock Graham claimed resembled the face of an elephant. According to the map, he should be there by now. The albino redwood Graham called the Ghost Tree, a half mile north of Elephant Rock. But he'd been walking for at least forty-five minutes. Maybe he'd missed it. Overlooked it somehow in the low-hanging fog.

Will balled the map in his fist and threw it into the underbrush. He sat down on a rotting log, contemplating the longest night of his life. It served him right for trusting Graham.

He knew he should go back to his truck and radio for help. If he could find his truck. But he couldn't unsee Drake's warning. He felt the weight of eyes on his back, following him at every turn. He had no choice but to keep going until he couldn't.

Newly determined, Will stood up and went searching for the map he'd cast aside. He would retrace his steps back to the rock and try again. But a light wind sent the scrap of paper fluttering with Will scrambling after it.

Finally, Will pinned it with his foot, securing it in a pile of leaves. When he bent down to retrieve it, he froze. A snow-white redwood needle rested beneath his boot. He looked up, casting the beam of his flashlight skyward.

The Ghost Tree didn't stand as tall as the others. But it looked so strange, so out of place, it stopped his heart. With its needles swaying in the wind and its stark color illuminated by moonlight, it lived up to its ghoulish nickname.

Drake had brought him here, fittingly. Both of them still haunted by the ghosts of the past.

A flash of movement in Will's periphery drew his eye and brought his hand to the Glock in its holster. Like a bride's veil, the misty fog concealed his view. It coiled low around the tree trunks, sweeping silently across the forest floor.

Will tucked the map back in his pocket and took a few steps forward. Again, a gentle stirring.

He rubbed his eyes, wondering if he'd imagined it all. Hunger and sleep deprivation could make you see things that weren't there, and right now, he was running on fumes.

Then, the snap of a twig. The sound as clean and sharp as the break of a bone. He withdrew his gun, backpedaling to take cover behind the Ghost Tree.

His tired mind played tricks, sending him flashes of that day outside the station in San Francisco when he'd shot Isabella dead. Little brain hoaxes meant to keep him on high alert, his heart pounding and ready for fight or flight.

The sounds grew louder, closer. Will's heart thumped loudest of all. He could feel it throbbing beneath his jaw. Finally, his finger on the trigger, he revealed himself, ready to end whoever, whatever had come.

A deer gazed up at him, looking just as surprised as he felt. Both of them stood stock-still, eyes wide and set upon each other. When Will laughed, the deer bounded into the woods, stirring the fog as it ran.

As the mist parted, he spotted a clearing ahead. Trailing the deer's path, Will jogged toward it, trying to make sense of what he saw.

A gaping hole in the earth. A heavy mesh gate laid to the side, stamped with the words DANGER: KEEP OUT. Will shined his light down into the darkness, hoping to find the bottom, but it seemed to go on forever. A rickety metal ladder led the way to hell.

He pulled Graham's map from his pocket. Near the X he'd made to mark the Ghost Tree, he'd written: *If you reach the collapsed section of Clawfoot you've gone too far.*

Lying on his belly, Will leaned into nothing. *Gone too far.* Way too far to turn back.

Will dropped from the last rung onto the floor of the mine. Far above him, the stars dotted the small expanse of sky visible from down here. He spun in a quick circle, aiming both his gun and his flashlight. Immediately, he spotted the collapse. A beam had cracked at its center, leaving a pile of rubble blocking the passageway. Will realized then he'd found Thomas's house of dirt and rocks.

Will walked the walls, wondering if he'd lost his mind to come down here. The perfect place for an ambush, and he'd gone in willingly.

To his right, the wall was solid rock. The other side, partially covered by an old shelving unit, was similar to the one they'd seen in the other section of the mine. Unlike those shelves, these were empty save for a thick layer of dust.

When Will saw the fresh drag marks in the earth, the fingerprints on the side of the unit, he knew exactly where to look. Crouching down, he saw it. A tunnel in the rock wall, just large enough for a man to crawl through.

Will tucked his gun back in his waistband and dropped to his knees. As he stared into the narrow passageway, he questioned his own sanity, remembering the K-9 officer's warning. *One wrong move, and the whole thing comes crashing down.*

Still, Will crawled forward, his back brushing up against the dirt ceiling of the tunnel as he moved. In one hand, he held the flashlight, the beam constantly shifting as he advanced. He imagined Drake waiting for him on the other side, ready to put a bullet between his eyes.

Halfway in, his breathing grew shallow, the tunnel's walls closing tighter around him with every desperate inhale. Frantic, he started to back out. But his clumsy effort sent bits of the ceiling crumbling to dust, which only made it harder to breathe and worsened his panic.

Then, he heard the faintest of sounds. Though it seemed to come from miles away, it cut through the static in his brain and pierced straight to his heart like the sharpest blade.

"Olivia!"

CHAPTER SIXTY-FIVE

Olivia's blindfold discarded, she could see everything now. Everything she wished she couldn't, bathed in the sinister glow of a camping lantern. She shivered in the cold, her skin like gooseflesh. Her injured arm had swelled to twice its size, a dark purple bruise circling her wrist beneath the cuff that bound her. She tried to raise her hands to touch the sore spot on her forehead, but they'd been shackled to her waist and tethered to the mine cart track. Despite her best efforts, she could only lift them waist-high.

Olivia sorted through flashes of memory. Thomas's bright blue eyes wide with terror. The sickening splash when his body broke the surface. His frantic cries for help. The gun barrel pressed to her flesh, as she'd been dragged down the trail and across a low point of the river. The squelch of the mud beneath her shoe when she'd stumbled and nearly fallen. The sound of Deck's voice—a port in a storm—before she'd been silenced.

"Again." Drake Devere lorded over where she knelt. His hair, long and wild and black as his heart. He pressed the barrel of his gun against the top of her head and ripped the thick tape from her mouth. "He better hear you this time."

She screamed as loudly as she could, hoping Deck wouldn't blame her for drawing him here. For not believing him. She knew now Drake had been there all along, stalking them. Sighting them from above like a hawk circling its prey. She felt certain he'd been the one to pilfer Emily's note from the kitchen. He'd been the source of the pricked hairs on the back of her neck.

When she'd realized Drake's cat and mouse game, she'd first tried to hold back. But that had gotten her nowhere. Earned her a swift slap to the face that had left her dizzy. Then, a hand closing over her throat until she saw stars. This time, Drake seemed pleased when Deck called her name, the sound of his voice growing louder. Closer.

"It won't be long now." Keeping the gun to her head, Drake pulled the tape back across her raw mouth, but she wouldn't give him the satisfaction of wincing. She closed her eyes for a moment, imagining herself anywhere but here. As she stilled her breathing, she heard quick footsteps approach through the water, sloshing their way toward her.

Deck stepped out of the shadows and into the lantern's gleam, his gun raised. As Drake sneered, Deck's face contorted in horror. His flashlight fell to the ground, snuffed out.

"Well, well, well. I must say I'm disappointed in you, Detective. With your hero complex, I expected you hours ago. You must be getting fat and lazy here in Fog Harbor without me." Drake's eyes volleyed between the two of them. "Love will do that to you. Is that it? I do hope so. It'll make our time together a lot more fun."

Olivia waited for more footsteps. But as time stretched, long as a rubber band, she realized Deck had come alone. Surely, he had a plan?

"You said this is between you and me, Devere. So why is she still here? Why is she injured?" Deck's pained gaze moved across her body, avoiding her eyes. She wondered how bad it looked.

"What can I say? A mind like mine needs constant stimulation. I told you I'd get bored." Drake cocked his head at Olivia, petting her with his free hand. Better that than around her neck again.

"I'm here now. Do whatever you want with me. Just let her go." Deck lowered his gun, placed it on the ground, and kicked it toward Drake. "Please."

A scornful laugh scraped from Drake's throat as he fisted Olivia's hair and pulled. She bit the inside of her cheek to keep from making a sound. "No can do. Without her, you can't pay your penance. You owe me, remember? For Isabella. For my freedom. You owe me ten times over."

"You've already taken from me. You humiliated me, escaping like you did. The media thinks you outsmarted me. Hell, so does my own chief. And I know you did something to Cyclops. He's been missing since yesterday."

"Poor kitty." Drake jutted out his lower lip. "He put up quite a fight, but you deserved a special message. It was a nice touch, wasn't it? Written in the blood of something you love."

"The blood you stole from the vet's office, you mean?"

Ignoring the question, Drake turned his attention back to Olivia. From the sheath on his pants, he produced a knife. The blade winked in the light as he turned it over.

Olivia's skin crawled as he squatted behind her. He kept the gun at her temple, while he pressed the blade against her thigh. Its cold touch sent a shiver through her blood.

"Olivia hasn't done anything to you. She doesn't deserve this." Though Deck's voice rolled out smooth as parchment paper, Olivia sensed the turmoil beneath. Beads of sweat were visible on his forehead. His hands, shaky at his sides. And he still hadn't looked at her. Instead, he kept his eyes laser-focused on Drake. "And neither did the Fox family."

Drake's cackling laughter echoed down the mine shaft. "You really are a pathetic excuse for a detective. *I* didn't kill the Foxes."

Olivia watched the truth settle onto Deck's face. She tried to speak through the tape across her mouth, to tell him what she knew, what she'd realized too late. But only strangled murmurs came out.

"All you shrinks like to do is talk." Drake traced the blade along her jaw, down her neck, across her breasts. The tip of it so sharp, it made a small hole in her thin T-shirt. He leaned down to her ear, and she gagged at the sour stench of his breath. "Talk, talk, talk."

Deck cried out as he lunged forward, grabbing for Drake. But Drake anticipated his rage, jabbing the barrel of the gun against her as he pulled her out of reach, the knife in his other hand pressing against her shoulder. "Careful with that temper of yours. One wrong move, and my finger might slip. Unless you want your girlfriend's brains spattered all over you?"

Until that moment, Olivia had been certain Deck had concocted a plan to get them both the hell out of here. But now, her heart in her throat, she began to wonder if he had any plan at all.

CHAPTER SIXTY-SIX

Will had no plan. No gun either. Just his damn hero complex, as Drake had called it, that had sent him running here like a total amateur, so intent to find Olivia he hadn't thought past it. He couldn't even bring himself to meet her eyes. He'd let her down. Though the realization hit hard, so did his resolve. No way he was letting that psychopath get the best of him again.

"I've spent a lot of time thinking about this moment, Detective. I wanted it to be perfect. When I saw you two canoodling on the beach, I had the lightbulb moment I'd been dreaming about since the day you put me in handcuffs. It's beautiful in its simplicity. I think you'll agree."

Will couldn't see what lay beyond the shadows, where the steel tracks disappeared into the pitch-black. But here, in the small circle of light, hope was sparse. Only Drake, his gun pressed to Olivia's head in one hand. The glinting knife in the other.

"Get over here." Drake dropped the blade at Olivia's knees, and she flinched.

Slogging forward, Will finally let himself look at her. The bruises laced around her neck, the angry bump on her forehead. Her swollen wrist. The fire in her eyes, still flickering despite it all.

"Pick up the knife," Drake directed. "Or she eats a bullet."

Will swallowed hard, reaching for the blade's handle. He felt his world closing in. He could hardly breathe. The knife felt strange in his hand, alive and hungry.

"Here comes the fun part," Drake said, raising the hairs on Will's neck. "You have a choice. Stab Olivia, or I'll shoot her in the head. Any way you play it, you'll live the rest of your life knowing it was all your fault. However short that may be."

The brutality of Drake's words rooted him to the spot like an animal trapped in quicksand.

"We don't have all day, Detective."

Will took a tentative step toward Olivia. No way in hell he could do it. But—the gun to her temple, a madman with his finger on the trigger—how could he not?

Just then, he spotted it. Behind Drake, a light pierced the dark mine shaft, glowing with the strength of a lighthouse beacon. Will didn't dare call out, but his heart leapt at the sight.

As the man came into view, Will found himself praying again. A prayer of thanks for sending him an armed rescuer. For sending him Wade Coffman.

Wade stopped a few feet short of Drake, holding his gun at his side, with wild eyes and his Steadfast Security uniform unusually disheveled. "What's taking so long? I thought you said you could make quick work of them."

Like birds on a wire, Will's scattered thoughts assembled themselves.

Coffman had been on duty the night of July Fourth.

He'd been at the Hickory Pit when Thomas panicked and ran.

Coffman wasn't a police officer. But he sure as hell looked like one. A four-year-old wouldn't know the difference.

"What're you doing, Wade?" Will asked, eyeing his own gun with desperation. It still lay on the mine's floor a few feet out of his reach. "What have you done?"

Drake grinned at Will, his teeth sharp in the lantern's light. "Go ahead, Wade. Tell the detective exactly what you've been up to."

Wade hesitated, frowning at Drake as he stepped closer. His jaw tensed when he spotted the damage to Olivia's face, her neck. "What the hell did you do to her? This wasn't part of the plan. We were supposed to be long gone by now."

"Did I offend your delicate sensibilities?" Drake scoffed. "You shot two children in the head at point-blank range. I hardly think you have the right to judge."

Wade drew his head back like he'd been slapped. But he didn't deny it.

"You're Dwayne Holt. *The bad man*." Will needed to say it out loud, to finally put a name to the monster he'd been chasing. The monster who lurked in Thomas's nightmares. "You killed the Foxes."

"*Ding, ding, ding*," Drake taunted. "Finally, the detective gets a clue."

Will ignored him, while Wade paced the tracks of the mine shaft, his head hanging and his free fist clenched. His gun in the other, poised like a snake. Unpredictable and ready to strike.

"I used to be Dwayne Holt," he said. "But he doesn't exist anymore. He's been dead going on ten years now, ever since Tim Overton put his entire family in the ground and walked away a free man. Dwayne died that day, even if his body didn't. I'm just the bitter shell he left behind. That's why I had to kill Thomas, too. I couldn't doom him to a life like mine. Death is better than that."

"Enough talking." Drake ripped the tape from Olivia's mouth, reclaiming Deck's attention. A sob escaped from her throat. "I want to hear her scream when you do it. Now, Detective. Now or never."

CHAPTER SIXTY-SEVEN

Will raised the knife. Searched Olivia's pained eyes. Found her spirit beneath the tears, darting like quicksilver. It gave him courage. Courage to try. He'd say anything, lie if he had to.

"Thomas isn't dead, Wade. I pulled him out of the water. He's alive. And he's going to be just fine."

Wade's face reddened, tears springing to his eyes the faster he shook his head. "No, no, no. That's a lie. He drowned. I threw him in the river. I watched him go under."

"Thomas drew a picture of this place. He identified Drake in a lineup. And soon enough, he'll ID you too. You tried to kill a little boy."

"It was for his own good," Wade yowled, wiping the snot from his face.

"No, Wade. It was for *your* own good. Just like all the rest of it. You murdered a police officer tonight."

Wade's mouth dropped open. He turned to Drake. "You *killed* him? I thought we agreed you'd only knock him out."

Drake lifted one shoulder, one corner of his mouth. "I got carried away. It happens sometimes."

"You're going to prison, Wade," Will continued, feeling the tension build between them. "For a long, long time. And I won't let them put you to death. That's what you want, isn't it? No, you'll have to live out the rest of your days without your family, knowing you did the same to Thomas that Tim Overton did to you."

"But Drake will be long gone by then," Olivia added, her voice steely, despite the fear written on her face. "He doesn't do well with partners. They always end up in prison, shouldering the blame. Or dead."

"Shut up!" Drake reared back, striking Olivia's temple with the butt of the gun. It was all Will could do to hold himself back, to wait. Just as suddenly, Drake's predatory gaze shifted to Wade. "You imbecile. You had two jobs, and you mucked up both of them."

His gun trembling in his hand, Wade remained indignant. "I told you, the cat got away. It climbed up a damn tree. What was I supposed to do? I did everything else you asked. I helped get these two here, didn't I? It's not my fault you're not man enough to finish the job."

The deafening crack of gunfire—one shot, then another—sent Will to the ground. He raised his eyes, dreading what he'd find. Then, scrambled forward blindly, charging at Drake with the knife. He didn't allow himself to look again but some things can't be unseen. Like Wade writhing on the ground in the glow of his toppled lantern, clutching his stomach, the blue of his uniform darkening beneath his hand. The hole in Olivia's flesh, blood spiraling in crimson ribbons down her thigh.

The gun skittered from Drake's hand as he fell back. Will grabbed for it in a frenzy, knocking it further from them both. With Drake crawling on his belly toward it, Will plunged the knife wherever it would land but only succeeded in breaking the blade against the rocky ground. Discarding the now-useless handle, he seized hold of Drake's leg, reeling him in like a fish.

Will landed the first punch. The snap of Drake's head satisfied him in a way he would never admit out loud. Finally, after all these months, he had the bastard in his grasp. If it came to it, he would kill Drake Devere with his bare hands.

CHAPTER SIXTY-EIGHT

Olivia's thigh burned white-hot. She rolled onto her side, watching her own blood waterfall onto the tracks. Tried to push herself up but the chain snapped her back down. Next to her, Wade moaned as he staggered to his feet. He stumbled forward, clutching his gun in his hand and aiming blindly. An errant step sent Drake's lantern skittering into the rock wall. Its bulb shattered. The only remaining light, a thin glow that emanated from Wade's overturned one.

Olivia's head felt floaty, like a kite lost on the wind. Even the desperate scrabble of bodies next to her, even Wade teetering nearby, couldn't tether her to the ground. Deck's service weapon glinted in the shadows, but with blood pooling under her leg, she felt too weak to reach for it. Too weak to fight, too. She curled into a ball and covered her head with her hands as if her own flesh and bone could protect her.

One blast, then another, shook the mine. Wade took another step forward and collapsed like a felled tree, his weapon beneath him.

Olivia waited, wondering where she'd been hit. A warm wetness spread around her shoulder, but she felt no pain.

She closed her eyes and surrendered to the dark.

CHAPTER SIXTY-NINE

A bullet to the back didn't slow Will down. Neither did Drake's blood, weeping from the wound on his shoulder, nor the darkness that spilled around them the moment the lantern cracked.

Drake kept coming too, grappling with Will as he struggled to get out from under Will's grasp. In his periphery, Olivia lay unmoving and far too quiet. When Drake's foot knocked against her, she groaned softly.

Landing an elbow to Will's gut, Drake finally pushed him off. They both lay there, breathing hard and waiting for a second wind. The metallic smell of Drake's blood gave him hope; his hands were sticky with it. Drake couldn't outlast him.

Will found his feet first and put them to work, scrambling to get to the gun before Drake. Just three, two, one more step. But as he extended his hand toward it, he hit the ground hard, Drake clawing at his waist and dragging him backward. The gun, painfully out of his reach again.

Will stared up into those eyes that had haunted the worst of his nightmares. He watched Drake's fist descend like a hammer, nailing his head against the track. Stars pinpricked his vision, tiny explosions of light. It reminded him of his first night in Fog Harbor. How many stars. How impossibly bright.

CHAPTER SEVENTY

A sharp grunt roused Olivia. Her eyes barely opened. With excruciating effort, she turned her head to the side.

She wished she hadn't.

In her mind, she screamed—*Deck!*—but it came out as a whimper.

Drake knelt atop him, both of their faces bloodied. He reared back, readying another blow.

With her last bit of strength, Olivia pushed herself up. Spotted the broken handle of the knife near her feet, where Deck had discarded it. A small portion of the blade remained intact. As Drake dealt another blow, she scooted as far as the chain would allow her and reached for it. Drawing it nearer with her fingertips, she wrapped her blood-slick hand around it and swung.

The blow glanced off the side of Drake's knee, as if she'd thrown a pebble at a giant. But when his head spun toward her, his teeth bared in rage, Deck seized the opportunity, landing a flurry of punches that rendered him stunned.

Olivia could only watch, spent, while Deck pinned Drake to the ground and wrapped his hands around his neck.

She drifted in and out again, her fading mind playing tricks. The inky shadows made it impossible to tell where Drake ended and Deck began.

CHAPTER SEVENTY-ONE

Will had long imagined his hands around Drake's neck. Had imagined throttling him. But in his wildest imaginings, it had never felt like this. So raw and real the connection between them. Drake's dark eyes bulged, his breath coming in terrible gasps. Drunk on his own power, Will pressed his thumbs into the small divot at the base of Drake's throat.

It felt too right to be wrong. Too good to be bad. As Drake swatted at his forearms, Will dug in harder and leaned in close, close, closer. Until he saw his own reflection in Drake's wide eyes. His features, distorted by anger, Will hardly recognized himself. What he saw so repulsed him that he lessened the pressure on Drake's neck.

"You're just like me," Drake rasped, a satisfied smile stretching his bloodstained lips. "I knew it all along."

Decker! Stop! Will couldn't tell if the voice came from his own head or from God himself. But it cut deep, its echoes spreading through every vein of the mine, impossible to ignore. Then, a light, so bright it blinded him.

"Decker!" The voice of God sounded a lot like JB's. Looked like him, too. Covered in sweat and dirt and wielding a flashlight with Graham alongside him. "He's not worth it."

Will stared at his hands, still fixed around Drake's neck. They'd taken on a life of their own, a dark life. Will couldn't seem to stop them, couldn't pry them away.

"He doesn't deserve to live," he heard himself say.

"I know." JB put a stern hand on Will's shoulder. "But that's not your call, partner. You need to help Olivia now. Understood?"

Olivia.

Will let go, slowly straightening his fingers, which for a moment stayed locked like a bird's talons in a claw grip. He stood with urgency, surprised his trembly legs still worked, and retrieved Drake's gun, along with his own. With JB's assistance, Graham rolled a semiconscious Drake onto his stomach, securing him in cuffs.

"Him too," Will said, gesturing to the heap of Wade's body. His chest barely moving, Wade clung to life. "He's our guy. He killed the Foxes."

While JB and Graham tended to Olivia, wrapping a strip of Graham's T-shirt around the wound, Will scoured Drake's pockets for the handcuff key that would release her. Turned them inside out. Searched the ground with JB's flashlight. Came up empty.

"Looking for this, Detective?" Drake's eye barely opened. The other had swelled shut. His head lolled to the side, and he stuck out his tongue at Will, mocking. The same way he had on the day he'd escaped. A silver handcuff key rested there, winking at Will from the pink, rolled center of Drake's tongue, until it disappeared inside his mouth.

"Shit. He swallowed the handcuff key."

"What about this one?" Graham offered the cuff key from the secret pocket on his belt. As Will expected, it wasn't an exact fit. Looking at Olivia's pale face, her drooping eyes, he panicked and tried to force it, nearly breaking off the end. Frustrated, he chucked the key at the rock wall.

Drake choked out a sputtering laugh. "This isn't over, Decker." Even half-dead, Will hated the sound of him.

Dropping to his knees, Will pulled at the chain that tethered Olivia to the track.

"The cuffs can wait. What we really need to do is break this goddamned thing."

"The EMTs will have something," JB said, patting the radio affixed to his waistband. "They're on their way."

"We don't have time for that." Will turned his attention back to Olivia, trying to rouse her. She clung to him, wobbly, mumbling unintelligibly. JB stationed himself on her other side to support her. "She's already lost a lot of blood."

"Deck's right. We need to get her out of here now. Coffman too." Graham rummaged through the pockets of his khaki cargo pants, producing an old Swiss Army knife. "Found it! I knew Uncle Marvin's rescue knife would come in handy one day."

Will held his breath—and Olivia—watching Graham saw at the rusty chain with a small steel-toothed blade. After a few minutes, the metal had weakened. With JB holding the chain taut, Graham positioned the damaged link on the tracks, giving it a hard smack with the butt of his gun.

The clang of metal on metal reverberated through the mine. Graham struck again and again until the chain threw off sparks. The beams of the old mine creaked in warning, and Will knew they had to hurry. A cave-in could happen at any time, triggered by something as benign as the vibrations of their footsteps.

"You... got... shot." Olivia barely managed the words, her voice so small beneath the raucous clanging. But at least she was still alert. Will wanted her to keep talking. "Wade... shot... you."

"He did." Will tapped his chest with his free hand, giving a nod to Graham. "But I never leave home without my body armor. Not when Drake Devere's involved."

He swore he heard Olivia laugh, even if it was all breath, just before the chain split open, finally freeing her. As the approach of distant sirens beckoned from somewhere above ground, Graham pointed down the long, dark tunnel opposite of where Will had come.

"This way," he directed, positioning Wade's body so he could hoist him in a fireman's carry. "There's a ventilation shaft that lets out in the grove behind Olivia's house. JB and I found it on an old map of Clawfoot. That must be how they got her down here so fast."

JB radioed the EMTs their exact location, as he pushed Drake ahead of him along the path. Will scooped Olivia up in his arms and moved as quickly as he could, while Graham brought up the rear, Wade slumped like a sack across his shoulders.

When a plaintive creaking travelled down the mine shaft, Drake cackled. Clawfoot had mounted its final protest. Will turned back in time to watch a support beam collapse behind them. Small rocks shifted and tumbled down, sending up a cloud of dust.

Drake dug in his heels, wrestling his hands from JB. As the rocks tumbled around them, Will wondered if this had been part of his plan all along. To end them here, buried in a mass grave of wood and earth and stone.

"Leave him!" Will bellowed to JB, still holding tight to Olivia.

Graham kept trudging forward with Wade, passing them, yelling over his shoulder, "C'mon! Hurry!"

JB's eyes volleyed between Will and Drake. Between freedom and duty. Life and death. For a moment, his feet cemented to the ground, paralyzed by indecision. Then, he moved with certainty, his choice made, just as another beam gave way, filling the tunnel with rubble.

"Are we... going to... die?" Olivia asked Will.

"Not if I can help it."

Will supported a still-cuffed Olivia from behind while she climbed rung by rung up the ladder of the ventilation shaft, out of the collapsing mine, and into the grove behind her house. He recognized that same redwood stretching its branches toward the sky, realizing he'd walked right over the shaft's entrance, unknowing.

Once Olivia arrived at the top, to the waiting arms of the paramedics, Graham and JB helped hoist Wade up in a stretcher, both men following behind. Finally, Will scurried up the ladder himself, pausing to take a last look behind him at the tomb of Drake Devere.

Overwhelmed by emotion, he collapsed onto the grass, JB and Graham breathless next to him. Above them, the morning had finally dawned, impossibly blue.

CHAPTER SEVENTY-TWO

Will paced the emergency room of Fog Harbor General, waiting for word on Olivia's condition. His side ached. His head throbbed. He had cuts and contusions in places he couldn't even see, and his ears wouldn't stop ringing. But knowing those two men would never take another life made the bruised ribs and mild concussion worth it. Fire Lieutenant Hunt assured Will they'd recover Drake's body as soon as the mine had stabilized. Wade had been hemorrhaging, his blood pressure dropping dangerously low by the time he'd arrived at the hospital. The prognosis was grim.

"Shouldn't you lie down, City Boy?" From his seat near Will's bed, JB glanced up, worried. "The doc's not gonna be too happy if he sees you getting all worked up. Besides, you're giving me a fright in that hospital gown. Some things you just can't unsee."

"Why isn't Graham back by now?"

JB consulted his watch. "He's only been gone five minutes. It'll take him at least that long to make it over to the ICU. We don't even know if she's out of surgery yet."

Will sucked in a breath, overwhelmed by it all. By Wade's unmasking. By Drake's twisted game. By how close he'd come to losing it. To losing *her*. The ER doctor had rushed Olivia straight into surgery to remove the .22 caliber bullet lodged in her upper thigh. She'd already gone into shock, requiring two units of blood.

"So what happened down there?" JB asked. "Wade Coffman? I didn't see that coming."

"Me either, partner. That's not even his real name." Will flumped back on the bed, eager to talk shop. He needed his mind anywhere but here. "Olivia discovered the case in Peter's files. His client, Overton, murdered Wade's—aka Dwayne Holt's—entire family and walked free two years later. Same MO as the Fox murders. Bullet to the head and torched the place."

"Sheesh. That'll turn anybody crazy. How'd he hook up with Devere? Match.com for psychopaths?"

Will shrugged, still uncertain. But the pieces had started to come together, forming a grotesque picture he never wanted to see again. "Drake admitted he'd been watching us. I think he saw an opportunity to use Thomas as bait. A way to get us exactly where he wanted, so he could carry out his revenge. Bullock's broken neck was Drake's handiwork, and Wade confessed to throwing Thomas in the water. Thought he was doing the kid a favor."

Graham pushed through the door, carefully balancing three cups of coffee. He doled them out with a lopsided grin that reassured Will. "Olivia's damn lucky. The doc said the bullet narrowly missed the femoral artery. There was damage to the muscle tissue, and she'll need physical therapy. But she'll be okay."

Relieved, Will took a sip and laid back against the pillow, staring up at the dingy white ceiling, a kidney-shaped water stain smack dab above his head. He felt grateful for that water stain. Grateful for the sickly-green pallor of the emergency room walls. For the lukewarm coffee and his stubborn-as-an-ox partner. Even for knucklehead Graham.

"Hey, Bauer," he said, feigning annoyance. "I thought I made myself clear. You weren't supposed to come looking for me. You were supposed to keep it to yourself."

Graham spun around, his eyes narrowed. A dart poised on the tip of his tongue.

"Kidding." Will chuckled, extending his hand to Graham. He still didn't like the guy. Still thought he made a lousy cop. But he couldn't deny the obvious. "Thanks, man. You saved my life. I owe you one."

With a hint of a smirk, Graham said, "Buy me a cold one at the Pit and delete that mortifying arm-wrestling video, and we'll call it even."

Will pondered for a moment, relishing Graham's discomfort, along with the knowledge that JB had made no such promise. "Deal."

"Stop, you two. I can't take it." JB shielded his eyes. "Can you imagine Batman and the Joker grabbing a beer? Luke Skywalker and Darth Vader splitting a rack of ribs? It's unnatural."

After his discharge a few hours later, Will navigated his way to the Post Anesthesia Care Unit on the hospital's second floor. He had to lay eyes on Olivia for himself.

When the elevator doors parted, Chief Flack stood outside the recovery room.

"Didn't expect to find you here," he said, shuffling toward her. His sore ribs protested every step.

"I let you both down."

Will joined her outside the glass, both of them looking in at Olivia. With her body bruised and battered, the rise and fall of her chest was a reassurance. The steady beep of the electrocardiogram was the best sound he'd heard all day.

"We could've lost her." The chief wiped a tear from her cheek so quickly Will wondered if he'd imagined it. "We could've lost all of you down there."

"But we didn't."

"No thanks to me. I should've listened to you. I should've trusted your instincts about Devere."

Will shook his head. "Don't beat yourself up, Chief. You couldn't have known. Besides, we're in the same boat. In a million years,

I would've never guessed Wade Coffman for our killer. I thought he was one of us. You know, one of the good guys."

"What are we going to do about Bauer?" she asked. "Mayor Crawley said he'd leave it up to me, though he made his position known."

"It's your call."

"I'm asking for your input, Decker. You say the word, I'll have him removed from the force and out of our hair for good."

Will studied Olivia as she slept. It scared him how his heart had bloomed like a daisy in a sidewalk crack. He could hardly bear it. But, when she stirred, her hand moving at her side, he realized how lucky he was.

Feeling generous, he said, "Give him one more chance."

Fog Harbor Gazette

"One Murder Suspect Dead, One Severely Injured in Shootout,
Mine Collapse"

by Jeanie Turtletaub

Authorities in Fog Harbor, California, confirmed that
escaped serial killer, Drake Devere, died yesterday, when
portions of a ventilation tunnel in the long-abandoned
Clawfoot Mine collapsed. Local security guard, Wade
Coffman, was also seriously injured in the incident and has
since been charged in the murders of Peter and Hannah
Fox and their children, Dylan and Lily Fox, as well as the
attempted murder of their four-year-old son. Coffman and
Devere are believed to have kidnapped the four-year-old
victim from a vacation home early Wednesday morning
and held him captive before leaving him in the Earl River
to drown. Fortunately, police and medical personnel were
able to revive the young boy.

Devere is also suspected in the murder of veteran
Fog Harbor police officer, Robert Bullock, affectionately
known as "Bulldog" to his colleagues. Bullock served
twenty-five years as a patrol officer and leaves behind two
adult children. Also kidnapped and harmed by Coffman
and Devere was local psychologist, Olivia Rockwell,
who our sources learned had treated Devere when he
was incarcerated at Crescent Bay State Prison. Rockwell
sustained multiple injuries, including a fractured wrist, a

bruised trachea, and a gunshot wound to the leg. She is listed in stable condition.

Though the extent of Devere's involvement in the Fox murders remains unclear, Fog Harbor Chief of Police, Sheila Flack, intimated that Devere may have been motivated by his desire for revenge against investigating detective Will Decker, who originally arrested Devere on multiple counts of murder several years ago. Misty Hubble, the founder of Devere's fan club—known as Drake's Devotees—petitioned to claim his body for burial in her hometown of Devil's Rock, Oregon. However, with no living blood relatives, Devere will likely receive a pauper's burial on prison grounds in the Crescent Bay State Prison cemetery. Coffman remains in serious condition at Fog Harbor General.

The four-year-old victim was released from the hospital following treatment for hypothermia and hypoxia.

CHAPTER SEVENTY-THREE

Olivia heard her name called from a great distance. Groggy, she fought her way to the surface, struggling to open her eyes against the harsh light streaming in from the hospital window. Each time she awakened, she remembered. The bullet hole in her leg, stitched and bandaged. The cracked bone in her wrist, reset in a cast. The lump on her forehead, turned bluish black. The slits of Drake's eyes, as dark as midnight. But, she felt nothing. Only a dull throb at the back of her brain and Emily's hand in hers. The benefits of modern medicine.

"Someone is here to see you." Emily smiled down at her, trying to hide her worry. "He's been lurking for a while now."

Olivia put on a brave face, trying to nod her head, when she spotted Deck hovering, the badge on his belt catching a ray of sunlight.

"I'll be out in the hallway," Em said, with the authority of a little sister turned big. "In case you need me."

Deck pulled up a chair, positioning himself next to her bedside. His hand rested on the mattress but he didn't touch her. She wished he would.

"How are you feeling?" he asked.

"Been better." Laughing hurt her throat. She took a sip of water from the hospital mug. "You?"

"If you're alright, I'm alright."

With effort, she turned her head to look at him, taking in his stubbled face. The brown eyes she kept falling into. "I'm alright."

"Well, then."

"Any news on Cy?" she asked, hopeful.

Deck hung his head. "No sign of him. But Doctor Jessup put up a flier at the office and JB's wife posted a few around town. He may still turn up."

Olivia patted the spot next to her, inviting him closer. He looked away, his jaw tight, leaving her cold.

"Em said Drake's body was recovered."

"I confirmed it myself at the morgue. You'll never have to see him again."

Though she'd already known it, hearing it out loud brought tears of relief to her eyes. She blinked them back before they had a chance to fall. "I'm so sorry I didn't believe you. I called you paranoid."

"Yeah. I remember. But it's thanks to you I'm not dead right now, so I'll give you a pass. You really know how to wield a broken knife."

She managed a wry smile but it drooped when she spotted the unease on Deck's face.

"I wouldn't have stabbed you, you know. I would have sooner stabbed myself."

She reached for his hand and tugged him toward her, giving him no choice but to join her on the bed. He sat gingerly. Like she might break. "Sure you would have. I'd have done the same. Drake gave you an impossible choice. It was smart pitting them against each other like you did."

She slid her good hand onto his knee, giving it a gentle squeeze.

"Did you know about Wade?" he asked.

"Not until that night. It was that phrase he used—'the devil's work.' Dwayne Holt had told the cops something similar. But even then, I wasn't sure until I saw him standing there with Drake, pointing a gun at poor Thomas."

"Funny how we always manage to both get it right."

"And wrong."

"You know what that means, don't you?" Her fingers fisted the center of his shirt, crinkling the starched blue fabric. He gave in, leaning toward her.

"If I want to be right one hundred percent of the time..."

"Then you better keep me close." Already, she could feel the warmth of him, as she mustered her strength and sat up to meet his lips. Later, she could blame it on the pain meds.

He looked at her, and for a moment, he hesitated, an unspoken fear in his eyes. "I fully intend to, Doctor." His mouth on hers—careful at first, then matching her insistence—left no doubt about that.

As soon as Deck left, Emily peeked in, grinning. "*Finally*. It's about damn time you two locked lips."

"I have no idea what you're talking about."

"But your cheeks do. They're blushing." Amused with herself, Em flopped into the chair Deck had left behind. "He's one of the good guys, Liv. So is Nick, FYI. And we're just friends. He's way too old for me."

Ignoring Olivia's groan, Emily withdrew her cell phone, tapping at the screen. "Look. He sent this for you. He said it was important, so he cc'ed me on the reply. In case you weren't able to access your email in the hospital."

Olivia studied the reply from Nick Spade, private investigator. Somehow, he'd managed to get his hands on the list of the VIP patrons at the Golden Steed, all proud holders of the happy horseshoe. Three pages worth of alphabetized names that cleared her brain fog in an instant.

After forwarding the message to Deck, Olivia went straight to the Cs, until she found it: Wade Coffman.

The night of July Fourth played back on a loop in her mind. The sound of a child crying. Wade's footprints in the sand. Thomas's terrified scream as Deck leaned in to show his badge. Behind him, all along, uniformed Wade Coffman had loomed in the doorway. A very, very bad man.

CHAPTER SEVENTY-FOUR

Will sat in his truck in the police station parking lot, his mind still at the hospital with Olivia, her hand grabbing at his shirt. The rest of her body, weak but not broken. He'd thought of telling her she'd been right. They should keep it professional. That he couldn't stomach it, the possibility of her in danger again. Him, to blame. He'd thought of walking out of that room as friends. But he'd come to his senses when he'd seen all of his fears reflected in her eyes. If she could throw caution to the wind, so would he.

While he trekked across the lot, Will's phone buzzed, notifying him of an incoming email. He stopped to take a quick peek at the list Olivia had sent, confirming Wade Coffman had been a proud owner of the happy horseshoe. Damn if Olivia didn't manage to out-detective him again.

"Detective Decker!" Will turned toward the sound of his name. Thomas's aunt Nora waved to him from the sidewalk.

"We're driving back to Santa Barbara today. But I couldn't leave without telling you how grateful I am for everything. It won't bring them back, but Thomas and I can rest a little easier knowing that Coffman's behind bars." She nudged Thomas until he looked up at Will with his mother's blue eyes. "What do you say to Detective Decker?"

"Thank you." Thomas extended his hands, Ranger Rob lying in the center of his palms. "I have a present for you."

"Are you sure you want me to have this?" Will took the soldier and held it with reverence. "I know it's very special to you."

"Ranger Rob will keep you safe."

"Thanks, buddy." Will tucked the toy inside his pocket, swallowing a lump. Maybe it was his near brush with death, or seeing Olivia bruised and bandaged, but that little boy sure knew how to tug on his heartstrings. He fully intended to break Woofie out of the evidence locker later and ship him overnight to Nora's house. "I'll put him in a place of honor on my desk."

But Thomas stared past him, scrunching his face. "Is that a cat?"

Will turned to see Dr. Jessup sauntering up the sidewalk. In his hand, he held a pet carrier. The plaintive yowling coming from inside it was instantly familiar to Will.

"Just the man I was looking for." Dr. Jessup set the carrier at his feet, giving it a good-natured pat. "This big guy was using Betty Jo Bryson's garden as a litter box. Her schnauzer chased him up a tree. Luckily, she recognized him right away from the flier in the office and coaxed him down. We treated him for dehydration, but otherwise, it looks like your tomcat is no worse for wear."

Will crouched down to look inside the carrier, hope beating its wings inside his chest, stealing his breath. Cyclops blinked back, with his good eye. Will grinned stupidly, fighting back tears for the second time that morning. Damn that cat.

CHAPTER SEVENTY-FIVE

A few hours later, the head nurse at Fog Harbor General summoned him and JB back to the ICU, where Wade remained shackled to his hospital bed. He'd been touch and go for a while but had regained consciousness that afternoon, telling the staff he wanted to clear his conscience in case he didn't make it through the night. For karma's sake, Will wished him a very long life in a very small prison cell.

Wade lay entwined in a tangle of tubes and wires, but the machine beside him affirmed the steady beat of his heart. Will tried to meet his gaze, man to man, but Wade stared ahead into nothing, pale-faced and shrunken.

"We're here to take your statement, if you have one to give."

Wade closed his eyes, opened them again, lost in an in-between world. A prisoner of his own vengeance, his shackles self-made. Though Will knew Wade had to pay for his decisions, he understood how the man had arrived at such a ruinous place.

"We don't have all day, man." JB folded his arms across his chest. "Are you gonna talk or not?"

Wade clenched his fists, saying nothing, until Will stood to go.

"And if you wrong us shall we not revenge?" Wade sounded like a wounded animal, fixing Will to the spot.

"Come again?" JB frowned at him.

"Shakespeare," Will explained. "Right, Wade?"

"*The Merchant of Venice*," Wade announced, still talking to the wall. "My mother taught English Lit at the high school, directed the drama club. That was her favorite play. She was voted teacher of the year three times running. And my father grew up on that ranch. He knew every acre like the back of his hand. My little sisters, Dana and Diane, they never made it past high school. All I wanted was justice for them. Justice for my family."

Finally, Wade looked at them, silent tears spilling down his cheeks. "I never knew it would go this far. Hooking up with that psychopath, Devere, it was pure desperation. He told me he could help get rid of Thomas, if I helped get rid of you."

"How long had you been planning to kill the Foxes?" Will asked.

"I'd been following them for years online. Since the trial. Every summer, they vacationed in Fog Harbor in their fancy beach house. They plastered their business everywhere. Their riches. Their mansion. Their perfect children in private school. All ill-gotten gains, earned off the corpses of the dead. Off my family."

"Is that why you took the job at Shells-by-the-Sea?"

"Right next door to Ocean's Song, it couldn't have been more perfect. For a while, I felt better here. Not exactly happy, but more alive. I started to wonder whether I'd go through with it. But that day on the beach tipped me over the edge. The moment I saw how Peter Fox lorded his power to make others feel small. When I watched that cop punch him in the face, I wished I'd done it. And I knew I wouldn't be free until I watched him die."

Will couldn't help but think of Drake. He knew how compelling that kind of anger could be. He'd felt it in his own hands. "And the firework show was the perfect cover. Instead of doing your rounds, you left the beach. You drove to Ocean's Song, expecting the whole family to be there."

"I got there a few minutes too late. I watched Peter storm out of the house, and I followed him. He took the cut-through, heading out of town." Coffman smacked the bed, a sudden intensity blackening his eyes, and the heart monitor beeped faster. "No way in hell I could let him get away. I flashed the strobe lights on the security car, and he pulled over. I'll never forget the way he looked at me when he rolled down the window. That moron was so drunk he actually believed I was a cop. I shot him in the head and set the car on fire, figuring no one would find it for a while. Then, I sped back to Ocean's Song on autopilot to finish the job. After I killed the first two, that's when I spotted Thomas peeking around the corner. I tried to catch him, but he ran outside. I shot the little girl and tried to torch the place. It was me, but it *wasn't* me. I wish I could explain."

Will had heard that one before. Rage could change a man into someone else, could blacken the soul and turn it to ash. "Did Peter recognize you when you stopped him?"

Wade scoffed. "Recognize *me*? I doubt he ever thought of me. I tried to speak with him at the trial, to beg him not to go through with Overton's charade. He had me escorted out... by *security*. The irony of it."

"Did he say anything before you shot him?"

Wade pursed his lips, sticking his nose in the air, as he imitated Peter Fox's last words on earth. "'Good evening, officer. Why am I being pulled over? I haven't done a damn thing wrong.'"

Outside the ICU, JB shook his head, dismayed. "We solved a quadruple murder, but it doesn't feel good."

"At least Thomas and Nora can have some peace now." Though even as he said it, Will wondered what peace looked like when you'd lost everything. When your entire world disappeared in one night.

After a moment of silence, JB clapped Will on the back. "You did good, City Boy."

Will side-eyed JB, waiting for the other shoe to drop. "What do you want?"

"Can't the Detective of the Year compliment his partner? No strings attached?"

Still suspicious, Will muttered, "Thanks, I think."

Will had gone halfway down the hall, when JB called out to him. "There is one thing. Get me out of this, will ya?" He held out his cell phone. Will chuckled as he read the subject line: *Introductory CrossFit, Saturday 8 a.m.*

That evening, Will pulled into the garage and eagerly grabbed the pet carrier from his passenger seat, along with a bagful of groceries. Cyclops had spent the day at the station, under Chief Flack's watchful eye. "We're home, Cy."

As soon as he cracked the carrier's door, Cyclops pushed his head through, meowing at Will's feet. Removing a small metal tin from the grocery bag, Will pulled open the tab, setting it on the ground.

Cy sniffed the canned salmon then made quick work of it, glancing up at Will occasionally to confirm his hearty approval. After, he trailed Will into the house, like he'd never left.

"Happy birthday, buddy." Will scratched behind Cy's ears, listening to his contented purring. "It's bound to be your ninth life by now."

EPILOGUE

Olivia smoothed her blouse. Even in the chill of the air-conditioned Mental Health Unit, the silk clung to her armpits. Her mouth was impossibly dry, though she'd been swigging water all morning. She'd expected nothing less from her first day back at work. Her nerves predictably on high alert inside Crescent Bay State Prison, where every man within a ten-foot radius had done something dreadful.

From her desk, she watched Leah exchange pleasantries with Sergeant Weber and retreat to her own office, giving Olivia a quick wave. Since Wade's arrest, Leah had taken it hard, blaming herself for hiring a madman. Olivia tried to tell her, to reassure her. Those kinds of men wore all sorts of disguises.

Olivia stood and walked to the door, trying to hide her limp. Better the inmates not see her weakness. Three weeks of healing had done wonders, but she'd need physical therapy to build her muscle strength before she could start running or boxing again.

With a silent nod, Javier Mendez made his way inside, taking his position in her patient chair. As soon as he sat, Olivia started the egg timer on her desk, questioning her own judgment. She should have begun with the depressed bank robber, not the stone-hearted killer leering at her as he petted his mustache. But she'd wanted a trial by fire to prove to herself she hadn't missed a beat, and now she had one. Blazing hot.

"I've been enjoying my single cell." His lips hardly moved when he spoke. "I wanted to tell you that in person. Face to face."

Olivia's throat constricted. Her own face, suddenly hot. She should never have written that memo. "You're welcome. After reviewing your mental health records, I felt it was warranted."

"Did you?" His dark eyes didn't waver. "I misunderstood, then. You don't want anything from me in return? I'm a well-connected man, and I always pay my debts."

All her questions about the General and her father—his death, his status as an informant—pounded at the gates, demanding to be asked. "There is one thing."

Olivia couldn't look away from the head of Javier's snake tattoo as he leaned forward, eager. "Name it, *Doctora.*"

"Ben Decker," she said.

"The dirty cop?" Javier's lip curled in disgust.

"Make sure nothing happens to him."

Olivia's first day back in the books, she made the turn off Pine Grove Road, anxious to get home. Emily had returned to San Francisco over the weekend to prepare for the fall semester, leaving her alone again. But it didn't feel lonely anymore, not with Deck around. She planned to meet him tonight at the Hickory Pit for their usual shop talk over two number fives. *Magnum PI* reruns—he'd bought her the complete series—and making out on her sofa afterward.

Right away, she noticed the motorcycles, parked in the grass adjacent to the house. She squinted against the sun until she spotted the men standing on her porch. Termite raised his hand to wave at her. His teenaged son, Scotty, by his side, his spitting image. Termite grinned shamelessly, as if his showing up on her doorstep wasn't a punch to her gut. The last time she'd seen him he'd been running away from the Oaktown Boys after they'd excommunicated him from the gang.

"What are you doing here?" she demanded before she'd fully exited the Buick.

"Good to see you too, sis."

"Don't call me that. Ever." Olivia shut the door and stomped toward him, her leg moving faster than it had since she'd been shot. Apparently, outrage worked as a cure-all. "And you didn't answer my question."

Termite wrapped an arm around Scotty, the scar on his bicep where he'd once been branded a member of Oaktown faded now. Scotty had covered his own Oaktown tattoo with fresh ink: a cross and barbed wire.

"We live here now. Scotty and me. We rented one of those old cabins on Wolver Hollow Road. Figured it'd be nice to spend a little time in the outdoors with my boy. Hunting, fishing. Getting back to nature."

Olivia glared at him in response. The only thing her half-brother could hunt was trouble. "And the Oaktown Boys are okay with that? I wouldn't have thought they'd be too keen on the idea of you settling down near one of their hangouts."

"We reached an understanding. I stay out their way. They stay out of mine. Besides, don't you think it would be nice to get to know your nephew? Spend a little family time together?"

When Scotty's lip curled at the suggestion, Olivia had to admit she felt the same. "Cut the crap, Termite. What are you really doing here?"

Grabbing her by the arm, he led her down the porch and around the side of the house, out of Scotty's earshot. "Word on the street is you've got a mole sticking its nose where it don't belong. I warned you not to make a stink about the General. Not to go digging. You're too damn stubborn for your own good."

"Mole? I don't know what you're talking about." She thought of Mendez. Nick Spade? Ben? "What's it to you anyway?"

Termite laughed, baring his yellow teeth. "Me personally, I don't give a rat's hiney if you want to get yourself killed. But the last time I saw him, I gave my word to your daddy I would protect you. Lord knows, I owed him that."

Stunned, Olivia followed Termite back to the porch, where Scotty sat on the step, waiting.

"We had a long day moving in, didn't we, son? I don't know about you, but I sure am hankering for some ribs from the Hickory Pit. Best damn barbecue joint this side of the Rockies." He cocked his head at Olivia. "Care to join us?"

A LETTER FROM ELLERY

Want to keep up to date with my latest releases? Sign up here! We promise never to share your email with anyone else, we'll only contact you when there's a new book available, and you can unsubscribe at any time.

www.bookouture.com/ellery-kane

Thank you for reading *One Child Alive!* With so many amazing books to choose from, I truly appreciate you taking the time to read the third installment in the Rockwell and Decker series. By now, I hope you've grown to love Olivia and Will as much as I do, and I can't wait to take you along on their next spine-tingling adventure.

One of my favorite parts about being an author is connecting with readers like you. You can get in touch with me through any of the social media outlets below, including my website and Goodreads page. Also, if you wouldn't mind leaving a review or recommending the Rockwell and Decker series to your favorite readers, I would really appreciate it! Reviews and word-of-mouth recommendations are essential, because they help readers like you discover my books.

Thank you again for your support! I look forward to hearing from you, and I hope to see you around Fog Harbor again soon!

TheLegacyBooks/

@ellerykane

ellerykane.com

ACKNOWLEDGMENTS

First, I owe a tremendous debt of gratitude to you, my avid readers, for joining me on this crazy adventure. Writing isn't always fun. Sometimes, it's the hardest work I've ever done. But hearing that my words have impacted you is a little bit of magic, and knowing that my characters have a special place in your heart makes it all worthwhile.

I am fortunate to have a fabulous team of family, friends, and work colleagues who have always been there to support and encourage me. For this book, I also relied on the knowledge and expertise of Fire Lieutenant Jeffrey Haughy, who taught me everything I needed to know about setting a beach house on fire. Though my mom is no longer with me, she gifted me her love for writing, and I know she's cheering me on even though I can't see her. Thanks, too, to my dad, who's never been a reader but thinks I'm brilliant anyway.

To Gar, my special someone and the unofficial president of the Ellery Kane fan club, for the countless hours of plot discussion; for the kick in the butt to keep writing; for the occasional bad review pep talk; and above all else, for guarding my heart like a dragon and believing in my dreams as fiercely as if they were his own. I couldn't have done any of this without you, and I wouldn't want to!

Every day I count my lucky stars that I have been fortunate to find an amazing editor, Jessie Botterill, and a fantastic publisher, Bookouture, who truly value their authors and work tirelessly for our success. Jessie's spot-on instincts, creativity, and sharp editorial lens have helped shape the Rockwell and Decker series into something special. I am incredibly grateful she took a chance on me, and it is a pleasure to team up with her and the entire

Bookouture family, including Kim, Noelle, and Sarah, who have worked so hard to spread the word about my books.

I have always drawn inspiration for my writing from my day job as a forensic psychologist. We all have a space inside us that we keep hidden from the world, a space we protect at all costs. So many people have allowed me a glimpse inside theirs—dark deeds, memories best unrecalled, pain that cracks from the inside out—without expectation of anything in return. I couldn't have written a single word without them.

Made in the USA
Middletown, DE
11 December 2021

55154399R00213